ELSWYTH THANE

THE
LIGHT
HEART

ÆONIAN PRESS

MATTITUCK

Republished 1978 by Special Arrangement
with Hawthorne Books, Inc.

Copyright © 1947 by Elswyth Thane

Library of Congress Cataloging in Publication Data

Thayne, Elswyth, 1900-
  The light heart.

  Reprint of the 1974 ed. published by Hawthorne
Books, New York.
  I. Title.
PZ3.T327Li   1978   [PS3539.H143]   813'.5'2   77-16219
ISBN 0-88411-951-3

AEONIAN PRESS, INC.
Box 1200
Mattituck, New York 11952

Manufactured in the United States of America

ACKNOWLEDGMENTS

As USUAL most of the research for this book was done at the New York Society Library, with the aid of Mrs. F. G. King and the obliging staff. Again Miss May Davenport Seymour of the Museum of the City of New York took time and trouble, and Miss Mary McWilliams at Williamsburg continued to be helpful. I am also indebted to what looks like half the British Army, including Major C. B. Ormerod of the British Information Services, Brigadier-General H. S. Sewell, Major Noel George, and an anonymous Blue (Royal Horse Guards) who supplied most comprehensive answers to a list of questions forwarded through the kindness of Lt. General Sir Charles Lloyd. In London, Miss Daphne Heard and Mr. Derrick deMarney went to untold trouble to find for me the contemporary books and periodicals which I could not go there and hunt for myself.

In case some younger readers feel that too much hindsight had gone into the handling of the First German War, I must add that to read the editorials, political speeches, and private correspondence of the years immediately before and after August 4, 1914, is pretty staggering. Almost all of it could just as well have been written at any time just before or after September 3, 1939. The last Emperor of Germany said practically everything Hitler ever said—and said it better. Hitler invented nothing —not even the German character.

E. T.

CONTENTS

vii

viii   *Contents*

THE
LIGHT
HEART

CHART OF FAMILIES AND RELATIONSHIPS

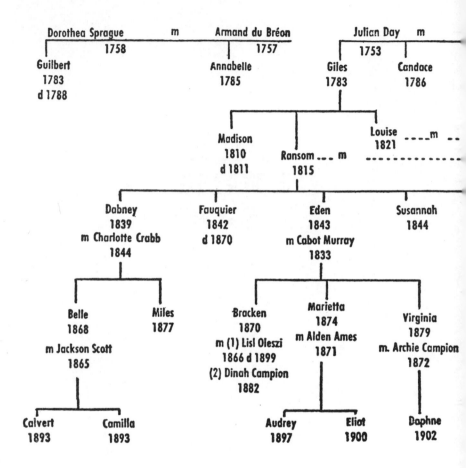

Dorothea Sprague   m   Armand du Bréon   Julian Day   m
     1758   1757   1753

Guilbert   Annabelle   Giles   Candace
1783   1785   1783   1786
d 1788

Madison   Louise   _ _ _ m _ _
1810   1821
d 1811   Ransom _ _ _ m
         1815

Dabney   Fauquier   Eden   Susannah
1839   1842   1843   1844
m Charlotte Crabb   d 1870   m Cabot Murray
1844   1833

Belle   Miles   Bracken   Marietta   Virginia
1868   1877   1870   1874   1879
m Jackson Scott   m (1) Lisl Oleszi   m Alden Ames   m. Archie Campion
1865   1866 d 1899   1871   1872
           (2) Dinah Campion
           1882

Calvert   Camilla   Audrey   Eliot   Daphne
1893   1893   1897   1900   1902

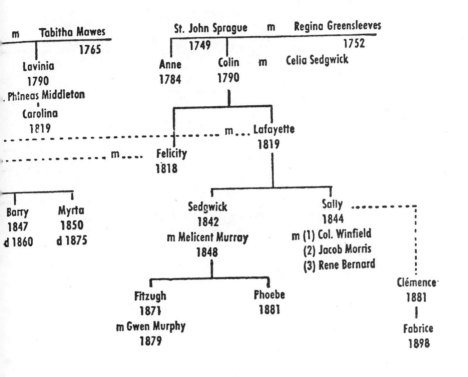

m   Tabitha Mawes
1765

St. John Sprague   m   Regina Greensleeves
1749   1752

Lavinia
1790

Anne   Colin   m   Celia Sedgwick
1784   1790

Phineas Middleton

Carolina
1819

m ... Lafayette
1819

m ....   Felicity
1818

Barry   Myrta
1847   1850
d 1860   d 1875

Sedgwick
1842
m Melicent Murray
1848

Sally
1844
m (1) Col. Winfield
(2) Jacob Morris
(3) Rene Bernard

Clémence
1881

Fitzugh   Phoebe
1871   1881
m Gwen Murphy
1879

Fabrice
1898

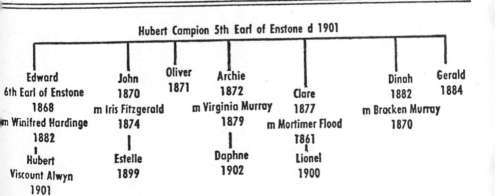

Hubert Campion 5th Earl of Enstone d 1901

Edward
6th Earl of Enstone
1868
m Winifred Hardinge
1882

John
1870
m Iris Fitzgerald
1874

Oliver
1871

Archie
1872
m Virginia Murray
1879

Clare
1877
m Mortimer Flood
1861

Dinah
1882
m Bracken Murray
1870

Gerald
1884

Hubert
Viscount Alwyn
1901

Estelle
1899

Daphne
1902

Lionel
1900

PART ONE

PHOEBE

>>

1

THE mockingbird woke her, singing in the mulberry tree outside her window.

She lay still, drowsy and at peace, listening to the babel of birdsong, which was full of the spring rapture of courtship. With the private satisfaction of the well-informed, she picked out the separate notes as Miles had taught her to do—the sweet *q—q—q* of the cardinal, the silvery boiling-over of the Carolina wren, the double metronome of the quail, the catbird mocking the mockingbird—and the mockingbird himself outdoing them all. The early morning hours in a Virginia garden were almost too noisy to be musical, she decided comfortably.

Gradually the small sounds of the awakening household formed their own familiar pattern. First there was the creak of the verandah door beneath her window as Uncle Micah, the old colored butler, opened it to the soft April air—and the brisk sound of cushions being plumped up in the cane furniture, and the swish of a damp broom on the matting. From the kitchen came a cosy smell of wood smoke and coffee, and the clink of kettles and cutlery. She heard the squeak of the windlass in the well and the gush of water from the wooden bucket into a pail—and a burst of half-suppressed laughter from one of the darky maids. Uncle Micah was the sober kind of clown, and always had them giggling with his straight-faced jokes. He was himself the last to consider his remarks funny, and even seemed a little hurt sometimes, as though he had been misunderstood—but he would have been disappointed if nobody laughed. . . .

Phoebe stretched herself in bed and smiled at the recollection of some of Uncle Micah's past jokes, which had become part of the family saga. The old colored man was a real wit in his way, and was indulged accordingly. Mother brought him up a bit short now and then, but Mother was raised a Yankee. Father tried not to let on sometimes, but you could see that Uncle Micah tickled him. Between Father and Uncle Micah there were mutual memories no one else could share now, except Cousin Sue Day—like after the battle at Fort Magruder just outside Williamsburg back in '62, when the Confederate Army retreated through the town, leaving its wounded behind, and Father was missing. Micah had gone down to the battlefield with Cousin Sue that night and they found Father wounded and pinned beneath the body of his horse. Micah's older brother, who was Father's bodyservant, was lying dead near by—killed by a Yankee bullet while he tried to reach his master with a fresh mount, and the horse he rode found its way home alone. Micah and Cousin Sue had brought Father back safe to the Days' house across the way, just one jump ahead of the Yankees. It was only thanks to Micah and Cousin Sue that Father had kept the use of his right arm, everybody said. And because his brother Judah was dead at his post, young Micah was promoted to be Father's bodyservant himself, and had pretty well run the Sprague household ever since, especially now that Mammy had got so old. . . .

Delilah, who was Micah's youngest daughter, came in softly with the hot water. She broke into a broad smile when she saw that Phoebe was awake and said it was a fine mawnin'—and went softly out again, the gentle clink of the polished brass hot-water cans following her from door to door around the big central hall at the top of the stairs.

Phoebe turned over on her back and her thoughts dwelt lovingly on her father, who was the most exciting and the handsomest man she had ever seen, and Phoebe was twenty-one this month. Father had been a captain of cavalry when Lee surrendered at Appomattox, but everybody called him Colonel now, perhaps because of his thick white hair, left long to the top of his collar in the back, and the old-fashioned black stock and frilled white shirt he wore with a frock coat and light trousers. Father was a lawyer, the best on the Peninsula, and lawyers had an answer for everything. Father said, "That's not the point," or "That isn't evidence, my dear," with a glint in his eye that held you right down to plain facts and dissolved a family argument into helpless laughter.

A door opened across the hall, where her parents slept, and her mother's light voice spoke on the threshold of their room. "Sedgie—don't forget Leah's medicine." His reply was inaudible to Phoebe, but Mother laughed, and the door closed and her feet ran down the stairs. Mother moved like a girl still, and weighed no more than she had when she was married, and she laughed a lot. Mother was the happiest person Phoebe knew. She entered each new day as though it was Christmas and would be full of presents. That was because she was so tremendously in love with Father, even now, at their age—in love so that it showed— showed enough almost to embarrass you, if you were their grown-up daughter. Of course everybody was more or less in love with Father; even Leah, the darky cook, who was taking medicine for her rheumatism, and to whom he was a sort of embodiment of God. (You couldn't let Leah have the bottle or she'd take it all at once, hoping for quicker results, as she had done before and made herself violently ill. So now they kept the bottle in Father's room and doled out to her one dose at a time.)

Even Cousin Sue Day, it sometimes seemed to Phoebe, was in love with Father. . . .

Phoebe lay still and contemplated Cousin Sue with affection. Cousin Sue wrote books. That is, she wrote books which got published regularly and brought in a lot of money. Well, not enough money, really, to run that big house and pay the doctor's bills for Great-uncle Ransom, who was eighty-seven. But quite a lot of money, all the same, just for writing. Phoebe was trying to learn to write books too, but nobody knew that except Cousin Sue, and of course Miles. Cousin Sue was never too busy to read the grubby little manuscripts Phoebe took her every so often, and to make the most brilliant suggestions, and she had promised to send one to her own publisher as soon as they got it good enough. You could always show Cousin Sue anything, tell her anything, without embarrassment. She would never laugh at you, and she always had time. That summer a few years ago when she went to England with Cousin Eden Murray for the Jubilee it was like being without an arm or a leg till they got her back again. The day she came home Father took her right into his arms, hard, in front of everybody—he didn't kiss her, he just held her, as though she was a child he had almost lost, and then he let her go and made some kind of joke, and nobody seemed to think twice about it. But Phoebe had thought about it many times. Cousin Sue had never married, though she must have had lots of chances. Could that be because Father had married a Yankee girl? Phoebe often wondered how it would feel if the man you wanted married somebody else and left you empty and alone. Would you take second best? Apparently Cousin Sue would not. What if Miles married somebody over there in Charlottesville. . . .

The door of her parents' room opened again and closed at once, briskly—that was Father—tall, quick, graceful, full of a youthful vitality that stimulated and cheered the most downhearted beholder. Almost simultaneously Fitz's door opened too, and she heard her father and brother greet each other heartily, and their crisp footsteps went down the staircase together. Fitz's wife, Gwen, had to stay in bed till noon, since her baby had come too soon and died. They said she lost it because she had been a dancer ever since she was a small child and had injured herself. Fitz had brought her back with him from New York four years ago, just before he went to the war in Cuba, and the family weren't sure at first what she would be like, being an actress. But she was beautiful and sweet, and even Mother was glad now that Fitz had married her. And she was so in love with Fitz. . . .

Phoebe sighed impatiently. There it was again. Father and Mother, Fitz and Gwen—everybody had somebody except herself—and Cousin Sue, who had only Great-uncle Ransom and three darky servants in that big house. Cousin Sue was a spinster. Phoebe wondered if at that age she too would be left over, looking after somebody old, being kind to somebody else's children. Well, unless Miles . . .

She didn't want to marry anybody but Miles, did she? Miles was Cousin Dabney Day's son, and lived at Charlottesville, where both he and his father worked at the University, Cousin Dabney as a professor and Miles doing odd jobs of tutoring until he could get on the faculty somewhere. Phoebe had been in love with Miles all her life. At least—there hadn't ever been anybody *but* Miles. And then, that awful year when they all went to the war in Cuba, Miles saw Virginia Murray at a family reunion and suddenly went right out of his mind.

Virginia was a cousin too, in a complicated sort of way, but the Murrays lived in New York. Virginia's mother was Cousin Sue's sister Eden, and her father was the brother of Phoebe's own mother—a Yankee, and the wealthy owner of a New York newspaper—the same paper Fitz was working for when he was up North and met Gwen. Virginia, who had spent half her life abroad anyway, eventually married an Englishman and settled down in Gloucestershire. But Miles didn't seem to forget her. And he hadn't been well since Cuba, he seemed only half alive, and had recurrent attacks of the fever he had got there. Maybe it wasn't Virginia any more, maybe it was all just the fever, but Miles was letting the years slip by, and while he was a wonderful friend and they liked all the same things and read all the same books, Miles just didn't propose. Phoebe sighed again, and buried her face in the pillow, while the mockingbird yelled his head off in the mulberry tree. It was spring in the Tidewater, and even the birds were in love. . . .

I must get up, Phoebe thought, or I'll have to ring for more hot water, and breakfast will be going in. But she lay still, wishing. She lay and thought about Miles, and his unaccountable behavior now that Virginia was married to the Honorable Archie Campion and had had a baby a month ago. Virginia had never looked at Miles anyway. Virginia was always a flirt. But her brother Bracken when he came down to Williamsburg with their mother to spend Christmas last year and bring his new wife—English too—Bracken had said Virginia was heels over head in love with Archie and had been ever since the Jubilee Summer. So there wasn't anything in it for Miles. There never had been. But Virginia was awfully pretty, and the Murrays had lots of money, and she had wonderful clothes. . . . Poor Miles had been dazzled, that's all it was. Virginia always made you feel like the little brown hen, with rather ruffled feathers. It wasn't surprising, was it, that Miles had been smitten. But need he go on—moping? Couldn't he do with something else now? And did anybody ever want to be second best?

Phoebe turned over on her back again and scowled at the ceiling. Suppose Miles asked her tomorrow. Well, the next time he came to Williamsburg, which would be in about a week's time, for her birthday. (The family always came to birthdays, from any negotiable distance, and there was always a party.) Suppose Miles did propose—next week. Would she say Yes?

Yes. She would. It was April again, and life sped by. And she had never dreamed of marrying anybody but Miles.

And yet—that look in her mother's eyes for Father—the way Fitz carried Gwen up and down the stairs since the baby, both of them laughing, with her arm tight around his neck—would that sort of thing ever happen to her with Miles? They all seemed to have such fun together—her father and mother—Fitz and Gwen—Cousin Bracken Murray and his English Dinah when they were here last Christmas. Phoebe asked herself if she and Miles, married, would ever carry on like that.

for anyone to see—so lightheartedly loving, so confident of each other, so *brazen*—so enviable.

Poor Miles, he would never be as much fun as Father, of course—but then, who was? Miles was very good-looking—tall, as all the men in the family were tall, Days, Murrays, and Spragues—excessively thin now, even for a Day, and on account of the fever his hair too was getting a little thin—so kind, so gentle, so patient if you were stupid, so ready to forgive if you were thoughtless. But that tender foolery, that shameless joy, that *shine* the rest of them seemed to have—would Miles do that for her? Would marriage with her do that for Miles? Wouldn't Miles perhaps limber up a bit if they were married? It wasn't Miles's fault, was it, that he had got fever in Cuba and it had hung on ever since, and probably always would. All the same, she couldn't help wondering—was it treason?—if when they brought Father back half dead from the battlefield at Fort Magruder it had ever occurred to anyone to say Poor Sedgwick. And she thought not.

I really must get up this minute, Phoebe told herself, and did so, and washed in tepid water as a penance for her tardiness, and went down late to breakfast, and kissed everybody all round the table, and asked Fitz how Gwen was feeling today, and said she was going over to Cousin Sue's right after breakfast, and Mother said Remember to take her back that crochet pattern I borrowed, and Father said Give her my love—he always said that, didn't he, when somebody went to see Cousin Sue, though he saw her himself nearly every day—and Fitz said Tell her I'll be over later on. . . .

When they rose from the table Phoebe ran back up to her room to get her newest manuscript and stopped to read it through again, and had to rewrite a page. By the time she got to Cousin Sue's it was nearly ten, and there in the drawing-room was Cousin Bracken Murray from New York, and nobody even knew he was coming.

2

BRACKEN had had a fairly sleepless night on the train and was feeling his years, which were all of thirty-two. Since the death of his father during the war in Cuba, Bracken had come to grips with things pretty suddenly, as the man of the family and the owner of one of New York's better evening newspapers. The newspaper was simple. He had been practically raised in the office and had gone to work as a leg-man when he left Princeton. But the family—that was a man-size job.

His father had always run the family without visible effort, ever since he married Eden Day in Williamsburg at the end of the War Between the States. Even though Cabot Murray was a Yankee, the Williamsburg family had leaned on him from the beginning, almost before he became a part of it. He had all the money in the world and the war had crippled finances in the South but that was not what made him valuable in the eyes of the clan. He had what the men who had recently been in Cuba called savvy. He knew what was what. He never dithered. And he got his way. Sometimes he had to buy it, but he always got it. He was worldly-wise, high-handed, hard-hitting, and utterly lovable. Beside him, his admiring son had always felt pretty small potatoes. And then quite suddenly Cabot Murray died and it was all up to Bracken.

Not that the other men in the family were weaklings or misfits. But they didn't run things. They didn't cope. And except for Fitz, none of them made any money. The Dabney Days lived at Charlottesville and were University-minded innocents. And the Williamsburg bunch never left the Peninsula if they could help it. True, Fitz Sprague had worked on the paper in New York for a while before he went with Bracken to Cuba as a war correspondent—but all Fitz really wanted to do was to write songs and musical comedies, which he was very successful at, and he could do that just as well in Williamsburg, and Gwen wanted to give up the stage and raise a family in a real home. Sue, with her invalid father to care for, had gone abroad just once, with the Murrays the summer of the Jubilee. If she hadn't, Bracken wouldn't have had to drop everything in New York and come to Williamsburg now.

The news he carried wasn't the kind you could set down callously in a letter, or deliver in a casual aside during a birthday party for a pretty young cousin. The news he had to tell Susannah Day was confidential, and he wondered if there was any way to cover up its arrival by saying he had been in Washington anyway, and so forth. She would have to decide about that herself. The family was always sublimely incurious, but a letter would have been more private—if you could have put it in a letter. You had to tell her this, as gently and tactfully as you could—hold her hands, produce a clean handkerchief, advise her what to do now—cope. He supposed she would want to keep it from Cousin Sedgwick, if possible, but how?

Walking thoughtfully through the quiet green streets from the railway station to Ransom Day's house, he appreciated even now the lost, sleeping-beauty charm of the little town. Williamsburg had been the capital of Virginia once, when the Royal Governor lived here and gave Royal Birthday Night balls in his handsome red brick Palace on the Green. George Washington went to those balls, wearing powder and a blue militia uniform with red facings, and a sword. Bracken's Great-great-grandmother Tabitha Day had had the whole French Army at her wedding ball at the Raleigh Tavern here in Williamsburg after York-town. But the capital had gone to Richmond by then, and the little Peninsula town with its red brick College buildings after Wren, and its low white painted houses behind white picket fences had got drowsier and drowsier. Disastrous fires had taken the Palace and the Capital and the Raleigh. Another war rolled over it in the 'sixties, wiping out whole families and their fortunes. The railway came in, and put its depot where the Palace gardens had once been. A young ladies' seminary stood on the site of the Capitol Building. What was left of Williamsburg now was shabby and charming and pathetic, and held its chin high—like the Days and the Spragues. Bracken loved the town, and he loved his relations who lived here. But Aunt Sue had really dealt him a handful of deuces this time.

She was so sweet. She was so pretty, with her neat little figure and her fading coppery hair and the misplaced dimple in her childlike smile. But she was a deep one. That year when they took her to England for the Jubilee, because his mother was convinced the darling should see something of the world while she was still young enough to enjoy her-self—that summer was when Aunt Sue really went and did it.

How those mockingbirds sang. . . .

And what was he going to say to her? He would be there in a minute, and Pharaoh would be opening the door and blessing his soul, and Aunt Sue would be so glad to see him, and he would kiss her on both cheeks and say—well, not straight off, not the first thing. And yet, why else had he come, with no warning? She would be so pleased to be surprised— But Bracken, what does this *mean,* why didn't you let us *know,* you're a week *early,* Bracken, for the birthday, and when can we look for Eden, and why didn't you bring your Dinah—?

What was he going to say then? Honey, you know that summer you went to England with us—? Well, of course she did, that wouldn't get him anywhere. Honey, you know that house I bought from a fellow named Forbes-Carpenter, the house Virginia's living in now with

Archie, the one Great-great-grandfather St. John was born in—? Naturally she knew it, she had lived in it herself for weeks. Honey, you remember Major Forbes-Carpenter—the man you wouldn't marry because of Cousin Sedgwick—? And Aunt Sue would probably get a little pink, and glance over her shoulder, because Gratian Forbes-Carpenter wasn't mentioned in Williamsburg, though all he had done was fall in love with Aunt Sue the summer of the Jubilee. . . .

Bracken was at the gate, at the steps, at the door—Pharaoh opened it with appropriate exclamations—Aunt Sue came running out of the dining-room—"Bracken, you *darling,* where have you sprung from, have you had breakfast, where's Dinah, aren't you going to kiss me, that's better, are you *starving,* why didn't you *tell* us, does anyone else know you're here—?"

"Sh!" he said, and laid his finger on her parted lips. "I'm incognito. I've come straight here from the station."

"Is anything wrong?" She caught at him. "Is Eden—?"

"Mother is perfectly well, and she knows where I am. So come into the drawing-room and I'll tell you about it."

"But you must have something to *eat,* Bracken, if you've been travelling all night—"

"Later."

With his arm around her waist he took her into the drawing-room and closed the door behind them. She stood quietly then, looking up at him, her eyes large and frightened.

"Bracken, I know it's something dreadful, don't break it gently, will you!"

"Very well, my dear, here it is." He took both her hands. "I've had a letter from Partridge in London." (Partridge was their solicitor.) "Honey, I don't know how else to tell you—Sir Gratian has been killed in South Africa."

Slowly, while he stood watching, her eyes filled with tears. Her hands gripped his, for steadiness. Then with a little sound, half gasp, half moan, she hid her face against his coat, and he laid his arms around her. "It was just one of those things that needn't have happened," he went on gently, to give her time. "The war down there is practically over—this was part of the necessary mopping-up campaign, and they'd put down a cordon at a place called Tarkastaad. The Boers rushed the Lancers and the British losses were heavy. It was a soldier's death, honey

—very quick, and with his boots on. He would have wanted it that way."

Bracken gave her his handkerchief, which she accepted gratefully. They moved together to a sofa and sat down, and she held to him still, shaking a little, her breath coming unevenly while she fought for self-control.

"I don't—mean to take it so badly," she got out. "It's only that there was so little I could do for him—and he deserved so much—and I gave him nothing—"

"You gave him a very bright memory," Bracken said firmly. "He had a beautiful time with us, that summer. It was probably his last leave in England, and he had a great deal to look back on. Don't think he wasn't grateful."

"If only I could have managed—if there had been two of me, so that one could have come back here, I—would have stayed with him—he would have retired by now—to raise dahlias, he said—"

"Don't cry, honey, he'd hate that. He wanted you to be happy. He did what he could about that. You see—in his Will he left you everything he had."

"What?" Sue lifted a shocked, tear-stained face.

"You aren't mentioned in the Will. He was too tactful for that. I am, though. The money is left in my name, with a sealed letter to me, putting it in trust for you. Apparently he went to Partridge in the Temple and arranged for everything before he left England that summer. His letter to me sounds as though he had had some sort of premonition that his time was about up—soldiers often do, I think. He arranged that if and when he was killed in action everything of which he died possessed would come to you—and this consists largely of the lump sum I had just paid him for the house. He never touched a penny of it. It makes a nice little nest-egg, you know."

"B-but I don't want it."

"I'm afraid you've got it, my dear."

"But it's *your* money, Bracken, that you gave him for Farthingale."

"Then I gave Farthingale to Virginia and Archie when they were married, and the money certainly isn't theirs."

"But it—it would be in *pounds,* wouldn't it? I can't—"

"The exchange is pretty good. We can have it transferred to your account here and—"

"No! Oh, please don't do that, Sedgie would be sure to find out! You'll

just have to keep the money yourself, Bracken, I don't want it, truly I don't."

"My dear soul, Wills are sacred things, we have to do as they say. And his says you are his heir—heiress, I mean. It gives you a good back-log in case the time ever comes when you don't want to go on writing books. You could live on the income anywhere in the world, very comfortably indeed."

"Oh, Bracken, please help me out of this, don't let Sedgie know, I'll *die* if Sedgie ever hears about it!"

"Cousin Sedgwick isn't a fool, Aunt Sue. He won't think anything scandalous just because—"

"But I'd *rather* he didn't know—don't you see, there was nothing between me and Gratian, really, except a fancy on his part. We were all so gay that summer, and he had been ill and dull, and it must have gone to his head a little. I thought he would have forgotten all about it by now."

"Had *you?*"

"N-no, but—"

"You were the nicest thing that ever happened to him, Aunt Sue. Don't take away his pleasure now."

She looked at him doubtfully, gravely.

"Do you—think he'd *know?*" she breathed.

"What do *you* think?" There was a silence while their eyes held. "I wouldn't risk it if I were you," he said.

"But—Gratian wouldn't want to make things difficult for me here—" She flashed a doubtful, confidential look at him. He was very young, but after all, Cabot's son was the head of the family now. "I don't know if anyone ever told you, Bracken, but at one time Sedgwick and I were very much in love, and—"

"And they wouldn't let you marry him because you were double first cousins. Yes, I've known that for a long time. It stood between you and Sir Gratian, didn't it? But you came back here, Aunt Sue, surely that's the answer to that. Anyway, Cousin Sedgwick is grown up now. It isn't going to break his heart to learn that a very gallant soldier of the Queen thought so highly of you that he wanted to endow you with all his worldly goods!"

"Sedgie would think I had—well, *given up* something, when I came back to Williamsburg. It would worry him. I won't have him upset. I could never make him believe, for sure, that I *wanted* to come home. We've got to find some way—"

The screen door of the verandah at the side of the house slammed heedlessly, and Phoebe's voice floated in from there: "Cousin Sue! It's me—Phoebe! Where are you?"

Sue seized Bracken's shoulders. Her eyes blazed up at him, wet and radiant.

"I know!" she whispered. "We'll give it all to Phoebe!"

"But—"

"Keep still. Let me tell her. You keep still." Then Sue raised her voice. "We're in the drawing-room, honey. Come and see who's here!"

3

BRACKEN spent the next half hour keeping still, by main force.

He kissed Phoebe's cool pink cheek, and took note of the clean shine of her brown hair and her pretty teeth and the really entrancing cleft in her chin, which came from the Murray side. And he watched Susannah Day, the authoress, spin her yarn.

According to Sue, he had come to Williamsburg solely on account of Phoebe's birthday, because Phoebe's present from the Murrays was going to be—guess what!—a trip abroad with them this summer!

At that point Bracken felt about as flabbergasted as Phoebe looked. It was true that he and Dinah and his mother were going to England within a month's time. It was true that this summer in England would be the gayest since the Jubilee Year, because the gay Prince of Wales was going to be crowned Edward VII. It was true that Virginia had urged them to spend all the time they could at Farthingale, which was not far from the Hall, where Dinah had lived before she married Bracken, and where her brother still lived with his wife and baby heir to the earldom. But it was not true that Phoebe had been included in his mother's plans.

They would be very glad to have her, naturally, and they might have thought of it themselves before now. Phoebe was a very presentable young woman, and had hardly been out of Williamsburg in her life. Undoubtedly it would do her good. And he saw what was in Sue's mind. She thought that by sending Phoebe abroad with a lot of pretty clothes and paying her expenses out of the legacy, she would have disposed of the embarrassing problem of Sir Gratian's Will. It was evident that Sue had no faintest idea of what Bracken had paid for that house called Farthingale down in Gloucestershire.

Phoebe was shaking her head, and looking bewildered and a little frightened.

"But, Cousin Sue, I'm not—not *ready,* I'm not equipped for a trip like that, I'd have to have new things to wear, and I—"

"Eden means to outfit you in New York before you go. I'll come along as far as that with you, I think, and help choose your clothes," said Sue recklessly. "If I can get away for a few days, I will."

"B-but it will cost so much money, Father couldn't—we can't just let Aunt Eden—"

"Nonsense, it's for your birthday present—your twenty-first birthday. The boys always have something special when they turn twenty-one! Eden wants to provide everything you need—entirely at her own expense, of course."

Phoebe looked at Bracken.

"It's awfully nice of Aunt Eden but I'm afraid—"

"So was I afraid once," Sue interrupted briskly. "And it didn't hurt *me*. In fact, it gave me a great many new things to write about, and increased my income." Suddenly, to Bracken's agonized inner amusement Sue flushed and stammered. "From my books, I mean, of course—they've sold much better ever since. It broadens your viewpoint, and—you'll be much more likely to turn out something worth publishing if you take this chance now, while you're young."

Bracken pricked up his ears at this.

"Is Phoebe writing?" he broke in.

"Yes, she is," Sue told him. "It's a secret so far, but it needn't be much longer. She's doing very well. All she needs is a little experience—a little life."

"Good," said Bracken, who had printer's ink in his veins. "Let me see something sometime."

"Not yet," said Sue. "After she's been to England, maybe."

"Well, I—I'll ask Miles what he thinks about it when he comes next week," said Phoebe, still dazed and sparring for time.

There was a silence. Bracken felt that Sue wished he wasn't there, and sat as still as possible, effacing himself. They all knew that Phoebe was in love with Miles, and that Miles wasn't doing anything about it, and it must be pretty embarrassing, but Phoebe herself had brought it up. He saw Susannah make up her mind to deal with it.

"I'm afraid it doesn't matter what Miles thinks in this case," she said gently. "Though of course he will want you to go when you have the chance. Let's see, the party is on Thursday, isn't it—I shall write Eden today that we will be ready to go with her when she returns to New York. That will give us plenty of time to get your clothes before sailing."

"B-but I never do anything without asking Miles—" Phoebe objected unhappily.

"I think it's time you did," said Sue, and they both stared at her, Bracken in delight, Phoebe in amazement. "Besides, I'm sure Miles would be the last person to stand in your way. Now, Bracken is going to have lunch here with me, and then we'll come over and talk to your father about it." Sue seemed to get her breath and relax a little, now that the first round, as it were, was over. She went to where Phoebe stood, still too transfixed to find a chair, and put her arms around the girl's waist and kissed her. "Well, we did sort of spring it on you, I know," she admitted ruefully. "Bracken had just sort of sprung it on me when you came in, and once you knew he was here we had to think of something —I mean, there wasn't much sense in trying to keep it from you for a few more days, you were bound to wonder why he had come."

"I was in Washington," said Bracken, rising to the occasion. "I knew I couldn't get away again next week for the party, so Mother thought I had better run down now and bring you my present—just a little something extra. Shall we let her have it today?" He put his hand in his pocket and glanced at Sue, who hesitated, for presents ahead of time were against the rules.

"Well, perhaps—just this once," she agreed as she was dying to see it herself. Bracken's presents were always fabulous, just as his father's had been in the old days.

Bracken drew out a flat jeweller's case wrapped in white paper and tied with gold cord, which Phoebe pulled off excitedly, clumsy with eagerness. Inside, on a bed of white satin, was a pendant made of turquoises, diamonds, and pearls, with whole pearl drops and a jewelled filament of chain.

"Oh, Cousin *Bracken!"* cried Phoebe, and went speechless and misty with pleasure.

"Let's put it on," he suggested, lifting it out with practiced fingers.

"In the m-morning?" said Phoebe, fascinated.

"It ought to go pretty well with that dress you've got on. Turn around."

He dropped the chain over her head and slipped the clasp home. Phoebe flew to the mirror above the mantelpiece to gaze at herself. The pendant from Tiffany's shone against the mended lace yoke of her last year's blue and white printed muslin as though it was lying on the very latest garden-party frock designed to be worn at Buckingham Palace. Phoebe's eyes were wistful.

"Would I see the King?" she asked, still looking in the mirror. "Would I really *see* him?"

"I don't know why not. I saw the Queen the year I went," said Sue.

"You'll certainly see the Coronation Procession from the best seats there are," Bracken promised. "It's too late to arrange for a presentation this year, I'm afraid. But we can go to Ascot and Goodwood—he's sure to be there, he never misses a horse race."

"It isn't just any king," said Phoebe, at the mirror. "It's the King of England. I wouldn't go across the street to see the King of Italy or— or the Kaiser."

"Wilhelm would hate to hear you say so," Bracken grinned.

Phoebe turned to them, standing very straight and proud, because of the pendant, with wistful eyes.

"Did *you* go to Ascot?" she asked Sue.

"I did. He was the Prince of Wales then, and he recognized Virginia all the way across the Lawn, because he had danced with her at a State Ball and she was saucy to him. He knew her, and they laughed like old friends."

Phoebe sighed.

"I *would* like to see the King," she said. "Just once before I die."

"You mean before *he* dies," said Bracken, but with understanding. "You're a much better risk than he is—the old boy's getting on a bit!"

"What do you wear at Ascot?" Phoebe asked, fingering the pendant.

"Frills," said Sue. "Big hats. Feather boas. The best you've got. It's terrific fun."

"I haven't got a big hat and a boa."

"You wait," said Bracken. "Just give Mother a chance. Time hangs heavy on her hands since both the girls got married. She needs another débutante to dress, to keep her spirits up."

"Oh, I'd never be like Virginia," Phoebe warned him. "I'm just a country cousin."

"So was I," Sue reminded her. "But you'll forget about that. You'll have the time of your life. I did."

"Couldn't you come too?" Phoebe suggested, holding out a hand to her.

"Only as far as New York, honey. I can't be spared here, longer than that. But you'll be all right with Aunt Eden."

"I think I'd better go round by the office and tell Father now—before lunch," Phoebe said.

"Tell your mother first, honey," said Sue, and Phoebe's eyes met hers gravely. Mother was a dear. But Father was so exciting, sometimes you almost forgot her. Cousin Sue had always taught them it didn't do to let Mother feel left out.

"All right. But then she'll tell Father when he comes home to lunch, and it won't be the same."

"Not quite, but it's better that way," Sue insisted quietly. "It's bad enough already that Bracken came to me before he saw them."

Bracken winced at this barefaced saddling of himself with a guilt which was not his, but Phoebe's glance was commiserating and innocent. She knew how that was too. You always went to Cousin Sue first. She talked people into things for you. It occurred to Phoebe belatedly that Cousin Sue had just talked her into going abroad right over Miles's head. Bemused, and fingering the new pendant lovingly, Phoebe set out for home.

In the drawing-room Bracken looked at Sue, one eyebrow aslant.

"*Well!*" he said admiringly. "You do think fast!"

"Eden won't mind, will she? She's always saying how dull it is without Virginia."

"She'll be delighted. Don't know why we didn't think of it ourselves."

"I shall pay for everything," said Sue firmly. "With Gratian's money, I mean. He would be glad if it gave Phoebe a good time, wouldn't he?"

"Undoubtedly. But you haven't disposed of the money, you know."

"I want her to have lots of clothes," Sue said extravagantly. "I want her to be dressed the way Virginia always was. Furs, even. And *all* her travelling expenses, mind."

"But, honey, if the legacy is properly invested here, Phoebe's holiday and wardrobe will all come out of the first year's income, no matter what you do."

Sue stared at him.

"As much as *that?*"

"Quite a lot. Farthingale wasn't a cheap house, it was fully equipped and in excellent condition."

"Well, it's all going to be Phoebe's, anyway," Sue said decidedly. "You've got to spend it on her, and invest it for her, without anybody knowing anything about it. Phoebe is the nearest thing to a daughter of my own I'll ever have, and I want her to—to—" She hesitated. "Well, to have everything," she finished abruptly.

"Am I to buy her a husband too?" he asked, and Sue's eyes were un-flinching.

"You're to buy her a chance to fall in love with someone besides Miles, yes."

"Well, I *am* surprised!" said Bracken. "I thought—"

Sue interrupted him levelly.

"Bracken, when I said I wanted Phoebe to have everything, I meant everything I have missed. It's all right in my case, because with me it was for Sedgwick. But you know as well as I do that Miles isn't Sedg-wick. Miles isn't—*enough*. Nobody ought to be an old maid because of Miles, it's—it would be too lonely."

He put his arm around her and his cheek against hers.

"I see what you mean, honey," he said.

"Don't think I'm sorry for myself, because I'm not." But she clung to him a moment gratefully. "What Sedgwick and I have had, all these years, has been—worth it. But that's not for Phoebe. Gratian is going to give Phoebe what he couldn't give me because it was too late."

"And what about poor Miles?" said Bracken. "If he sees danger of her being snatched away from him like this mightn't he pull up his socks and ask her to marry him?"

"I hope not," said Sue gravely. "I do hope he won't ask her before she goes. It may be very wrong of me, Bracken, but I want Phoebe to have something—well, something *more* than Miles!"

4

THE decision had been made before Bracken left Williamsburg that evening, but there was still time to write to Miles before he arrived for the birthday party. As she sat at the little desk in her bedroom, tearing up sheets of notepaper and beginning again, Phoebe found it a very difficult letter to compose.

She felt a necessity to apologize to Miles for not consulting him—and at the same time there was no real reason for Miles to object, as there might have been if, say, they had been engaged. This sudden, drastic break in their established routine underlined uncomfortably the equivocal position she was in with Miles. In her own mind she belonged to him, and had no existence separate from him. And yet because he had not claimed her, either openly or in private, she had no official standing, even with herself, as his property. She was actually quite free to go to England, quite free to fall in love with somebody there as Virginia had done, if it came to that—except that she preferred to consider herself dedicated to Miles. But the letter she wrote to him now must carry no assumption that he couldn't get along without her, or would miss her unduly. Likewise, it must not contain any indication of her own growing exasperation, amounting almost to humiliation, that she was so willing and anxious for an understanding between them which he was too indifferent to make concrete.

By the time she had finished and sealed the final version she was very nearly fit to dispense with Miles voluntarily—tired of a bondage of her own making, tugging crossly at chains which were invisible to everyone but herself—even, apparently, to Miles.

The letter took Miles by surprise, and roused in him old, uneasy memories. First of all he found himself wishing that the Murrays would stop throwing their money around and leave things alone. And then his fair, well-balanced mind reminded him that Phoebe had a perfect right to go abroad in luxury if she got the chance, especially since she wanted to write novels like Aunt Sue.

After that, his thoughts lingered unwillingly, unhappily, on Virginia Murray, who was now Virginia Campion. He had, he thought, got used to the idea of never seeing her again. In fact, he preferred never to see her again. Virginia was nothing to him. She had never been anything to him but a bright comet flashing across his calm, studious horizon. She had looked up at him through her dark lashes, smiled at him her closed, curved smile which was always as though she knew something you didn't know—she had waltzed in the circle of his stiff, careful arm, and chattered to him of her curtsey before the old Queen, and the conquests she had made in London the summer of the Jubilee. He was on his way to Cuba then, and you couldn't ask a girl to marry you when you might be blown to bits a month later—at least not a girl like Virginia Murray.

He had returned from Cuba without a wound, but was tormented by that persistent fever and a digestive ailment which came of the food and water he had had on the campaign. Before he had begun to get himself together again Virginia was off once more for England, where she suddenly married Archie Campion without even coming back home first. Miles was at that time a very sick man, with nothing to do but lie about and brood. In normal circumstances he might have got over it in a normal way, and seen for himself that Virginia would never have made a college professor's wife. As it was, with his health broken and his mind insufficiently occupied, Miles became a blighted being who had loved and lost. Because she was now unattainable, Virginia increased proportionately in desirability until he had convinced himself that she was the only woman in the world, La Belle Dame Sans Merci, Circe, Dulcinea, Eurydice—Miles's love-making, if he had ever got down to it, would have taken a very classical turn.

So, during a slow and tiresome convalescence with many relapses, Miles came to live more and more in a misty world of his own, nursing the might-have-been, coddling bereavement, dwelling on frustration, courting heartbreak—he was still young enough, at twenty-two, to dramatize a thwarted love, and his dreamy, bookish temperament was favorable to solitary yearnings. He even, at one time and another, contemplated the monastic life.

His parents very wisely, at first, let him alone, hoping he would right himself as his health returned. But there was created, between his mental depression and the recurrent bouts of fever, a sort of vicious circle, and instead of getting well Miles showed a tendency now, at twenty-five, to become a chronic semi-invalid, patient, studious, self-effacing—half alive.

Through it all, Phoebe had stood by him staunchly, always sympathetic and soothing, ready to read aloud to him till she was hoarse, anxious to absorb books he had already read and listen to him discuss them for hours, always serious-minded, undemanding, considerate of his feelings, tacitly recognizing his broken heart, and offering with both hands her generous, flattering friendship as a makeweight in his celibacy. And now she was going to England. Suppose, like Virginia, she never came back. . . .

Disturbed by emotions he had thought permanently shelved, Miles went for a walk on the Lawn at Charlottesville in the late afternoon shadows and sunlight, and faced things he had shirked with impunity too long. Was he to go on like this, he asked himself desolately, for the rest of his life, losing girl after girl into limbo, or was he going to put his foot down before it was too late and have a wife like other people? The family expected him to marry, he knew. Fitz had married, and then Bracken had taken to himself the younger sister of Virginia's English husband. Miles was the last, and it was his turn.

Pacing slowly under the old green trees across the closely mown grass between the classic pavilions, Miles contemplated marriage for himself and found himself, as always, shrinking back into his shell. He liked his life as it was. He had his own room in his parents' spacious house— a rather Spartan, monkish room, with a plain white coverlet on the bed, plain white curtains at the windows, a writing-table in the best light, books all along one wall and all across the mantelpiece. He could read in bed—read all night, when he was having one of his bad times. . . .

The life-force in Miles had flickered very low. The possible introduction of a woman into his tidy, self-centered days and nights presented to him mainly problems and unwelcome readjustments—even a woman so familiar to him, so well-versed in his ways, and so eager to please as his Cousin Phoebe Sprague. He viewed the ensuing loss of his bachelor privacy almost as squeamishly as a girl. A wife would always be there, morning, noon, and night; at breakfast when he wanted to read the newspaper, at luncheon when he was allowed to bring a book to the table, at dinner when he supposed it would become necessary to make a change of dress. She would be in his room when he went to bed and wanted to read before turning out the light—in his bed when he woke up in the morning. Would he ever be alone again, and how did married people bear it? What would you talk about with a woman, shut up with her seven days in the week, three hundred and sixty-five nights in the year? Even with Phoebe, who had an educated, serious mind, for a woman, what would you talk about all that time?

Walking up and down in the lengthening shadows of the lovely grounds, his tall body stooping a little, his hands behind his back like an old man, Miles tried to think how his mother and father managed. He knew they were happy together, for it was plain to see. His mother was a notorious chatterer, and always had been. It amused his father, a smiling, silent man on whom the perpetual patter of her words fell like the gentle rain from heaven. Apparently his father dearly loved to hear her and was endlessly diverted. Miles wondered if she ever stopped, even when the door closed behind them in their own room at night—and was embarrassed at his own thoughts.

Phoebe could be silent, he knew. Perhaps if he and Phoebe lived with his parents after they were married his mother would be company for her and he wouldn't have to—have to what? Entertain her? She would share his room. Everyone would think it very odd if she didn't. The room where now, if he closed the door on himself, no one had any right to intrude. And there was another thing—he faced that too, reluctantly. There might be children, crying and making a noise, running about getting into things—his sister Belle's babies were an awful nuisance, she said so herself. Phoebe's child and his—what would it be like? Could it be trained to behave, and not yell?

By now Miles was very near to begging the whole question, as he had done many times before. Let Phoebe go to England—let her stay there, if she wanted to, and have some other man's babies, as Virginia was doing. Let her leave him in peace with his books and his irregular hours, reading till dawn, sleeping after lunch, foraging for milk and gingerbread alone at midnight. No woman could fit herself into his erratic, selfish habits. No woman was worth the effort it would be to him to change them now. No woman—except possibly Phoebe Sprague.

Last summer when they went to Williamsburg for Aunt Sue's birthday, which was in August, and the fever came back on him in the hot weather and he had to go to bed in his father's old room in Grandfather Ransom's house and miss the party—Phoebe had made iced drinks for him, and came up in her party dress and sat with him most of the evening so he wouldn't feel out of things—her hands were so cool—he had begged for her hands on his face. . . . That time he ate the plum pudding at Cousin Sedgwick's at Christmas and couldn't eat anything for a week afterwards but milk and eggs—couldn't get out of bed, even, to come home, till after New Year's—Phoebe had read to him; Carlyle, they were reading then, and her voice sent him to sleep when nothing else could. . . . The touching way she always handed over to him her little manuscripts, anxious and embarrassed while he read them . . . the pretty way she flushed and sparkled when he praised them . . . the earnestness with which she listened to his judicious criticisms. . . .

With him to help her, Phoebe might become a successful novelist like Aunt Sue. That would be something to talk about together, wouldn't it? Perhaps they might collaborate on a book. His step quickened on the grass. They got on so well together, never any quarrels or misunderstandings. Phoebe was much too sensible to quarrel. They understood each other. She would never find anyone in England who understood her as he did. They were such old friends, lifelong friends—surely friends would be happy together, married? If he was going to marry at all, it would have to be Phoebe, she never got on his nerves, never raised her voice, never took offence. He thought of her honest, shining eyes, waiting for his smile, and the cleft in her funny little chin—he thought of her cool, quiet hands on his hot face. . . .

Miles had bought a seven-volume edition of Fanny d'Arblay's diaries bound in blue moiré, for Phoebe's birthday present. Before the shop closed that evening he returned it and got his money back. Then he walked three doors down the street to a jeweller's and bought a garnet ring, set in gold, with chip diamonds. It cost him more than the books. It cost him all the cash money he had saved up. It even cost him his peace of mind for a long time to come.

5

PHOEBE was glad that her Aunt Eden Murray arrived in Williamsburg before Miles did and was there to back her up. (Trust Bracken's mother, who had been Cabot Murray's wife, never to betray by the flick of an eyelash that the idea of Phoebe's going abroad with them had been Sue's and not her own.) Phoebe was not sure what she felt the need of protection *from*—she did not flatter herself that Miles would care very much whether she was in England or Williamsburg. But she had decided to go without asking his opinion first, and she had some dim idea that for this Miles might be reproachful.

He wasn't, though. He was smiling broadly and she thought he looked uncommonly well when he bent his lean height to give her the customary cousinly kiss. And, "That's a pretty dress," he said of her last year's pink lawn, freshened up with black velvet ribbon, which he had never noticed at all when it was new. Phoebe's eyes were very bright. Perhaps Miles was actually limbering up. And she had a new dress for the party— hyacinth-blue foulard with white spots, trimmed with lace medallions and white satin ribbon—the sleeves were deeply belled at the wrist above pointed lace cuffs. It was a present from Mother, who had money of her own which she was always afraid of using for fear of hurting Father's feelings, because she had inherited more than he could ever earn. Mother said she didn't care about the money, let it rot in the bank —but at times like birthdays she cheated a little. Phoebe suspected that Father knew.

Miles didn't wait for the new dress. The same evening he got there they went for a walk down the Jamestown Road past the College, and he listened with genuine interest to what she had to tell him about the proposed trip—how unexpected it was, and how good it would be for her writing, and how they all said she was sure to see the King—and of course, Phoebe added with some diffidence, she would see Virginia too.

"I wonder if having a baby has sobered her up some," said Miles in his slow, smiling drawl, and Phoebe laughed.

"I don't think *twins* would have any effect on Virginia," she said without malice, and added casually, "It will be interesting to see what kind of man she married."

"If he's anything like his sister Dinah, I reckon he's all right," said Miles, for the whole family had given Bracken's Dinah its heartiest approval, even if she was a ladyship with another brother who was an earl.

"Can I—give Virginia a message from you?" Phoebe asked, bracing herself invisibly against whatever his reply might be.

"Nope," said Miles placidly. "I've nothing to say to Virginia, nor she to me." They walked along in silence, while the sunset faded behind them—they were on the homeward lap now, and dusk was drawing in as they approached the campus of William and Mary College. Easter vacation had emptied the lawns under the high, spreading trees. It was a setting towards which Miles instinctively gravitated, and when they came to the gate in the low brick wall he turned her into it, saying, "Let's have a look round—wish I could get a job here, don't you?"

"Oh, Miles, that would be wonderful! We could really see something of each other then, and get some reading done together!"

"Would you like that?" he asked gravely, looking down at her from his great height as they moved side by side into the shadow of the trees.

"Well, of course I would! It's much more fun reading with you than alone, and—and—" The words drifted away rather breathlessly.

"Reckon you won't have much time for reading this summer," he suggested, but without reproach.

"I hope to," she insisted seriously. "I want to do some sightseeing, and know what I'm looking at. It's not going to be all new clothes and parties, Miles. I am going to learn a lot in England, to help my writing."

"I bet Virginia hasn't even seen the Tower of London yet!" he remarked ruefully with a shake of his head.

"Then I'll make her go with me and be educated!" she laughed, falling in with his mood as she always did, pleased that he was taking everything so easily tonight, for that was a sign that he felt well, and wouldn't have to leave the party and go and lie down. "I'll show her the spot where Anne Boleyn died, and the cell they kept Raleigh in!" she boasted gaily. "I've got a guidebook of Aunt Sue's, and she said I could mark things like that, that were really important."

"It wouldn't be any use trying to educate Virginia," he murmured. "She hasn't got that kind of brains. Reckon Virginia was mostly made to be looked at. A fellow can talk to you, though, with some hope of bein' understood—part of the time, anyway."

It was a left-handed sort of compliment, but Phoebe lapped it up gratefully—even with its implication that she wasn't much to look at herself. And then, having thought it over, Miles made an amendment.

"I don't mean you aren't pretty too, because you are," he added gravely. "In a different sort of way."

"Why—thank you, Miles." Phoebe's cheeks were pink in the dusk.

"You know, all of this has got me pretty scared," Miles went on, and their steps slowed to a stroll. "Never you mind about Virginia—that's all in the past. I never—never got far with Virginia, you know, and I reckon it's just as well, she wouldn't have cared much for Charlottesville. Do you suppose she has ever read a book since she stopped doing lessons?" he queried with a slanting, confidential look.

"I'll find out and let you know," Phoebe promised. Her heart had begun to beat rather fast.

"Doesn't matter," said Miles. "What matters now is you. I worried myself a good deal about your birthday present, because I know you like diary books, and I thought I'd found just the thing. And then at the last minute I changed my mind. I'm kind of scared now maybe I was wrong."

"You mean I don't get a book from you this time?" She tried not to sound disappointed.

"Well, that depends. If you—if you don't like what I got instead, I can still get you the books." Miles hesitated, put his hand into his pocket, and took it out again. "Phoebe, I think you're right to go abroad with

Aunt Eden, I wouldn't try to stop you for the world. But before you go I'd like to say—to sort of stake out a claim."

"To *what*, Miles?" Her heart was pounding in her ears now. They stood still in the dusk under the elms, facing each other, while Miles sought for words.

"I—don't know what I'd do without you, Phoebe—and I thought maybe this would remind you to come back home."

It was still light enough for her to see that in the palm of his hand, held out to her, was a small square box—the kind that rings came in. She took it with a gasp and opened it on the little garnet set with its circle of chip diamonds. Something like pity for Miles engulfed her in a paralyzing wave. It was so pathetic a gift beside Bracken's magnificent pendant—and beside the intrinsic dignity and value of any book.

"Will it fit?" he was asking anxiously above her, and she hesitated, holding the box—which finger was it meant to fit? Rather clumsily Miles took the ring from the box and reached for her left hand. "It's an engagement ring," he said simply. "If you're willing to marry me when you get back from England."

Phoebe stood still in the dusk and felt the ring slide on to her third finger. Her throat had closed, her eyelids stung. For some foolish reason, now that the thing she had dreamed of for years was happening she only wanted to cry. Having placed the ring on her finger, Miles put an arm around her waist, and drew her diffidently a little nearer.

"Is it all right?" he was saying in a worried sort of way. "It does fit, doesn't it? Will you marry me, Phoebe—along about Christmas time, maybe?"

"Oh, Miles—I've loved you all my life, you know I have!" She put out a hand to his shoulder, looking up at him. They were kissing kin, she had felt his lips a thousand times before now, briefly, at his arrivals and departures in Williamsburg. His first lover's kiss was quick and shy and undemanding, and over too soon. She leaned against him, shaken, swirling with her own delight, and felt the heavy beat of his heart beneath his jacket.

"I'll do my best to make you happy, honey," he said with his familiar, unself-conscious humility, and she put her arms around his thin shoulders and held him more closely than he was holding her.

"You *will*, Miles—there couldn't be anybody else—I *will* be happy with you!"

"If I should get that job in Louisville next year—you wouldn't mind living in Louisville?"

"With you it would be fun! Just the two of us setting out together, like pioneers!"

"Louisville isn't exactly the backwoods any more," he drawled. "The trains run pretty regular now."

She held to him, laughing, with brimming eyes. This was the way she loved him best—joking in his sober way, poking mild, unacrimonious fun at her—easy and cheerful and feeling well, and surely she could make sure he would always feel well, if she never worried him and always watched what he ate and kept him from getting bored and low in his mind by always being interesting and cheerful herself. And he said she was pretty. When she began to earn a little with her writing and could dress better she could be prettier, for him. And finally he would forget all about Virginia.

It never occurred to her, in the flurry of her own emotion, that Miles had not uttered the word love.

6

So PHOEBE's birthday party turned into a betrothal party, with extra ceremonies and gaieties. Miles enjoyed it all immensely, feeling that he had done the right thing for once. Phoebe was radiant and oddly inclined to choke up with happiness and whatever else it was that flooded through her when she looked at the little garnet ring. Sue and Eden, after refraining from a single telltale glance at each other, talked it over in Sue's room the evening before they left for New York.

"I suppose it was only to be expected," Sue said ruefully. "But I don't pretend it's going to be the same thing, sending Phoebe abroad with a ring on her engagement finger! Miles doesn't realize, of course—but what he's done is to bar her from half the fun she was meant to have."

"Meaning a few harmless little flirtations?" Eden asked sympathetically.

"Meaning," Sue corrected her steadily, "a chance to find the sort of thing Virginia found."

"Then you think Miles won't quite do," said Eden, turning her own handsome rings in the lamplight, and wondering at her sister's profound and unspinsterly wisdom.

"Oh, Eden, you, of all people, know very well what I think! Miles is

a dear, Lord knows we're all devoted to him. But think of your Cabot
when you first fell in love with him—remember Sedgwick when he
was Miles's age. What *is* it that Miles lacks?"

"Or don't they come the way they did when we were young?" Eden
mused.

"Of course they do, look at Bracken!" Sue pointed out triumphantly.
"He's the younger generation, and whatever it is that Miles hasn't got,
it's in Bracken. And in Fitz too, since he found himself."

"Poor Miles has been ill so much since Cuba," Eden began. "Perhaps
if we could get him really *well*—"

"So has Fitz been ill," Sue reminded her obstinately. "I don't mean
to be hard on Miles, he's Dabney's son—but there's no *grip* to him, Dee,
no—no—" Sue spread her hands helplessly, and Eden nodded.

"He certainly hasn't swept her off her feet," she agreed. "But he's
what Phoebe wants, Sue, don't forget that. She has always trailed after
him like a puppy, ever since they were babies."

"How can Phoebe know what she wants?" Sue asked rebelliously.

"You knew. I knew. And we had seen no more of the world than
Phoebe has. We'd be wrong to meddle, Sue. People must find their own
destiny."

"But I wonder if they do," said Sue. "Sometimes I think destiny
needs a good strong push from behind."

Eden smiled at her affectionately.

"You can't write Phoebe's romance as though it was in one of your
books, honey. She's a human being, not a pen-and-ink person you've
concocted out of thin air. Phoebe's got to write her own love story."

"You're right, I know," Sue conceded doubtfully. "But if only he
hadn't got that ring on her finger! No self-respecting man will look
twice at her, now that he can see at a glance that she's spoken for!"

"Well, of all the matchmaking little busybodies!" said Eden admiringly. "It's no joke to lose them to an English husband, Sue, I can
tell you that! You ought to be thankful Phoebe is going to settle down
here, with Miles."

"But I didn't want her to settle down at all," said Sue. "Not like that,
anyway. I wanted her to have *fun*, Dee—*you* had fun. You had Cabot.
Do you honestly believe it will be any fun to marry Miles?"

Eden sighed suddenly, and her slender body wilted in the chair and
she put up a hand to shield her face from the fierce, searching eyes of
her too-knowing little sister.

"When you put it that way—no," she confessed behind her hand. *You had Cabot*—his hard, leashed strength, his all-seeing, possessive eyes, his big, gentle hands, his laughter—his irrepressible, irreverent, invigorating laughter, even in bed—how on earth did Sue know, so surely, about such things as rowdy laughter in bed, and sense that lack in Miles? *You had Cabot*—there was a world of wistfulness, even of envy, in those words. And Melicent had Sedgwick. But Sue knew, somehow, what she had missed, and insisted on it for Phoebe, who was Sedgwick's child. "I suppose we couldn't persuade her to leave off the ring this summer," Eden said thoughtfully, behind the shielding hand.

"I suppose that wouldn't be fair to Miles," said Sue, and sighed again. "No, I reckon he's been and done it. Maybe marriage will bring him out some. Gwen did wonders for Fitz, though that wasn't at all the same thing."

"Phoebe's happy, anyway," said Eden. "She wanted Miles, and now she's got him. We mustn't interfere."

"Oh, no," Sue said hastily. "We must never interfere."

In New York the following week they bought Phoebe the loveliest clothes they could find, and Eden's obliging dressmaker worked day and night to complete the outfit before sailing time. Phoebe watched her own Cinderella transformation with an almost impersonal fascination, as though she stood aside and saw some other girl enjoying all this good fortune. There were printed muslins and figured foulards and embroidered voiles, evening frocks in white lace and blue satin and mousseline de soie—velvet tea-gowns trimmed with fur for chilly days, other tea-gowns of crêpe de chine and kilted chiffon (you wore tea-gowns at breakfast in English country houses)—an opera wrap of white velvet and miniver—tweeds for the country with neat matching toques —chiffon blouses for the theater, white linen for river parties, a lace and tussore silk coat for Ascot, a grey walking costume trimmed with chinchilla—slippers and parasols and boas and fans, gloves in three different lengths, and hats and hats and hats. . . .

When Phoebe protested belatedly about extravagance and began to show an inconvenient interest in the prices of things, they reminded her that she would have Virginia and Dinah to live up to—and suggested that she call it a trousseau, with which to impress all Charlottesville next winter and make Miles proud. The summer would be just a sort of dress rehearsal for her début in Charlottesville as Miles's bride. And besides, if the King should happen to look her way . . .

PART TWO

OLIVER

Farthingale.   *Summer, 1902.*

>>

1

THEY sailed at the end of the month, for Bracken wanted to deposit his mother and Phoebe safely in Gloucestershire and say Hello all round before he and Dinah dashed off to Spain to see the coronation of young King Alfonzo, which was to take place in Madrid a few weeks before that of Edward in London in June.

The voyage would have passed uneventfully if it had not been for Miles's ring. Phoebe laid it on the shelf above the wash-basin in the *Ladies* when she went to wash her hands before lunch on the second day out. And being unaccustomed to wearing a ring at all, and becoming engrossed in a discussion of the ping-pong game in the ship's gymnasium where Dinah had just royally trounced her, Phoebe forgot the ring and left it there on the shelf. When she rushed back for it half an hour later any number of other people had washed their hands at the same basin and the ring was gone. The purser, who was wearily familiar with countless tearful women who had done the same thing, was as sympathetic as he could manage to be, and pinned up a notice offering a reward, but the ring was not returned.

Phoebe wept piteously and begged to know what she was going to tell Miles, and was advised to say nothing about it till she got back, and by no means to let it spoil her enjoyment of the summer. But she remained inconsolable for hours. Eden remarked privately to Bracken that Sue would probably be pleased to hear of the loss, and Bracken said no doubt it was Fate. Anyway, the very next day the first officer suggested that Phoebe might like to see the engines, and the day after that the ship's doctor, a most delightful man, asked them all to take coffee and liqueurs with him in the lounge after dinner—it was Phoebe he wanted to talk to—and the day after that the Captain invited her up on the bridge.

They arrived at Liverpool on a cold wet day and went straight down to Virginia at Farthingale to see the baby, who had been born in February and christened Daphne. Virginia happened to have had an easy time during her first confinement, and therefore was convinced that people made too much fuss about having babies. She would not get it into her head that things sometimes went far otherwise, and told everybody that she meant to have another just as soon as possible, as there was absolutely nothing to it—if, the implication was, you knew how.

Eden, who had always nearly died, held her peace with a slight effort for the sake of Dinah, who was serenely hopeful that some day soon she would start a baby herself and was delighted to hear how simple it was. "Of course it's a bore not to hunt, if it's coming in the winter," Virginia would add carelessly. "I shall manage better next time. Winifred had her little Hubert in November and was out again before the season ended." Winifred had married Dinah's and Archie's brother Edward, who had succeeded to the earldom the year before on the death of their father. The earlier splendors of the Hall, a fine Georgian pile which was the preferred seat of the Earls of Enstone, were reviving under Winifred's vigorous reign, for she was an heiress with a half million in coal.

Dinah considered that Edward had been very lucky to get Winifred —who had married him at eighteen when she was just out and had not taken time to look round. There was nothing wrong with Edward, of course—unless you compared him to Archie, who was Dinah's favorite brother. Edward had tried very hard for Virginia once, against his own better judgment, but she had chosen to marry a mere Honorable instead of becoming Edward's countess, and Dinah for one quite saw why. Edward would be an unimaginative lover and a domineering husband. In Winifred, young as she was, he had got a wife who domineered right back at him, in a perfectly well-bred way, but she didn't have that chin for nothing, and she took to horses and the sporting, strenuous life at the Hall with enthusiasm. She rode well and fearlessly over stiff wall-country which required nerve and decision and staying power, danced equally well and tirelessly at the Hunt balls, and managed the rather complicated household at the Hall to the admiration of all beholders.

The old Earl had had five sons and two daughters, of whom Edward was of course the eldest. Then came John, who was a successful Conservative M.P. and seldom left London where he lived in an ornate little house in Eaton Square with a dull and browbeaten wife and one small daughter. Oliver was a captain in a Lancer regiment and had gone to South Africa with Kitchener and carried dispatches under fire and got the D.S.O. Having been severely wounded in the same fight which had killed Gratian Forbes-Carpenter, Oliver had arrived back in England at the first of the year, trailing clouds of glory, and was now convalescing on sick leave at the Hall. Archie, who had married Virginia Murray, came next, and was known in the family as the brainy one, being a great reader of books and a rising young barrister in the Chancery Court. Clare, the family beauty, who had come out the year of the Jubilee, married for money and had an establishment in Belgrave Square and a bull-necked, doting husband in the City, and an infant son. Dinah, who was so young when Bracken fell in love with her that he had to wait for her to grow up a little, was now only twenty, but carried off her position as a famous journalist's wife with complete aplomb. And Gerald, the youngest, was still at Eton.

Phoebe said it all sounded rather like the family intricacies at Williamsburg and was prepared to assimilate all of Virginia's and Bracken's acquired relations as easily and with as little shyness as the youngest members of a large family usually show in the presence of other people's brothers and sisters and their offspring. The more Phoebe heard about life at the Hall, and at Farthingale, the more it seemed to her that England was going to be just like home.

She didn't see them all at once when she reached Farthingale on that wet afternoon about tea time. Archie would not have a motor car because he said they smelled, so a smart barouche with matched bays was waiting at the station—horses, Virginia was accustomed to point out with entire good humor, had no smell whatever.

The carriage passed through a backward countryside—the village of Upper Briarly was a mile and three-quarters from its railway station on the banks of the little river Windrush, which ran right down the middle of the only street, with a triple-arched stone bridge above the old ford. The Hall lay on the left across the river when you had driven through the village, and Farthingale was a mile farther on. To reach the house you came up an avenue of chestnuts which made a dramatic turn and presented the west front to view—golden Cotswold stone, with a sharp, steep roof-line and narrow mullioned windows in rows, and a branch of the Windrush flowing almost level with its clipped grassy banks at the edge of the green lawn. Only the bravest flowers were out in that inclement spring—lemony primroses, forget-me-nots bluer than the pale English sky, wallflowers, daffodils—Phoebe had seen pictures of Farthingale, but she exclaimed with delight at the reality.

Tea was waiting before the drawing-room fire, and Virginia in ruby velvet and old lace flung herself into her mother's arms with touching abandon and began at once to tell about the baby. You would have thought nobody had ever had a baby before. Eden listened politely to a lot of things she already knew, and drank hot tea out of the old Worcester cups, and realized once more that Cabot was gone forever and would not be with her when she first beheld her remarkable grandchild. Dinah and Archie were full of family news, to which Bracken and Phoebe attended with interest, and then they all adjourned to the nursery to admire Virginia's achievement, which Archie said irreverently looked to him pretty much like all the other babies he had ever seen.

Phoebe took to Archie at once. He was like Dinah in a way—fair, with a fine jaw-line and small bones. He was clean-shaven and wore an eyeglass and by all accounts looked marvelous in his barrister's wig and gown. Phoebe felt acquainted with Archie on account of Father, recognizing in him the same dry lawyer's logic, the same glinting wit, the same amusing air of having summed up. Virginia's slim brunette beauty and vivacious ways set him off to advantage, too. They were a delightful pair, still visibly enchanted with each other, though they tried to hide it with understatement and golden-wedding airs. Phoebe could see that Archie was the one for Virginia, and that Miles would never have done. But one couldn't say that, could one, to Miles? Any more than one could confess in the first letter home that one had left his poor little ring on the shelf in the *Ladies*.

2

It had been arranged that they should dine quietly at Farthingale the first evening, in case Eden was tired, and all go to lunch at the Hall the following day. Easter had passed, but the Hall was still fairly full of visitors, though John and his family had returned to London and Gerald had gone back to school.

There were five house-guests at the Hall from outside the family, Virginia explained to Phoebe as they all sat round the drawing-room fire at Farthingale that first evening—Charles Laverham and his sister Penelope, who had married Tommy Chetwynd last winter; and a girl called Rosalind Norton-Leigh, who had been bridesmaid to both Clare and Dinah, and her mamma who never let Rosalind out of her sight if she could help it—a *ubiquitous* woman, Virginia said, but one would put up with far worse for Rosalind's sake. Then there would be Edward and Winifred, of course, and Oliver, who was still on sick leave, and Clare and her husband, Mortimer Flood, who was rather a wart but meant well and you got used to him.

Charles Laverham had got the V.C. in South Africa, Virginia went on, and when Phoebe, whose head was by now swimming with names, which was understandable but would sort itself out in time, failed to look sufficiently impressed, Virginia elaborated on Charles.

"You don't get the V.C. except for 'conspicuous bravery in the presence of the enemy,'" she informed Phoebe. "Charles is a captain in the Blues—the Horse Guards, you know, with the shiny breast-plates and the plumes—Bracken will take you to see them in Whitehall when you get to London. Charles went out to South Africa with the Household Regiment and saw a lot of fighting."

"What did he do," Phoebe asked, "to get the V.C.?"

"Nobody knows, he won't talk about it!" Virginia sighed resignedly. "Oliver won't talk about his D.S.O., either. Men are funny. But the Queen herself pinned the medal on Charles's chest while he knelt in front of her chair, and it must have been a real satisfaction to Victoria, I should think—Charles is just the last word in soldiers. He's six foot three to begin with, and his helmet and plume must really scrape the sky."

"No Guardsman can be less than six feet," Dinah reminded her. "I remember Oliver was pretty sick about that, he lacked a little less than an inch no matter what he did, and he had set his heart on joining the same regiment because he and Charles had been at school together. But the Lancers are almost as good, I always think," she added loyally. "Of course there's less foreign service with the Household Troops and Charles likes to be in London. Do you think he's in love with Rosalind?" she inquired of Virginia in entirely unconfidential tones.

"It won't do him any good if he is," Virginia replied decidedly. "Rosalind's mam*ma* has made up her mind that Rosalind must Marry

Well. She's spoilt two good chances already that I know of, people that Rosalind might easily have been very happy with—shooed off by Mam*ma* because they hadn't enough Prospects! And Charles's prospects, even though he's a lamb and any girl would be lucky to get him, don't go beyond the regiment."

"Isn't his uncle somebody or other?" Dinah asked idly.

"Marquis of Cleeve, no less! But Uncle Cleeve has two healthy sons of his own, about Charles's age. One is in India, and one is still in South Africa, and of course something *might* happen to them both, but it isn't very likely. Charles has enough to live on, from his own father who died a few years back, but barely enough. It's an expensive life in a regiment like that, as anyone knows, and Charles *will* play polo. I doubt if he'd give up his precious ponies for any woman on earth."

Archie looked across at Bracken.

"Isn't it frightening to hear women talk?" he inquired with a shudder. "They're as cold-blooded and impersonal as a surgeon, and as rude as a gossip column in a servants' hall paper. These two have vivisected Charles Laverham and hung him up to dry before our very eyes, all with the best will in the world!"

"Well, what have I said?" Virginia challenged him. "It's nothing against Charles that he's a long way from being Cleeve's heir, and that Mrs. Norton-Leigh wouldn't consider anything less than fifty thousand a year for Rosalind!"

"Doesn't Rosalind have anything to say about it?" murmured Eden, who had married for love and got money as well.

"Not very much," Virginia admitted cheerfully. "Rosalind is pretty vague about life still, and very much under Mam*ma's* thumb. It's not like Clare, marrying this man Flood with her eyes open and her wits about her. Rosalind doesn't—" She glanced round quickly, remembering there were gentlemen present. "—doesn't know *anything,*" she finished with a comprehensive gesture. "I shan't allow my Daphne to grow up with blinkers on like that. She's going to know exactly what's what, from the beginning."

"Judging by her mother," Archie put in gently, "Daphne was born knowing a lot of things Rosalind will have to find out by trial and error."

The chat around Virginia's fireside that evening had more or less cleared things up for Phoebe, but when she walked into the white drawing-room at the Hall next day at lunch time bewilderment set in again. Ten people awaited them there, clustered casually about the two fires in the long room, with its Gainsboroughs over the mantels and its crystal chandeliers and its fragile Adam furniture and old needle-point and brocade draperies. There were six in their own party, and everybody knew everybody except herself, and introductions were interrupted and sketchy, and it was difficult to decide which was which and who was married to whom.

It began to simplify at luncheon when Edward and Winifred took their places at the ends of the table, and wives were naturally not seated next to their husbands. By a process of elimination Phoebe made out Penelope and Tommy Chetwynd, Clare and Mortimer Flood. Then the lovely creature next to Archie across the table must be Rosalind, and the pretty woman with the overdone hair was her mamma. Phoebe tried hard not to stare at Rosalind, who typified in her slim person all the romantic heroines Phoebe had ever imagined.

Rosalind had softly waved dark hair abundantly dressed and seeming to make her little head too heavy for its slender neck. Her eyes were dark blue, with the longest eyelashes God ever gave a woman. Her brows were arched and quizzical, her rather large mouth curved in a somehow expectant smile, her chin was pointed and young. She was not more than eighteen inches at the waist, and her voice lilted like a child's. She was plainly on good terms with Archie and was enjoying herself with him so much that one could observe her without being caught. The man on her other side was devoting himself to Eden, and was either Charles or Oliver, Phoebe wasn't sure which. He was big enough for a Guardsman, heaven knew, with brushed-looking dark red hair and a rather plain, square, honest face which expanded into a most engaging grin at intervals. But all the men at the table seemed enormous in their country tweeds, except Archie, who looked oddly boyish and brittle in this hefty company.

Eden was on Edward's right, and Phoebe on his left found herself undergoing a sort of catechism as though she was not more than ten years old, obediently answering her host's blunt, friendly questions while he placed her in his mind, docketed and pigeon-holed her, with her precise position in Virginia's family, her experience—or lack of it—in travel, her attitude towards dogs and hunting, and so forth. Phoebe could ride, for all the family rode, and understood horses. But she was not a passionate sportswoman and had never cared about riding to hounds. This was obviously a black mark against her character, and Edward showed his disillusionment by joining the conversation with Eden.

Phoebe sat in rebuffed silence for a few minutes, eating, and then became very conscious of the presence on her left, which had to be either Oliver or Charles, and she was still not sure which. Whoever he was, she was afraid of him, for he was the best-looking man she had ever seen, and she was sure that a country-mouse like herself could be of no possible interest to him, and dreaded the moment when she must try and entertain him. She had already seen in incredulous stolen glances before they left the drawing-room that his dark hair fitted his well-shaped skull like a cap, that his dark mustache was clipped more closely than was the fashion and showed the curve of his upper lip above his white teeth when he smiled, and that his brown eyes shone and dazzled in his tanned face—so that if you were not accustomed to holding your own with so much masculine splendor, and Phoebe wasn't, you looked down, and away, and couldn't think of anything to say.

"Has Edward been bullying you?" said the voice on her left, sympathetically. "You look sort of trampled on."

"I said the wrong thing," she heard herself confessing impulsively. "I don't hunt."

"Heavens above," he murmured. "That's a social error in these parts."

"Yes, I begin to think it is." A silver platter came down between them, creating a pause, and then was removed. "Are you the V.C. in the Horse Guards or the D.S.O. Lancer?" she inquired then, still trying for her bearings.

"That's the V.C. over there," he said, indicating the man on Eden's right. "I'm just one of Kitchener's messenger boys."

"Then you're Dinah's brother," she discovered with some relief.

"Yes, I'm Oliver. I don't wonder you've got a bit mixed up."

"Was he wounded too?" she inquired, looking at Charles, who was guilty of conspicuous bravery.

"Got nicked in the arm somewhere. We've both had sick leave, but he's back on the King's duty now. You'll see him swanking about in the Procession, on Coronation Day."

"What did he do?"

"When?"

"To get the V.C."

"Oh, that. Pulled some other bloke out of a hole, I suppose, at the risk of his own neck. That's what most of 'em are for."

"Don't you *know?*"

" 'Fraid I don't, as a matter of fact. I wasn't there."

"Well, why don't you *ask* him?"

"Couldn't do that, he'd probably tell me to go boil my head!"

"Aren't men funny," she mused, echoing Virginia.

"And do you flatter yourself that women aren't?"

There was laughter in his words, and she turned her head to share it with him and was caught by his eyes—clear brown, with dancing amber lights, the whites very white, like his teeth, in his tanned face. They were the *livest* eyes she had ever seen, as though they were charged with electricity, and they were very kind. . . .

"Now tell me when I was born, my favorite flower, and what I had for breakfast," he suggested quietly, and she realized that she had been gazing at him openly and flushed. "Do forgive me," he added quickly before she could speak. "But you were looking through me as though I were plate glass. What *did* you see?"

"A soldier," she said. "I—never knew a soldier before, except my Cousin Miles and he was only an amateur and didn't like it. Do you?"

"Very much indeed. It's a good life—keeps you busy, no time to brood over the state of your soul or your liver. That's all taken care of for you in the Regulations."

"You wouldn't change?"

"Not till they kick me out for old bones!"

"I don't know much about the war in South Africa," she said seriously. "I should like to understand it better."

Oliver laughed outright.

"So should I!" he said. "So would Charles, no doubt!"

"So should I what?" said Charles, looking round at his name.

"Miss Sprague was saying she would like to understand the war better. I tell her she's not alone in that."

"She's got lots of company up at the War Office, I should think," said Charles. His voice was rather light for so big a man, and had a sort of softening overtone like a burr, which came of his Gloucestershire up-bringing and which Eton had failed entirely to eliminate.

Edward then gave it as his opinion that they were a lot of bl-blithering fools at the War Office and that General Buller ought to get the sack, and Winifred said what about the b.f.'s at Westminster while he was about it, and the conversation became general and rather heated. Phoebe thought she could see Bracken making mental notes on the state of public opinion in England and she sat silent, wondering about Rosalind and Charles, weaving romance around them and Rosalind's ambitious mamma. And by the time the dessert came in she had become so aware of the man on her left that she felt him like a tingling in her fingertips.

Life, and a zest for living emanated from Oliver Campion like a fragrance. His casual humor, baiting Edward good-naturedly, kept ripples of laughter running through her. Once when his elbow accidentally touched hers she started as though the tweed sleeve had burned her. She was obsessed by the need to look and look at him, imprinting his lean brown sparkling face on her memory, and like a man who triumphs over the fumes of a heady wine and by sheer will power holds his behavior to a normal pitch she forced herself to keep her eyes turned from him and her mind on what was being said by the rest of them. He's like Father, she found herself thinking dazedly in her inner turmoil. He outshines everybody else without trying. And again, sealing her own doom with the knowledge—Father must have been like this when he was young.

"What *are* you thinking of, all by yourself?" said Oliver's low voice on her left, and Phoebe, caught off guard, blurted out the truth.

"You remind me of my father," she said, and his eyes searched hers briefly for any sort of double meaning or transatlantic jest, and found only a troubled honesty.

"That must be rather a compliment," he said then.

"I thought there was no one like him," she explained simply. "But you are. When he was your age, I mean."

"Thank you," said Oliver. "I should like to say, if I may, that I never dreamed there was anybody like you."

For a moment more, surrounded by that noisy, contentious luncheon table, they looked at each other, and then realized that their hostess had risen.

They said no more to each other until the general good-byes, when he took her hand in a warm, hard clasp, and remarked, "My leave runs through July, so you'll see a good deal of me, I expect. Do you like to ride without the fox and hounds?"

"Very much."

"Good. I've got just the horse here. May I bring him round tomorrow morning about ten?"

"Thank you, I'd like to if—if Virginia has nothing else planned."

"She'll lend you to me," he promised confidently. "The anemones are out, and you must see them at their prime, they don't last long."

Phoebe was very quiet on the drive home, which she made in the dog-cart with Bracken and Virginia, while the others followed in the barouche. Virginia rattled on to Bracken, who was anxious to hear about everything which had happened since he was last in England the previous autumn, and then suddenly she said, "What did you think of Oliver, Phoebe, isn't he a duck? I was terribly afraid you might get stuck down with Mortimer, who bores us all to tears, poor dear. The best I hoped for you was Tommy Chetwynd, who is all sorts of a fool but rather sweet. When I saw you'd drawn Oliver, I knew you'd be all right."

"Yes, I—he's charming," said Phoebe rather breathlessly, and Virginia sighed and scowled at her slipper toes.

"If only Maia was a little *easier,*" she said. "Oliver is such a light-hearted soul, and she does grind him beneath her chariot wheels!"

"Who is Maia?" Phoebe asked automatically.

"The girl he's going to marry, dammit," said Virginia. "We none of us know quite how it happened, and we none of us can bear her, isn't it awful? She made such a dead set at him you'd think *any* man would have run like a stag, but darling Oliver just put his silly head into the noose like the gentleman he is, and there we are!"

"What *is* the matter with that girl?" Bracken demanded. "And am I going to meet up with her while I'm here? You've all got your knife into her, and nobody can give me any clear reason why!"

"She's up in Yorkshire now. She has to spend a lot of time there because her mother is dead and her father is an invalid," Virginia explained. "Sometimes I think Maia is only marrying Oliver to get away from home, though of course he's beautiful to look at and lets her order him around to her heart's content."

"How did she meet him, then?"

"She was in London when he first came home from South Africa and was so ill, and probably he hadn't seen a woman for months. Clare had taken her up for some reason, though she's sick of her now, and Maia was always underfoot in Belgrave Square, and then suddenly, *wham,* she had him!"

"Well, I'm still waiting to hear what's wrong with her," Bracken insisted equably, and Virginia gave another impatient little sigh.

"It's hard to say, it really is. She's pretty in an exotic sort of way. You see, her father made his money in tea, and married out in Calcutta, where Maia was born. Nobody in England ever saw his wife because she died out there, and while everything *appears* to be all right, one does sort of wonder—"

"Great Scott, not some sort of *mixture!*" cried Bracken.

"Oh, no, that is, not *recently,* of course, and some of it is very good blood, at that—but Maia *is* rather sallow, and her eyes are set in a rather odd way—"

"But the Army is very fussy about such things," Bracken pointed out.

"Oh, Oliver must know all about her background, of course, or he would never—and since his commanding officer allows the marriage it pretty well proves Maia's pedigree, I suppose. It's only—well, I happen to know Charles hates it. And besides, she isn't nice to Oliver."

"How do you mean? She must have been fairly nice to him or he wouldn't—"

"I think it's because she's uncertain of herself," Virginia said thoughtfully. "And she takes it out of him. She likes to tyrannize in little ways— she makes him wait on her hand and foot—fans, scarves, gloves, shut the window, open the window, please do this, don't do that—and there's something stingy about her mouth. Mind you, she's a beauty in her way, and knows how to dress to bring out her good points. But she's one of those *tight-lipped* women!"

"Oh, Lord," said Bracken, with perfect comprehension at last.

"Oliver deserves better," said Virginia with her unexpected, acute perception. "A woman who marries a professional soldier ought to be the sort to fling herself into love head first and not care if it drowns her. Rosalind could do it like that—I've always sort of hoped Rosalind and Oliver would take to each other seriously, but they give no signs at all, I suppose because they've grown up together and she's got used to him—but no woman could resist him if he really tried."

"But you just said Maia did fling herself at him," Bracken objected.

"Till she got him, and not the same way I mean. Oliver is wasting himself on a woman who will make him beg for everything he gets from her," Virginia prophesied gloomily. "And she doesn't even think he's funny. *I* think Oliver is awfully funny, don't you, Phoebe?" she asked suddenly of the silent figure beside her. "I saw you two laughing together like anything."

"Yes, he—said some very funny things, I thought," Phoebe agreed hastily, while the green world beyond the dog-cart tipped and spun before her eyes and she felt something beating in the roof of her mouth which seemed to be her heart. Oliver had put his silly head into the noose. Oliver was engaged to be married. But so am I, Phoebe told herself as though reassuring a small, whimpering child. So am I engaged—to Miles.

3

BEFORE nightfall Oliver was inclined to regret his hasty offer of a horse and the anemones, for he found he could think of nothing else but seeing Virginia's American cousin again, and he was forced to remind himself that there was no sense in that, because of Maia.

It was a new sensation to Oliver, who had always been a free soul, to have to remember Maia.

Like everybody else, except possibly Maia herself, he was still uncertain exactly how it had happened, though he hated to admit that even to himself. He had been confined to his rooms in London by bad weather and his wound, and Clare insisted that he needed cheering up and would be better off in her Belgrave Square establishment. His batman, on whom he depended for everything, had had a bad go of fever and was able only to creep about to do for them both, and needed a bit of leave himself. Under Clare's persuasion, Oliver arranged for Simmons to go to his own people near Oxford for a month and allowed himself to be transplanted, bag and baggage, to Clare's luxurious household, until he should be well enough to leave London and enjoy a bit of air and mild exercise at the Hall.

He had been given his own sitting-room in Clare's house, and he got very dull in it, keeping rather quiet because of the unhealed hole in his back, playing patience and reading himself blue by choosing all the wrong sort of books. Maia had been a diversion. She was easy to look at, she brought him grapes and gossip, and she poured out his afternoon tea and plumped up his tired pillows and didn't seem to mind that he was seedy and low in his spirits. Having had very little experience of being ill, Oliver was impressed at how pleasant a woman's ministrations can be. One day he kissed Maia's hand as she did him some trifling service, and was not rebuked. The next day when she came her eyes were expectant, and it was raining outside and cosy inside, and life was beginning to flow back into him, and still he was tied to his invalid routine and the doctors wouldn't let him off the lead—he was bored—she was kind—he was grateful—she was clever, passing so close to his chair as she moved about the room that her soft skirts dragged across his feet, bending above him so that her perfume reached his nostrils, offering his teacup with lingering, manicured hands—sympathetic, entertaining, preferring his company to gayer surroundings—he said too much—she was too willing—there was no retreat.

After she had gone he sat a while alone in the dusky room, bidding good-bye to certain cherished aspects of his existence—contemplating the possibilities of the new life ahead. He suspected within twenty-four hours that he had made a mistake, and promised himself that no one else would ever suspect, least of all Maia. He had always maintained that you could make a life with whatever you had, if you tried. He would have an attractive wife, with money of her own, who knew how to be a pleasant companion and who would be a suitable mother to the children he would like to have before he got much older. What more could a man ask, he would demand of himself in his solitude. The rapture and agony and intricacies of falling wildly in love? That was for people in novels. Besides, he was getting on for that sort of thing—thirty next birthday. Where had the time gone? Where had his love affairs gone? Two or three in India—one or two in Egypt—no better than Maia, any of them, if you came down to it. Except the first. And she had had a husband.

Thus Oliver, a born philosopher with a light heart, assumed the inevitable consequences of making careless love to his sister's friend, and looked forward with interest to what could be done with a marriage he knew dismayed his relatives. He would show them all. He would be happy with Maia, he would start a family of his own, and the rest of them would see that he knew perfectly well what he was about. You could always be happy with a woman if you took a little trouble to make her happy, unless she was an absolute harpy. All it req ired was a little care and consideration, a little tact and good management, and a life could be built, a home could be founded. In most countries except England it was seldom done any other way. Sometimes the rapture came later.

And then, sitting on his right hand at a family luncheon party in the country, was this slim grave girl with the dignity and reserve of a princess, and the eyes of a troubled child. What had given her that look in the eyes, he wondered during the laggard hours which had to elapse between the luncheon and ten o'clock the next morning—patient and good and obedient she looked, as though she had been taught to watch and not touch. It was against nature that a person so young should have so much the look of *waiting,* so that whatever it was she didn't have you longed to give to her quickly and coax her to smile. She had smiled, of course, at luncheon—they had laughed together more than once—she had beautiful teeth and a cleft in her funny little chin. But she had only laughed on the surface, there was something deep and still and unstirred inside her. She must take things very hard, he decided, and that was always a mistake. In his soldier's fatalistic scheme of things, you had to take life as it came and make the most of it, without wishing it was different, or you would never be happy at all. You lived whatever was ahead of you up to the hilt and enjoyed it the best you could, whether it was a hand-to-hand fight (in which, be sure, there was a certain joy) or a dull spell of footling maneuvers with never a glimpse of the enemy and with manifold bodily discomforts—or, if it came to that, marrying Maia. There was always something to be said for most of it, and the main thing was, you weren't dead. But the little American had allowed life to puzzle her. There was something she hadn't solved. Her search for the solution was visible in her steady, unembarrassed gaze, which questioned and appealed. You wanted to hold out a hand to her and say, Mind the step—now you're all right—it's quite safe, just follow me. . . .

Maia always seemed to know exactly where she was going.

All that was chivalrous and tender-hearted in Oliver had risen up to answer the little American's unconscious need. She seemed to have so much to learn, there seemed to be so much ahead of her, and who was there to see that she didn't go blundering about in the dark and hurt herself? Because she would hurt herself, she was endlessly vulnerable in her present unfledged state. She hadn't learned to cut her losses. She hadn't learned to laugh things off.

He wondered how he knew so much about her, for he had never had second sight before. But long after his lamp was out and the fire had died on his bedroom hearth, he lay in the dark and thought about Phoebe Sprague and how she could be armored against circumstance. It was not his affair, of course, to try to protect from unknown eventualities a perfectly strange girl who had a large, capable family of her own as a bulwark. But so far they didn't seem to have been much good to her. They had left her to grope. That was it. Phoebe was groping. And her outstretched, seeking hand had touched his heart. Pleased with the high literary tone of his metaphors, he fell asleep.

The idea of Phoebe as a lost child who must be seen safely into competent hands was waiting beside his pillow when he awoke. While he bathed and shaved and dressed in riding clothes, he turned over in his mind various words of wisdom he might utter during their ride. But you couldn't just say suddenly, out of the blue, Look here, my dear, life is really a lot easier than you might think. She would question your right to give her advice. She had a right to tell you to mind your own business. Besides—maybe he was all wrong about the girl, maybe the next time he saw her she would have all Virginia's insouciance, or Rosalind's heedless ingrained gaiety, or Maia's cool audacity. He had no real reason to think he knew her inside out on the strength of sitting next to her once at luncheon. But he did. That was the funny part. He did know her, right down to the bottom of her transparent soul.

He supposed of course Virginia would have mentioned his engagement to Maia, so there would be no misapprehensions on Phoebe's part if they saw something of each other while she was at Farthingale. It was a beastly nuisance, though, not being free. A year ago—Oliver paused, with somewhat the sensation of having tripped over his own heart, and stood with a military brush in each hand, looking into his own eyes in the mirror of the chiffonier. A year ago wouldn't he have undertaken to make quite sure that Phoebe Sprague would be properly looked after for the rest of her life? Good Lord, what have I done, said Oliver to himself in the glass. No. It's not possible. One doesn't fall in love at first sight at my age. Besides, I'm already in love with somebody else. Supposed to be, that is. . . .

He put down the brushes absently and went to stand at the window of his room, which looked out over the sunken garden. This really won't do, he said to himself in astonishment. I must get her off my mind somehow, this is preposterous. The best thing is to see her again and find out how wrong I am and stop imagining things. She doesn't need me, there are heaps of people to look after her. A girl like that is bound to have a dozen faithful admirers at home. . . .

But somehow he knew she hadn't. No matter what he told himself, he knew that without him Phoebe Sprague was going to get hurt. And she was certain to be without him.

His heart was beating considerably faster than it had done in the cordon at Tarkastaad as he rode up the chestnut avenue to Farthingale, leading the best horse in Edward's stables which wore a side-saddle, and his lips were drawn in a rather one-sided smile. He could not but be amused at his own youthful sensations. He had outgrown all this long ago. Women no longer made his heart beat like that.

But this one did.

4

PHOEBE was waiting for him in the drawing-room, dressed for riding. It occurred to him forcibly all over again how she had the somehow pathetic gravity of all very young things—kittens, puppies, colts—you wanted to laugh, but you felt like crying too, because they were trying so hard.

And Phoebe, who had wakened at dawn feeling as though it was her birthday, and had been unable to go back to sleep, was thinking dizzily as he tossed her into the saddle, But there must be *something* wrong with him, *nobody* could be so good-looking all the way to his bones— either he's a heartless flirt, or—or he drinks too much, or—well, no, that would show, wouldn't it, what sins don't show, because those are the ones he's got. . . .

Meanwhile, when they had dealt with the weather and the horses and the state of everybody's health since yesterday—

"Tell me about your father," he was saying. "You've roused my curiosity about him."

"I've never tried to describe him before," she confessed, at a loss. "Where I come from, everybody knows him. I did try to write about him once, but Cousin Sue said it wasn't any use, paper was too cold and flat to hold him. Cousin Sue has had nearly twenty books published," she added with a certain pride.

"Yes, I know. I was in Egypt the year she came to England, so I never met her. My major did, though—and fell heels over head in love with her, I believe."

"With *Cousin Sue?*" cried Phoebe incredulously. "I never knew about that!"

"Perhaps you weren't supposed to. Nothing came of it, and he was killed in South Africa, poor chap. I never got it from him, of course, Virginia told me about it after I came back."

"Does Cousin Sue know he's dead?"

"Sure to. Bracken would have seen to that, wouldn't he?"

"She's never mentioned him." Phoebe rode in thoughtful silence. "Isn't it strange what can go on inside of people you see every day and you never suspect a thing! It makes you despair of ever knowing what anyone is really like, inside."

"Usually it's none of your business," he suggested, and she laughed uncertainly.

"That's true, I suppose. But if you marry someone—it would be convenient to know then, wouldn't it?"

"Perhaps you do know then, after a time, anyway. I admit Maia is still a closed book to me, but I'll manage somehow, I hope." There, that had to be done, in case Virginia had not warned her.

"I—could I ask you a question?" she said hesitantly.

"Anything you like," he assured her, wondering.

"Well, suppose you had given a girl an engagement ring—your Maia, suppose—and she lost it. What would you do?"

"First, I'd smack her for being so careless. And then I suppose I'd get her another ring. Why?"

"You wouldn't be angry—or terribly hurt? She wouldn't—needn't be afraid to tell you?"

He turned in the saddle and looked at her straightly with those little amber flames in his eyes.

"Look here, are you engaged to somebody? And have you lost the ring?"

"Mm-hm." She nodded guiltily and her beautiful full lower lip came out a little. "To my Cousin Miles back home. I left the ring on the washbasin in the lavatory on the ship, and when I went back it was gone. I—don't know what to say to Miles, and I thought you m-might help me."

"Because I remind you of your father?" he smiled, and her eyes filled piteously.

"Well, we always say nothing ever looks so bad after you've told Father," she said.

"God help me, I've no idea what he would say now," Oliver began. "But as for myself, I should just like to ask, Do you love this fellow Miles and is he in love with you?"

"Yes, of course. What a funny thing to ask. We're engaged."

"Then how can there be anything you're afraid to tell him?"

"Well, for one thing—he's not like you."

"And Father," he interpolated.

"And Father," she agreed gravely. "You see—Miles always takes things very hard."

"I wish people wouldn't do that," Oliver remarked. "Doesn't it seem to you that part of growing up is to find some way of facing things and not minding—too much?"

"It's not good for Miles to be upset," Phoebe said obstinately.

"Oh, dear, oh, dear," murmured Oliver, looking straight ahead of him. His jaw was rather set.

"You see, Miles got fever in Cuba," the hesitant voice beside him went on. "He's never been well since he got back. He may never be *quite* well again. You have to be careful, because you never know how things are going to strike him."

"Must you do this?" he said after a moment.

"Must I—what?"

"Marry a man who can't face things," he said, and threw up a hand quickly before she could reply. "No, sorry, I never said that. You know best, of course. Forgive me."

Phoebe stole a glance at his profile and thought it looked, for him, rather grim. In that instant he turned, and caught her eyes upon him, and gave a sort of half-laugh, and held out his gloved hand to her as they rode.

"I'm not much good as a father, am I," he said ruefully. "Try me as a friend, will you? I'll do my best."

Phoebe put her gloved hand trustfully in his and said, "I feel better now, anyway," and Oliver said, "Good," and gave her fingers a quick squeeze and dropped them. Engaged, he was thinking with his closed, one-sided smile. Both of them, then. Well, that settled that. All cards on the table now. Everything understood. Better that way.

"I like what you said about growing up," she was saying with some diffidence. "You think it's childish to cry over spilt milk, is that it?"

"Foolish, at least. There's likely to be lots more in the cow."

She laughed her surprised, rather belated laughter, as though she had caught the joke just in time.

"You do know how to enjoy life, don't you!" she said enviously.

"I'm enjoying it very much this morning," he replied, and the words were warm and comforting. "Perhaps I'm too easily satisfied. It's spring, after a fashion, and the sun is coming out, I've got a good horse and a lovely companion—but suppose I was saying to myself, it won't always be spring, and at the end of the summer you must rejoin the regiment, marry Maia, set off for India, or Egypt—God knows where—and you may never see Phoebe Sprague again." He was not looking at her now, his eyes were on the edge of the wold ahead of them where it met the pale, misty sky. "If I allowed myself to think like that I should be utterly miserable in no time," he said, almost as though he had forgotten she was there.

It was impossible not to take the words at their full value, impossible to discount them as a mere pretty speech—futile to throw up conventional defences of misunderstanding or indifference, even if that had been a game Phoebe knew how to play. She felt herself flooded through with a warm tide like a blush, and her hands were shaking on the reins. She spoke impulsively out of her own swift insurgent need, casting herself on his mercy for guidance in this unforeseen, exciting thing that had happened to her because of him—so different, so much more compelling than anything that had ever happened because of Miles.

"And can you teach me how not to mind—too much—before the summer ends?" she asked humbly, and his expressive face turned towards her, lit with amazement and ungovernable delight, so that she had to look away, and fixed her blurred gaze on her horse's ears. Oliver reached for her bridle and brought the horses to a stop.

"No, let me see," he commanded softly. "Look at me, Phoebe."

She obeyed him slowly, but willingly, her lower lip a little out.

"You feel it too, then," he said, very low. "You would, of course, it couldn't happen to just one of us. It began at luncheon yesterday—didn't it?"

"At first I thought it was only me," she confessed. "But just now, when you said—I realized you must have noticed—something—yourself—" Her voice died away breathlessly, her eyes hung on his steady gaze, shy but not embarrassed, sweet and very candid.

"It was rather like noticing a landslide," he remarked at last. "And yet I tried all night to think I was imagining things. Tell me—what's it like with you? Can you think straight? Can you sleep? Can you hear what people are saying to you, and give a coherent answer? Can you get on with your life in any way, shape or form?"

"No," said Phoebe, looking back at him fearlessly.

"Nor can I. Thank you for being so honest. Let's go on being honest, shall we? Now that it's happened to us, what would you prefer to do about it? Stop right here, which means both of us run like hell and pretend it never was at all—or try to cope with it, get what we can out of it while it lasts, and then let it go—or smash up everything and start again, with two very bad consciences and the whole world before us? And I haven't even the right to ask you, remember that."

"Let's—cope with it," said Phoebe, looking at him.

"Try to be just friends, knowing very well it will never be enough? That's the hardest way of all, I think."

"Half a loaf," said Phoebe, wondering how she dared.

"I'm not sure," he murmured, and his eyes were compassionate. "It depends on how hungry you are, perhaps."

"I seem to be starving," said Phoebe, realizing it at last.

"So am I. Famished. It won't be simple, you know. People have so many eyes. And the walls have ears."

"There must be nothing for them to see or hear," she said bravely.

"Only when we're alone like this will I even dare to look at you—like this. Promise you won't mind if I seem to snub you when they're watching."

"But I shall mind, like anything. And I shall give myself away with every breath I draw, I'm afraid. You won't believe me, but nothing like this ever happened to me before, and I'll be thirty in the autumn. How old are you?"

"Twenty-one."

"Are you, really?" He found this surprising, and searched her defence-less face with his quick, shining eyes—so candid she was, so without veneer and worldly wisdom, as though she had grown up in a convent. What sort of engagement must it be, then, to have left her so unknowing? "What about this Miles?" he heard himself demanding, rather abruptly for him. "Do you mind my asking, he does seem to come into it, rather!"

"He's my cousin. I've loved him all my life. I thought."

"You're sure you want to go on with it?"

She nodded.

"I can't back out on him now. You—feel the same way about Maia, don't you?"

"Yes, I must. It's been announced. But this isn't what I want for you —you were meant for something *more,* you know that, don't you."

"I reckon this is all," said Phoebe and tried to smile, and heard again in her mind Virginia's sage words in the dog-cart—*a woman who marries a professional soldier ought to be the sort to fling herself into love head first and not care if it drowns her*—and I *don't* care, Phoebe told herself valiantly—I *wouldn't* care what became of me if only Oliver went with it—the ends of the earth—come hell or high water— for better, for worse—oh, *Oliver*—

"How honest you are," he marvelled as though he read her thoughts, not touching her, just holding her bridle, while the horses fidgeted at a standstill in the road.

"It's not much use trying to hide it from you," she sighed. "Just sitting there beside you at the table yesterday—it was like being very drunk, I should think—is it always like this to fall in love?"

"No." He was very grave. "Only once in a million it's like this. It's a sin not to do something about it, you know."

She shook her head.

"I couldn't go back on Miles. He doesn't know how to stand up to things."

"And so I must pay the penalty," he objected unfairly and repented. "Oh, I know—I can't jilt a woman, it's like cheating at cards, it won't do! So I'm no better than you are. If I were, I might try to change your decision."

"No, don't try," she said quickly. "Don't let's waste time arguing about what can't be helped. Let's just be happy, while we can."

"You learn fast," he said, watching her.

"If only I can! We've got—how many weeks?"

"My dear, we shall have only hours together, all told."

"But even *hours*—when I can talk to you—when I can learn from you —it's better than nothing!" she insisted hopefully.

He gave his half-laugh, and dropped his hand from her bridle and the horses moved on slowly, side by side.

"I wonder how well I have learned the lesson myself," he said. "I talk a lot. Now we shall see."

"I don't want to make trouble for you," Phoebe said with her touching docility. "Would you rather we ran?"

"Lesson Number One," said Oliver, and again all she could see was his profile. "*Never* apologize. You have made all the trouble in the world for me, and it's *much* too late to apologize!"

"Well, I'm s-sorry," said Phoebe, drooping in the saddle. "Maybe it would be better after all to just ignore the whole thing and avoid each other."

"If you talk like that I shall really forget myself," Oliver threatened, and he was laughing again, because she was so young and so dignified, and so ignorant still of what was before them. Phoebe glanced at him doubtfully when he laughed, confused, but contented just to be in his company, and eager for further revelation.

"What do you want me to say?" she asked.

"Whatever you like, in heaven's name!" he told her firmly. "Will you do that for me? Will you always utter whatever comes into your funny head, and trust me to make some sort of intelligent guess at what you mean and what the answer is?"

It was what she had done half a dozen times already, with no thought of the pitfalls such a course might present to two people so little acquainted as they were. Even with Miles, she had learned long since, it was dangerous to say the first thing that came into your head, and she and Miles had grown up together. But with Oliver there were no pitfalls. One could relax. One could *let go,* and coast along on his quick comprehension, his uncanny perception, his embracing good will and indulgence. With Oliver there was no thin ice, it was firm footing all the way. One day of him was all you needed to be sure of that. Phoebe drew a long breath, as though someone had opened a window somewhere inside her.

"Well, then, to begin with, suppose I meet Maia now," she said frankly. "I feel as though this would be written all over me if she came into the room."

"I'll try to make sure that you don't meet her—at least when I am in the same room," he promised with equal frankness. "You must watch out for Virginia too, she's pretty quick." His eyes rested on her, searching, smiling, and kind. "Darling, you do understand me, don't you. I don't expect anything of you—and I won't demand anything. There's nothing to feel uneasy about, I promise you." And he could see quite plainly that what he was trying to convey had not even crossed her mind. Such small risks as stolen kisses and perilous meetings at odd hours and dangerous whisperings in corners would never occur to Phoebe. Except when they were alone, she meant to snub him. It was a bleak prospect for a man whose blood was singing in his veins, but clearly Phoebe would not comprehend the possibility of anything else. "You'll have nothing on your conscience when you go back to Miles," he added with an inward sigh.

"Nothing but not loving him," she said ruefully. "It's queer—I might never have known that I didn't. How *can* I feel that I've known you forever, when it's not yet been a whole day!"

"They do it with mirrors," he told her fatalistically. "We aren't supposed to understand how it happens, we're just supposed to say Thank you, and take what's given to us."

But we aren't taking it, thought Phoebe, in her uncompromising way. We're making up our minds to let it go. Shall we be punished for thinking *we* know best and doing what *we* think is right? How do we know it's best? You're not supposed to go back on your plighted word, of course. But then why has this other thing happened to us when it's too late? Surely it was meant for something. Suppose we're wrong after all, to let it go. . . .

Meanwhile they left the road, dismounted, and walked through a grassy glade to where the anemones grew beside a stream. Led on by his skilful, sympathetic questions and his attentive silences, Phoebe found herself with all reserves down, telling how she happened to come abroad with her wealthy cousins all of a sudden, as a birthday present, and how Miles had proposed at last just before she left Williamsburg, and how they had bought her a trousseau in New York, and how she hadn't come to England just to go to parties and wear pretty clothes, but to see things mentioned in the guidebooks and make the most of her opportunities and broaden her mind so that she would be able to write books too, because Cousin Sue had done very well at it, and there wasn't any money at home except Mother's and they couldn't use that, and Miles would never make much as a teacher, and anyway she *wanted* to write books, she always had wanted to since she was a little girl. . . .

It was a thing he came back to more than once, this writing of books. It seemed to amuse him, in a quiet way, that she should want to; it impressed him that Cousin Sue had made a success of it and a living for herself and Great-uncle Ransom, and he wanted to know how you began, and where the words came from, and he appeared to consider it something tremendously clever and difficult to do, the way playing the violin had always seemed to Phoebe. She could guess that he didn't read much himself; a soldier wouldn't have time for books and no place to own them either, on active service. But she wondered how anybody so fascinating as Oliver was could at the same time be so illiterate and not seem to mind, and found she didn't mind either—

The novelty of each to the other was complete, the differences of background and habits of thought to be explored were endless. They seemed to have nothing in common but their blind, urgent need to know more of each other, to ask and answer personal questions, to marvel and discover and admire—that and the singing of their veins.

When finally they left the anemones and returned to where the horses waited, he stood still a moment looking down at her beside her stirrup before she mounted.

"I begin to think we can do it after all," he said, while his quick, caressing gaze played over her face from the cleft in her chin to the broad, childish brow.

"Do what?" asked Phoebe, breathless, her face upturned to him.

"And then I'm not so sure," he murmured, and raised her left hand in both his, pushed back her sleeve and set his lips against the inside of her wrist above her glove. "Just this once," he said lightly, and let her go. "I *will* behave. I promise." He offered his locked hands for her foot. "Up you go!"

She looked down at him from the saddle while he arranged her skirt with a deft, impersonal touch.

"Where does conscience begin?" she inquired soberly "Or haven't I got one?"

"You've got one," he said, and moved to his own horse and swung up in the easy cavalryman's way. "But it's not altogether your conscience I'm afraid of."

She considered this cryptic statement of his in silence until they regained the road. Glancing once at her preoccupation, he noticed with a pang that she carried her left wrist cradled in her right hand as though his lips had left a bruise, and he sent up a wordless prayer that he might be granted wisdom and self-control for two.

5

VIRGINIA and Archie always took a furnished house in London for the Season, and went back and forth to Farthingale a good deal for weekends. Archie had resigned himself to this extravagant state of affairs when it developed that Virginia's father had arranged a generous marriage settlement for her in addition to her original inheritance in his Will, which in itself had been almost enough to scare Archie off entirely lest people should think he was fortune-hunting. But as Virginia often pointed out, their having a house in Town simplified things for Bracken and Dinah because the family could be together during their visits without their having to assume responsibilities themselves, and they didn't have to stay at a hotel. Thus it was already arranged that they should all use a convenient little mansion in Hill Street during the Coronation festivities, and Bracken could see his old friends there and collect some new ones.

Virginia discovered that Bracken was rather cultivating the German Embassy this summer, for dark reasons of his own. After a year of ill-health the old German Ambassador had died about Christmas time, and Count Paul Wölff-Metternich had succeeded him, and the Embassy had some new blood and was humming with activity, social and, said Bracken significantly, otherwise. The recurrent Anglo-German tension had eased off a bit again, now that the Kaiser had got it into his thick head that England was going to win the war in South Africa in spite of persistent Continental crowing to the contrary, and Wilhelm had decided to be congratulatory to his Uncle Edward, instead of egging on the other side as he had done in the beginning. But Bracken nursed an obstinate, uncomfortable conviction that England's next war would be with Germany, and Archie was inclined to agree with him. Whenever they started talking like that Virginia would beg them not to be morbid, and would invite them hastily to come and see the baby taking the air on the lawn in her pram, or some such domestic diversion.

Official Court mourning for the old Queen had ended, peace in South Africa was rumored, though prematurely, for guerrilla warfare still dragged on, and England was putting itself *en fête* for the coronation of a very human King who loved to go to the theater and the races and gay dinner parties with bridge to follow. By his wish the dull mid-afternoon Drawing-rooms of his mother's reign had given way to brilliant evening Courts, where the new electric light at Buckingham Palace could show off the gowns and jewels and flowers and uniforms, and where refreshments were served and the hock cup was said to be something to dream about. The first evening Court of Edward's reign, in March, had gone off in a blaze of success, and the ordeal for débutantes was found to have been mercifully mitigated. There had been no presentations during the past year of mourning, and the lists for the Coronation Summer Courts were crowded. There was some excitement in the family therefore when Winifred as the new Countess of Enstone received her cards for the evening of May twenty-fourth, to be presented by her husband's aunt, Lady Davenant, who had sponsored Clare the year of the Jubilee.

Bracken and Dinah would be off for Spain on the twelfth, having delayed in order to attend the party Winifred was giving at the Hall just before the family departed for the Town house in St. James's Square. Winifred's parties usually turned out to be miniature balls where everybody wore their absolute best, and there were caterers and a band down from London, and the floral decorations were beyond words, and everyone ate and drank a great deal and danced until dawn.

Phoebe looked forward to the evening as her own début, and after much indecision was going to wear the white chiffon trimmed with pink ribbon and trails of tiny artificial pink roses on the deep berthe and the triple flounce at the bottom of the flaring skirt. A wide pointed pink satin girdle emphasized her narrow waist, and the slippers and fan which went with it were pink too.

Maia's father was having one of his bad spells and she could not leave Yorkshire, so it came about quite naturally that Oliver as the nearest unattached bachelor should be paired with Phoebe, leaving Rosalind to Charles, because as Winifred put it they were used to each other and one didn't have to worry. Eden was as usual attended everywhere she went by her faithful shadow, the rector—a saintly, silent man with iron-grey hair and a deeply lined, ascetic face, whose modest sum of happiness was just to bask in Eden's presence, demanding nothing, uttering little, and exuding a pathetic sort of beatitude that she had come back to England once more, where he could look at her, fetch her tea and cakes, open doors for her, keep track of her needlework and handkerchiefs and fans, place fire-screens and chairs to her comfort, and strive single-mindedly to anticipate her every wish. "Mother's beau" Virginia called him, but without ridicule, for everyone loved him and sympathized with his unself-conscious devotion. Eden had long since ceased to be embarrassed by him and accepted his homage as simply as it was given, and even went so far as to invent little needs to make him happy if things got slack. His wife had died many years before, and he lived with an elderly sister who kept house for him. He seemed to have no idea of trespassing further on Eden's more recent bereavement, probably because he recognized the hopelessness of trying to be anything more to her than he already was—a cherished and reliable friend.

Rosalind and her mamma had come over to Farthingale for the weekend of Winifred's party and the Hall was full of new guests, though there was always room there for Charles Laverham and the Chetwynds whenever they chose to run down from London. Oliver quite naturally wanted to see something of his sister Dinah, and was always in and out of Farthingale to luncheon, tea, or croquet on the lawn. With Rosalind staying under the same roof, Phoebe now had an opportunity to observe at close hand the girl she was convinced would be the unconscious model for her newest heroine, in the book she planned to write as soon as she got home again. Virginia was devoted to Rosalind and Archie said she had a very soothing effect on him, like a glass of sherry at the end of a hard day. Rosalind laughed rudely at the idea that any of his days were hard, and said she would ask him for a character when she came to get married.

Phoebe seized the opportunity one day when they were strolling across the lawn a little behind the others, who had come out after tea to admire the lupins in the border, and asked Oliver why on earth he had not fallen in love with Rosalind as Virginia wanted him to. Oliver raised his eyebrows.

"How women matchmake!" he said. "Rosalind is a darling, and I'm exceedingly fond of her, but I should feel somehow incestuous if I married her!"

"But you're not related, are you?"

"Not a bit. But anyway—" He gave her a droll, sidelong glance. "—heaven preserve me from Mam*ma!*"

"Virginia says Mam*ma* has spoilt Rosalind's chances more than once."

"I can well believe it."

"And that rules out Charles too, doesn't it?"

"Very likely. Is Charles in the race?"

"It's hard to tell. He's so nice to us all."

"That's the Guardsman in him! Keep them all guessing, is their rule! You might wake up some morning and find it was you he was after all the time!"

Their eyes met intimately, secretly smiling, and Phoebe shook her head.

"I'd rather it was Rosalind," she said. "Oliver—what about when we all go up to Town next week? Shall I be able to see you *ever?*"

"Oh, that's all arranged for," he said easily. "I shall be there too. I have to see a lot of doctor people, so I shall be staying at Belgrave Square again. Except for a run up to Yorkshire for a few days."

The quiet words still lay between them when they rejoined Virginia and the rest beside the lupins.

The days were passing fleetly for Phoebe, in alternate exhilaration and despair. There were times when she told herself that nothing mattered except that she had seen him, knew he was in the same world, and hadn't got to live and die without ever dreaming there was such a man as Oliver to love. And there were other times when life without him seemed too empty and hopeless to contemplate, and Williamsburg and

Miles were something some other girl had lived, and there was no place there, at all, for Phoebe Sprague, and she tried to think what she might do in order never to go back. In these moods she was likely to find Oliver's effortless composure, his casual ways and good spirits rather infuriating, and she was even inclined to believe that he didn't really want her and wasn't suffering as she was—until at a glimpse of his face in a moment of unguarded repose, a quick glance from his changing eyes, she knew, with repentant certainty, that it wasn't that Oliver didn't care, it was just that he knew how to live, and she ached with compassion for him, who was going to have to beg for everything he got from Maia. Oliver wouldn't beg from any woman. He would just do without. And she, Phoebe, was the girl he should have had—she who had thrown herself head first into love and was now drowning in it.

Oliver and Charles and the rector all dined at Farthingale the night of Winifred's party, in order to escort their respective charges from door to door. That made ten for the carriages, and things divided up so that Phoebe and Oliver made the drive with Dinah and Bracken in the motor car Bracken had insisted upon hiring for his own use, and they of course arrived before the others.

"I suppose I shall have to use discretion here," Oliver murmured above her dance card, and just then Bracken tweaked it out of his fingers, remarking that he had taught Phoebe to dance himself, by gum, and that gave him rights, and Oliver said, "Put me down for the supper dance, you silly ass, I hadn't finished." So it was Bracken's hand and not Oliver's which set the initials O.C. opposite the supper dance, underneath his own for a waltz, and Phoebe realized that the two best-looking men in the room were squabbling over her dance card, which was about all any girl could ask at her début, and she never saw the card again till it was full.

Then she was waltzing on a still uncrowded floor with her hand in Oliver's, both wearing white gloves, and his arm around her waist. Her head swam and she was short of breath, and Oliver was covering a lot of ground and making her ruffled skirts swirl just for the fun of it while there was room, and it was one of the times when the present golden moment was worth anything which might catch up with her later on.

The floor filled up as more and more guests arrived, and partners came and went, with Oliver at discreet intervals, until they came to Bracken's waltz, which was the last before the supper dance. As she walked with him towards the ballroom, which was also the picture gallery, they encountered Clare, who wore a worried look and asked if they had seen Oliver. Bracken pointed him out, leaning up against a door-casing chatting with Eden and her rector, and Clare said, "He oughtn't to be dancing so much, but he's having such a good time I hate to say anything."

"But I thought he was quite fit again," said Bracken.

"Well, he's not, you take my word for it," Clare told him rather sharply, for she had always idolized her brother Oliver as the handsomest one of the five. "He'd murder me for mentioning it, but Edward says the poor boy is never out of pain, and it's high time he saw the doctors again."

"Phoebe's got him for the next, and supper," said Bracken, and added to her, "You'd better sit it out. But don't let him catch on."

Phoebe nodded, and the bright, beautiful evening fell to bits all around her as she moved out on the floor with Bracken. Oliver in pain, overdoing it, having a good time, and nobody daring to stop him. Anguish rolled in on her, blotting out the lights and the music. She faltered in Bracken's arms, and he glanced down at her quizzically.

"Tired?" he said. "You've been at it without stopping ever since we came. How does it feel to be the belle of the ball?"

"Bracken—Oliver's wound—is it bad?"

"Pretty bad, I guess. He kept on going after he was hit, and got some kind of complications. It won't kill him, but he's got to go lightly for a while, and he's not the kind to do that."

"But he's rejoining the regiment this summer, he says."

"At this rate they won't take him back before the end of the year. He caught a piece of shrapnel as big as your fist somewhere in his back, but he took his message on through, and they gave him a medal, and he's a blooming hero and entitled to a bit of rest. But don't for God's sake try to baby him or he'll dance all night just to show us. He's an obstinate beggar, you know. Enjoying yourself?"

"Oh, yes—it's wonderful," she assured him automatically, through a mist of apprehension and anxiety to get back to Oliver quickly and make him sit down, to make sure that he was all right and that the wound wasn't killing him, to search his gay, smiling face for signs of the pain he was never without. So that by the time Bracken's waltz was ended and Oliver came up to them it was all she could do to stand quietly while he and Bracken exchanged a couple of friendly insults and Bracken left them.

"Mine again at last," Oliver murmured then, so close his breath was on her cheek. "I know I've been caught watching you, but I can't help it and anyway everybody else is doing the same. You're a great success, you know, are you enjoying it?"

"Oliver, let's skip this one, I've been dancing steadily and—"

"By all means, let's go outside where it's cooler." With his hand at her elbow they crossed the corner of the ballroom and passed through the French windows on to the terrace. "Even a full moon," he remarked. "Amazing how Winifred arranges everything, isn't it!"

"Oliver, please, I—want to sit down—"

"What's the matter?" He looked down at her in the moonlight. "Something has upset you. Tell me."

"I—your wound—" she stammered, and her fingers found his arm and held to it, briefly aware even now of the surprising hardness of the muscle beneath his sleeve. "I never thought—ought you to dance so much?"

"Who's been talking to you? Clare? What a meddlesome girl she is! I'm perfectly all right, please don't think twice about it."

"You could *die*," she whispered, "and I wouldn't even *know*—not till somebody like Virginia got round to write a letter—"

"I shan't die of this one anyway," he said cheerfully. "And I may never get another. They say our next station will be Delhi and that's dull enough, God knows!"

They had reached the terrace steps, leaving the open windows of the ballroom behind them. Only one other couple was in sight, strolling away from them on the gravel walk that ran towards the sunken garden. Phoebe hesitated on the top step, looking out blindly on the moon-drenched world, and he paused a little below her, waiting.

"No?" he queried, and his teeth gleamed in a smile. "I suppose you're right not to trust me further." He had been drinking Edward's champagne. Not too much of it. But if he didn't look ahead this was a very glorious evening, though his back was hurting like mischief and he suspected that he had pulled something loose in spite of the taping, and the doctors would not be pleased with him when he got back to them on Monday. He pointed away to the left, where the silver thread of the river showed. "That path leads to a little temple among the trees on the riverbank," he told her. "It's sheltered on three sides, and if we walked down to it, which wouldn't take much over five minutes there and back, I should kiss you — just once — and we'd neither of us ever forget it as long as we live. So you see how right you are to stop here."

Phoebe's eyes rested a moment on the path where it wound into the shadow of the trees. Then she moved deliberately down the steps like a sleepwalker and with Oliver at her side started towards the riverbank.

The columns of the little marble gazebo glimmered white in darkness so dense under ancient beeches that there might have been no moon at all. When they reached it they were screened on all sides except the one towards the placid river on which a broad band of moonlight lay. Oliver set an arm around her waist to draw her further into its shelter and then caught her to him possessively so that his face was buried in her hair and hers was pressed into his coat, and her voice was a muffled wail he could hardly hear.

"Oliver, tell me how to bear it! I didn't know it would be like this! How can you be so gay, how can you laugh and say silly things and fool them all the way you do! You've got to *help* me, you're so much wiser than I am, you've got to *teach* me, before I can get along without you, you *promised* to teach me—"

"I didn't promise anything of the kind," he said quickly, and his arms were hard and urgent. "That's not what I want to teach you, I'm no such smug, bloodless ass as that, what do you take me for?" His lips found hers. . . .

"That's more than once!" she gasped after a minute, and hid her face against him again.

"And you will never forget it as long as you live?"

"As long as I live."

"You come half way," he discovered with satisfaction. "You don't withhold. It's taken you the same way it has me. You've no choice either, have you! This is forever. No, don't answer. Don't move. Don't think. Not yet."

And Phoebe, standing quietly in his embrace, her face hidden in his coat, was thinking without any astonishment, Here it is, for me—the laughter and the shamelessness and the *shine*—the confidence, each in the other, the reckless loss of time and space, the froth in the blood, the gay, giddy slide towards oblivion—what Gwen had, and Dinah, here it was for her, not with Miles—it would never happen to her with Miles. . . .

"I love you," said Oliver against her hair. "It's time I said that, isn't it! Ever since that first day at lunch, when you were so lost and so dignified. If I'd never seen you I would have lived a life of sober rectitude and never guessed what I was missing. If you'd never seen me you could have married your Miles and lived happily ever after—on a moderate scale. There is nothing moderate about this, my dear. I shall still love you—immoderately—when you're ninety. I shall be ninety-eight then—years of discretion, for most people. Not for me, loving you."

"Oliver, we m-mustn't—"

"Don't say it, I know all about that, say you love me, it's more important. Well, hurry up, *say it!*" he commanded, crushing her, and she said it, laughing, to ease the painful pressure on her ribs. "You see, brute force does it every time," he remarked, releasing her a little. "How would you like to be beaten every now and then, just to show which one of us is the master?"

"I'd love it," she murmured, nestling, and felt his lips quick and hard and brief on her throat.

"Phoebe, you asked me not to argue, but it's no good, darling—let's throw in our hand, I'll see it through if you will. Ah, what a *niggardly* thing to say! Phoebe, we shan't ever have enough money, and we'll have to live wherever the regiment takes me, but we'll always have this! Will you face the music with me and then marry me, Phoebe?"

For a moment there was no answer, and he thought she was trembling, and found her shaken by silent sobbing, and her cheek was wet against his. Then she straightened slowly, fighting for control of herself, and sniffed like a wretched child.

"I must be the most awful trial to you, going all to pieces like this—could you lend me a handkerchief?—thank you. It must be the champagne, I'm not used to it. I promise not to snivel any more." She dabbed at her eyes again, and returned the handkerchief to him. "I'm all right now," she assured him bravely. "It's a mistake to dance with you, I think. We must sit out the rest of them—somewhere in plain sight of everybody!"

"Have you said No?" he asked very quietly.

"Yes, Oliver, I've said No. Don't let me even think of it again. It's too demoralizing."

"You're quite sure this is the way you want it," he said, while his hands lingered on her shoulders.

"You know it's the only way there is," she sighed, and started resolutely along the path which led back to the terrace and the ballroom.

But now he had kissed her, and she knew what it was like. When the party finally ended, and she was safely shut up in her own room at Farthingale, she took off the white chiffon dress with the little pink roses, so much admired, which was destined to wind up like herself at Charlottesville with Miles—and panic set in. I can't, *I can't,* said Phoebe, and threw herself down on the bed and pulled the eiderdown over her head and cried herself to sleep in the dawn.

6

THEY found London covered with scaffolding like a town under siege— seats were building along the route of the Procession, besides deal plank balconies and Venetian masts from which drapery and festoons were to be slung. Parliament Square was almost obliterated, and Whitehall was eclipsed with raw timber. Westminster Abbey had sprouted an Annex at the great West Door to provide space for the King to robe in. Archie reported that his club had been transformed into something that looked like an out-size poultry-hutch, and certain bilious members were complaining bitterly.

Bracken and Dinah got off for Spain, Winifred was absorbed in fittings and Court curtseys, Rosalind received with characteristic levity the news that she was commanded to the same State Ball that Charles and Edward and Winifred were to attend—she had been presented at a Drawing-room the year Clare came out—and Oliver was deposited, fuming, in hospital for observation, where he remained exactly three days and then turned up in Hill Street, announcing that he had got five tickets for them all to see the Boxing Horses at the Royal Aquarium show that night.

"What," said Eden incredulously, "are Boxing Horses?"

"Horses that box," said Oliver, and explained that Charlie (dun color, fourteen hands) and Cigarette (black, with four white stockings, fourteen hands two) boxed three rounds with twenty ounce gloves, shaking hands and taking corners just like prizefighters. Cigarette was said to use its left glove even more scientifically than some human boxers, and a natural antipathy lent realism. Their two-legged seconds wore evening dress, which gave the whole thing tone.

Everybody, including Eden, was enchanted at the idea, and they had a very lively evening, starting with dinner at Gatti's and finishing off with champagne and rarebits back in Hill Street about midnight.

"Thank God it wasn't my stomach that got hit!" said Oliver piously, filling his plate at the chafing-dish, and Archie heartily agreed that to get shot in the appetite would be really too much of a good thing.

"Well, now that we've been intellectual and seen the Horses," said Oliver, sitting down rather carefully though nobody caught him at it, "how about something really vulgar, like *Zaza?* Is Phoebe too young for *Zaza,* do you think?"

"Perhaps not, but I am," Eden said decidedly, and they jeered at her till she gave in and consented to go, on condition that they would take her to see *Ben Hur* the following night, and she wanted to sit in the stalls, please, and not in a box, because even the King had sat in the stalls for *Ben Hur* as it was the best place from which to see the chariot races. She was enthusiastically promised stalls for *Ben Hur,* and threatened with Ainley in *Paolo and Francesca* if she gagged at *Zaza,* and Oliver took his departure with everyone in the best of spirits.

But the day after *Ben Hur* he went up to Yorkshire, and Phoebe was devastated by waves of what she identified with horror as plain old-fashioned jealousy, because now he was with Maia and she had no part in his days and no place in his thoughts. Before the end of the month Bracken and Dinah were back from Madrid, where they had attended the Royal bullfight, among other Coronation festivities, but Dinah wouldn't look after the horses came in.

Meanwhile Miles's letters arrived regularly, about once a week—painstaking, well-thought-out love letters, rather full of quotations and literary allusions, and always containing some confident reference to their coming life together. Phoebe answered them scrupulously as they came, giving him carefully watered-down accounts of the luxurious, entertaining life she was living, practicing just a little on her novel with descriptions of Rosalind, Charles the V.C., and the thronging, hearty, horsey life at the Hall, where a printed notice hung in the main entry: *You are requested to keep the hall doors shut, on account of the animals in the park.* And the spotted deer did come in, she explained, and had the maids screaming in corners like the Scottish Express—Oliver's simile—until some big brave footman would arrive to usher the intruders outside. Doggedly Phoebe tried to include in each reply some intimate personal paragraph which said she loved him and missed him, and wished he could have come too—and that was out-and-out fiction.

There was no reason for Oliver to write to her from Yorkshire and he didn't. But she found herself wondering what his letters would be like, and what sort of letters he was accustomed to write to Maia, and how an envelope addressed to herself in his handwriting would look—and she thought of a great many things she could have written to him if it had not been for Maia.

The official end of the war in South Africa was posted on June first, and there was rejoicing in the streets of London, though nothing like Mafeking Night at that, everybody said. They all went out into Piccadilly Circus and Trafalgar Square with Bracken to see the fun and were thoroughly jostled and thoroughly enjoyed it. The fourth and last Court was said to have been greatly enlivened by the good news, and the big military review at Aldershot, which would be attended by the King and Queen, acquired a new significance.

Lady Shadwell, who was Eden's dear friend and had presented Virginia at a Drawing-room five years before, gave a ball on the Friday night before Aldershot, which brought out many brilliant Diplomatic and Court personages, and a Royalty or two, and for which everyone had saved a new gown. Rosalind and her mamma were among the guests, and there would be Eligibles present. Charles Laverham was invited, because Lady Shadwell had always been very fond of his father. And of course the household in Hill Street were going.

Bracken and Lady Shadwell were known to have had their heads together over the invitations, so there was no doubt that the German Embassy would be represented. Dinah sighed, because she had a constitutional aversion to Germans. But she was developing a highly intuitive and diplomatic side which Bracken put to shameless use when he wanted something he couldn't get by more stereotyped methods. "She looks so damned guileless and above-all-that-sort-of-thing," he would say with pride. "And half the time she pumps them dry and brings me just the leakage I'm looking for!"

Dinah's assignment for that evening was less irksome than most. There was a new military attaché at the German Embassy who was known to be very much in the Ambassador's confidence—a Prince whose name carried the significant *zu* which meant that the family still occupied the original estates from which the title came, instead of the *von* which might be landless. His father in Germany was a Serene Highness, very old and in poor health, and Prince Conrad was likely at any time to be called home to assume his hereditary dignities and responsibilities. Meanwhile he enjoyed himself in London, seemed to be possessed of unlimited spending money, had an almost perfect command of

English and an almost fatal way with women. He had had a wife once somewhere in the past, a twice-hyphenated German princess, but she had died childless. It was well on the cards that Prince Conrad would marry again.

Bracken's Dinah looked very fragile and harmless, waltzing with him —dove to his eagle. He was tall and magnificently built, and perhaps because his mother had been a Polish countess famous for her beauty, he had not the usual Prussian look, except for the monocle, rimless and without a cord, fixed permanently in his right eye, his erect military bearing, and his rather parade-ground style on the dance-floor. He was clean-shaven, with a high forehead from which the dark straight hair was receding a little; his eyes were piercing and deeply set, with the Polish melancholy in their thin, curving lids; his nose was big and bold, and his mouth was strong, full, and well-modelled above a brutal chin. He wore the spectacular uniform of a senior Hussar regiment in the German Army—black, braided in silver, with the slung pelisse or jacket, very tight trousers, and polished Hessian boots. He looked, Phoebe thought enviously for he did not ask her to dance, like something out of *The Prisoner of Zenda.*

"Dinah's got him hooked, I can tell," said Bracken, with a chortle, as they circled the floor together towards the middle of the evening in the Prince's wake. "He's chatting away like mad, and she's got on her aren't-you-clever-I-never-know-what-it's-all-about expression. And then she'll recite to me everything he says, before we go to bed tonight."

But what the Prince was saying to Dinah at that precise moment was, "Tell me, please, who is the young lady in blue who is dancing with Captain Laverham?"

It was Rosalind, of course, looking like an angel in shaded layers of blue chiffon, with deep vertical tucks at her miraculous waist and a bodice cut well down off her slender shoulders. Her dark cloudy hair was massed around her little head, her big, engaging mouth was smiling, and she danced without seeming to touch the floor.

"Will you present me?" inquired His Highness, and Dinah thought, Oh, Lord, Mam*ma* will approve of this!

Unwillingly when the dance ended she crossed the floor with him to where Rosalind and Charles had paused, and made the introduction. Prince Conrad bowed from the waist and kissed Rosalind's hand, and asked for a dance. She gave him an extra which came later in the evening,

Dinah's next partner came up, the Prince bowed again and strode away towards the buffet.

"Fee, fi, fo, *fum!*" said Rosalind irrepressibly, almost before he was out of earshot. "Shall I be safe, do you think?"

"Unless he wants a war here and now, you will be," said Charles, rather through his teeth, and Rosalind cried, "Charles, I forbid you to say 'war' again! It seems as though I hear nothing else these days! The war is over, hadn't you heard, and there is not going to be another one!"

"You forbid that too, I suppose," said Charles, smiling down at her with visible affection.

"The King will forbid it!" said Rosalind confidently. "If he doesn't know how to handle Uncle Willy I don't know who does!"

"Who, indeed?" murmured Charles, and Dinah said, looking as though butter wouldn't melt—

"Prince Conrad has just been telling me how it is naturally to the interest of Germany to behave towards England with the respect which is demanded by the dictates of international courtesy." Her delicate echo of the almost imperceptible accent brought laughter from her hearers.

"In other words, please don't take any notice of anything Willy says when he makes a speech, because the rest of Germany isn't responsible for him," said Charles ironically. "They do hate it, though, that we won the war in South Africa with a volunteer Army and Navy!"

"Now, stop it, Charles, do stop!" Rosalind commanded. "You have got a perfect bee in your bonnet about Germany, and Bracken always makes you worse! I won't listen to you!" She danced away from him with a new partner, and made a little face at him over her shoulder as other couples swirled in between them.

Rosalind was an accomplished pianist, and with more study and practice might have equalled almost any professional on the concert stage, and her mamma always saw to it that she was given an opportunity to play at the houses of their friends. Virginia called it putting Rosalind on the block, but no one could resist hearing her if they got the chance. Rosalind herself loved to play, and always performed without self-consciousness and with a childlike, touching docility when it was required of her.

She and Prince Conrad were drinking hock cup together near the buffet when she was summoned to the piano, and he walked along beside her, saying, "You do this often—play for all these people?"

"Oh, yes—they seem to like it and it doesn't hurt me," she assured him casually.

"But—excuse me—you are very good-natured. In Germany if we wished for a pianist at a gathering of this kind we should have a paid entertainer."

"Well, these people are all our friends, you know," she reminded him. "Three or four in Mamma's drawing-room at tea time, or fifty couples here tonight, what does it matter, so long as they like my music?"

"You will play, no doubt, some German tunes?" he suggested, and Rosalind, who had intended Chopin but never played from notes, cast round hastily in her memory.

"Very well—Beethoven," she agreed, and added with her gay good will towards everyone, "To please you!"

Prince Conrad gave her a gallant smile, and escorted her all the way to the piano, where Lady Shadwell stood awaiting them.

"His Highness thinks I should be paid for this," said Rosalind to her hostess. "You may expect a thumping bill in tomorrow's post!"

"Miss Norton-Leigh is pleased to make fun of me," said His Highness gravely. "I am not yet entirely acquainted with your English procedure."

"She's always so generous," Lady Shadwell remarked imperturbably. "And Queen's Hall would be lucky to get her."

"I am sure," said His Highness, and composed himself near the piano to listen.

It was Virginia's habit when she was in Town on a Sunday during the Season to give little luncheon parties where she served champagne and the events of the past week were discussed without reservation.

On the Sunday after Lady Shadwell's ball the Chetwynds were among those invited to Hill Street, and almost before the greetings were spoken Penelope said, "Do tell us what happened Friday night, it's all over Town that Rosalind Norton-Leigh took the German Embassy single-handed!"

"Oh, you mean Prince Conrad," said Dinah thoughtfully, and added, "It wasn't quite as bad as that."

"And Prince with a *zu!*" cried Penelope. "Mam*ma must* be pleased!"

Dinah said, "Don't, darling, you make my blood run cold," and, "He doesn't seem to have that effect on most people!" Penelope assured her shrewdly. "I hear he's most frightfully distinguished-looking, hasn't got a straight back to his head and doesn't wear his hair *en brosse,* has pots of money and hardly any accent, and will be a Serene Highness when his father dies, which will be any day now—and he's supposed to be a great chum of Bracken's."

"That last is a slight exaggeration," said Bracken judiciously. "I admit I have a sneaking liking for the fellow—he hasn't got most of the more obnoxious shortcomings of his race. To see anyone I care a hoot for marry him—that would be a different thing altogether."

"But surely even Mam*ma* wouldn't encourage anything like that!" said Archie in an appalled sort of way.

"Wouldn't she *just!*" said Penelope.

"Well, then, Rosalind wouldn't have anything to do with it," said Archie. "She's got too much sense."

"Aren't you all rushing things a bit?" Tommy put in sanely. "The fellow seems simply to have been taken with a pretty girl—she *is* a dashed pretty girl. But she hasn't got sixpence of her own, and she's no match for one of those stiff-necked Embassy nabobs."

"I think it's time we changed the subject," Virginia began, and just then the door opened to admit another guest.

"Prince Conrad zu Polkwitz-Heidersdorf," said the butler, and Virginia went forward in the graceful pose of a woman who knows she is going to have her hand kissed.

PART THREE

HIS SERENE HIGHNESS

London.   *Autumn, 1902.*

»»»»»»»»»»»»»»»»»»»»»»»»»»»»»»:»»»»»»»»»»»»»»»»»»

1

AT BRACKEN'S request, Virginia had placed His Highness between herself and Dinah at luncheon—what *is* Bracken after, she wondered with one corner of her busy hostess's brain—gun calibers—North Sea fortifications—invasion maneuvers—it would all be Greek to Dinah, and anyway the man would never *tell* her—what does Bracken *expect?*

Not even Dinah knew. She merely memorized Prince Conrad's conversation when she had led it by some casual reference to the outlook in South Africa now that peace had come, or the presence of Kruger as a welcome guest in Europe, or the anti-German movement in Poland, or the activities of the Pan-Germans in Austria, or the troublous state of the chronic Balkans, or the recent long-distance interchange of acrimonious comment between the German Chancellor in Berlin and the British Foreign Secretary at Birmingham—the last having brought forth the pacific remarks she had quoted at Lady Shadwell's ball. The new German Ambassador's policy seemed all friendliness, and a hint appeared to have been given from high places that the German Press was to moderate its rancor against England. Dinah was aware that in Bracken's viewpoint the reckless attacks on England in German newspapers, quite unrestrained by the laws of libel or Prince Conrad's rules of international courtesy, were part of a deliberate plan to create a permanent anti-British feeling in Germany, so that the German nation might be ready to enter into some coordinated plan of future conflict with England—just as soon as the German fleet was big enough. Germans did not love England as a rival to their own ambitions of colonial expansion. And it was a fact, said Bracken, that the German colonies were so far not remarkably worth fighting to extend or even to keep—which was due in part to the secondary fact that Germans who colonized preferred to go anywhere but to lands where they would find the already too familiar German official.

Prince Conrad looked almost as impressive in his correct morning clothes as in full dress uniform at the ball, and his manners were good, if his sense of humor was practically nonexistent. The light, running banter of Virginia's luncheon table, often carrying what might sound to an outsider like downright deliberate rudeness, seemed more than once to perplex him under his highly collected, affable exterior. Archie and Bracken perpetually scored off each other with all the affection in the world, egged on by their laughing wives, who sometimes changed sides just to make it harder. Tommy and Penelope Chetwynd always wrangled happily about everything under the sun, made fun of each other, called each other liar and wench and traitor and thief—it was part of their youthful game of being in love with each other. And Lady Shadwell, who had come with Charles Laverham, sat on them all with matchless irony whenever she felt like it. And yet nobody took offence.

Prince Conrad's melancholy dark eyes followed the uninhibited laughter from face to face around the long table. Already there were grounds for half a dozen student duels in any self-respecting society which had not run hopelessly to seed. He was surprised—and interested —to observe also that the Americans had no self-respect either. One had assumed since the affair in Cuba, and events in the Philippines, that they might be made of sterner stuff. It was plain, however, that their womenfolk had no reverence for them. He turned to the American journalist's pretty English wife, placed on his right hand by the thoughtfulness of his hostess. He had hoped, of course, for little Miss Norton-Leigh, for he had taken the trouble to ascertain that these people were among her closest friends. Her absence was not mentioned or explained. He accepted it philosophically, and met Dinah Murray's innocent upturned gaze with an encouraging smile.

Towards the end of the meal, Bracken, whose subconscious eye was always on Dinah when she was pumping them for him, became aware by a kind of wireless telegraphy that she had struck some kind of bonanza. He saw her ask a quick, concerned question, saw Prince Conrad's grave confirmatory nod, saw Dinah's swift glance round the table as though she looked to see if anyone had overheard. And then, reading her lips, he saw her say, "May I tell them?" The Prince gave his consent with a small, almost disinterested shrug. Then Dinah's eyes met her husband's across the low centerpiece of flowers.

"The King is ill," she said, and somehow the quiet words carried to the corners of the room so that all other talk ceased.

There was a second's polite incredulity, while everyone realized the source of her information.

"He was at Aldershot last night," Bracken said then.

"He is still there," said Prince Conrad, almost indifferently. "But he was unable to attend Church Parade this morning."

"B-but what ails him?" blurted Virginia.

"The usual thing with him—a chill." And after the slightest pause for his effect, Prince Conrad added gently, "The Queen will take the march-past tomorrow—alone."

"You mean it's *serious?*" gasped Penelope.

"These things are always likely to be serious with him. His chest is weak, as everyone knows."

Their minds all darted the same way—towards the succession. The Prince of Wales, long accustomed to deputize and represent, was more than adequate to fill his father's place when the time came.

"It would be a great pity," Prince Conrad continued with every appearance of resignation to the inevitable, "if the Coronation arrangements should have to be postponed—or cancelled."

If the phrase had been in his vocabulary he could have congratulated himself then that he had got right in amongst them that time. They were like a dozen heedless, hoydenish children come suddenly upon disaster to one of their number.

"He always rallies," Archie reassured them at once. "There will be a powerful incentive to quick recovery, don't forget. He must have been looking forward to this month's ceremonies a very long time."

"Yes, he is turning sixty-one," Prince Conrad reminded them sympathetically.

They rose from the table soon afterwards in a much subdued mood, and began to break up in desultory talk in the drawing-room. Just as Prince Conrad was taking his leave Bracken was called away to the telephone. He returned, very poker-faced, to find His Highness gone. A little ring of strained, silent people awaited him.

"A rumor of the King's illness has just been confirmed," Bracken told them quietly. "All his public engagements are being cancelled several days ahead."

There was a long, taut silence. Then—

"But how did the blighter *know?*" demanded Archie, and his eyes sought Bracken's.

"Makes you think, doesn't it," said Bracken. "How they know everything. Almost before it happens."

2

So PHOEBE didn't see the King at Ascot, though she wore her white spotted muslin trimmed with lace and pink chiffon roses *appliqué,* and her toque was made of pink roses and osprey. Oliver came back from Yorkshire in time to accompany them on the opening day, and turned out like the rest of the men in their party in morning clothes and a grey topper, which consoled Phoebe in some degree. They all went down in a coach, which was great fun, but left her no opportunity for so much as a word alone with him.

The Queen made the semi-State entrance down the course in a carriage which also contained the Prince and Princess of Wales and the venerable Duke of Cambridge. Even on Gold Cup Day, the nineteenth of June, the King was prevented by the advice of his physicians from enjoying his favorite sport. People counted off the days on their fingers till the twenty-sixth, and remained hopeful. He had still a week to go.

On the twenty-third their Majesties returned to Buckingham Palace, driving in an open landau from Paddington Station, escorted by a party of the Blues *en cuirassier.* The King looked pinched and ill, but he raised his hat and smiled at his welcome from the crowd which paused to see him pass, and everybody drew a long breath and said There, *that's* all right.

The following morning, while a little group of holiday-minded people were clustered round the gates of the Palace to see the foreign envoys drive in for their official reception, a bulletin was posted on the railings, which was read with rapidly spreading consternation: *The King is suffering from perityphlitis. His condition on Saturday was so satisfactory that it was hoped that with care His Majesty would be able to go through the Coronation Ceremony. On Monday evening a recrudescence became manifest, rendering a surgical operation necessary.* The names of four famous physicians were signed.

Bracken received the news promptly from Fleet Street where the words: *The King seriously ill—Coronation postponed* had been hastily printed in pen and ink on sheets of paper and posted up in the windows of newspaper offices, in front of which people stood staring, rooted to the pavement. He went straight down to the Mall, accompanied by Phoebe and Dinah who pinned on the first hats they came to, caught up boas, parasols, and gloves, and begged to go with him. The crowd in front of the Palace had grown enormously, and the carriages of the special ambassadors and princely representatives in their gorgeous uniforms were still arriving to attend a ceremony which could not take place. The official announcement that the Coronation had been indefinitely postponed had now gone up as well.

Bracken, with a white-faced, speechless girl on each arm, circulated among the orderly, almost silent throng which waited patiently, faithfully, for any more crumbs of information which might be forthcoming. He was looking and listening, but never taking notes, for his early reporter's training under Cabot Murray had made him practically independent of the grubby bit of paper and pencil stub of the journalistic profession. Never write it down, his father used to hammer home. As soon as they see a pencil they will dry up on you. Look them in the eye and remember.

So Bracken was looking them in the eye, and saw tears more than once. People he knew turned up in the crowd, conversed briefly, shook their heads ruefully, agreed that it certainly didn't look too good, and drifted away, late to their engagements. People he didn't know allowed themselves to be drawn into conversation. The King was never spoken of by name or title. *He,* they said, often without the *h,* and it was spelled with a capital letter.

At two p.m. a second bulletin told them that the operation had been successful, but that it must be some time before the King could be pronounced out of danger, and a few people turned away with thoughts of lunch. Many of them stayed, and many more came, and were still there at six and even at eleven-thirty p.m., when new bulletins reported progress, less pain, and the taking of a little nourishment.

Some of the scaffolding and decorations came down at once—in St. James's Street the overhead floral festoons were dismantled that same afternoon, while in other streets the erection of stands went on for hours

after the news was known. Months of preparation involving the dis-
location of every aspect of business in London had suddenly come to
nothing. Bracken and the two girls stayed in the streets all day, lunching
briefly at Gunter's on food which might have been sawdust, and going
out again to watch and listen and wonder. They went to Westminster
and learned that Crown officials had been just putting the finishing
touches to the arrangements in the Abbey when the message from the
Palace came. A full choral rehearsal of the Coronation music was just
beginning, and everything came to a stop among the swathed ceremonial
chairs and canvas-covered carpets while the announcement was read.
The Coronation Litany was then intoned by the Bishop of Bath and
Wells, the blessing was pronounced by the Dean of Westminster, the
choir and orchestra were dismissed, and the Abbey was solemnly locked
up in charge of the Earl Marshal until further notice.

For the next three days and nights the anxious crowd lingered around
the Palace gates until the small hours, reading and discussing the latest
bulletin, and newspaper men were grimly reminded of the death watch
outside the high grey house at Osborne only eighteen months ago, while
the old Queen was dying—and of the winter dawn which showed the flag-
staff bearing the Royal Standard at half-mast. Then it was announced that
the King was making satisfactory progress and the bulletins were cut
down to one a day.

The Queen and the Royal Family deputized and filled in and carried
on, and the visiting Continental Royalties and representatives called at
the Palace, paid respects, left messages, and by the twenty-fifth most of
them had departed from London. Some of the decorations were still to
be seen, wilting in the weather which was mostly vile. Virginia objected
volubly to a rather pompous statement by Cardinal Vaughan to the effect
that "the finger of God has appeared in the midst of national rejoicing,"
and declared that it was most unfair always to blame God for everything
that went wrong, it made Him such a spoil-sport, and besides it was so
obviously the finger of Somebody Else.

On the day when the King ought to have been driving triumphantly
through his capital, the military camps in Kensington Gardens for the
accommodation of the troops which were to have kept the streets along
the route were breaking up, and the Army Service Corps wagons were
trundling the paraphernalia away to the railway stations. In place of the
crowning at Westminster, a service of intercession for the King's recovery took place at St. Paul's—and similar services were held by the

Catholics at St. Ethelreda's, the Jews at Bevis Marks Synagogue, and the gorgeous East Indians with their carpets spread in the field at Fulham.

Even more than the general flatness produced by the sweeping away of the carefully organized and rehearsed festivities, there was a sense of acute personal anxiety. The head of the family was stricken. The big genial man known to his mother as Bertie, known all over the world for his love of sport and good living, his annual cures at Homburg and Marienbad where he went to drink the waters and watch the lawn tennis, his informal stop-overs in Paris and Biarritz, his diplomatic yachting tours in the Mediterranean which, it was said, caused his German nephew some loss of sleep—the man-about-town, the *bon vivant* with the weak chest who still, by virtue of his kinship and his seniority, held the whip hand over the ambitious German Emperor—the fabulous, naughty, romantic, pleasure-loving prince who had lived to be a king at last—was the crown to be snatched from him on the very eve of his anointing?

The strange, uprooted days went by on tiptoe, and July came in, and he was known to be making an almost miraculous recovery, though he had still a long and difficult convalescence before him. The Coronation could take place, it was thought, in the autumn—though naturally there could never again be gathered together so imposing a list of foreign and Colonial visitors as had been present in London in June, and the King would be unable to undergo a ceremony of the original length and elaboration, which would have lasted several hours. The nation resigned itself with characteristic cheerfulness to a semi-State ceremony, much curtailed and simplified, and gave thanks that the King had been spared for that.

Balls and entertainments were still being doggedly given, for everybody had new gowns which had to be paid for and might as well be worn, and it was the Queen's express wish that the trades-people should not lose too heavily on their expectations by what was universally known as the national Trouble.

Therefore Virginia proceeded with her plans for a rather exclusive evening revel in aid of her favorite charity, known as the Mabys—the Metropolitan Association for Befriending Young Servants—which dealt with the girls brought up and trained in the workhouses and sent out to service in their early teens. Most of them were, of course, orphans, or had been deserted as unwanted infants, or merely left by drunken or irresponsible relatives to be brought up by public charity. Until a group of young society matrons undertook to see that life was a bit less perilous for these less fortunate creatures they had passed out of the knowledge of the Board of Guardians as soon as they left, voluntarily or by request, their first situation. Since Virginia had been taking an interest in their welfare, all her friends were most liberally supplied with deserving tweenies and under-housemaids, and the girls' gratitude often amounted to embarrassing Cockney tearfulness.

Instead of the usual bazaar where people had to buy things they didn't want at outrageous prices, Virginia intended a sort of amateur concert party where everybody paid through the nose for a ticket and could there- after enjoy themselves. Phoebe, whose brother Fitz wrote musical comedies and had married a music-hall actress, was naturally expected to contribute something pretty fancy to the program. She and Gwen had done a cakewalk together at one of the amateur Christmas shows in Williamsburg, and she said rather doubtfully that she supposed she could remember her steps, which Gwen had arranged and taught her, and could probably guess at most of Gwen's if somebody like Rosalind wanted to try. Gwen had worn the trousers and done the man's part. Rosalind said at once that she would love to wear trousers, and did they think Archie's would fit her with a little taking in? Phoebe then at- tempted to draw the costumes she and Gwen had worn, which they had made themselves, with Mammy's help, and Virginia's dressmaker was consulted. Before long, Archie's tailor was also involved, and private re- hearsals went on every morning in Hill Street in an upstairs room which was furnished as a schoolroom and could be cleared to the dimensions of a small stage.

Archie came home to lunch one day because he thought he was starting a cold, and heard the gramophone playing and wandered upstairs to see where everybody had got to. He paused at the schoolroom door un- observed and beheld a most unusual scene.

Phoebe, with her hair coming down and her skirts pinned up so that her ankles showed, was dancing with Rosalind, who wore a frilly lace blouse above what he at once identified as a pair of his own grey flannel trousers, reefed in at the waist with a pale blue leather belt and turned up at the bottoms and sewed in a wide hem. Rosalind carried his new Ascot topper in her right hand and his gold-headed dress cane which Virginia had given him for Christmas in her left, twirling it like a band- master with a very accomplished wrist. Both girls were bent backwards at an incredible angle, with their feet kicking very high in front of them, as the infectious beat of *The Georgia Campmeeting* blared from the gramophone in one corner, which was tended by Eden and Virginia sitting in wooden schoolroom chairs in enthralled attitudes and quite oblivious of his presence.

Back and forth, in and out, pivoting, bowing, strutting, the two girls danced absorbedly till the record ended and Eden said, "That's it— you've got it!" and they collapsed on each other's shoulders with breathless laughter.

"What *is* going on up here?" Archie said then, and they all discovered him, and Rosalind shrieked and got behind Phoebe who spread her shortened skirts to hide the desecrated trousers from their owner.

"Isn't it going to be *wonderful?*" demanded Virginia. "It's the cakewalk for my party. *You* know, that new dance everyone is doing in Paris —it's a darky dance to begin with, and Phoebe knows how, Gwen taught her. We're having costumes specially made and they're going to wear dark grease paint like Othello and bring down the house."

Archie said No doubt, but what about his trousers, and Virginia assured him they were only borrowed and not hurt a bit, and his tailor was making the ones Rosalind was going to wear on the night, and he was to let her have the bill.

Just then the luncheon gong went, and the girls flew away to tidy up, and Archie and Virginia descended together to the dining-room.

"I say, does Mam*ma* know about this?" he asked on the stairs.

"Yes, in a way—and Rosalind is going to play some Chopin too, before she puts the make-up on. You don't know what a relief it is to her to do something besides play the piano at one of these charity do's, and she's caught on like anything—Phoebe says it might almost be Gwen herself."

"Mm," said Archie thoughtfully and sneezed. "Well, for one thing, it ought to put His Highness thoroughly off, I should think. Not sufficiently *fürstlich.*"

"Darling, are you starting a beastly cold?"

Archie said he thought he might be, and Virginia insisted on his having a good stiff shot of whiskey before lunch, and by the time the girls came down decently clothed he was soothed and comforted and at peace, and the cold seemed to be receding.

3

PHOEBE had been enchanted by Rosalind's fragile beauty and childlike good spirits since the day they first met at the Hall. Rosalind's eighteen-inch waist, her slender neck supporting a royally poised head loaded with soft dark hair, her soaring brows and fantastic eyelashes, above all her chuckling, irrepressible laughter, always made Phoebe feel like a rather staid maiden aunt, though they were nearly of an age. And Rosalind, affectionately recognizing both the wordless, humble admiration Phoebe had for her and the amusing contradiction in their temperaments, had taken to calling her Granny, but in such a way that it was somehow a compliment, and Phoebe rather enjoyed playing Conscience to Rosalind, picking up after her, finding the things she had mislaid, reminding her what time it was and what she had promised to do.

Her protective attitude came partly from her growing conviction that Rosalind's mamma was very little good to her, either as a confidante or a standby. Mrs. Norton-Leigh was as shallow as ditch-water, and yet she was pretty in what Virginia called a well-preserved way. Having been widowed, as she was fond of pointing out, ridiculously young, with two great galumphing girls on her hands—Rosalind's younger sister Evelyn would make her début next year if only Rosalind would get married and out of the way—Mrs. Norton-Leigh always had a string of rather second-rate admirers, most of them younger than she was, or else a great deal older, to occupy her time and attention. A girl who danced less lightly than Rosalind over the thin ice which formed the foundation of that brittle home in one of the Terraces near Regent's Park, might have found the behavior of her mamma a trifle embarrassing, or might have realized a sobering lack of maternal care and understanding. But Rosalind was used to her life, she had never known any other, and she accepted it philosophically and got a certain detached sort of amusement out of Mamma's affairs. The late Mr. Norton-Leigh, dead of a fall in the hunting field years ago, had left them comfortably though not lavishly provided for, and the pretty little Regent's Park house had no strings of debt to it. But Mamma was extravagant, and since she could not get at the capital, he had seen to that, she always found it difficult to make ends meet, especially, she would remark with an acid note in her languid, discontented voice, having to dress both herself and Rosalind on her income, and what it would be like after Evelyn came out too she daren't think.

Phoebe, who was accustomed to love and tenderness at home, sometimes yearned over Rosalind's uncherished state, though she would remind herself sensibly that Rosalind didn't know what she was missing. Phoebe often felt more maternal than Mamma, and Rosalind went on being pathetically gay and uncomplex and trustful towards life, which so far had given her no hard knocks, and if only she married the right man, someone kind and thoughtful like Charles Laverham . . .

"Would Rosalind have to marry just anybody who asked her if he happened to have enough money to suit Mamma?" Phoebe asked one day as she and Virginia were driving back to Hill Street from one of Mrs. Norton-Leigh's afternoon At Homes.

"It looks that way," said Virginia darkly. "I'm sorry I took you there, it was a raffish crew this afternoon. That woman gets worse and worse."

"They looked all right to me," said Phoebe, "except some of the men were rather odd, I thought."

"Very odd, indeed! Poor old Mr. Norton-Leigh must be revolving in his grave, Lady Shadwell says he was rather a dear."

"I didn't see Charles today. Couldn't he get off?"

"Charles? He wasn't even asked! Mamma isn't taking any chances on a young man without Prospects, that might produce Complications!"

"But if Rosalind were really in love with someone who wasn't rich—and was *not* in love with someone who *was*—"

"It wouldn't matter to Mamma."

"But—that's *medieval!*" cried Phoebe in honest horror.

"People like Mamma belong to the Dark Ages," said Virginia, with a sigh, and they ruminated for the length of Portland Place.

"Charles would be the one, of course," Virginia said as the carriage reached Oxford Street. "Since it can't be Oliver, as I'd hoped. You might think Charles is just a thick-headed Guardsman, but he's great fun, really, when you know him."

"He does seem just the least bit—well, *stodgy,* compared to Oliver, for instance," said Phoebe carefully.

"That's just his Horse Guards face. Charles has a great deal of dash, as a matter of fact, when he lets himself go. Wait till you see him play polo! There is a legend that he once jumped his charger over the mess table laid for a banquet, without disturbing so much as a wine glass."

"*Really?*" cried Phoebe, entranced, for this was sheer Ouida-ism. "Whatever *for?*"

"Some silly wager or forfeit in the mess, I suppose. And he must be cleverer than he lets on, back of those casual ways, because he never seems to get himself involved with some sticky woman, the way so many young officers do. Well, of course, Charles must have had some kind of—romance before now," Virginia acknowledged broadmindedly. "But nothing anyone can point to, not for several years anyway. Of course there was the war, and that broke things off for a lot of them, but they mostly tripped themselves up the minute they got home. Look at Oliver!"

There was silence, while the carriage worked its way out of Bond Street towards Berkeley Square.

"Is she really so dreadful?" Phoebe asked then.

"Who?" Virginia's mind had gone ahead to the dinner she was giving that evening, and what she would wear, and whether the flowers had come, and what Archie would say to her afterwards for putting that tiresome Abbott girl next to him, but it had to work out that way, eight was always a difficult number. . . . "Who?" asked Virginia, groping for the subject they had left some minutes before.

"Maia."

"Oh, *that!*" said Virginia. "She's dreadful, all right! We none of us can imagine what Oliver was thinking of. I'm perfectly certain she took some sort of mean advantage."

"You'd think Oliver could take care of himself," Phoebe remarked with deliberate sarcasm. "A great big man like that!"

"You'd think so, wouldn't you!" Virginia agreed cheerfully. "But he's so *polite!* And so far as that goes, I used almost to get qualms myself sometimes—if Archie hadn't *wanted* to marry me, I honestly don't see how he could have got out of it!"

"But—didn't he *ask* you?"

"Not really. I sort of asked *him.*"

"*Virginia!*" Phoebe stared at her.

"Well, it came to the same thing, I guess. But of course with us it's all right, I know that now."

"But how do you suppose Maia—" Phoebe paused helplessly.

"There are ways!" said Virginia. "Home at last! Not even for Rosalind will I go there again and be *ogled* by the objectionable men you always find in that woman's house!"

"Do you call Prince Conrad objectionable?"

"Perhaps not. Only dangerous. But he's new there."

"Dangerous how?"

Virginia gave her a wise, oblique, amused look.

"Hadn't you noticed?"

"I didn't notice anything, except that he can't be bothered with me if Rosalind is in sight!"

"Lucky you!" said Virginia, and the carriage drew up before their door.

Closer association during the rehearsals for their cake walk cemented a real friendship between the two girls, who seemed to understand each other almost without words, and with few outward demonstrations of affection. The bond as it grew went very deep, but Phoebe was taken by surprise one afternoon when, as they were walking back to Hill Street after fitting her costume at the dressmaker's in Hanover Square, Rosalind said suddenly, almost bashfully, "You know, I'm going to hate it when you have to go back to America."

"Are you going to miss me?" asked Phoebe, rather pleased.

"More than anybody I've ever known."

"We have had fun together," Phoebe agreed, much touched and a little at a loss.

"I don't mean just the fun. I've got a feeling you and I could be friends —lifelong friends, I mean, even when we're quite old—when we could look back on this summer from our bath-chairs in the park and think how gay it was—how *free* we seemed to be—and being old wouldn't matter so much if you were there to remember things with."

Phoebe put her hand through Rosalind's elbow and they walked on together, in step, without saying anything more for a few minutes.

"Do you dread getting old?" Phoebe asked sympathetically at last.

"Not just that—everybody comes to it, and some people do it very nicely. But sometimes I do wonder where I'll be. And just lately I've been wishing you could be there too, and not way off in Williamsburg, wherever that is!"

"It's funny you should say this," Phoebe said slowly. "Because just lately I've been sort of wishing I needn't go back."

"Not even to be married?" asked Rosalind, and glanced quickly at her, and away again.

"Sometimes that all seems rather—remote."

"Don't you love him? Or shouldn't I ask?"

"Well—not as much as I thought I did, anyway. But that doesn't let me off. I'm going on with it."

"I was hoping Oliver wouldn't let you," Rosalind said gently, walking in step, with Phoebe's hand in her elbow, and felt Phoebe's fingers jerk against her arm.

"Oliver? What's it got to do with him?" Phoebe gasped.

"I know I shouldn't have mentioned it," Rosalind began uncertainly, very grave for her. "You've kept it well hidden, both of you. But it makes my heart *ache*, Phoebe, you were made for each other!"

"I don't—know what you mean, I—I—"

"Darling, *don't* try to lie to me, I know I had no right to say a word, but if only you *could* marry Oliver and stay here in England, then I would have somebody to be old with, and in the meantime we'd all be so happy together!"

"But how did you—" Phoebe was appalled, and felt hot and cold by turns, as though she had somehow betrayed a secret that was only half hers. "Do you think anyone else has noticed anything?"

"No, of course not. Do you remember the night of Winifred's party, when Clare told you Oliver shouldn't dance so much because he was always in pain? I happened to be standing close by, though you didn't notice, and I happened to see your face. And then when he came to claim his next dance, I happened to see his. And when you came back to supper from wherever you had been, I had a good look at both of you, and then I knew."

"Well, good heavens, if it was as plain as that—"

"It wasn't plain at all," said Rosalind firmly. "I just *happened* to notice. And I know Oliver pretty well, don't forget."

"Rosalind, you aren't—you couldn't ever be in love with him yourself?"

"With Oliver?" Rosalind laughed the spontaneous, *fat*-sounding chuckle which came so strangely from her delicate throat. "It wouldn't be decent! He's like my own brother! Can't you save him from Maia? Has this Miles of yours got a lot of money or something?"

"None at all."

"Oh. Then why do you have to marry him?" asked Rosalind, for whom life had always been kept so simple.

"I've promised."

"You mean your people would make a fuss?"

"It isn't my people," Phoebe explained patiently. "It's Miles. He counts on me. I couldn't go back on him."

"But if he hasn't got any money you might not be able to come back to England every year!"

"Perhaps never. This trip was just a present from Aunt Eden."

"Oh, but you've *got* to come back sometimes, I shall be wretched if you don't!"

"We can write to each other. Always."

"I shan't be much good at that, I'm afraid," said Rosalind, whose idea of correspondence was thank-you notes and bread-and-butter letters.

"You could tell me—the news," said Phoebe, not quite steadily, and

Rosalind glanced into her face again, and tightened her elbow on Phoebe's hand, pressing it against her side.

"Yes—I'll try to do that," she promised.

"And you'll be getting married yourself, you know," Phoebe reminded her, and Rosalind sighed.

"I suppose I shall, and what a bore *that's* going to be!"

"If you don't mind my asking—isn't there anybody you love?" Phoebe ventured.

"If only there *was!*" cried Rosalind unexpectedly, and her animated little face was quite tense and distraught, so that Phoebe could hardly believe her eyes, for here it was again—things going on inside people you saw every day and you never guessed. "What's the *matter* with me, Phoebe? Why can't I *care* about somebody? Even if it broke my heart, I'd rather that than never know what it's like at all!"

"You've got lots of time yet," said Phoebe uneasily, not knowing how to meet this unforeseen side of the carefree, butterfly-minded Rosalind who had seemed never to give a thought to anything beyond her newest frock and the next dance.

"No, I haven't," said Rosalind flatly. "If I don't marry this Season Mamma will wash her hands of me, she says so herself. It's Evelyn's turn, you see."

"Maybe we'd better both just give up and be old maids together," Phoebe suggested thoughtfully. "We could have a stuffy little house somewhere and keep cats, and get queerer and queerer."

But Rosalind could not be won back to laughter so easily.

"They think Mamma is too particular about whom I marry," she said, and her brows were knitted and her blue eyes were dark with unaccustomed apprehension. "But it's my fault, really, that I'm so long about it. That is, I did refuse to marry Lord Meriton—over and over again I refused. Mamma was furious with me. But he was way past forty and *totally* bald and no taller than I am, and I should have had to just move in with his first wife's belongings and live with them, and she'd hardly been dead a year, and the whole thing just gave me the creepy-crawlies, and not more than forty thousand a year went with it, and besides he was always patting my hand, and it *sounded* so silly! And then there was Sir Angus McBride's son Willie, I balked at him too, and Mamma simply took to her bed that time—but I'm *quite* sure he wasn't altogether right in the head, and I should have been frightened to death to live in the same house with him. One time when he was waiting in the drawing-room I went in, thinking Mamma was already there, and she hadn't gone down yet, and when he saw me he had some sort of fit—he grabbed my hands and began to kiss them, and then he grabbed *me* and tried to kiss my face—it was horrible, and I pushed him so hard he sat down plunk! on the sofa—luckily it was there behind him—and I ran out of the room and met Mamma on the stairs and told her he wasn't well and to get him out of the house quick—and she must have thought so too, because I've never seen Willie McBride since!"

"Maybe the poor boy was just awfully in love with you," said Phoebe, bewildered by all these confidences, for now that Rosalind had begun to talk she seemed unable to stop, though they had reached Hill Street and would soon be at home.

"Oh, but it can't be like that!" cried Rosalind. "I mean, I can't imagine Oliver— Oh, please don't mind my asking, will you, but—what's it like to love a man?" And as Phoebe hesitated, feeling inadequate and a little embarrassed, Rosalind hurried on. "I know it's wrong of me to mention it, but Mamma won't let me read novels, and I can't get anything out of *her,* and I'm almost never alone with people like this, and you seem so *sure* of everything! Phoebe—you and Oliver had a *look* that night at the Hall—I made up my mind then that if ever I got a chance I would ask you, even if it made you angry, because somehow I've got to *know*—what had happened between you?"

And Phoebe said, confession drawn from her by the other's compelling, unself-conscious need, in which there was no taint of curiosity, but only a terrified ignorance trying to right itself—"He kissed me—in the little belvedere down by the river. It was the champagne, I reckon—and a sort of good-bye. It won't ever happen again."

There was a silence. They had come to the foot of Virginia's front steps, and Rosalind halted there and put the toe of her shoe on the edge of the bottom step and poked it with her parasol, looking down.

"Was that all?" she asked, very low, and Phoebe glanced at her in open astonishment.

"Of course it was all!" she said rather sharply, for in the first place she and Oliver had not been gone much over ten minutes, and what did Rosalind *mean,* what did she think—? Phoebe started up the steps.

"Please don't be cross with me for asking," said Rosalind, and her slim body drooped as she followed slowly up the steps, dragging her parasol like a tired child. "I don't think you've any idea what it's like to have to guess at everything, and wonder, and not *know*—"

Just then the door was opened to them by Virginia's powdered footman, who said he was to tell them that tea had just gone in. That meant that Archie and Bracken were home, and everybody was in the drawing-room in a relaxed and talkative state of mind.

Within five minutes after she and Rosalind had joined them, Phoebe was almost willing to believe she had dreamed the conversation on the way home, for Rosalind was exactly as usual, cheeking Archie, laughing at Bracken's jokes, and making a pig of herself over the coffee cream cakes.

4

THE announcement of the King's remarkable recovery, which would make it possible for his coronation to take place early in August after all, was made on the day of Virginia's entertainment, and brightened everything up to a degree. Bracken decided to wait over in London till he got the story he had come for, and they all promised Phoebe that she would see the King after all, and Dinah said Thank goodness now everybody could stop having the jumps and settle down.

There was a dress rehearsal of the cakewalk in the schoolroom behind closed doors that morning, and considerable mystery had grown up over what they were going to wear, as nobody but Virginia and Eden and the two girls knew. Eden had not raised objections to Rosalind's appearance in trousers, for she had seen Gwen's performance in hers and considered them actually more modest than Phoebe's short skirts. Rosalind's mamma, who as a rule hardly let her out of sight away from home, was going through some sort of *crise* with her current admirer, and was trying a new hair tint which hadn't come right, and was pleased that the dresses (*sic*) were to come (at Virginia's expense) from that new house in Hanover Square which was supposed to be terribly smart and dressed Lily Langtry and Margot Asquith. Consequently she had allowed her customary vigilance to lapse a little, in the comforting belief that Eden's chaperonage would do, temporarily, as well as her own. Eden, of course, believed in allowing a responsible girl like Phoebe more discretion than Rosalind had ever been granted in her life, and while Phoebe never went out in London alone, they did go together as far as Hanover Square unattended.

As a matter of fact, it was only Phoebe's dress which was being made by *Lucile,* who had designed a gorgeous riot of cerise and yellow furbelows with a tremendous pink ostrich plume in the wide-brimmed hat. Rosalind's outfit was being scrupulously tailored to her ridiculous measurements, and consisted of very narrow satin trousers striped in cerise and white, with a fawn-colored poplin coat, a spotted Ascot tie, a white silk shirt, a brocade waistcoat, and an exaggerated pearl-grey topper, with patent leather boots and grey spats.

It made her look incredibly long and slender, and the make-up—dark *café-au-lait*, with a reddened mouth which only enlarged her own generous one without losing its shape—showed up her vivid blue eyes in a startling way. She never for one moment looked like anything but a girl wearing trousers—but she wore them irresistibly, without self-consciousness and without any noticeable modesty either.

Archie, who was by experience better able to see into Mrs. Norton-Leigh's mind than either Eden or Virginia, awaited her reaction to the cakewalk with a kind of fearful joy. Archie anticipated that Mamma was going to get a real facer, and that Prince Conrad was likely to be less heard of in the future; which was all to the good any way you looked at it. The sort of ladies German Royal diplomats could consider seriously as future wives did not black up and wear trousers, even in the name of charity. The trouble, as Archie knew very well, was that the blighter was so filthy rich he could afford to marry a penniless girl if he wanted to—though not without considerable opposition in some German quarters. Archie surmised that opposition never bothered His Highness much. But he would never stomach the coon dance, that was one thing.

Archie was not posted where he had a good view of His Highness during the cakewalk that evening, but Charles and Oliver, leaning up against the wall at the side of the room, were. And they both saw him take out the immovable monocle from his right eye, polish it on his white silk handkerchief, and replace it, to bestow renewed attention upon the two dancing figures on the little stage. It was an unconcious music-hall gesture which sent the angry blood into Oliver's ears. At the same moment he felt Charles stir impatiently beside him and glanced round with an unspoken query.

"Swine," said Charles under his breath, and Oliver's smile was small and grim.

"Somebody's got to ride him off, I'm afraid," he murmured. "You aren't going to leave it too late, are you?"

Charles accepted the implication that Rosalind was his property without any futile obtuseness, in the tacit understanding which always existed between him and Oliver.

"We've had false alarms before," he replied in the same experienced murmur which barely moved their lips.

"But not so much smoke," said Oliver.

"It's not possible," Charles reminded him. "She hasn't a bean. His family would raise the most almighty row."

"He has the look of getting what he wants," said Oliver. "Watch out for him, that's all."

"Easy to say," Charles objected, with a smothered sigh. "But what can I do when I come down to it? I never get a chance to talk to her without Mamma breathing down our necks."

"I'd do something all the same, if I were you, old boy. And pretty damn' quick."

So Archie had guessed wrong, and was to be cheated of his private gloat. Mrs. Norton-Leigh was sitting beside Prince Conrad, and after one dazed, near-hysterical moment when she recognized the capering hoyden in the striped trousers as her own child, she was quick to sense in the motionless figure at her side an alertness and a concentration so complete that it was perfectly safe to steal a glance at his face in the light which came from the stage. Just as she did so, he made that offensive gesture of wiping his monocle, and all her intuitions sprang to attention. His Highness was not displeased. He was most tremendously entertained!

Her eyes returned shrewdly to the stage. So far from unsexing Rosalind, the clothes she wore only accentuated her fragility and grace. She moved like a sprite, impudence personified, her white teeth gleaming in her wide, carmine smile. Her gallantry towards her flitting, coquetting partner buffooned all the male gallantry in the world. Her strutting triumph as the beruffled Phoebe obediently twirled and backed and filled to match her steps parodied masculine conquest from the beginning of time. It was all there, subtle, cruel, and hilarious—the thumbing of the female nose at masculine vanity, in her cocky, grinning, graceful, rampant coon.

Rosalind brought down the house, and such spontaneous applause had seldom been heard in jaded Mayfair. Prince Conrad was putting his white-gloved hands together as heartily as anybody.

"Charming," he remarked audibly, and his monocle gleamed as he turned his head towards Rosalind's mamma, smiling his indulgent appreciation. "Perfectly charming. I congratulate you on your—lenience of mind—to permit such a departure."

Mrs. Norton-Leigh, who had not permitted it at all, beamed back at him knowingly.

"It is the American influence, I fear," she said complacently. "One has to move with the times. One cannot, in this day and age, bring up one's daughter to be a prude."

Prince Conrad's left eyebrow, the one not engaged by his monocle, rose judicially, and he said, "I have no doubt, however—and I should prefer to think—that your daughter's innocence is proof against the lack of—ah—restraint which is becoming so fashionable in what calls itself the younger set."

Mamma backtracked hastily. She prided herself on being able to read men, and she had long before now classified Prince Conrad as the kind who liked his women straight from the convent or else out of the music hall. The imitation sophistication which most girls attained in their first season would never attract him. He must not be allowed to think for a moment that Rosalind made a habit of escapades like dancing in trousers, however much this one performance had enlivened his interest in her.

"I know every thought in my dear child's head, Your Highness," she assured him sentimentally. "As you must have noticed, she is rarely out of my sight, and I do not encourage—confidences between her and other girls of her age. I think I am safe to say that she has no ideas of anything beyond what I have chosen to give her."

"I am sure," said His Highness, nodding approval, and having been clever enough to pick up her cue, Mrs. Norton-Leigh for the first time acknowledged in her secret thoughts the most daring and far-fetched hope she had ever entertained—and allowed herself to contemplate the possibility of Rosalind as a princess, eventually a Serene Highness, married to a fortune not a dozen Englishmen of any rank could boast— one of the largest fortunes in Europe, everybody said. The Schloss at Heidersdorf was believed to have over three hundred rooms and as many servants; the estate was as large as an English county, and the Kaiser always came for the autumn shooting. There were also a palace in Berlin, a villa on the Riviera, and several small houses and shooting-boxes. And it wasn't as though one had to overlook things with regard to the man, either, for Prince Conrad was young enough, magnificent to look at, and had delightful manners—of course one could not expect fidelity from that type, but Rosalind would learn, her mamma felt reasonably sure, that too much fidelity in a husband could be very tiresome. . . .

It was from that night, Virginia always said direfully, looking back, trying to see where everything had started to go so wrong, it was from that very night, in the house in Hill Street, with the consent if not the connivance of Mamma, that Prince Conrad began his open, shameless, pitiless, but flattering pursuit of Rosalind Norton-Leigh.

5

OLIVER had returned from Yorkshire his usual smiling, imperturbable self, and there was less opportunity in London for Phoebe ever to see him anywhere but in a room full of other people. She confessed to herself meanwhile that he had become—the word was chosen in desperation—an obsession. It was difficult to attend to what someone else was saying to her if Oliver was in the room. The effort not to gaze at him with open adoration became a form of agony. She watched his hands, stealthily, as he lighted a cigarette or carried round the teacups in the drawing-room. She listened to him with her eyes fastened somewhere else. When she was alone she day-dreamed of him shamelessly, recalling all the time they had had together, imagining other meetings in impossible, more untrammelled conditions.

She was in love—headlong, schoolgirlishly in love for the first time in her serious-minded life, and she sat back and saw herself indulging in it with surprise and a kind of admiration. She had never known, because of Miles and the sober, undramatic devotion she had always had for him, the exhilaration and despair, the giddy ups and downs of this new unbridled emotion. It made her feel young and irresponsible, and altogether like somebody else. One result was that she had developed a soft, confiding, sunny look she had never had before. She laughed more easily, her eyes were bright and kind and friendly to everyone. Loving Oliver had somehow made her love other people more too, and the world had become a dear, generous, revealing place with largesse at every turn of the path.

Because she was still intrinsically self-contained and because she put up all the barricades she knew to guard herself and Oliver from discovery, the new, enriched Phoebe was not as visible to the eyes of observers as she might have been. They all thought how she had blossomed, and gave credit to the New York wardrobe and the broadening influence of travel and wider acquaintance, and they said what a good thing it had been for her. And they all accepted as a matter of course the inevitable association with Oliver, for he came and went as one of the family and was always encouraged to do exactly as he liked because of being on sick leave and having such a horrid time with his back.

He and Phoebe had not been really alone together since those few minutes in the little belvedere during Winifred's party. They had ridden in the mornings in Rotten Row, encountering a great many people they knew—Phoebe always looked forward to seeing Charles Laverham there, on the days he was not on King's Guard Parade, wearing what she called his bewitching get-up and which was known in the Regulations as dress blue patrol—tight blue trousers with a red stripe and polished Wellington boots and spurs, a white cross-belt over his blue tunic, a blue pill-box cap with a chin-strap, and sword slung. Off duty in the evenings he always wore ordinary clothes, which they preferred not to call mufti, and Oliver being on leave never wore uniform at all. Curiosity aroused by Charles's splendor, Phoebe made Oliver describe his own uniform—blue with a white plastron and facings, and a drooping white plume in the Lancer cap with the Polish-style Czapka top. She longed for a photograph, and dared not ask.

They had dined and gone to theaters, always in a party of four or more. They went to Hurlingham to see Charles play in an inter-regimental polo match, and that was another coaching trip arranged by Bracken.

One day in the midst of tea in Hill Street Oliver inquired rather too gently how Phoebe was getting along with the guidebook, and she looked up to find him leaning towards her, his face very near, his eyes laughing at her. Phoebe's cheeks grew pink.

"You think I have got very lightminded," she said defensively. "But Virginia says it's no time to go sightseeing while the town is full of visitors, and that I had much better leave it till after the Coronation."

"It becomes you to be lightminded, if that's what it is," he said, so that anyone could have heard if they had cared to. "Own up, my dear, you're a much happier person than you were when you first came to England."

Phoebe gazed at him in amazement, for when she came to England she had been happy about Miles and now she was miserable about Oliver.

"Am I?" she said blankly.

"You're living," he said. "You're waking up. You're having fun. Your eyes and your hair and your teeth all shine with it."

"Oh?" said Phoebe, and her lower lip came out. "Were my eyes and my hair and my teeth so awful before?"

Oliver laughed at her joyfully, and she found it difficult to believe that he was the same man whose arms had been so hard and his lips so urgent in the little temple by the riverbank. A pang went through her. Had Oliver decided up in Yorkshire that Maia was the one, after all? Because if Oliver loved her, Phoebe, the way she loved him, and was going to have to live without her, he couldn't be so *rollicking* about things, teasing her, making these personal remarks when people might overhear. The pang had lasted perhaps three seconds when Oliver said, still laughing, "You're priceless! I don't think I can bear it!"

"Bear what?" asked Phoebe stupidly, for if he could laugh like that—

"Bear to have you marry Miles," he said, and she sent a panic-stricken glance around the room to find that the others were all absorbed in their own conversations and were taking no notice of what Oliver said to her. "It's quite all right," said Oliver, amused. "No one is listening, and my back is towards them, hadn't you noticed? Yours isn't, though, and you really must try not to blush like that, do you want to give us dead away?"

"You m-mustn't—" Phoebe began, and buried her face in her teacup.

"I know I mustn't." He sighed gustily. "I was just suddenly taken with it. You get more fascinating every day, and I have to just grit my teeth and see it happen."

Phoebe was genuinely interested in that, and looked up at him over the teacup.

"Why do I?" she demanded. "How?"

Smiling his closed, rather one-sided smile, he studied her upturned face, and she found she could not meet his eyes for long.

"Shall I tell you?" he wondered then.

"Please do!" Nobody had ever called her fascinating before.

"Promise not to throw that at me?" He pointed to the empty cup in her hand and she set it down on a little table at her elbow. "You're in love," said Oliver, his back to the room. "With me. It makes you very beautiful, and me very humble. We're playing a dangerous game, my dear, but so far they haven't caught us out, I can't think why."

"Oliver," said Virginia from the tea-table, "bring Phoebe's cup, do you want her to starve?"

Oliver rose at once and returned to her with the cup, and his own from the small table.

"We were planning to see some pictures," he said easily. "Does anyone here want to go to the Tate with us tomorrow?"

"No," said Virginia rudely, filling Phoebe's cup. "It will be packed with Colonials and Americans, improving their minds. Wait till after the Coronation, and they'll all have gone home."

"And we shall all have gone back to the country," Oliver reminded her. "I'm taking Phoebe to the Tate tomorrow. If nobody will go with us, we'll go alone. She must see the Pre-Raphaelites."

"Pictures make my feet hurt," said Virginia. "And Mother has seen Pre-Raphaelites *ad nauseum*. Take Phoebe to see them if she's fool enough to go with you, and come back here for lunch."

"Thank you, I will. By the way," said Oliver, waiting at the tea-table for the replenished cups, "I heard from the Medical Board this morning. They won't let me rejoin before October at the earliest, and meantime I've got to footle about with some kind of asinine treatments at Leamington or somewhere."

"Oh, Oliver, how *sickening!*" Virginia paused to look up at him with the sugar-tongs in one hand and his cup in the other. "Does that mean you can't come down to Gloucestershire?"

"Only for weekends, I'm afraid."

"And will they make you drink those nasty waters?"

"I keep telling you, it's not my tummy, it's my back," said Oliver patiently. "Let's not go into details, shall we, not at tea time, anyway. I'm supposed to be lucky not to be shut up in hospital for weeks on end."

"Will this upset all your other plans?" Virginia dared to inquire, for they were all dying to know the worst and he had told them almost nothing since he came back from Yorkshire. "Will you and Maia have to postpone things, or hadn't you set a date?"

"We can't look far ahead on account of her father's health." Oliver replied without apparent effort. "But if both her old crocks can pull themselves together, and she can find someone to take over up there while she's away, it will be sometime this autumn."

"You'll beat Phoebe, then," said Virginia in all innocence. "She and Miles are going to wait till Christmas, so all the family can be there."

"It's always a good idea to have a gallery, I think," Oliver remarked. "Maia wants the whole show—St. Margaret's, red carpets, crossed sabres, *The Voice That Breathed o'er Eden,* with all the stops out! I shall hear from the regiment about it, of course."

"Shall you be able to come down for some cubbing before that, anyway?" Virginia insisted.

"Doubt it, you know. They've got some notion I shouldn't ride." He carried Phoebe's cup back to her, his own in his other hand, and settled himself again beside her. "It appears I'm a very sick man and must be humored, and I've a sudden fancy for Pre-Raphaelites, Phoebe, *will* you go to the Tate with me tomorrow?"

Phoebe said hastily that she would, and Virginia began to give her impressions, mostly adverse, of that year's Academy, and Oliver sat facing the room the rest of the afternoon and behaved.

The next morning when he put Phoebe into a hansom to drive down to the Embankment, he said, "I don't really give a damn about the Pre-Raphaelites, but it was all I could think of which was sure not to interest Virginia. We now have a couple of hours to ourselves, with all London looking on, I feel like a schoolboy on a treat." The cab turned into the lower end of Park Lane and he reached for her hands in her lap, gathering them firmly into his. "I am holding your hands in both of mine in a cab," he explained simply, "because then whenever I cross this particular bit of pavement and look up at those trees in the Park, I can say to myself, This is where I held her hands in both of mine on the way to the Tate. And I thought of taking you there in the first place so that there would be one place in London where I could go by myself and remember that we were there alone together—how you looked, what you wore, what you said—it doesn't much matter what you say, you know, it's bound to sound brilliant and original to me!"

"Otherwise I would be afraid to talk!" said Phoebe, and they laughed together and their fingers tightened.

"And what are you wearing today?" he continued, while his eyes ran over her, asking questions. "A white straw hat with a bow and feathers— a blue dress—what's it made of?"

"Shot voile, with shirrings. These are called pagoda sleeves," she told him with amusement.

"Shot voile with shirrings, whatever they are, and lovely lace under your chin—" His eyes lingered on her chin. "And a blue parasol with a mother-of-pearl handle, and—" He looked to see. "—white gloves. I think I can remember all that, for the rest of my life."

"Oh, Oliver, don't make it sound so dreadfully *final!*" she cried, and her eyes filled with tears.

"My dear, I'm not being dismal, just the opposite! I'm very—elated. I've got you all to myself—barring the cabby and the policeman on the corner and several dozen other people. We can say what we like to each other, there is no dangerous opportunity to kiss you, and we don't have to be back in Hill Street till lunch time! I think we're very well off, if you ask me! Burne-Jones is going to be rather a bore, of course, but you've got to look at him because they'll ask."

"Have you been there before?" she inquired, and Oliver admitted that he had.

"With Clare," he added quickly, so that Phoebe would be sure her image in that setting would not be impinged upon. "She made me go, as a gentle sort of outing last spring when I was getting well. And I thought at the time what a suitable place it would be for an assignation. Almost nobody one knows ever goes there! It's not half as obvious as the British Museum, which must be quite crawling with people one would have to pretend not to see!"

"I've been there," said Phoebe, and, "I'll bet you have!" Oliver laughed. "How were the mummies?"

"Very dead," said Phoebe. "I liked the statues best."

"You did?" He was interested at once, as always when she expressed an opinion. "Why?"

"I don't know. Perhaps because I had never seen any real ones before. There was a head of Caesar—" Phoebe frowned out at Hyde Park Corner, seeking words to convey to him what she had felt about the head of Caesar. "He was good," she said, groping. "If he looked like that, I mean. He would have been nice to know."

"The Gauls didn't think so," Oliver suggested, watching her, and she shook her head gravely.

"I would have *liked* him," she said, and turned to Oliver, her hand still in his. "I thought of you that day at the Museum, and I thought what fun it would be, to see the things with you. Shall I ever be able to enjoy anything again without wishing you were there to share it?"

"Perhaps not. Shall you mind that horribly?"

"No. It was before I met you that I was lonely."

"We haven't begun yet to be lonely, that's all still to come," he said, much moved. But there was nothing gloomy in the way he said it, nor resigned. He was merely not unwilling to acknowledge the impending tussle with his own rebellious heart. And when she was silent, he said, "Now tell me what you're thinking."

She looked at him directly, without self-consciousness.

"I was thinking you didn't know me very well," she said. "And I was wondering how it is that someone who is practically a stranger could matter to you very much."

"Know you? I was *born* knowing you!" he cried. "Else how does it happen that everything you do and say seems so exactly right to me, as though you couldn't possibly have done or said anything else but that? How is it that when I come into a room where you are, I have come home, no matter whose house it may be? Why was I so sure from the first day I saw you that I wanted to keep you with me always, and do what I could to see that you were properly treated and had everything you wanted? My dear, I've known you since the beginning of time!"

There was a silence full of choking, forbidden things, and soon the cab stopped outside the imposing façade of London's newest picture gallery.

They enjoyed themselves in the long, quiet rooms, which were not after all full of the Colonials and Americans Virginia had prophesied. Phoebe had not seen enough pictures to be surfeited, and it was always exciting to her to come upon the original of something she had seen reproduced in the books she had read and the engravings and postcards that had found their way to Williamsburg. To Oliver her fresh viewpoint and undisguised enthusiasms and sudden, instinctive, first-glance likes and dislikes were enthralling to explore, and he set himself by a receptive silence or a provocative question to draw out of her the characteristic comments he delighted to hear.

Sometimes as they paused before a picture his hand would rest lightly at her elbow. Sometimes as they moved on to the next her shoulder would brush his sleeve, and their eyes would meet and linger, and the smiles they shared had little to do really with the words they happened to be saying, but were born just of their satisfaction at being together, their pleasure in each other's looks, and the mutual knowledge that they were in love.

It was a clear, uncomplicated happiness which took no thought, for the moment, of any further fulfillment, and knew no regrets that it must end. What they said to each other mattered less than that they were able to converse together at all, and they talked sensibly enough most of the time so far as anyone could have overheard. And Phoebe was thinking, even while she laughed, Here it is again, like being drunk—not caring what went before or what comes after—not even caring that it won't last—how can I be so *happy* when I know it can't last—I never felt like this with Miles. . . .

But she said nothing of that to Oliver, and if he saw her eyes cloud over briefly, and he saw everything, he was too wise to say just then, Tell me what you are thinking. The bad moment passed, and they went on into the Burne-Jones room and sagely appraised *The Beggar Maid* and wondered how long it took her to learn to behave like a queen, and if King Cophetua had ever been sorry for his impulse. And it occurred to Oliver that probably she had had the same look in the eyes that Phoebe had had at luncheon that day at the Hall, when there was nothing to do but undertake to look after them and see that they came to no harm; and he thought, At least Cophetua was free to follow his impulse. . . .

But there was nothing in his lean brown face to show the stab of angry frustration that shot through him as he realized anew how he had tied his own hands and made himself useless to Phoebe before he ever saw her—she needed him, and reached out to him as Maia never would, but now she must be allowed to put her funny little chin in the air and keep her word to Miles, while he fulfilled his own pledge as per *The Morning Post* and *The Queen: The engagement is announced and a marriage will take place between Captain the Honorable Oliver Campion of the 25th Lancers, brother of the Earl of Enstone, and Maia Marguerite Douglas, only daughter of Francis Merton Douglas, of Merton House, Darceydale, Yorkshire.* . . .

When they came out of the gallery they walked for a little way along the Embankment, strolling with the noonday sun warm on their faces, and Oliver thought, I can come back here too—flecks of shadow on her blue dress from the leaves—tiny spangles of sunlight through her hatbrim on her face—I should have kissed her chin when I had the chance that night—I shall always see her looking up at me if I come and stand here—do I *want* to be haunted like this?—damn my back. . . .

Phoebe saw his mouth straighten with pain, and said anxiously, "Oliver, ought you to walk any more? Let's take a cab."

"Not just yet," he said, and drew her over against the stone wall above the water. "Just stand there a moment and let me look at you. Would you do me the favor to smile?"

Phoebe smiled, and then they laughed together, and guiltily remembered the time, and when they were in a cab driving north, Phoebe asked again about his back. Though it had been aching like a bad tooth for the past half hour Oliver said, "Darling, I'm perfectly all right, it's just those silly asses at the Medical Board," so convincingly that she believed him and thought no more about it, and everything shone and sparkled again all the way to Hill Street.

6

GOODWOOD without the King was dull and the weather was beastly. The polo season at Hurlingham finished with the Hurlingham team defeating the Horse Guards, the sacred Blues, six goals to four, and Charles took a bad spill over the boards and everybody said he could have broken his neck. One of the last brilliant affairs of the waning Season was a reception at the German Embassy in Carlton House Terrace, which Bracken and Dinah attended and to which Rosalind and her mamma were invited at the request of Prince Conrad. He danced three times with Rosalind—the absolute Diplomatic limit—and took her in to supper and saw that she met everyone of importance, and she was taken special notice of by the Ambassador. Prince Conrad also arranged that the Norton-Leighs should be invited to visit after the Coronation at the same country house in Scotland where he himself would be staying, and Mamma allowed herself further glittering dreams of tiaras and sables and motor cars on a Royal scale.

On August ninth, when Phoebe at the window of Archie's club in St. James's Street actually saw the King returning, crowned, from Westminster, Oliver was beside her to point out Charles Laverham riding in the escort, or she could not have been sure which one of the magnificent mounted figures in plumed helmet and shining cuirass she knew.

"How can you *tell* which is Charles?" Virginia asked unbelievingly, for they all looked alike to her.

"By his place in the guard," said Oliver. "But even without that, you can always tell a man you know on a horse as far as you can see him —by the set of his knees, and the line of his shoulders, and the way he holds his elbows—"

"That one holds his elbows just like all the rest," said Virginia captiously, and Oliver laughed and said So he did, and let it go.

"It *is* Charles, though," said Rosalind, watching him out of sight. "Somehow you can't miss him, but how do we *know?*"

"Perhaps because we love him," said Oliver very low, and Rosalind replied without embarrassment, "Yes, we do, don't we. There's nobody quite like him."

Oliver glanced at her as though he was half-minded to say more, but held his tongue. Her pure little profile was towards him as she watched the distant, red-plumed rider that was Charles turning into Piccadilly. Oliver knew that her words had been the simple truth with no secondary meaning for Rosalind. Anyone who had known Charles for years, as she had, knew that there was no duplicate, on or off a horse.

London emptied very fast after the Coronation, and they began at once to take down the stands, which added to the general desolation. The King went off in his yacht for a cruise along the Scottish coast. The Norton-Leighs departed for the house-party in Scotland in Prince Conrad's reserved compartments, with the understanding that they were to come to Farthingale for a week later on, before Phoebe had to sail.

Virginia's lease, already extended, on the Hill Street house expired, Archie's club was closed for cleaning, and they all said how pleasant it was to be back at Farthingale again. Clare and Mortimer and little Lionel were at the Hall, with Edward and Winifred and little Hubert, though the babies were seldom seen except when they took their daily airings with their Nannies in the park, for they were kept stowed away on the rather barrack-like nursery and schoolroom floor in the west wing which Dinah had so recently left, and where young Gerald and his visiting chums still slept when he was home for the holidays.

The announcement of Rosalind's engagement to Prince Conrad was not altogether unexpected, and there was no reason for it to take everyone who loved her by such outraged surprise, and yet that was the general reaction when it appeared in *The Morning Post*. The marriage was to take place during September, which was not the most fashionable time of year, but Mrs. Norton-Leigh dreaded that the death of Prince Conrad's aged father in Germany might occur to diminish with mourning the splendors of a Royal wedding and its attendant festivities, and so she gave easy consent to what seemed to onlookers His Highness's indecent haste.

When the promised visit to Farthingale had been ruthlessly cancelled because of the trousseau and other obligations in Town, a letter arrived from Rosalind in which she implored Phoebe on tear-blotted pages not to sail before the ceremony, because she had set her heart on Phoebe's being one of the bridesmaids.

Phoebe showed the letter to Eden and entreated her for a postponement of their sailing date, which was more than a week too soon as it stood. Eden showed the letter to Bracken, who said "Poor little beggar, of course she must have Phoebe at the wedding if she wants her," and arranged at once for them all to sail on a later boat. He also gave Phoebe a large check to buy a wedding present with, just as though it was her own money. "Find out what she would like from Dinah and me and let me know," he said. "We must do this up right."

Rosalind's letter had said that the gowns and underclothes were all to come from *Lucile* in Hanover Square, which was of course frightfully expensive, but the trousseau was one of the gifts of the bridegroom to the bride, in view of the exalted position she would be expected to fill as his wife. Virginia looked dark when she heard about that. "And how does he know so much about *Lucile's* underclothes?" she inquired, for it was the first London house to supply sets of rainbow-tinted cobwebs trimmed with lace in place of the fine embroidered linen and muslin which even Royalty wore. Most English wives considered them immodest and succumbed by degrees, a nightgown here, a corset-cover there, and then either a dozen of each or no more at all, according to their husbands' reactions. Prince Conrad's order for his bride was six dozen of everything, in tints to match the dresses, which were to be designed especially so as not to obliterate the lines of Rosalind's lovely *fausse maigre* figure—a job after *Lucile's* heart, for she always leaned towards the theatrical, and even actresses had been known to hesitate at their own reflections in the mirrors of her little grey fitting-rooms.

There was some discussion, quite friendly and shameless, at Farthingale and the Hall of how Charles Laverham would feel about Rosalind's engagement. Oliver, who alone really knew, contributed nothing, until Virginia taxed him with looking sphinxish.

"You men always stick together," she accused him. "Have you seen Charles since it happened?"

"No."

"Nor heard from him?"

"No."

"Aren't you going to *do* anything?"

"Dear heart," said Oliver gently, for he was very fond of Virginia but found her rather difficult when she started asking questions, "there are times when one does best to mind one's own business."

"But *somebody's* got to stop her!" cried Virginia.

"Abduction has gone out," Oliver reminded her. "You can be put in jail for it nowadays. Besides—how do you know?—maybe Rosalind likes the prospect. It's not every girl who has six dozen of everything from *Lucile* at the bridegroom's expense, is it?"

Virginia said he had a vulgar mind, and gave him up.

The next day Oliver went back to London to see his doctors, he said, and there was Charles at the club.

"Thank God," he said at sight of Oliver. "Look here, you've got to help me out, old boy. Reinforcements signalled for."

"Reinforcements dispatched at the gallop," said Oliver sympathetically. "Tell me what I can do."

Charles thought a couple of whiskeys and soda might help them to think of something, and they sat down in a corner and went to work on it.

Shortly after noon the next day, at the hour when fashionable carriages turned into the Park at Grosvenor Gate for the daily drive, Charles and Oliver took up a casual-seeming patrol near the Achilles Statue to wait for the Norton-Leigh landau and matched greys. Both were grave, for Charles and Oliver, and as nervous as actors on the first night. Oliver's task, and it was not an easy one, was to get the carriage stopped in order to pay his respects and take the opportunity to wish Rosalind happiness on her engagement—Charles was under no illusion that the carriage would stop for him alone, but Oliver was almost one of the family and was considered harmless by Mamma—and Oliver must then somehow hold Mrs. Norton-Leigh in conversation long enough for Charles on the other side of the carriage to get in a few unnoticed words with Rosalind.

As they paced up and down together, greeting even in their preoccupation the passersby whom they knew, Oliver was racking his brain for topics sufficiently interesting to enlarge upon, and inventing messages from Eden and Clare. Charles was rehearsing in his mind the fewest and quickest words in which to convince Rosalind that he must see her alone, somewhere, somehow, and soon. It wasn't a very good scheme, or a very easy one to carry out, but it was the best they had been able to evolve.

"Here they come," said Charles, looking rather the way he always looked when the first wailing notes of the *"Charge!"* fell on his ears in action. "Come on, old boy, buck up!"

Oliver stepped to the side of the road and raised his hat. The carriage slowed and came to a stop, and Mrs. Norton-Leigh extended to him a tightly gloved hand and began to inquire after the family at the Hall and how his poor back was. . . .

When it was over and the Norton-Leighs drove on, Oliver was perspiring freely and Charles, rather white around the mouth, had extracted a promise from Rosalind to write him a note that very night telling him where he might see her for a few minutes without being overheard by Mamma. He had no idea where that might be, and hadn't much hope of it, really, when he opened the note at his club the next morning.

> Dear Charles—[it said]
> You're very mysterious, and I can't think what you're up to, but if you want to come to the dressmaker's on Friday I shall be there for a fitting at three. Phoebe and her aunt are coming up to Town for a few days because I am full of appointments and poor Mamma has to have a tooth out and can't go about with me. They will be staying at Claridge's and I expect Phoebe and I shall be allowed to go as far as *Lucile's* alone, and I can see you there in the fitting-room before I change.
> They are very obliging about letting you in without having to go through the show room, and I know people do meet people that way, though not the girls who are fitting their trousseaux because they are allowed to see their fiancés at home. I'm afraid it will look very queer, but it's all I can think of to suggest, and Phoebe would never say a word if we asked her not to.
> Yours sincerely,
> ROSALIND

Charles at once consulted Oliver, who raised his eyebrows.

"Sounds like a French farce," he said. "Just the thing for Marie Tempest. Do I hide behind a screen?"

Charles called him all sorts of a fathead, and said if he were to turn up at Claridge's in time to walk to Hanover Square with the two girls Phoebe's Aunt Eden would surely seize that opportunity for a little peace and quiet on her own and not think it necessary to come along. Which proved to be the case. Bracken kept a hired motor car in London for his mother's use, and when it had brought Rosalind to Claridge's Eden took it on to Regent Street to accomplish some shopping of her own while Oliver escorted the two girls to *Lucile's* on foot. The motor was to be waiting to drive Rosalind home when they finished.

So Charles found himself discreetly admitted to a small grey room lined with mirrors where Rosalind awaited him with her hat off, beside a rack of unfinished dresses to be tried on—among them the unmistakable silver tissue and Brussels lace of the wedding gown. The door closed softly behind the young saleswoman who had guided him there.

"Well, Charles, what on earth is it all about?" Rosalind demanded at once. "I don't know how I ever dared to do this, Mamma would have the roof off if she knew." And as he only stood looking at her helplessly from just inside the door, she went on almost impatiently, "What *is* it, Charles, you're very odd, all of a sudden!"

Charles cast away his hat and gloves on to a small grey upholstered chair and took a step forward, looming enormous in the boxy room.

"Look here, my girl, you can't marry this fellow, you don't know what you're doing," he said abruptly.

It was the wrong beginning. Rosalind stood very straight facing him, looking cornered and defenceless, her small head with its heavy crown of dark hair held very high.

"I know quite well," she said. "I shall have a most interesting life, marrying into the Diplomatic Corps. Vienna may be our next post, and I shall hear the best music in the world, there. And if ever Conrad should be sent as attaché to Washington I could go and visit Phoebe, because she lives in the same state."

They were such pitiful, childish reasons for marrying a man you were not in love with—couldn't possibly be in love with, Charles thought, watching her. If she had said money—titles—the famous castle at Heidersdorf—the prestige and luxury of Prince Conrad's station in the world—but to hear music in Vienna—to visit Phoebe in Virginia—they were fairy tales to amuse a little girl.

"But you don't understand," he tried again. "This man is a stranger to you, in all his ways—he's a Continental—he's a *German!* Their ideas are very different from ours, you don't know what you're getting into!"

"I think I can take care of myself," she insisted with pathetic dignity, and Charles blundered on with no one to tell him he was taking the wrong line entirely, to question her judgment, when he might have said instead that he loved her and had always wanted to marry her himself.

"You're about as able to take care of yourself as a three-weeks-old kitten," he asserted. "You haven't even had the chances most girls do to find their feet and get their eyes open. If he was one of our kind, I'd bite on it, I promise I would. But this fellow is a damned outsider, and I'm damned if I'm going to take it lying down!"

"*Charles!* What language!" Rosalind covered her ears, and he reached her in two strides and took her hands down, imprisoning them in his.

"Rosalind, you've got to listen to me—seriously—"

"Don't, please—" She pulled her hands away from him and backed against the wall. Her blue eyes were dark and shadowed in a face suddenly gone white. "You've no idea how I hate being pawed," she said, and Charles's expression went from astonishment to compassion to despair.

"Oh, my God!" he said, just above a whisper.

"Will you please stop s-swearing at me?"

"It's not swearing, it's praying," said Charles. "Have you said that—about being pawed—to his Nibs?"

"Mamma says it will be different after I'm married."

"Why?" said Charles.

"You've got no right to come here and ask impertinent questions!" she cried, and her lips were quivering.

"Of course I've got the right, I've loved you ever since you wore your hair down your back, and I've never thought of marrying any other girl but you!"

She stared up at him incredulously.

"B-but, Charles, that's impossible, you haven't—you couldn't—"

"I couldn't afford you," said Charles steadily. "Yes, that has been made quite plain for years. I was trying to hold my tongue so as not to make trouble for you, but this is too much, I can't have this."

"You m-might have said—something—in time—"

"Well, what was the good of my saying anything, I should only have been warned off! Then I saw this fellow was after you, and I knew you were being thrown at his head. But I couldn't believe it would really happen, at least not so fast. I thought something might save you. Rosalind —think. His father will die, and he'll go home to his estates, and you'll have to go with him. You'll have to live there, in Germany, your children will be German children, you won't hear a word of English spoken from one week's end to the next—"

"I'm allowed to have an English maid," she interrupted quickly. "And he has promised we'll come home to England every year, no matter where we may be."

"Then he's lying," said Charles, and fear suddenly showed in her white face—livid, childish fear that wrung his heart.

"Oh, *no!*" she cried. "He *promised!*" And she caught at Charles with small, cold, fumbling hands, her face upturned to his as a child looks for reassurance. "Charles, you're only trying to scare me out of it! You must do him justice, he's been very kind, very—respectful. He says I may always do exactly as I choose, and we'll have a house in England for the hunting! I didn't ask him, he suggested it himself, he wants me to be happy, he said—" She tore herself out of Charles's cradling hands and dropped down on the nearest chair with her arms across the back of it and her face hidden against her wrists. Charles stood where he was, looking down at her.

"Child, you can't do it," he said in his light, slurred voice with its casual-seeming but perfect articulation. "You must tell them—at once. Whether you marry me or not, and I mean to do what I can about that, you must get rid of this blighter today."

She was not crying. She rocked her head slowly, listlessly, on her crossed wrists without looking up, and her voice was flat and hopeless.

"It's no use, Charles. I can't stand up to them. I did try. But it's cheaper to go on."

"Cheaper! At the price of your whole life?"

"You don't know what it's like with Mamma," she said. "She gets an idea in her head and she never lets go. Besides, it's Evelyn's turn, next year. And he's better than Lord Meriton—or Willie McBride. I can't go through all that again. I might as well go on."

Charles went down on one knee beside the chair and laid his arms around the small, quivering figure, but she clung desperately to the back of the chair and would not yield.

"My dear, let me try," he said. "Let me talk to your mother—"

"No—please—you'll only make it worse—"

"Then come away with me," said Charles quietly. "Now. This minute. And hang all the consequences. I'll keep you safe."

Slowly she raised her head to look at him, and he saw her white face as though she had been stunned, as though any minute now she might begin to come to.

There was a discreet tap on the door. When they did not answer at once it was repeated, more insistently. Rosalind's dazed blue eyes went on past Charles's face to rest on the panels of the door behind him.

"Yes?" she said.

A girl's voice spoke through the door.

"I'm sorry, Miss Norton-Leigh—but I was to say the fitter has been waiting, and she has another appointment at four-thirty."

"I'm ready," said Rosalind. "Just one minute." Her wide, unseeing look came back to Charles where he still knelt beside the chair. "You'll have to go," she said tonelessly.

"Rosalind—"

"Thank you for trying to help. But it isn't any use. You'll have to go now."

He rose, and picked up his hat and gloves and turned to speak again. Her forehead was resting on her crossed wrists on the back of the chair, her face was hidden.

"A message to me at the club," he said, "before it's too late—"

She made no answer. He looked back through the narrowing crack of the door as he closed it behind him. She had not moved.

7

PHOEBE came in with the fitter and watched Rosalind stand listless and docile while gown after gown was put on her, pinned, snipped, altered, discussed, and removed. When they had finished it was tea time and Eden's motor was at the curb. They got in and were driven off smoothly towards Regent's Park.

For more than half the way they sat in silence. Then Rosalind said, very low, "Charles asked me to go away with him."

"You mean *elope?*" Phoebe's eyes were round. "Oh, Rosalind, *do* it! There's still time!"

Rosalind turned her head to look at her friend, withdrawn and defensive.

"What's the good of that?" she asked. "There'd be an awful row, and when the dust settled I'd be married anyhow—to a man with no money at all instead of to a man with lots. I don't see much point in that."

"Don't you love Charles?"

"No. I don't think I do. If I did it might be different, but I never thought of such a thing till this afternoon."

"But he's English," Phoebe said. "You wouldn't ever have to go away and live on the Continent."

"He said my children would be German," said Rosalind, frowning at the chauffeur's back, for she had not thought much about the children either.

"And if there should be a war—" Phoebe began carefully.

"I should come straight home in that case."

"But it might not be possible to come—especially if you had children. Your son would be a prince. He would be the heir. You wouldn't be allowed to bring him with you."

"Perhaps I shan't have any children," Rosalind said slowly. "Sometimes one escapes that."

"Do you want to?"

"I don't know. If they're going to be German it will seem very strange —and rather uncomfortable, I should think. I shall get them an English nurse, anyway. Conrad had an English nurse when he was little. It's the fashion in Germany. And French governesses. The boys have German tutors when they're old enough."

"Are you going to see Charles again?"

"No. I told him it wasn't any use. Besides—" She hesitated. She wasn't in love with Charles. But compared to the unknown ahead of her he looked very safe, very usual, very comforting and restful. She sighed. "It's too late now," she said. "Don't tell a soul, will you. It wouldn't be fair to Charles."

Phoebe promised and the motor stopped in front of Rosalind's house. Phoebe watched till the door opened and then was driven back to Claridge's for tea.

Rosalind found her mother propped up on the sofa in the drawing-room wearing a skittish lilac tea-gown and holding a lace handkerchief to her face. Opposite her, in his well-cut English clothes, sat Prince Conrad. He stood up as Rosalind appeared in the doorway—she noticed how he moved all in one piece, it was a way Germans had, and stood erect with his feet together, no lounging—and Mamma said, "Oh, there you are at last, my dear. His Highness was kind enough to come and inquire how I had survived at the dentist's, and I persuaded him to wait for a cup of tea."

Prince Conrad bent over Rosalind's hand till his lips touched her glove.

"What I waited for," he said in his formal, almost unaccented English, "was a glimpse of you. I hear you have been trying on dresses. Are you tired? Shall I go?"

But just then tea came in, and Rosalind had to sit down and pour out for all of them, and answer Mamma's searching questions about the dresses and what was still to be done on each of them. Instead of boring Prince Conrad, the conversation seemed to elicit from him the most intelligent interest. It developed to Rosalind's surprise that he knew all about the dresses, and had been to Hanover Square himself to see the designs and to choose the furs, which had been shown to him on living models.

In the midst of it Mrs. Norton-Leigh set down her cup rather suddenly and said she really must go and lie down, she did think her face had begun to swell—which it had. Prince Conrad gave her his arm as far as the door and saw her sympathetically into the care of her maid, Gibson. She looked back from the threshold to where Rosalind remained stranded at the tea-table.

"Give His Highness some fresh tea," she said. "You will have to keep each other company today, I'm not fit for anything." And she tottered away, supported by Gibson.

As Prince Conrad returned across the room, Rosalind knew a moment's terror, and then reminded herself that this was no Willie McBride, and thought, Mamma did it on purpose. But she was still far from guessing that Prince Conrad had requested, even required, her mother to leave them alone together that day, and had received as a warning an account of the Willie McBride episode. Suppose he wants to kiss me, Rosalind thought—I can't go on with this—suppose he—

She reached for his cup on the corner of the table and he said, "Please, no—don't trouble. Come and sit here, you will be more comfortable."

It was the sofa.

She rose and moved obediently to sit on the end of it, and he placed himself casually in the middle, where his knee brushed her skirt, and took her left hand in both his. He had already put the ring on her finger in her mother's presence some days before, and he sat looking down at it —an impressive sapphire, which was her birthstone—in a silence she found impossible to break.

"It is time, I think," he observed in his too perfect English, "that you ceased to be afraid of me." His piercing, melancholy gaze, lighted by the immovable eyeglass, came up to her face. "Your hand is cold, and it trembles in mine." He chafed it gently in his fingers. "Will you answer me a question? I would like the truth."

She nodded speechlessly.

"Are you in love with somebody else?" he asked.

"No. Of course not," she assured him in some confusion.

"There is no Of course about it," he remarked placidly. "I come into your life. I am a good match. You are advised to accept me. I do not flatter myself, you see. But that is not to say that you have never had—dreams, shall we call it—of marrying someone quite different."

"No. There's nobody. But I don't— I think it's only fair to tell you that I'm not in love with you."

"You have said so before." He smiled, with tolerance and affection, his fingers chafing hers. "I do not expect that so soon. But I am relieved to know that I have no rival."

He raised the hand he held and turned it over, and laid a lingering kiss in its small moist palm. She felt the bold, heavy curve of his lips and started, and found she could not draw her hand away. It was a very slight liberty he took, to put his kiss in her palm, but it was her first experience of the strong attraction he had for nearly all women, and she thought, dizzy and surprised, I don't know—it may not be so bad—

Then he was looking at her again, his arm sliding along the back of the sofa as he leaned towards her.

"You see," he was saying softly, "I am no ogre to eat you! You need not fear. And tell me another thing. Are those eyelashes *real,* or do they come off when you wash your face?"

"*Nothing* comes off when I wash my face!" she told him indignantly. "And none of my hair spends the night on the dressing-table, either!"

"I am very glad to hear," he said, and her cheeks flamed while his deliberate gaze probed the mystery of her waved pompadour and intricate coils. He smiled again, more and more broadly, and then he laughed, disproportionately, and his hand possessed hers more closely against the front of his coat. "I shall remember," he said, laughing. "When the night comes that I take it down for myself—nothing falls away with the pins, eh?" His other hand came up from the back of the sofa to catch her chin between finger and thumb. "Oho, she has spirit!" he said. "She will talk back to her clumsy prince, English fashion, when he puts his foot in it!"

"Don't German girls defend themselves from slander?" she demanded, removing her chin with a little jerk from his grasp.

"Ah, let us not talk of German girls, they are nothing to do with us! They are always dull, and say Yes and No, and have thick ankles!"

She tried to smile at him gallantly, tried to meet him halfway, the beginnings of coquetry awaking to his experienced approach.

"But you haven't seen my ankles," she remarked, pink-cheeked at her own audacity.

"Yours I can imagine," he said easily. "You have small bones everywhere, like a doe's, that I could break in my hands."

"That's not a pretty simile," she objected hastily.

"To say I could break you in my hands? It is true. But you will be quite safe. I am not a bad-tempered man, I am very easy to get along with, you will see."

"No doubt you are," she said, playing up the best she knew how, "so long as you get your way!"

"But you will give me my way," he said confidently. "It will be your pleasure to do so when you have learned—learned how happy it is in your power to make me. Heretofore, I swear it, there is no woman I cannot do without. I come—I go—it makes no matter to me. But always I say to myself, Conrad, I say, your time will come. Somewhere is the woman you will possess at any cost. Make sure you are free to take her, I tell myself. And so what happens? The years go by, and I am still not married again, and there is still no heir after me. My father is anxious. People make up foolish stories about me, some of them not altogether —savory. But I do not mind, no. I am still free. I still come and go. Once, twice, I think possibly—but always I am wrong. Always they know too much, or too little, they try too hard, or they are too—unpromising. Then I see little Rosalind, and I know at last I am undone. True, it is not what was most desirable for me in many ways. It is not a title, it is not a fortune, but I have both. It is not experience of the world, to uphold my position. It is not a figure to furnish me with strong heirs. It is not even sophistication, to keep me amused. What then is this magic you have for me? Because it is magic, and I am bewitched."

His hard, unsparing eyes ran over her, from her hair down across her face and body to the hand he held, while she sat mute and unresisting and a remote corner of her brain reminded her hysterically of the rabbit and the snake.

"Perhaps it is your stillness, which nothing reduces to fidgets—for I have tried," he was saying. "Or your beauty, which does not come off at night—I believe you. Or your naked fear of what I may do next—ah, yes, I can see!—but that will pass. Or your courage, to make a marriage you do not understand and cannot but dread. Whence comes so much courage, in a thing my two hands can span? Perhaps that is what holds me fast, so that I must see more of this courage, I must try it still further, I must hold it in my arms—I can see your heart beat in your throat, but you sit quite still beside me. You don't try to escape. You don't cry quarter. Perhaps it is that that I— But how thoughtless I am, to press you so," he broke off in apparent chagrin. "Believe me, it was not intentional. You take one quite out of oneself. Always remember, if I hurt you—and no doubt I shall—it was not my intention. Always remember I shall be sorry, when sanity returns. It will always return, I promise you. In all but one way. As for that—you are the woman I cannot live without possessing. Try to thwart me in that now, and you will find no sanity anywhere—no mercy. Little love, there is no need to look at me like that! You will find me the tenderest of men, for your happiness is mine. Your lightest wish shall be my law, and it shall be my joy to anticipate even the wish. Do you like baubles? It will take a little time for me to learn your taste. If I make you presents you do not care for, please do not hesitate to say so—we can send them back and choose others."

He paused, and his gaze rested on her rigid face, amused, penetrating, but kind. He was somehow much nearer than he had been when he first sat down, and when she tried to draw back she met the corner of the sofa. He put his hand into his breast pocket and took out a small plush case and flipped it open to reveal a brooch set with diamonds and sapphires which would have taken any woman's breath away.

"Tell me then if this sort of thing appeals to you," he said, and watched the spontaneous surprise and pleasure she was showing. "Yes? How right I was to bring you sapphires. A pity that there are none as big as your eyes." He removed the brooch from its white velvet bed, adding with a contemptuous flick of his fingers towards the modest pearl and coral affair pinned to the lace of her blouse, "Take off that thing you are wearing and let us see how this one looks there."

Rosalind removed her own brooch and put it down on the table, holding out her hand for the new one. He ignored her gesture and laid the box aside.

"Allow me," he said firmly, and his fingers were at her breast, deftly fastening the gift in place. "And what do you say to your lover now, eh?" he suggested as he finished.

"Th-thank you very much," she whispered. "I shall—treasure it always."

Again he was amused, leaning towards her.

"You are altogether enchanting," he said. "I am very fortunate. May I?"

His head came down. She felt his weight above her and shut her eyes.

The kiss, which was the first between them, claimed her completely, violent, intimate, and long. When he let her go she was shaking, and caught her breath audibly.

"Forgive me if I startled you," he said quite gently. "With you it is difficult to contain oneself."

He began again to kiss her hands, opening her passive fingers to expose the palms, holding them against his face. Rosalind set her teeth and let him have her hands, while a rising tide of panic, hot and cold, engulfed her—I can't go on—it's nothing like Willie McBride—*but I can't go on*—

"Such cold hands," he murmured against her fingers. "The time comes soon when I warm them against my heart—such a little iceberg she is, but we change all that—little love, you must have confidence, I will be kind—"

"I'll t-try to please you—" she got out, feeling that she owed something to his ardor.

"Please me? But how can you do otherwise while you still breathe?" He rose, keeping her hands in his, and drew her up facing him. "I must go now, while I restrain myself. Soon there will be no necessity for that between us. In the meantime—see how patient I am!" Again he clipped her chin between his finger and thumb, tilting her defenceless face to his gaze. He was smiling, but his eyes were bright and strange. "How your Conrad has been brought to his knees at last!" he marvelled. "A scrap of a thing like you, to bind the eagle with chains! No doubt you will learn soon enough to take advantage of that. Until then—ah, yes, be but a little afraid of me, it becomes you!"

He pinched her chin playfully and released it, bent formally to kiss her hand, and left the room without a backward glance.

She stood where she was, holding her chin and shaking, her knees unsteady. But he promised to be kind, she thought dizzily—he's really very fond of me—that was a nice speech about binding the eagle, an Englishman would never have said that—I wonder if I *can* have power— Beneath repulsion curiosity stirred, for his ruthless, conquering magnetism had reached her a little. What next? When he no longer restrained himself, what then? The time was coming soon when he would not have to go away at all. Her heart was beating heavily under the sapphire brooch.

She dropped down on the sofa with her face in her hands, and found herself thinking of Charles, who she was sure had never kissed anyone like that in his life. But probably if you were going to marry him he would. Probably they were all alike, and it didn't make much difference which of them you married. Only—it seemed fantastic to suppose that one would ever feel afraid of Charles. . . .

She tipped over against the cushions which Prince Conrad had crushed behind them and lay still, her face hidden. I can't go on with this—not even for the sables—not even to go to Washington and visit Phoebe— not with him—there's something awful coming, and I can't stop him then, I shall have to pretend to like it—I'm frightened—he *likes* me to be afraid—I'd rather it was Charles. . . .

8

VIRGINIA gave a dinner party at Claridge's the evening before Rosalind's wedding, and everybody was there, Prince Conrad foregoing the usual bachelor spree without visible regret. It was much the same company who had sat down to lunch on Phoebe's first day at the Hall last May, with some additions such as His Highness and a Count Chlodwig von Lyncker who had recently arrived at the German Embassy from Berlin and would be best man, and a few of the Norton-Leigh set, and Lady Shadwell, who was lending her house in Buckinghamshire for the first week of the honeymoon before they went to Paris—Prince Conrad having been explicit in his wish not to begin with a seasick bride.

But it had been a difficult table to plan, with Rosalind necessarily on Archie's right and Prince Conrad on Virginia's left; with Mrs. Norton-Leigh on the host's left and Charles anywhere but next to her or Rosalind; with Oliver demanding to take in Phoebe, and Dinah begging not to have to sit next to Prince Conrad. Dinah lost on that, though she had Charles on her other side for consolation, and Virginia took Oliver on her right as, she said, moral support.

It was all very decorous and candle-lit and discreetly gay, and everybody drank the proper toasts and said the proper things, and Oliver was just beginning to think maybe he was all wrong and everything was for the best, when Phoebe leaned across him and said confidentially to Virginia, "What was Clare saying to you before we came down?"

Virginia stole a glance at Prince Conrad, who was occupied with Dinah, and leaned towards Phoebe and said, "Don't listen, Oliver. Clare is convinced that Rosalind is going to back out at the last minute. She's scared stiff, poor lamb."

And Phoebe said, "Clare should have *told* her!"

"No *time!*" Virginia reminded her significantly. "Besides, Clare is no help, she says nobody told *her!* Dinah tried to talk to Rosalind upstairs, but Mam*m*a was on top of them instantly!"

"Does this really mean what it seems to?" Oliver asked, bewildered, and they glanced uneasily at him and at each other, and returned to their food.

It was beyond even Virginia to explain even to Oliver that Rosalind's abysmal ignorance, rigidly enjoined by her mother, had brought her to the verge of hysteria, and that nobody could get to her with a few private words of encouragement. But Virginia, acknowledging in spite of herself Prince Conrad's personal magnetism as most women of any experience did, had remarked to Archie while they dressed for dinner that evening that His Highness scared the daylights out of her in an exciting sort of way, and that Rosalind might be better off than they thought if only she could learn how to manage him. Archie said no daughter of his would ever marry a German, and Virginia asked with interest if he was going to take himself seriously as a father and be difficult about the man Daphne wanted to marry when she grew up. Archie replied that if it was a German he was going to be very difficult indeed. Jerking his white tie into a perfect bow, he added that Mam*m*a was a cockatrice, and would never go to heaven when she died.

Having been married herself without even girlish sentiment on the side of her unfortunate husband, who never realized how utterly he had failed during his brief, conscientious courtship to reach her heart, Mrs. Norton-Leigh was firmly convinced that if girls knew what to expect on their wedding night few of them would ever marry at all, and the human race might soon become extinct. Her bland preservation of an unmentionable mystery overcast with some unpleasantness had by now reduced Rosalind to a state of nervous apprehension far worse than would have resulted from the rudest facts, and even commonsense had ceased to function for her. In the beginning she had tried to tell herself that since Dinah and Virginia were so content there was nothing in marriage for her to dread. But as the days passed and she never saw Prince Conrad alone again, nor had any further opportunity, owning to the vigilant presence of Mamma, to become accustomed to the small privileges which were rightfully his as her fiancé but which he mostly forebore under Mamma's eye, that argument became specious and the answer was tormentingly plain—Dinah and Virginia had been in love with their bridegrooms. As for Clare—Rosalind's mind would flinch away from the memory of Clare's lifted brows and careless shrug that time she had said, "My dear, don't be a goose, one gets used to it—and the baby is fun once you've got it."

Sitting between Archie and Bracken at Claridge's that night, Rosalind was vividly aware of Prince Conrad at the other end of the oval table, his eyeglass turned attentively on Dinah who seemed to be telling some sort of story which amused him. Dinah knows how to entertain people, she thought—Bracken has taught her—Bracken would be easy to live with—you wouldn't have to worry about anything with him. Her eyes went on to Charles, smiling his wide, transfiguring smile at Eden, who was looking up at him with affection—Charles was plain until he smiled, and then he radiated friendliness and charm, and made you feel clever and beautiful and confident—you didn't have to be sophisticated to amuse Charles, and he never expected anything of you more than you knew how to give—

The now familiar churning of her midriff which was sheer nerves and made it impossible to eat laid hold of her again. Tomorrow night at this time she and Conrad would be dining alone together at Lady Shadwell's house in Buckinghamshire—she wouldn't be able to eat, and he would notice, for nothing escaped him, and he would realize that she was paralyzed and witless with fright, which would be the ultimate humiliation—

"Drink your champagne, quick," said Bracken's voice on her right, and she reached for the glass. It shook and wobbled in her hand as she raised it, and clinked against her teeth. She gulped the cold wine, choked a bit, and gulped again. When she set the glass down it was immediately filled by a watchful footman, and Bracken said, "Steady, now. Not all at once. If you handle that stuff right it will get you through almost anything."

She looked up at him piteously.

"I thought I was going to faint."

"Nothing of the kind, you're all right, it's just strain. You'll live through it, everyone does."

"Did Dinah—w-was Dinah—"

"Dinah was a wreck by the time I got her away for the honeymoon. All those fittings for clothes—all those presents to deal with—all these parties—weddings are hard work for the bride!"

But Dinah was in love, she thought again dismally, chewing up a piece of roll and forcing it down. Dinah *wanted* to be married, she was the happiest girl I ever saw, even while we were putting her into her going-away dress. Dinah went *dancing* to meet him at the top of the stairs. . . .

"Rosalind, you must eat something, child." It was her mother's voice from across the table. "Try and eat the chicken, it's delicious, and you'll want your strength tomorrow."

Rosalind picked up her fork. It slipped from her cold fingers and fell to the floor. She sat helplessly, her head down, while the footman brought her another, and Bracken talked on comfortably beside her, telling some cheerful anecdote she made no effort to comprehend. "Look at me and smile," she heard him say, and obeyed. "More champagne now. Drink up."

He pulled her through the meal that way, and she was wordlessly grateful to him. But Bracken would not be beside her tomorrow night. . . .

When the dinner ended at last they drove home to Regent's Park in Prince Conrad's brougham with the Polkwitz-Heidersdorf coat-of-arms on the door. He sat with his back to the horses and made polite conversation with her mother. The champagne Rosalind had drunk on Bracken's advice had made her head sing, rather, and she sat beside Mamma in what she felt was doltish silence all the way, hoping she would still be fuzzy when she got to bed and could drop off to sleep that way. At the door he said, "May I come in to say Good-night?" and to her relief Mamma replied, "Positively No. I do not approve." "Perhaps you are right," he commented without resentment, and solemnly kissed their hands and departed.

They went straight upstairs and Mamma saw her to bed with a hot water bottle at her feet, keeping the maid Gibson in the room the whole time. At last she was left alone to lie dully waiting for the champagne to put her to sleep, determined not to cry and spoil her eyes for tomorrow and be forever in disgrace.

It was much too late now to send that message to Charles at the club and go away with him as he had suggested. It had been too late ever since the afternoon when Conrad had said he could not live without possessing her. *Try to thwart me in that now and you will find no mercy anywhere—* If Charles attempted to rescue her it would ruin him in the regiment— Army men couldn't afford scandals. Charles had been the soul of tact tonight—so much so she could hardly believe the scene in the fitting-room had happened—no private glances, no tendency to whisper, no reminder of his offer—just Charles. It had been hard to meet his eyes, and she gave up trying. He would be at the wedding tomorrow, and she would have to tell him Good-bye. . . .

The sickness flared again in her middle and by now it was partly hunger. It wouldn't do to see too much of Charles from now on, with the strange interview at *Lucile's* between them and her own belated knowledge that with Charles one wouldn't have been so nervous. But Conrad wouldn't understand, he might think she had been in love with Charles, and it wasn't that, it was just that one had known Charles all one's life, and he wasn't a stranger, and he would be—compassionate. . . .

She got up and put on the light and poured a glass of water from the carafe. When she turned out the light again the window showed faintly grey. She went to it and stood looking out at the dark blur of trees that was the Park. The last time. She shivered in the cool September air and went back to bed and felt for the hot water bottle, which was only lukewarm now. Awful to catch cold and have a runny nose at one's wedding. She curled herself crosswise in the bed, hugging the bottle, thankful for the dark and the solitude. The last time. Oh, Lord, I'm going to be sick—

She ran to the wash-basin and hung above it, damp and weak. The spasm soon passed, for there was very little inside her to come up. She crawled back into the rumpled bed, wearing a dressing-gown over her nightdress for warmth. Her teeth were chattering now, but that gradually passed too, under the eiderdown.

Crossing her arms, she tucked icy paws against her own ribs and waited for the shivering fit to let up. *Such cold hands—the time comes soon when I warm them against my heart.* . . . The words became suddenly significant, and what had passed for a figure of speech was illumined by his real meaning, and terror closed her throat. She battled with it, face down against the pillow, arms across her breast. But he only meant to be kind, he said I would be safe, he is really very considerate— Clare must have gone through this and it didn't kill her—I must pretend I know all about it and not cry quarter—*whence comes so much courage?*—if he ever *guessed*—but he will, he sees everything, you can't deceive him, he knows how frightened I am—I must try to please him, though, Mamma said you must do just as they say if you want things to go well—*but you will give me my way when you have learned how happy it is in your power to make me*—me, to have power over him— *no doubt you will learn soon enough to take advantage of that*—how did he mean?—I must find out how—Clare winds Mortimer around her finger, and she doesn't love him, I know—I wish Clare would have talked to me, I'm sure she doesn't always do just as Mortimer says—she didn't marry a prince in the Diplomatic Corps, though—I shall never be able to live up to that, suppose some day he is ashamed of me—no title, no fortune, no experience of the world, no figure to furnish him strong heirs—*you have small bones everywhere that I could break in my hands* —if I don't please him—if I tried to escape—but he *is* kind, he will be good to me, he really cares for me—he won't hurt me, and if he does he'll be sorry, he said so—*a scrap of a thing like you, to bind the eagle with chains*—Charles would never have thought of himself as an eagle, he couldn't have kept his face straight—I mustn't think about Charles any more, I must think about Conrad—I shall be Your Highness—my son will be a prince—Conrad will be pleased if I furnish him a son soon, and I'm almost as big as Virginia and *she* had a baby the second year—he doesn't want a German girl with thick ankles, he wants me—I should be proud—he thought my eyelashes came off, though—and when the night comes that he takes down my hair—that's tomorrow—less than twenty-four hours away—well, at least he won't be disappointed in my hair, and I look quite nice with it down—I always want to scream when he takes me by the chin, it makes me feel *trapped*—perhaps I'll get used to it— I mustn't jerk away—I mustn't let him notice—it will be easier if I don't annoy him, and it's too late now, I've got to go on—I shall do exactly as he says about everything and just hope for the best—it may not be so bad, he seemed to like it when I cheeked him that day we were alone— *be but a little afraid of me, it becomes you*—oh, I *wish* it was only Charles. . . .

9

"THE marriage of Prince Conrad zu Polkwitz-Heidersdorf and Rosalind, elder daughter of the late Mr. Hugh R. J. Norton-Leigh and Mrs. Norton-Leigh of Dorset Terrace, Regent's Park, N.W., was celebrated in St. Margaret's Church, Westminster, on the after-noon of Tuesday last. The church was very beautifully decorated for the occasion with white flowers and ferns, and the aisle was arched with palms. The service, which was fully choral, was con-ducted by the Reverend Canon Merryweather, assisted by the Rev-erend Cyril A. Browne, and the Reverend D. C. F. Cholmondeley.

The hymns included 'Lead Us, Heavenly Father' and 'O Perfect Love.'

"The bride, who was given away by her mother, looked very lovely in a gown of white Duchesse satin embroidered with lovers' knots in diamonds and silver, the transparent yoke and sleeves of Brussels lace. The skirt was vandyked at the foot and finished with numerous frills of mousseline de soie. The full Court train hung from both shoulders and was composed of silver tissue covered with Brussels lace and lined with white satin and trimmed with trails of real orange blossoms. Over a tiara of the latter a silver-embroidered tulle veil was arranged. Her ornaments consisted of diamonds and sapphires, the gift of the bridegroom, as was her bouquet of white orchids and orange blossom. Her train was carried by two little girls dressed in soft white satin with lisse overskirts and wearing wreaths of pink roses.

"There were ten bridesmaids, whose dresses were of white chiffon over satin which was inserted with point d'Alençon. The tucked bodices had yokes and fichus of lace and there were deep waistbands of pale blue Louisine. Their hats were of white tulle and straw. The bridegroom presented each of them with a diamond and sapphire pendant and bouquets of long-stemmed La France roses artistically tied with a knot of forget-me-nots and pale blue tulle. Count Chlodwig von Lyncker attended His Highness as best man. Both wore the uniform of the German Emperor's 18th Hussars, with decorations.

"While the register was being signed 'There Shall a Star from David Come Forth' from the 'Christus' of Mendelssohn was beautifully rendered, and the bridesmaids distributed fragrant wedding favors of natural white roses and forget-me-nots among the congregation. After the ceremony a reception was held at the Earl and Countess of Enstone's house in St. James's Square which was lent for the occasion, the bride's charming home in Regent Park not being large enough for the great circle of guests and relatives who were present. There was a gorgeous array of presents, the jewelry in two big cases attracting much attention.

"The newly married pair then left for Shenstone Lodge in Buckinghamshire, placed at their disposal by the Dowager Marchioness of Shadwell, where they will spend the first part of the honeymoon. The bride travelled in a dress of white cloth embroidered in gold in a floral design, the bolero opening over a front of point d'esprit net, and a large black picture hat. Among the beautiful dresses in her extensive trousseau was a ball gown of Malmaison pink chiffon. . . ."

Thus *The Queen and Court Circular* the following week.

But to Oliver, seated on the bride's side of the church and perspiring gently in sympathy with Charles who was somewhere behind him with Lady Shadwell, the whole thing became unadulterated nightmare, and the reception, at which he was expected to drink champagne at tea time, was even worse. Charles, every inch a Guardsman even in morning clothes, looked everyone straight in the eye and got through it with the utmost aplomb, so that you would have sworn it was nothing to him whatever.

Phoebe had some idea by now of how Charles felt, and was weighed upon by a conversation she had had with him in a corner at a dance a few evenings before. She had mentioned, hoping to comfort him a little, the serious, schoolgirl pact that she and Rosalind had made—to write to each other once a month for the rest of their lives, never to lose touch even if they never saw each other again. Charles had looked even more cheered by this than she had expected him to. "Jolly good idea," he said. "I could never have managed anything like that myself, but now we shall be able to keep track of things, through you." His honest hazel eyes met hers directly. "But can you make sure she gets your letters?" he added. Phoebe asked stupidly what he meant. "I suppose you realize," said Charles with laborious patience, "that she'll be amongst strangers— she'll be Royalty, and Diplomatic, at that—cut off from the rest of the world by an army of servants and reams of deportment and protocol. Her letters will be filtered through a dozen hands. They may even be read. You must be prepared for that." Phoebe stared at him in horror, for letters were private property. Phoebe said they wouldn't *dare*. "My good child," said Charles kindly, "you don't seem to have taken it in even now that she's going to live amongst the enemy. Her friends will be suspect. Her utterances will be subject to censorship. She won't be an Englishwoman any more, with an Englishwoman's rights and privileges. She will be *Durchlaucht*—a Highness—she's marrying a German." The word jarred the air between them. "They hate us, you know. They'll discourage all her home ties, once they've got her over there. If there is a war, we may not be able to reach her at all. But you could, from America. That's why this is so important. You can be the link. You must be. The chances are they won't object to you, if you're wise. Be a little careful about what you write to her, won't you. Don't give anything away, I mean. Nothing they can get hold of to use against her." Quite bewildered, Phoebe asked bluntly if he meant she wasn't to mention him.

"I shall want you to mention me now and then, if you will," he said. "But as your friend, not hers. I can't write to her, of course. The blighter's got his eye on me, he must have heard something, God knows what. He's the sort to have spying servants, I shouldn't wonder." Phoebe said Rosalind was allowed to have her own maid, and Mamma was giving her Gibson, who had been with them for years. Charles brightened again. "Then get hold of Gibson," he said urgently. "Tell her to make sure of the letters. Gibson's no fool, and she won't take any nonsense from a German footman, we can be sure of that! Give Gibson your address—a permanent one. We can count on her." Phoebe promised, feeling unreal and melodramatic, like someone in a play. I wouldn't dare *write* this sort of thing, she thought. But there was nothing melodramatic about Charles, looking rather more stolid than usual in his formal black and white, speaking in his low, casual-seeming voice which made the most commonplace words beautiful. "Oh, Captain Laverham," Phoebe gasped, throwing away tact and discretion, *"why do you let her?"* He looked down at her in silence, his plain face quite expressionless under his inbred self-control. "I've done all I can," he said then. "There's still time—if she chooses."

But Rosalind had not so chosen. And Phoebe, holding her bouquet and wearing Prince Conrad's gift pendant and feeling the tears slide slowly down her cheeks, had heard the impressive Church of England marriage service with a leaden heart—for Rosalind certainly, and in a dim but growing apprehension for herself . . . *an honorable estate, instituted of God in the time of man's innocency . . . not to be enterprised, or taken in hand, unadvisedly, lightly, or wantonly, to satisfy men's carnal lusts and appetites like the brute beasts that have no understanding; but reverently, discreetly, advisedly, soberly, in the fear of God. . . .* But not honorable without love, Phoebe argued passionately as the grave, mellifluous voice flowed on. And not advisedly, in the fear of the man to whom you committed your life. . . . *I require and charge you both, as ye will answer at the dreadful day of judgment when the secrets of all hearts shall be disclosed, that if either of you know any impediment . . .* It was Rosalind's last chance, and it passed in the resonant rumble of the clergyman's voice sweeping relentlessly into those sobering vows, now full of a new significance to Phoebe, which should be taken with a deep and solemn joy, she was thinking, not in fear and misgiving. . . . *Wilt thou obey him, and serve him, love, honor, and keep him . . .* When her time came to speak them it would not be to a terrifying stranger like Prince Conrad, but to dear, good Miles, the idol of her childhood—and the only frightening thing about Miles was that he wasn't Oliver, and that in her secret soul she was forsworn before she began. Rosalind was spared at least the guilty knowledge that she belonged by every impulse and desire to somebody else, Phoebe thought. Rosalind's conscience was clear, as her own would never be, for Miles. . . . *I take thee, Rosalind* . . . that was Conrad, rich and clear, but with a German *r* to her name. . . . *I take thee, Conrad* . . . Almost voiceless she was, but somehow still audible in the vaulted hush of St. Margaret's, unfaltering, unhurried, but breathless, like a child repeating a well-learned lesson. . . . Then Conrad again, rolling his *r*'s in his emotion . . . *With this ring I thee wed, with my body I thee worship, with all my worldly goods I thee endow* . . . and then the grave overtones of prayer . . . *O Eternal God* . . . *send thy blessing upon these, thy servants* . . . *may ever remain in perfect love and peace together* . . . *world without end*. . . .

It had a dreadful finality, Phoebe thought, like a burial service—with or without love, war or no war, for better, for worse—happy like Dinah, resigned like Clare to a good bargain, confident and content like Virginia, in desperate courage like Rosalind—half-hearted and resolutely gay as she herself would be for Miles when the time came—there was no turning back when you had got as far as the altar. And Oliver? World without end for Oliver and Maia too. . . .

At the reception in Edward and Winifred's house in St. James's Square, Rosalind stood in the receiving line with her chin well up, no whiter in the face than was suitable for a bride, and smiled docile indulgence as each new guest addressed her twitteringly as Your Highness. Prince Conrad towered beside her in his black Hussar's uniform with the silver braiding and the slung pelisse, reminding everybody of Rupert of Hentzau, and laughing good-naturedly more than once when someone said so. His manner towards his bride in the presence of her friends was exactly the right mixture of conquest and devotion to make chills go up and down the spines of the more impressionable ladies, who were inclined to assure one another in asides that Rosalind was really a very lucky girl, but God help her if she tried to cross him.

In her becoming bridesmaid's gown Phoebe drank champagne with Oliver and Charles and observed their masculine aplomb with envy and respect as the reception guests swirled round her. Men knew how to hide their feelings behind trivialities, knew how to swallow the lump in their throats and keep the tears from welling up into their eyes. She wondered how they did it. Charles, she was sure, was on the rack. And Oliver's thoughts during the ceremony must have been much the same as hers—the single long look he gave her now as he raised his glass told her that. But neither of them betrayed himself in any way. Both were armored in immaculate and smiling composure, while she felt miserably tearful and ready to weep if anyone said Boo. It was too late now for Rosalind and Charles. But for herself and Oliver . . .

She set down the champagne hastily, convinced that it was giving her ideas. The time had come to help the bride into her travelling dress.

Mamma was in Rosalind's room, of course, and the bridesmaids milled about in chattering confusion, admiring themselves in all the mirrors, They unhooked the diamond and silver encrusted wedding-dress and dropped it around Rosalind's feet, and it was Mamma's hand which steadied her as she stepped out of the shining circle—its weight attested the magnificence of the gown, and the diamonds were real. Then for a moment Rosalind stood alone, straight and slim in her sheer lacy petti-coats, waiting for the other dress to be put over her head. Her eyes met Phoebe's sympathetic gaze, and she tried to smile.

"You *will* write to me?" she entreated. "You *promise* to write to me every single month?"

"As long as we live," Phoebe promised solemnly, and they reached for each other's hands. Rosalind's were icy. The white travelling dress came down between them, and their fingers parted reluctantly.

Rosalind stood like a doll while the dress was fastened. Someone said, "Oh, heavens, her shoes and stockings!"—they made her sit down—the maid Gibson, who was to go with her to Buckinghamshire and eventu-ally to Germany, knelt at her feet—Gibson's hands were steady and unhurried—Gibson's face, bent gravely over the bride's shoelaces, was calm and kind—Phoebe waited till Rosalind stood up again, and then caught Gibson's arm.

"Look after her, won't you!" she said urgently. "Don't leave her—no matter what happens, don't ever leave her!"

Gibson's plain face softened in an understanding smile.

"That's not likely, miss," she said quietly.

"And if anything *should* happen—be sure to let me know, whatever and whenever it may be. All the address you need is Williamsburg, Vir-ginia, U.S.A. You can remember that, can't you?"

"Yes, miss, I'll remember."

"And, Gibson—always make sure my letters get to her." The woman's eyes, half surprised, half comprehending, rested on Phoebe's earnest face. "I shall always write once a month, or send a message." Phoebe said. "If ever she doesn't get them there's something wrong—something on your end of the post. And you must find a way to let me know."

"I'll try, miss. But you don't think they'd ever—"

"She's Royalty now," said Phoebe with that uneasy, recurrent sense of theater which Rosalind's affairs produced in her. "She'll be among strangers, except for you. Enemies, maybe. You must watch over her."

"I will, miss."

Gibson turned away competently, unalarmed and self-possessed, to pick up Rosalind's hat, and Phoebe stood struggling with her own emotion, dreading to make things worse by breaking down at the last minute. Rosalind's face in the mirror as she adjusted the hat was set and expressionless, with an odd glitter in the eyes. The throb of the pulse in her throat was plain to see just below the jawbone. The net frills at the front of her dress were visibly jarred by the beating of her heart. Her fingers shook and fumbled at the hat-pins.

Then they kissed her all round, being careful of her hat, and her lips were cold on Phoebe's cheek. There was a knock at the door and word was passed that His Highness was waiting.

Phoebe saw him put his hand possessively through Rosalind's arm as she joined him, and found Virginia standing beside her. Together they watched Rosalind go, and then turned to each other, feeling old and sad and very fortunate themselves to be left behind. "Thank God for Gibson," said Virginia simply. "I want to see Archie. I just want to *look* at him."

Archie was not far away, but Phoebe's unspoken desire to look at Oliver was cut off in its prime by his departure on foot with Charles, who everybody would have agreed ought not to be left to himself that evening. Oliver preserved a comradely silence as they strode northward from the square into Duke Street where Charles's chambers were, and as they came opposite the door Charles said in his unemphatic way, "Like a drink?"

Oliver expressed a pious hope that a stiff whiskey and soda might mitigate the barbarous introduction of champagne into his system at that time of day, and as they mounted the single flight of carpeted stairs to Charles's rooms they were apparently absorbed in a discussion of why champagne was so agreeable at lunch, or even at eleven, so helpful at dinner, so essential at supper, and so utterly loathsome in the middle of the afternoon.

The unembarrassed silence fell between them again as Charles set out a decanter and siphon. Oliver sat with one knee over the arm of a big chair, watching his host and debating with himself. At last he said, "Charles, old boy, I'm afraid I'm going to confide in you."

"*Must* you?" said Charles amiably, and approached him with an amber-filled glass in either hand.

"I know it's rotten, but I can't come at the answer any other way. I think first of all, I'd like to ask you a rather personal question, if you don't mind."

"Oh, very well, fire away," said Charles, and their glasses saluted each other briefly. "Cheers," said Charles, and they tested the strong drinks and approved.

"Just tell me this," Oliver said then with some diffidence. "How on earth do you do it?"

"Do what, old boy?"

"Watch the woman you love marry another man," said Oliver brutally, and took a long thirsty swallow.

There was an endless pause while Charles, moving with his cavalryman's effortless ease, shifted a chair to suit him and lowered himself into it, facing his friend. When he spoke it was in the same even tones he would have used about the polo score or the weather.

"Well, for one thing," he said, "at first you're fool enough to hope that you can bear it. You're quite wrong, of course, because you never can. Bear it, I mean."

"So what happens?" Oliver asked, his eyes on the glass he tilted against the light.

"Oh, nothing much," said Charles with the ghost of a sigh. "You seem to hunt a bit, and fish a bit, and drink a bit—and you bore every woman you're put next to at dinner, no matter how hard she tries, because your heart's not in it."

"What else?" said Oliver, when he stopped.

"Then, of course, there are the nights," said Charles academically. "Sometimes they're not much fun either."

"What do you do about that, as a rule?"

"A Turkish bath helps. A bottle doesn't. I've tried both."

Oliver rose, glass in hand, and prowled restlessly about the room until he stood at the window with his back to Charles.

"You're a better man than I am," he said simply. "But I'm lucky, I shan't have to stand there and see her swear her life away, out of my keeping."

"At least *I* don't have to go and do likewise," said Charles, and Oliver glanced at him quickly, and away. "I can be alone in my misery, and I confess I'm rather looking forward to that."

"I don't mind telling you this whole business today has got me thoroughly rattled," Oliver confessed. "The things you have to swear to! Even at best it's enough to make you think twice!"

"It's the little American, isn't it," Charles suggested gently. "I know, I know, we don't mention names and all that rot. But you began this, old boy, and I should just like to say before you regret it to the extent of dotting me one, if I were you I'd bust everything wide open and have her at any price." He buried his face in his glass.

"Jilt Maia *now?*" said Oliver in quiet horror. "I'd as lief cheat at cards!"

"Doesn't it occur to you that you'll be cheating them both if you go on as you are? Besides, I thought your C.O. was dead against your marrying Maia."

"He was, rather. But I talked him round."

"Outwitted yourself, eh?" Charles grinned sympathetically. "That can be very humiliatin'."

"I do feel the most awful ruffian, you know," Oliver said with contrition.

"Oh, you are that," Charles agreed readily. "But little Miss Sprague can't see it, bless her."

"I say," said Oliver. "How did you guess? Who it was, I mean."

Charles pondered the lowering tide in his glass.

"I think you ignore one another too thoroughly," he decided. "It's a bit overdone, old boy."

"Lord, do you think anyone else has noticed?"

"Doubt it. People are damned unobservin'. The decanter's nearer you than me. Help yourself."

"Thanks. How would it do to get absolutely blazing tight for once?" Soda fizzed briefly into Oliver's glass.

"Can if you like," said Charles. "I always have the most damnable head the next day, though, and if I remember, so do you."

"Oh, awful. I suppose because we're ruddy amateurs. Chaps who make a business of drinking seem to get along all right," said Oliver enviously.

"Look here, am I being a nuisance, or hadn't you any plans for this evening?"

"I have one ticket to the Alhambra," said Charles. "We could turn it in and get two together if you'll join me. I'm not damn-all keen on my own company, if you must know."

"Good. Nor am I. Let's hang together on it, shall we? Have a whopping great dinner somewhere, eat like pigs, drink like fish, and sleep through the show! I'm only killing time till tomorrow afternoon, anyway, when I am permitted to take Phoebe shopping for presents for the family in Williamsburg, and then to Gunter's for tea. It's got to be all very cheerful, and it's got to last us a long time. They sail at the end of the week."

The choice of a suitable place to dine involved considerable discussion, which Charles entered into with apparent zest, and all the while he was thinking what a lucky dog Oliver was, with a whole afternoon ahead of him in which to be cheerful, and Charles could not but compare that to the wretched ten minutes he had had with Rosalind in the fitting-room at *Lucile's*. After dreading through many sleepless hours the moment when he would have to say a final Good-bye to her with all the world looking on, he was spared that last ordeal, for she had been swept past him on Prince Conrad's arm on her way to the motor, and there was just that second when her eyes, searching among the faces grouped round the door, had found him. And that was to be his memory —her white face, with its set, gallant smile, and her eyes, unnaturally wide and dark, meeting his as she passed beyond his reach.

Each time it came he flinched and stirred and frowned like a man in pain, and knew that there was no relief but what time could bring, and that grudging and small. Gradually this first sharp agony of loss would fade, he supposed, into a drag endurance, just as for Rosalind some kind of familiar routine would bring a form of reassurance and confidence. People got used to things, he had heard, even amputations. People could get used to almost anything. Meanwhile Oliver was suffering too, and taking it well, and they could always hang together.

10

LIKE Oliver, Phoebe had been killing time till the promised shopping tour. But the American mail arrived that morning, and in it was a letter from Miles, who had got the job in Louisville, telling all about the house he had found there for them to live in, and how his mother had sent his Mammy's youngest daughter (who was named October because she was the eighth child, though her birthday was in June) and October's son (who was called Septimus because he was born in September) up from Charlottesville to look after him and to be her household staff when she came to Louisville after the wedding. Reminded thus of the perennial family joke of the darkies' names, so familiar as to require no comment from Miles, Phoebe felt homesickness wash through her in a warm, unexpected wave. She had been going over her shopping list, to make sure that after today nobody would be forgotten, and counting up what remained of the extravagant check Bracken had given her to buy presents with. Today was just to finish off the odds and ends. They would have to go back to the artificial jewelry place in Oxford Street to get some kind of gaudy brooch for October and one of the horse-shoe scarf-pins for Septimus. Oliver would think that was fun. And dozens of embroidered handkerchiefs from Peter Robinson's for everybody—he could help choose them. And another silk scarf from Liberty, and then to Hamley's for toys for Belle's and Marietta's children. By that time they would want tea!

Phoebe sat biting the pencil thoughtfully. A whole afternoon to themselves—did Cousin Eden suspect anything, and was she being tactful and kind, or was it simply that they all looked on Oliver as a kind of relation? Phoebe had thought a good deal about Cousin Sue lately, and Oliver's story about the major who had fallen in love with her and later been killed in South Africa. Cousin Sue must have brought back a secret to Williamsburg too. Phoebe found comfort in the thought. If things got too bad, one could always confess to Cousin Sue about Oliver, and she would understand. It would be nice to be able to talk about him to somebody—sometimes—not to have to lock this shining thing away in darkness and silence for the rest of her life.

It would feel very strange, going home to Williamsburg now—like trying to crawl back into the chrysalis after one's butterfly wings were grown. Cousin Sue would know how that was. In Williamsburg one would meet again one's own age of innocence, full of simple joys and without taboos and reservations—childish, bread-and-milk days forever outgrown now that Oliver Campion had bereft one of reason and peace of mind, and taught one the art of easy laughter and gay, foolish talk and lighthearted living of the sunny days as they came.

Oliver never burdened today with the encroaching complications of tomorrow or the stale worries of yesterday. Oliver took what came and was grateful, kissed, and let go. Oliver knew better than to fight destiny tooth and nail for favors. Destiny couldn't be bullied. It saved a lot of useless effort not to try, and left you time and energy to enjoy what you already had in your hands. Almost she had learned from Oliver to count their meeting as a prodigal gift of chance, and not a meagre glimpse of paradise withheld. "But suppose I had never seen you at all!" he had cried once, and the idea of this hypothetical loss had come nearer to upsetting his equanimity than the almost certain prospect of never seeing her again.

His was more than a soldier's fatalism. It was a whole philosophy, deep and strong and sustaining. They had met, in spite of terrible odds against it. They had loved at first sight, without wasting time, and snatched golden hours which nothing could ever take from them. They were just that much ahead of other people, who had to make do with ordinary lives which ran in ruts. But for the grace of God they would have gone in ruts themselves to the end of their days.—Easy to say, easy to believe, while their hands could still touch. But now the night was drawing in. Now one went back to Williamsburg and married Miles, who was a worrier. And Oliver? Oliver would have to beg for everything he got from Maia. . . .

Phoebe pushed the thought away hastily. Not yet. Not today. Today was still theirs, and must be free of shadows, undefaced by tears. She must tell Oliver about October and Septimus—that would make him laugh. It didn't take much to tickle Oliver, he met all one's jokes half way.

Their last afternoon together went the way it was expected to—cheerful and foolish and content, as though it would never end—no tension, no tragedy, no yearning silences. He's such *fun,* Phoebe thought, for she couldn't get used to that, after Miles. It's like floating, to be with him. Everything else can wait, you are so happy *now.*

Finally they were sitting at one of Gunter's corner tables, Oliver's back to the room, and the tea had come, in hot, gleaming pots, and toasted buttered scones and a silver tray of iced cakes and pastries. And then a pause crept in on them, while he watched her pour the tea.

"What nice hands you have," he said, not as though he had just discovered them, but rather congratulating himself on an old, remembered delight. "I shall always see your hands like this, pouring out my tea."

"*Both* milk and sugar," she said, wrinkling her nose in distaste. "Like a nursery. There you are."

Their fingers brushed as he took the cup and Phoebe kept her eyes down.

"I spent last evening with Charles," he said. "To avoid the general effect of a wake, we got drunk and went to the Alhambra. Case of the blind leading the blind. Tonight we're going to try what a Turkish bath will do."

"I wish *I* could get drunk," said Phoebe recklessly, and he shook his head.

"Charles says it's no good in the long run," he said. "And I fancy he's right about that."

Phoebe accepted a scone, dripping with butter, and bit into it.

"You know, if I were writing a farewell party like this in a book," she remarked, "I should have said the girl couldn't eat a thing. Shows you how wrong I'd be. We're both of us ravenous!"

"Maybe that comes later," he suggested. "When we start pining. Promise me not to go into a decline, or anything silly like that."

"No," said Phoebe. "I shall begin my book instead."

"Going to put me in it?" he asked, it seemed hopefully, and she laughed.

"Not a word of you! I wouldn't know how, any more than Cousin Sue has ever written Father."

"What's the book about?" he asked with interest. "You never talk about it. Would you rather not?"

"I don't think there's much to talk about till we know whether it is a book or not," she said sensibly. "One that can be published, that is. I've got a lot of notes and a lot of ideas, and it's not a bit autobiographical, that's one thing to be said for it. Most first novels are likely to be, but I think I've passed through that phase now."

"How do you know what to write?" he marvelled. "I thought since you were going to write novels I'd like to know more about 'em, so I went into that place in Piccadilly and bought some, and now I'm more at sea than ever."

"What did you buy?" she inquired curiously, touched at the picture of Oliver determined to improve his mind because of her.

"What the man gave me. He picked out the ones he said were going very well just now, and I carried 'em away, and sat up most of the night with 'em. What I can't understand is, how do you know what the people are going to say to each other?"

"They're your own people. You can tell them what to say," she tried honestly to explain. "Of course once a character is drawn, if he's alive and right, he's likely to tell *you*."

"And you don't have to live through everything you write about?"

"Heavens, no, that would be impossible! Of course travelling and knowing people and seeing how they react to things always helps in the end. But Cousin Sue wrote a successful book about London in the eighteenth century long before she had ever been here at all, and every last detail was correct. A writer is supposed to *know* things—it's a sort of sixth sense. I'm not sure yet if I've got it."

"Did your Cousin Sue ever write about poor old Forbes-Carpenter?"

"Never. None of us at home ever dreamed of such a thing. Darling, don't you be alarmed, I'm not going to use you for copy," she assured him, laughing.

"I think I should be rather flattered if you did," he said, and seemed to mean it. "But at least you will write me letters sometimes?" he added anxiously, and Phoebe hesitated.

"Would that be—all right?"

"To the club," he said, unabashed. "And what about you, had I better not? Or shall we send each other a single red rose once a year, like *The Prisoner of Zenda?* You see, I can't make up my mind to lose you entirely."

"Miles wouldn't understand," she said thoughtfully.

"Jealous?" he asked with a quick frown.

"No, not like that. But he would wonder and worry. He would be afraid I had known someone here that he couldn't ever measure up to. And he would be right, which makes it awkward."

"Then you'd rather I didn't write at all," he said gravely.

"Not to Louisville. But—once in a while—you could send something by Dinah in New York. She wouldn't ask questions, would she, and Miles wouldn't notice if it came in a letter from her. Or is that terribly dishonest, and tempting Providence?" She lifted guilty, questioning eyes. "Maybe if we're going to do this thing right we ought to make a complete break from the time I sail."

Oliver sighed, and passed his cup for more tea.

"We had to come to this sometime, didn't we." Neither of them spoke till she handed the newly filled cup back to him. "I still find it impossible to believe that this is the last time you will ever do that," he said suddenly. "It seems so utterly right and natural, to sit across a table from you and wait for my tea. We did it years ago—we shall be doing it years hence. Nothing else is conceivable."

Phoebe stared at him dumbly, conscious of a perverse satisfaction that at last Oliver seemed to be hurting the way she did, that for once his light touch had failed him. Much as she loved him for the lift of his spirit and his casual, tender humor, she needed to know that Oliver had his bad moments too. And he, whose gaiety had been for her protection from the rough reality of their impending separation, felt himself sliding down hill into blackness and was powerless to find a foothold on his way to the bottom. He had witnessed the bleak vacuum in which Charles moved now that Rosalind had gone. The same purgatory was just around the corner for himself. He leaned across the table to her.

"Phoebe—it's only jilting we'd be guilty of now—not the other thing, in the Commandments. It makes me a cad, but I'd commit a worse sin if I marry Maia now, loving you like this. You saw Rosalind's face yesterday, I can't let you— Phoebe, we've tried, but suddenly I can't face it. Let me tell Maia. Go home if you must, and tell Miles. And then come back to me and let's start again, together."

Phoebe sat looking down at her empty teacup through a blinding blur, her hands knotted in her lap, striving for composure. She had not expected anything like this. She was taken off guard, and it softened her very bones. But she heard her own voice, rather dim and far away, telling him about Miles's letter that morning, and the house in Louisville, and how the family were expecting a Christmas wedding—

And then she heard Oliver interrupt her crisply, a thing he had never done before.

"All right," he was saying. "That's enough. It was a crazy idea. Please forgive me." He signalled for the bill and paid it with the change for the tip, and waved it away, so there was no need to wait.

Phoebe gazed at him piteously.

"You aren't—offended?" she begged, and he gave her his small rueful smile which did not show his teeth.

"No, I'm anything but offended," he assured her gently, and helped her gather up her parcels. Outside in Bond Street he put her into a cab and told the driver to take them to Claridge's.

She sat silent beside him in the hansom for the short drive. It was ending all wrong. The bright bubble had burst in their faces. An agony of doubt invaded her. Had she ruined everything? Had she answered wrong? Was there any other possible answer to give him?

As the cab turned into Brook Street his hand caught hers out of her lap and raised it, glove and all, to his lips.

"I'm terribly sorry," he murmured. "I never meant to cave in like that. Don't hold it against me, will you!"

"I—" she began faintly, and the cab came to a stop in front of the hotel.

Oliver handed her out, asked the driver to wait, gave the parcels to the doorman, and held out a formal hand.

"I won't come in if you don't mind," he said quietly, and smiled down at her in the usual way. "Tell them I had to dash off to meet a man at the club!"

"Then—good-bye." Phoebe put her hand in his.

He refused the word, with a little jerk of his chin.

"God bless you," he said, and stepped back into the cab, which moved away at once.

Phoebe walked blindly to the lift, and arrived at their sitting-room on the second floor, where she found Eden alone, reading an evening paper.

"We got all the things," she said unnecessarily. "The boy is bringing them up. Oliver had to go on to the club."

"Did he, dear?" Eden's response was deliberately vague, and she pretended not to notice the quiver of Phoebe's chin, returning gravely to the paper after one discerning glance. "Come and look at this," she said, and Phoebe bent to read over her shoulder: *His Serene Highness, Prince Hugo zu Polkwitz-Heidersdorf, is gravely ill at his castle in Silesia. On account of his great age, considerable anxiety is felt because of the repeated heart attacks which have recently become more and more frequent—*

"Virginia said Rosalind would have to go into mourning before she got any good of that trousseau!" Phoebe cried. "Prince Conrad will be sent for, won't he. Bracken thinks he'll have to leave the Diplomatic for good when his father dies."

"Well, Beryl Norton-Leigh has brought it off," Eden sighed. "She'll get a Serene Highness for a son-in-law even sooner than she had any right to expect, and her daughter will be one of the richest women in Europe—without a penny of it to call her own!"

"Wasn't there some kind of marriage settlement?" Phoebe asked.

"Entirely controlled by her husband!"

"You mean Rosalind can't write a check?"

"Rosalind won't even have pocket money. Her credit is good any-where in Europe if she wants to buy a diamond necklace. But if she only wants a *pfennig* in her hand she will have to ask her husband for it."

"Oh, how awful! Perhaps I could slip something in my letters some-times."

"American money?" said Eden and shook her head. "No. It's no use now." She threw down the paper and ran a hand across her forehead as though it ached. "Perhaps I should have interfered somehow—I did try, but Beryl always bit my head off—I couldn't see my way to any-thing more—it's going to haunt me for the rest of my days. Archie says if there's a war Rosalind's life will be simply unbearable—"

"I don't know," said Phoebe tersely. "It's funny what you can bear."

And she went off to her own room to remove her hat.

PART FOUR

JOHNNY

New York.   *Spring, 1903–1911.*

>>>

1

BUT before the boat reached New York Phoebe knew, for certain, that she had answered wrong.

It was no good telling herself that when she saw Miles again she would feel differently. Every turn of the screw which carried her away from Oliver made Miles more impossible. She promised herself that as soon as she got to New York she would send Oliver a cable, but when she tried to word it nothing came. The last day out she wrote him a letter—and tore it up because it sounded to her like a self-conscious heroine in a very amateurish novel. How do you tell a man you have refused to marry that you have changed your mind? Simplify. Reduce it to a cable again. Bracken always said that for good reporting you should remember your word-rate, and if you weren't cabling pretend you were. *Dear Oliver—I was wrong. Please forgive me.* Then what? *I want to marry you after all.* Well, hardly, in so many words. But what other words were there for the same thing?

Oughtn't she to see Miles first? Would that be fairer to him? And then write to Oliver saying, I'm free, what about you? But that cornered him. That left him no choice whatever, made no allowance for the pressure put on him by his own surroundings and code of behavior. That forced him to jilt one girl, no matter what he did.

Stick to it, then. See it through, as you said you were going to. He's given up by now, don't open it again. Let him make what he can of his life with Maia.—The familiar sharp pain which was plain, old-fashioned jealousy wrenched at her heart. Maia didn't deserve him.

137

Maia wouldn't come half way. And as for herself, to see it through with Miles was beyond her now.

Once her feet touched American soil Phoebe knew what she wanted, and that was Cousin Sue. She left New York the following day and sat pushing the train all the way to Williamsburg. Then another night had to pass before she could get Cousin Sue alone. But at last, on a sunny morning at the end of September she sat in the drawing-room of Great-uncle Ransom's house, with the door closed, and told Cousin Sue with laughter and tears and unconscious pathos all about Oliver Campion.

Sue listened almost wordlessly, supplying a tactful handkerchief midway, until Phoebe came to the end and said, "So what am I to do now? Which of them must I tell first? What can I say to Oliver?"

"None of it really matters," Sue said without hesitation, "so long as you *tell* Oliver."

"You do think I should?" Phoebe quavered hopefully. "I wrote him a letter on the boat but I couldn't have sent it, it sounded—childish!"

"Write him another," said Sue. "Tonight. Never mind how it sounds. Just tell him."

"B-before I tell Miles?"

"Tonight," said Sue.

"And Miles too? Should I write to Miles tonight as well?"

"Yes," said Sue, and sighed, for her conscience gave a twinge. "Poor Miles. But it's best for you. Oliver is the one for you."

"Oliver told me about a man named Forbes-Carpenter," Phoebe remarked, and watched Sue's cheeks get pink. "Then it's true! He did fall in love with you! But you came back to Williamsburg. Why?"

"It wasn't the same," Sue said, confused and defensive. "Gratian was a dear, but—the only man I ever loved was here."

"*Father,*" said Phoebe in an awed whisper, watching her, and Sue nodded.

"We are three times cousins," she said. "It wouldn't have been right for us to marry. But I want you to promise me one thing. Never mention anything you heard in England to him."

Phoebe promised solemnly, and Sue's dimple showed.

"It's none of his business," she said defiantly. "But if he should find it out now from you, after all this time I've kept it from him, he'd have a fit. Besides," she added more seriously, "I came back. That's all he needs to know. But there's nothing like that standing between you and Oliver, and Miles can get along somehow. I know that sounds heart-less, but Miles isn't really the marrying kind, I sometimes think."

"Well, but there's Maia to think of," Phoebe reminded her, and Sue shook her head.

"She wouldn't want him if she knew how it was," she said.

Phoebe wasn't so sure.

Dear Oliver—[she wrote that night at the little desk in her own room]

I feel the most awful fool, but I've gone back on everything I said—except that I love you. I'm writing to Miles tonight when I finish this, to tell him so and break our engagement. I want to come back to you if you will have me.

Please don't mind that I say it without any maidenly flourishes, in words as bald as an egg. Everything else I can think of to say sounds theatrical and girlish. I suppose being a writer makes one self-conscious when it's something real like this, so that you always wonder if you're turning phrases. Later, perhaps, when we know where we are, I can write you a love letter—my first. They weren't love letters I wrote Miles this summer, they were works of art.

I realize that I am taking you up on something you said on an impulse some time ago now, and you may not find it convenient to make good your offer. Please don't just go out and drown yourself in embarrassment if you can't manage it, and must go on with Maia. No matter what I do, I can't marry Miles, anyway. I'd rather be an old maid.

Yours always,
PHOEBE

It wasn't very good, but it would have to do. She sealed and stamped it, and took another sheet of paper.

Dear Miles—[she wrote]

I have got to ask you to forgive me, because I fell in love with a man in England and I want to marry him. I tried to think it would pass and everything would be the same again when I got home, but it isn't. I have written him to say that I am asking you to let me go.

Oh, Miles, I did try, and I'm so terribly fond of you still, but not in the marrying way. I hope you won't let it upset you, and I hope you won't think too badly of me. But it wouldn't be fair to marry you, feeling the way I do about somebody else. And the worst of it is, I can't even return your ring, because I lost it. I don't know how I could have done such a thing, except I wasn't used to wearing a ring at all, and I thought so much of it I always took it off when I washed my hands—and one time I forgot it and when I went back for it of course it was gone. I can't begin to say how sorry I am.

Sincerely,

Phoebe

This one also she stamped and sealed and sat a moment with both letters in her hand—so easy not to send them, even now—so easy just to let things drift, and perhaps by and by it wouldn't matter so much. . . .

Phoebe's lower lip came out. She rose, and ran down stairs and out into the warm autumn dusk, and carried her two letters to the post office and pushed them through the slot. And then, further to burn her boats, she went home and told a surprised and interested family what she had done.

It would take, say, ten days for the letter to reach London, and at least ten more for his reply—or would he cable? Being Oliver, he was sure to cable. If he did, she could be with him again in a little more than a month. If only she had *stayed,* there would have been only one letter to write. If she had stayed, she might have been Oliver's wife by now. . . .

But the tenth day came and went, with no cable from London. And when nine more had gone, and she had told herself over and over that cables weren't private enough for what Oliver had to say, and of course he would write it, a letter came from Dinah in New York, enclosing one from Virginia—Oliver had married Maia very suddenly, without the elaborate church ceremony Maia had always intended, and they had gone away to the Lake Country for the honeymoon.

Phoebe found herself face down and crosswise on the bed in her room with the letter from Dinah and its enclosure under her hand. She was not sure how she had got there, but the door was closed and she was safe from observation for a while. Finally she sat up and smoothed out Virginia's letter and read it slowly again, with dry eyes. Virginia was indignant, for she considered that Maia had forced Oliver's hand. It was all because Maia's father, invalid though he was, had succeeded in acquiring a wife, a sympathetic (and impecunious) widow of the neighborhood, who apparently asked nothing better than to take charge of a peevish, well-to-do, and not unattractive man barely into his sixties, whose ailments were more than half imaginary. And Maia, who had hitherto only longed to escape her own bondage, now chose to be out-raged and humiliated that her services were no longer required, and had flounced up to London and descended on Clare, announcing her will-ingness to be married at once, in what she stood up in, rather than be beholden and subordinate to the intruder for another hour. Oliver, wrote Virginia, had risen magnificently to the occasion. And so they were married, very quietly, at St. Peter's in Eaton Square, about a week after Phoebe had sailed, or she and Dinah and Bracken and Eden could all have come to the wedding, added Virginia innocently. It was at least a little less depressing than Rosalind's, and Maia had looked divine, though she was a bit of a gum-boil and would never be as good to Oliver as he deserved.

Phoebe sat still on the edge of the bed, taking it in. Her letter to Oliver must have arrived in London just after he departed to the Lake Country with Maia, and would be waiting for him when he returned. There was no way now to get it back or stop him from reading it. He would go into the club some day in the usual way, a reasonably happy man who had done the right thing and was entitled to enjoy what he could make of his life. And they would hand him her letter, which turned his kind-hearted, philosophical marriage into a bitter farce, with laughter by the gods.

What would he do? Nothing, how could he? What would he reply to her, who had now made hash of both their lives? Would he write at all? Better, perhaps, if he didn't.

Gradually other aspects of the situation than Oliver's began to emerge from her dazed thoughts. Miles would probably feel sorry for her now and offer himself once more, as consolation. She could never face Miles again. She could never face any of them, here in Williamsburg. Oliver had let her down before all her world—they would never be able to understand how powerless he was to do otherwise in the circum-stances. They would think he had trifled with her. Or that she had misunderstood and magnified a casual flirtation. . . .

Phoebe slid off the bed and stole out of the house, carrying Virginia's letter. When she got past the gate she ran.

Sue was alone in the drawing-room doing up the corrected page-proofs of her latest book to send back to the publishers, when the tornado struck. She shut the door and made Phoebe sit down and get her breath, while she read Virginia's letter with great thoroughness, making up her mind meanwhile. It had gone all wrong, her gift and Gratian's, to Phoebe. They had bought her the chance to love, and brought heartbreak upon her as well. And humiliation. That was the hard part. One had to be able to hold up one's head.

Phoebe was crying into the back of the sofa, and Sue leaned over and laid her hand on the shaken shoulders.

"Don't spoil your face," she said gently. "We've got to lay plans now. We're going to New York."

Phoebe looked up at her with streaming eyes, and her breath caught on a childish hiccup.

"N-New York? What for?"

"We're going to get you out of this at once. Phoebe, you will have to keep a secret. From your father. Can you do that, for me?"

Phoebe nodded, her tears arrested by bewilderment.

"When Gratian Forbes-Carpenter died he left me all his money—quite a lot. He hadn't anybody else, you see, but I won't touch it, I don't need it, I meant it all for you some day. I'm going to give it to you now, enough for you to live on in New York and write your book and forget all about both Miles and Oliver. I can arrange for you to be independent there with Eden to look after you, of course—but I want your father to think that Eden is paying for it all, and not me, the same as when you went to England."

"W-was that you?"

"It was Gratian," said Sue. "He would want you to have this money, since I can't use it here. I have everything I'll ever need. I shall have to talk to Bracken. We'll tell them at home that Eden is lonely and wants you for a visit, and that I have to go to see the publishers about my book. I can go with you and be back here by Saturday."

"You mean I can *stay* in New York—as long as I like? And pay my own way?"

"Thanks to Gratian, you can. Eden will say it's nonsense for you to pay anything, and in a way it is. She has plenty of room at the house, and you must live there under her roof, at first anyway where you'll be safe. But Bracken will give you an allowance each month, from Gratian's money. Till you can earn with your writing."

"Maybe Bracken would give me a job on the newspaper. They do hire girls, to do the weddings and things."

"We can ask him," Sue nodded, remembering what it had done for Phoebe's brother Fitz when Cabot Murray gave him a job on the paper a few years before. "But I want you to work hard on your book now. You ought to be able to make something out of it. And work is the best pain-killer I know."

"Then I won't have to stay here and have everybody sorry for me," said Phoebe, tears drying on her cheeks.

"Bless me, no!" cried Sue, who had been through all that herself. "And you're not to be sorry for yourself, either. Some day you'll be able to see that you're the better for having known Oliver, hard as it is."

"I can see it even now," said Phoebe steadily. "He taught me—well, just about everything, I reckon. He was—" She caught Sue's shoulders, looking up earnestly into her face. "You're not to blame Oliver for this," she insisted. "Everyone else will. But you've been in England, you know how they are, especially in the Army. Oliver had given his word to Maia. We both knew that from the start. We never really lost sight of it—and of Miles. It would have been desperately hard for Oliver if my letter had got there before the wedding, I knew that. It's probably better for him, some ways, that it didn't. If only I hadn't written it *at all* —but you won't hold Oliver to blame, will you?"

"No," said Sue, smiling. "There is no blame. Except possibly to you, for not having the courage to follow your heart when he asked you."

Phoebe stood up, both hands at her temples in an unconscious gesture of distraction.

"It's this writing books!" she cried. "You try to do the thing that will *read* well! I *know* I saw myself as the heroine of one of your romances! You wouldn't allow one of them to break her troth, would you?"

"I might, now that you mention it," Sue said thoughtfully. "I still could. It hadn't occurred to me, that's all."

2

OLIVER's letter was forwarded to New York, and Phoebe read it alone in her room in Eden's Madison Avenue house. Everyone had been the soul of tact, and Bracken had given her the first month's allowance at once so she would have pocket money, and had had a typewriter sent up from the office for her exclusive use. She had bought a supply of paper and carbons, and begun her book. A little later, when the society editor's assistant got married, Phoebe was to have a chance to work on the newspaper.

She opened Oliver's letter with cold, nervous fingers. Miles's had been bad enough, with its magnanimous tone which almost amounted to relief on his part that she had changed her mind. Miles had taken it with dignity and restraint. It was far worse to face Oliver's unfamiliar handwriting.

> My darling—[he began]
> Fortunately I was sitting down when I read your letter—as I realized when I came to in an armchair at the club with a whiskey and soda nearby. It was my first day in Town, and I hadn't had my letters sent on to Coniston because I wasn't expecting anything. Not anything like this, anyway.
> You must know by now from Virginia what happened after you sailed. Nothing seemed to matter to me very much, and I just went with the tide because, since it was going to happen sooner or later, I thought I might as well get on with it. A fine state of mind, but there it was.
> If you think I am taking it as casually as this sounds you are wrong, but you won't be such an idiot, I know. I'm just a thick-headed soldier, my dear, and I don't know how to write letters, so perhaps you will never know what this message from you has done to me. But in spite of everything, I am proud that you had the confidence in me and the courage to send it, even as things have turned out. It is something that will go with me all the way.
> But what does this mean to you? You won't change back again, I think, however much encouraged to do so. Or is that only my selfish wish, that I have no right to entertain? Do what is best for your own happiness, my dear, and love someone if you can, for you were not meant for loneliness and regrets. And forgive me, if you can, for losing the way.
>
> OLIVER

Phoebe sat still with the tears dripping down on the page, till Oliver's precious words were blurred and damp. Then she blotted them carefully and put the letter back in its envelope and laid it away beneath her handkerchiefs in a bureau drawer, and went back to the typewriter.

The book was published late the following autumn. It was fresh, it was young, it was gay, and it caught on. By the time the advance copies arrived she had begun another, and was doing a series of special interviews for Bracken which had caused favorable comment in the newspaper world. Bracken said she had the touch.

Johnny Malone, who worked in the City Room, said she was gilt-edged, and had nominated himself as her permanent and exclusive watchdog, first because of his old friendship with her brother Fitz, and second because he at once fell in love with her. He took her to Martin's, and saw that she met the right people. He took her to Churchill's, and taught her the latest dance-steps. He took her to Guffanti's, and showed her how to eat spaghetti without cutting it. He kept her laughing, with his own brand of slangy, hard-boiled wit.

The first time Johnny proposed she almost accepted him out of sheer gratitude. To be wanted by somebody again—not to look a fool to herself any more—to be desired again, and treated tenderly, for one's own triumphant sake—it restored her self-respect to know that Johnny was in love with her, for it had been a blow to her pride as well as to her heart that Oliver had not been able to accept the offer of herself when she made it.

Johnny was first of all a good playfellow, honest and kind and devoted. He was nice to look at, with a smiling snub-nosed Irish face, very clean, and a rather stocky build, sufficiently tall. But she had to admit to herself from the beginning that she was not going to be in love with him. It was no good wondering why, or if, or when—she just wasn't. So she said No, and Thank you, and Can't we be friends, and she couldn't help thinking the whole thing sounded like something she had written, or that *somebody* had written. . . . Johnny took it very well, and said who said they weren't friends, and that she hadn't heard the last of it.

When Dinah and Bracken set out in June, 1904, for their annual visit to England, Phoebe refused without a pang their cordial invitation to go along, and was able to keep on laughing with Johnny. England was over, for her. If ever she went abroad again it would be to visit Rosalind at the castle at Heidersdorf, and to look up the Spragues' legendary Aunt Sally in the South of France on the way. Aunt Sally was Father's only sister, who had been a great belle in the 'sixties and had buried three wealthy husbands since then, and now lived in Cannes in more-than-Oriental-splendor and rather dubious company, Cousin Eden said, but Phoebe was convinced that she would make a wonderful story if you could get it. Phoebe and Johnny often talked about Aunt Sally and the story that could be written about her, until one time Johnny said,

"Let's us get married and go to Cannes on our honeymoon and see Aunt Sally." And Phoebe had laughed at that too, but not in a way to hurt his feelings.

The second book, in the spring of 1905, was surer, and went a little deeper, and commanded some respect. The third one swept the country with mounting sales. The fourth one topped the third, for Phoebe had found a formula more or less her own and was developing an easy, original style which caught on. Each summer Dinah and Bracken went to England, and each summer Phoebe refused with thanks to accompany them. Each summer Johnny proposed the honeymoon in Cannes and was gently laughed off.

Two things never changed, while the years slipped away. No one ever measured up to Oliver in her heart. And every month she wrote a letter to Rosalind in Germany. The replies were more irregular, but they always came. Prince Conrad's father had died before Christmas the year of Rosalind's marriage, and just as Virginia had prophesied, all the lovely dresses had to be put away for a year's mourning and by then much of the trousseau finery was out of style and had to be—very lavishly —replaced by Paris dressmakers. The honeymoon had been cut short by a summons to the old man's bedside, and after the funeral they had returned to England only briefly to wind things up there at the Embassy, before Prince Conrad assumed the dignities and duties of a reigning prince on his ancestral estates in Silesia. His mother had been dead for many years, and his Aunt Christa on his father's side ruled the *Schloss* at Heidersdorf, so that his English bride's position was bound to be equivocal and uncomfortable from the beginning.

At first Rosalind's letters tried to conceal her own disillusion and despair and were merely schoolgirlish, brief, and disappointing to Phoebe, whose pen obeyed her thoughts freely instead of standing between them and the paper. Patiently she began to ask questions, and open discussions, and try to get at the real Rosalind again as though they were still face to face. Gradually Rosalind's letters changed, got longer, less stilted, more amusing, as she attempted to convey to Phoebe the fantastic, infuriating, often ludicrous life of a German princess who also happened to be an Englishwoman. Phoebe naturally begged for more of this, and Rosalind's pride and reticence gave way before her growing need of a confidante.

Phoebe was able to gather that Prince Conrad had little inclination to back up his English wife against his Prussian aunt, and various awkwardnesses accordingly developed. That is, filtered through Rosalind's indestructible levity they became awkwardnesses, whereas a different temperament would have magnified them into tragedies. Phoebe began to save the letters from Rosalind, and to read bits of them aloud to her friends, until a sort of Heidersdorf saga took shape in New York, and people were eager for the next chapter. But a desolate homesick strain ran through all the letters. Conrad seemed not to think it necessary to keep his promise that Rosalind should go home to England to visit every year, and extravagant holidays at Nice and Biarritz and St. Moritz were not the same thing. In 1906 she had a son, and barely survived the birth, and was months convalescing, but even the baby did not still her perpetual sense of exile.

News always came too from England, through Virginia and Dinah's yearly visits there. Virginia had had another girl child, with her customary ease and dispatch. Clare and Winifred each produced another boy, neck and neck, said Archie. But Dinah had begun to wonder. Anyone could do it, even Maia was expecting. She alone had failed.

Oliver never wrote again, and Phoebe never tried to communicate with him. Word of him would arrive obliquely, from time to time, through Dinah or Virginia. He had rejoined the regiment the same autumn he married and they went out at once to India, where Maia lost her first child, a boy. Then in the summer of 1908 a girl was born in England, and lived. Charles had got a Staff appointment at the War Office, with the rank of brevet major, and was highly thought of there. This news was duly passed on to Rosalind by Phoebe, and was not referred to in her reply.

Miles wrote often to Phoebe as he had always done, almost as though nothing had ever happened between them beyond their lifelong friendship, and she was grateful to him for his lack of dramatics over the broken engagement. It almost seemed, as Cousin Sue had once said, that Miles was not the marrying kind; almost as though he felt let off.

Time slid by with little to mark its passing except new successes for Phoebe, whose books paid better than Sue's had ever done, and started a vogue for rather stylized, understated, somewhat glib romances with a deft touch. Their author also created a vogue—the well-groomed, well-bred, expensively dressed bachelor girl who never indulged in sticky love affairs, whose rejected suitors remained her devoted friends, and whose unapproachable heart became a mystery and a challenge.

Feeling grown up and fully fledged, she left Eden's Madison Avenue house and took a picturesque apartment in the upper Twenties, with a colored maid from home to look after her. She furnished it herself with cheerful chintzes and ginghams, and there was always a wood fire in the black marble grate in winter and an iced drink in hot weather for the weary or convivial dropper-in at tea time. And there was always Phoebe, slim and sweet and smiling and a little aloof, with her brushed, shining hair and the Murray cleft in her chin.

Johnny Malone saw it all from the reserved seat section, offering marriage at fairly regular intervals, accepting the inevitable negative with the best of grace, striving not to agonize over the growing list of his competitors nor to drink too much in his hours of despair. Johnny outlasted them all. He had seen her first, and no late-comer ever dislodged him from his pre-empted position as watchdog and court jester. A deep and comfortable affection existed between him and Phoebe, punctuated by flare-ups of Johnny's much-enduring desire.

Because of Oliver Campion and what he had taught her, and in view of several episodes besides the perpetual devotion of Johnny Malone, there was something soft and chastened and appealing about Phoebe. She had none of the usual stigmata of the unmarried career girl. She was not angular or brittle or aggressively self-sufficient. She expected to have doors opened for her, and chairs placed, and things handed. She was utterly feminine, and enjoyed being treated by infatuated males as though she was a little half-witted.

The twenty-one-year-old Phoebe who had set out from New York to see Edward VII crowned had been sturdily determined to stand on her own feet, earn her own money, and prove that she could take care of herself, even after she married Miles—for she had expected to look after Miles, rather than the other way about. Having done all these things—except looking after Miles—apparently with the greatest of ease, the present Phoebe found it nothing to wave flags about, and preferred to conceal from her admirers the embarrassing fact that she got more for her serial rights than some of them could earn in a year's hard work at their own respective jobs. The young Phoebe of the past had even contemplated woman's suffrage with open-minded interest and approval. Nowadays Phoebe said "suffragettes and people like that" with the implication that one did not know them. She was not by nature a crusader in any cause.

Quite suddenly, in the middle of the 1910 London Season, King Edward died. Bracken and Dinah had just arrived in England and

Bracken was therefore on the spot for the funeral, and for the proclamation of George V, whose coronation was announced for the following summer at the end of Court mourning. It was disturbing to Phoebe to realize that Edward's reign had lasted all of nine years. Her thoughts turned inward and backward unbidden, and she found her eyes wet with tears—a luxury she seldom allowed herself any more.

She brushed them away impatiently, and went to the typewriter and turned out a reminiscent, nostalgic piece about the year of Edward's crowning, which was bought by a famous woman's magazine and regarded with such enthusiasm there that they offered her a handsome sum, plus expenses, if she would go to England and report to them exclusively on next year's ceremony.

It tempted her. Bracken would be pleased and proud. She was sure of a welcome at Farthingale, and the idea of seeing Virginia's offspring appealed to her. She wondered what Charles was doing by now, and realized that she had actually lost track of Oliver and did not know where he was stationed. She went to the mirror above the black marble mantelpiece in her little chintz drawing-room, and eyed with some misgiving the glossy young woman who looked back at her—the elaborately waved brown hair, the discreetly carmined lips, the high-waisted, clinging gown were not what Oliver would expect. And while Phoebe felt they were a distinct improvement on his remembered image of her, and thought it would be rather fun to present him with this new version of herself which success and self-reliance had wrought—she wondered. Men didn't change much between twenty-one and thirty, but women grew up, and sometimes they even grew old. Phoebe, turning thirty, was more beautiful than she had ever been, as Johnny could have told her with his eyes shut. But would Oliver behold the change without a shock?

Anyway, what satisfaction would it be to see him now, with Maia looking on possessively and doubtless bringing out all the worst in one? None whatever. Besides, it would be dangerous. The door was safely shut now, he was Maia's husband, the father of a child. Don't open it. Don't risk one's hard-won immunity, one's carefully preserved peace of mind, by flying round the same old candle-flame. Characteristically, her writer's mind jeered self-consciously at the worn-out simile. She acknowledged an increasing tendency to edit even her own thoughts with a mental blue pencil poised for clichés and sentimentalisms. Soon she would just turn into a manuscript, she thought impatiently, with no human spontaneity left.

She turned restlessly away from the mirror, running critical, dissatisfied eyes over the homey, deliberately shabby room. Unpretentious Surroundings of Successful Lady Novelist. Her lower lip came out. All right, I'll do it over, she thought. Something expensive and artificial and becoming. Empire. Récamier sofas. Or I might go all rococo. That would jar them!

At this point the doorbell rang, and she heard Delilah greeting Johnny, who had not been invited this afternoon but whose appearance was a godsend in her present fractious mood. She flew at him, almost embraced him, made him effusively welcome, and asked Delilah to bring cocktails.

Johnny stood still in the middle of the carpet and eyed her with a narrow, sidelong, suspicious look.

"What are you up to now?" said Johnny.

"Why should I be up to anything?" Her gaze was wide and limpid. "You drop in—I invite you to sit down and have a drink—anything unusual in that?"

"You haven't been so glad to see me in years," said Johnny, unimpressed. "What's on your conscience?"

"I haven't any," said Phoebe, all impudence and charm.

"That's right, you haven't. What do you keep where it ought to be? An umbrella stand?"

"I was just thinking," Phoebe began, ignoring that, "it's about time I had this room done over. What would you suggest?"

"Hunh-unh," said Johnny, sinking into his favorite place on the right-hand end of the sofa. "Let's not. I'm so used to it."

"That's what I mean," said Phoebe. "How would you like something in old blue and gold?"

Johnny shuddered and shut his eyes.

"Or Nile green and white?" she added brightly.

Johnny groaned.

"You'd make a horrid husband," she told him. "Every time I wanted new chair covers you'd say the old ones were best."

"But in other ways," said Johnny alertly, "I assure you I'd give satisfaction."

Phoebe's eyes fled before his, and Delilah came in with the cocktails. It was bragging, but Phoebe could not resist telling him about the offer from the woman's magazine, and how she had made up her mind to refuse it after all because—it seemed best to give a reason—she had so many things to do. Johnny promptly brought up the honeymoon in Cannes, and she refused that too, and there were no hard feelings. But gradually a silence overtook them, for Johnny had something on his mind. Finally he said, "Phoebe, whatever happened to you in England that time?"

Phoebe was startled, but almost contrived not to show it.

"What makes you think—" she began.

"Oh, come off it, honeybunch, you've got some sort of kink about England, I've known that for years. Sometimes I think it would do you good to get it off your chest. You fell in love, didn't you."

"Mm-hm," she said, turning the glass in her hand.

"And I suppose he was a bum," said Johnny.

"He was not! He was in the Army!" She bit her lip too late.

"What does that prove? So was I in the Army once. When we fit the war in Cuba I was in the Army, and I knew lots of bums who were in it too."

"Well, he wasn't one of them," she reminded him tartly.

"Are you going to love him all the rest of your life?"

"No. Well, anyway—it's finished. I shall never see him again."

"Then why do you carry this white banner emblazoned with a strange device?"

"Do I?" She looked at him doubtfully.

Johnny set down his empty glass, removed hers from her unresisting fingers, and took both her hands.

"I don't know how old you are, my angel, and I don't care—but I do know I have been courting you for eight years off and on, and I was on the safe side of the law when I began. You'll be an old maid, sweetheart, if you keep on, and I'll be doddering—but still faithful. It seems a pity, though, to let so much good time go to waste."

When she didn't answer, and didn't object, Johnny laid cautious arms around her and drew her over against his shoulder where she sat passive and thoughtful, and so he kissed her and she even let him do that.

"At last!" he murmured, and became more possessive, until she stirred drowsily and drew away from him, and went to stand beside the window, a hand on the curtains, looking down into the summer twilight.

"Don't rush me," said Phoebe, and Johnny, with his record of eight patient years, put his head down in his hands and rocked with silent laughter. "Johnny, I've never led you on, have I. All this time you've wasted—I never held out any hope."

"Never," Johnny agreed at once. "It was entirely my own idea. I wasn't ambushed into it. You discouraged me every foot of the way. Till now," he added, brightening.

"I haven't promised anything," she reminded him guardedly.

"Nope. Not yet." He stood up and followed her to the window.

"Go away, Johnny, I'm trying to think."

"I'd rather you didn't. We were doing fine without it."

She looked up at him gravely, from beside the window, the light full in his face—his honest, boyish face, with its sleepy eyes and generous mouth and the well-trimmed mustache—his look of humble watchdog worship. *How would you like to be beaten every now and then,* a dim voice asked her across the years, *just to show which one of us is the master?* Something inside her crumpled, and she put up both hands to her eyes.

"Sweetheart, what is it? Have I said the wrong thing?" Johnny stood over her, trying to take away her shielding hands. "Phoebe, what have I done? I apologize. Phoebe, *don't* freeze over again, you were being so soft and sweet. Come back, Phoebe, the ghosts were all laid and we had just begun to be happy."

"The ghosts aren't laid. It's no use, Johnny. Go away and find some other girl who will treat you better than I have, all these years."

"I don't want some other girl," said Johnny obstinately. "I guess what it comes to is, I'd rather be kicked around by you than be kissed and cuddled by somebody else. It's got to be a habit with me now."

"You must break it, then. It's wasting your life."

"The only part of my life that's wasted is the part I have to spend away from you. Such as the nights. Was it so bad, when I kissed you just now?"

"No. I liked it."

"Well, then!"

"But that's drifting!" she cried rebelliously. "I can't do it! It isn't fair!"

"It was a nice piece of drifting while it lasted," he said. "Phoebe, are you sure you're not just writing a book? Are you sure if you saw him again he wouldn't look like everybody else? Are you sure you could tell him from me in a crowd?"

"Yes, Johnny, I'm sure."

"Well," said Johnny vaguely, "that's that. Had I better go now?"

She stood looking at him helplessly from across the room. She would have been the first to admit that her maternal instincts were not very highly developed. She was sorry for Johnny, but she had no impulse to mother him, or any other man who had worn because of her that look of aching despair. Perhaps if Johnny had not asked, if he had not apologized—if Johnny had been the master and shown her that he was, he could have had her then, for she was lonely, and longing for love. But, "Had I better go now?" said Johnny, and lost her forever.

"I wish it was different, Johnny," she said miserably, and what she meant was that she wished Johnny was different, with a hard, irresistible grip to him not to be denied.

"I wish it was," said Johnny, and picked up his hat. "Well—you haven't heard the last of it, you know."

The door closed behind him, and she laid her arms along the edge of the mantelpiece and hid her face. *I shall still love you—immoderately —when you are ninety. . . . Oh, Oliver . . .*

3

SHE and Johnny didn't exactly avoid each other after that, but they did spend less time together as the year ran out. Around Christmas time Phoebe was surprised to receive a telephone call from Bracken, who asked to see her privately. She invited him to tea, and looked her best to receive him.

Bracken came straight to the point.

"Ordinarily, I believe in a strictly hands-off policy as regards the private life of my employees," he began almost at once. "But you are wrecking Johnny Malone. Have you any idea of marrying him, ever?"

"No. I've always told him that."

"Then you can have no objection if I send him out of town."

Phoebe stared.

"I need a good man in Madrid," Bracken went on. "Johnny speaks Spanish and he's due for a promotion, if he can stay sober. He'll never call his soul his own so long as he can leave it on your doorstep like the milk, and I've watched you trample him long enough. It's Johnny's unhappy destiny always to adore women who dangle him. Virginia did the same thing, till Archie put a stop to that. I'm going to rescue him from you by shipping him to Madrid before it's too late."

"Will he go?"

"Well, of all the conceit!" said Bracken wonderingly. "A good newspaper man goes where he is sent."

"I see," said Phoebe. "This is a form of blackmail. Marry Johnny or kiss him Good-bye."

"I only wanted to make sure you had no honorable intentions," Bracken said coldly.

"I'm afraid I haven't."

"Then he's on his way."

He was, too, by the middle of January. And with him went much of life's charm and cosiness in the apartment in the upper Twenties.

Phoebe was aware of an increasing restlessness and dissatisfaction with her existence, and in March when a long-delayed letter arrived from Rosalind telling of another difficult birth which the baby did not survive and from which she was slow to recover, Phoebe suddenly made up her mind.

She would go to Germany for the summer. She should have gone long ago. And possibly to Cannes. Not to Madrid. Certainly not to London.

PART FIVE

ROSALIND

Heidersdorf.   *Spring, 1911.*

‣‣

1

ROSALIND'S reply to Phoebe's letter asking if she might visit Heidersdorf that summer was a cable, journalistic in its contempt for the word-rate from the middle of the Continent: *Jumping for joy at prospect seeing you again. Come straight here might all go Cannes together. Conny says you must not put us in a book. Love.* ROSALIND.

Well, Phoebe thought, and read it again. Rosalind was sounding very much like herself. *All* go to Cannes together? That might be rather a circus. Conny says . . . *Well.*

It was not necessary nowadays to draw on Sir Gratian's legacy when Phoebe wanted to go abroad. Her own bank account stood the strain of an embellished wardrobe, a first-class passage on the new Cunarder *Lusitania,* and a sufficient letter of credit for several months in Europe. She sailed early in May, standing somewhat thoughtfully at the rail on the boat deck as the big liner slipped down the harbor. Several people she knew well were on board, and she would not lack for companionship during the voyage. Most of them were bound for London and the Coronation festivities in which Phoebe firmly refused to take an interest.

She would disembark at Havre and go from Paris by way of Metz and Dresden to Breslau, where Rosalind would meet her with a motor for the drive to the *Schloss,* which stood on a pinnacle of rock commanding a magnificent view in the Sudeten-Gebirge, "a picturesque mountain region," according to the guidebook, "reached by a light railway and thence on foot" from various hyphenated villages, a few of them with "(inn)" in parentheses. Phoebe, who liked to be comfortable and was particular about the condition of the sheets when she travelled, had no desire to sample the inns of the Sudeten-Gebirge if a *Schloss* in the luxurious French chateau style was available, and she preferred a motor car to her own feet at any time.

She leaned her elbows on the rail and watched New York fall astern, while her mind slid back ruefully to a spring day nine years ago when she had stood like this, with Miles's ring on her finger and adventure before her. Having just experienced her thirtieth birthday, she was now inclined to an increasing reflectiveness, amounting sometimes to a gentle melancholy. I am very well preserved, she would remark to herself with a pitying smile when she woke bright-eyed and becomingly dishevelled and surveyed herself in the bathroom mirror before brushing her teeth. And with that round, childish brow and full lower lip and the candor of her steady eyes, she would have passed for twenty-five at any hour of the day, and often looked even less.

Leaning on the rail of the *Lusitania,* eastward bound, she quite naturally began to think of her first voyage and its unforeseen events and consequences. First, she had lost poor Miles's ring. Then she had met Oliver and never been the same again. It was because of Oliver, wasn't it, that she stood here now, free, independent, successful—empty-handed. Without knowing Oliver, she would have been Miles's wife these past nine years—probably she would have had several children by now, no reputation as an authoress, and no money of her own (unless Sir Gratian's) to spend on a European holiday. And she asked herself seriously, would she have been better off?

She had become the least faithful of all the family about going home to Williamsburg for Christmas and birthdays. The rest of them always went. But it was tactfully understood in the family that for Phoebe it was difficult, because of that unfortunate business with Miles. And while Miles himself appeared to bear her no grudge, Phoebe had found it convenient to beg off sometimes from the traditional family anniversaries and reunions. She saw the Murrays often in New York. Since Great-uncle Ransom died a few years ago, Cousin Sue was free to visit Eden frequently, and Fitz and Gwen came north every winter to stay with Bracken and Dinah and see the shows and attend to his music sales. There was only Father, to take her back to Williamsburg—and of course Mother too, but Father was the one you couldn't do without forever. But now he always set her dreaming about Oliver, who had a daughter too —Hermione (in four syllables, with the accent on the long *i*) would be three years old this summer. Phoebe was sure that Maia had chosen that name. And did Hermione feel about Oliver the way she herself had always felt about Father? . . .

The same young man wearing a belted topcoat and a soft hat passed along the deck behind her for the third time with an inquisitive, lingering glance—Phoebe was aware of him with a growing impatience, whereas such glances had once stimulated and then amused her. Another sign of being thirty, she thought. Too much trouble to play up to stray young men with admiration in their eyes. A fine thing. This boy would get himself introduced. Then he would offer cocktails, want to dance, want to sit in the moonlight and tell the story of his life. And she would be bored. A fine thing. Obviously it was time she had a holiday. Or something.

Phoebe took her elbows off the rail and marched towards her stateroom, giving the young man a brief, level look as she passed, designed to set him right back on his heels. Before she reached the bottom of the companionway she heard his feet at the top, and as a consequence she was scowling when she ran into the first of several convivial acquaintances in the main square, whom at one time she had considered a welcome addition to the passenger list.

She escaped from them too and shut the door of the stateroom behind her, thankful that she had insisted upon sole occupancy. The wind was freshening, and as she began to take her gay new dresses out of the suitcases she felt the first gentle lift of the bow as it met the sea. Maybe they'll all be seasick and leave me in peace, she thought vindictively, for she was a good sailor herself. What is the matter with me? Rosalind will think I've turned into a sour old maid, she reflected. Well, maybe I have. I wonder what Rosalind has turned into.

She had been wishing lately that she had kept all Rosalind's letters and could refresh her memory on their half-forgotten contents. The idea had crossed her mind in the very beginning that it would be fun to write Rosalind in a book—the irrepressible and unimpressible English girl set down in a pompous little German circle ruled by her in-laws, before whose opaque self-esteem she could at times hardly keep her face straight. But Phoebe had formed an unbreakable rule as a novelist never to draw on her friends or her friends' friends for copy, but always to cut her stories out of whole cloth. Besides, as time went on and Rosalind's little tragedy of homesickness and loneliness and misunderstanding began to emerge, the whole situation became too poignant and private to go into print.

And now Prince Conrad said that she must not put them in a book.

The self-conscious conceit which could instantly suggest such a thing riled her—likewise the type of mind which could suppose that a guest would thus repay hospitality. As a gesture of defiance to His Serene Highness, Phoebe had packed several of the little ruled notebooks in which she always made her jottings for a new story. Just for that, she would keep a sort of journal of this summer in Europe. Just for that, she had put down, as they came back to her, various items of Rosalind's past letters. Just for that, if she happened to feel like it, she would write a book about her visit to Germany.

The notebooks appeared early in the course of her unpacking on shipboard, and the one already begun she laid out on the bedside table. She often thought her way back into Rosalind's letters as she was falling asleep, and brought up impressions and highlights she had thought forgotten. When she could talk to Rosalind a great deal more would doubtless occur to her. And already she had recognized in herself a malicious itch to get her pen into Prince Conrad. Of course I *never* write about real people and I'm not going to begin now, she told herself again, hanging up dresses in the wardrobe, which was too short for them. But he *is* asking for it. . . .

When she went down to the dining-saloon she found herself assigned to a large cheerful captain's table, and became without visible effort the brilliant Miss Phoebe Sprague.

2

DROPPING off to sleep that first night out, lulled by the afterglow of champagne at dinner and liqueur brandy with the coffee, and by the drowsy creak and swing of a very gentle swell, Phoebe sent her thoughts back to Rosalind. It had become a sort of bedtime game to reconstruct her ideas of what she was going to find at Heidersdorf.

There would be first of all that growing dread, mentioned over and over again in Rosalind's accounts of conversations in her own drawing-room after dinner—Rosalind's dread, not Germany's, of war with England. Even Conny, she wrote, had begun to feel that it was sure to come, and seemed to be slipping all his old ties with England, one by one. They no longer went over for the hunting, as he had promised they always would; the leased house in the English countryside had never materialized; they had not attended the Court of St. James for years; and they went to Vienna and Paris, not London, when they wanted to shop and hear music and renew friendships.

Rosalind's mamma and younger sister Evelyn made visits to Heidersdorf, as did a good many other people from England, and she spent some time among the gay international set on the Riviera, and in Switzerland. She still wrote wistfully of England as "home" but she saw very little of it any more, and apparently accepted exile as all a part of the unwelcome bargain she had been forced to make with her destiny— but Evelyn had succeeded in marrying a baronet during her first London season and now lived in a dear little Elizabethan house in Surrey. He hadn't such a lot of money, but he was kind and stupid and he thought Evelyn was quite perfect in every way, and—she hadn't got to live with her in-laws, and anyway, they were English in-laws and wouldn't have been hard to bear.

It was very odd, Rosalind had remarked in a recent letter, how England got on Germany's nerves. She had lived all her life in England without hearing a tenth as much about Germany as one heard about England in Germany in a week. They couldn't let it alone. Even among themselves, and regardless of herself as an Englishwoman, they had to go on telling how superior Germany was in every way; they had to make fun of the English, whose low voices annoyed them into sinking their own robust tones to a funereal mumble in derisive imitation; they said there was never anything to eat in England except mutton and apple tart; they deplored the English flower arrangement which allowed everything to straggle all over the vase instead of wiring each separate stem so that the blossoms stood up straight like soldiers; they were sure the English always ate a meal before they left home in order to appear to have small appetites and leave food on their plates when they dined out.

But the worst of all was when they talked of *invasion*—the invasion of *England*—as a feasible and perhaps an advisable thing to do, because the German Army was angry with the English newspapers, which were angry with the German Press—and because they said Germany had no friends, only enemies, who were jealous of her growing power. The Kaiser swore high and low that as Victoria's grandson he was England's best friend, and kept up a pretence of affection for his Uncle Edward, but although they exchanged visits at Cowes and Kiel, Windsor and Friedrichshof, they scarcely ever met without there being some kind of row, and international complications were sometimes narrowly averted. There was a natural antipathy between the two men, as between the nations.

Prince Conrad said it was a great pity, but was not inclined to discuss it sympathetically with his wife, her letters had made that pretty plain. He had always deplored the savage tone of the German Press towards England, Rosalind recalled, even in the old days when they were all in London. But even the Kaiser talked too loud, said Rosalind, and his ministers lived in dread of the occasions which called for public utterance by him, and always had to suppress and smooth over and deny for days after he had made a speech somewhere. If he got on to his pet subject—the "encirclement" of Germany, and her vulnerability, placed as she was in the center of Europe and exposed to attack on all sides, and of Germany's wrongs (all still pending) at the hands of envious nations who wished her ill and would not recognize her good, her *benevolent* intentions in building a fleet as large as she could, but to defend herself only and never to challenge (perish the thought!) the British Navy—when he got started like that, God only knew what his obsession might lead him to say before he could be diplomatically shushed again.

And yet, Rosalind would add with an almost visible shrug of her shoulders, the Emperor was a delightful companion when he chose to be, though his humor was likely to be of the coarse schoolboy variety, with puns, horseplay, and practical jokes. When he came to Heidersdorf for the shooting and during maneuvers, he always asked her to play to him after dinner, and once he refused to kiss her hand till she had taken her glove off. (The old goat, Johnny Malone had remarked, when Phoebe read that page to her friends in New York.) But for all his rather flamboyant gallantries, Wilhelm believed that women were meant only for *Kinder, Küche,* and *Kirche,* as he did not deny when you taxed him with it, said Rosalind, who on her part as hostess to their imperial guest must have given her husband some bad moments.

The Crown Prince, Rosalind reported once a little while before his marriage, with an almost audible giggle, was even more so than his father, and was apparently making a collection of her handkerchiefs, which he tucked away in the breast of his coat with sentimental glances which someone else was bound to see sooner or later, and he wrote her notes signed *Forever yours*— Conny, of course, would only laugh, so long as it was the Crown Prince, who was so "susceptible" that he was not allowed to travel in England for fear his virtue would be unduly taxed by so many lovely women and too friendly girls in a country notoriously lax about chaperonage, as every good German knew. Rosalind had to speak to him very severely and tell him that she would not be flirted with in such an obvious and banal fashion. Fortunately he took it meekly.

Germans were likely to be so touchy. They called it sensitiveness. They had to be perpetually humored and placated, both as a nation and as individuals. Even Conny, who had been out of Germany so much and presumably knew how to behave, took offence at the oddest things, and had to be coaxed into a good humor again. For instance, he had promised her an English nurse for the first baby, and then when the time came his Aunt Christa tried not to allow it, and it wasn't until Rosalind had made herself quite ill and run up a fever that he had given in and kept his word—and then, because she had held out against him and got her own selfish way, he had not spoken to her for three days. (Well, *really,* said Phoebe in exasperation, reading that letter.) Also Aunt Christa thought it was nonsense to insist on sterilized milk, though even the German doctor had ordered it. Conny, said Aunt Christa, had drunk only raw milk fresh from their own cows, which had never set foot off the home farm where they were born and weaned and bred, and had therefore never associated with any inferior cattle from which they might conceivably catch diseases—and look at Conny now, Aunt Christa would conclude triumphantly, could you ask for a man in better health and of a finer physique? And the answer was No, laughed Rosalind, and squeezed in at the bottom of the page the information that Conny's son was drinking sterilized milk all the same, and doubtless the cows all had hurt feelings.

Phoebe smiled in the dark, while the *Lusitania* ploughed eastward and the wind began a faint shrill singing in the rigging. Rosalind wouldn't change, not with all Germany trying to squash her. Prince Conrad must be mightily amused with her still, in spite of the passages with Aunt Christa. Fancy marrying a man who wouldn't take your part in a family row. I wouldn't stand for that, thought Phoebe comfortably on her pillow. I'd—well, I'd walk out on him if he wouldn't stick up for me. What's a husband for, anyway? Oliver's wife would be like Caesar's —she couldn't be wrong. But Oliver wasn't a German.

Rosalind said Conny *would* smoke in her bedroom—even cigars—so that one's sachet never had an earthly, and sometimes after an evening in the drawing-room with a houseful of guests and all the men puffing steadily, even one's hair smelt of smoke when it was brushed out at bedtime. But how shocked they would all be if Rosalind herself had lighted a cigarette, though everyone knew that nowadays even Queen Alexandra smoked cigarettes. Everyone in Germany knew, and considered it merely a further symptom of the decadence and slackness of English society—they could go on about that for hours, and because you had married a German you had to sit still and say nothing, and even though Conny had lived in England and knew it was not decadent a bit he would not take up the cudgels, and fixed you with a glassy eye if you dared to fidget while the lies grew taller and taller.

It was very odd, Rosalind had once confided, how Conny sometimes reverted and behaved exactly like a German who had not travelled at all. German men put their heels together and bowed and kissed your hand and paid elaborate compliments—but it never occurred to them to open doors for you, or wait on you at tea, or see that you had the most comfortable chair, or carry things for you. Of course Conny did all these things because he had been in the Diplomatic and because he knew she expected them of him—and of course at Heidersdorf the doors were opened by powdered footmen in knee-breeches who were there to do nothing else, and tea was handed round for you unless you were absolutely *en famille*. But in Germany you were "only" a woman, subject to a lord and master who permitted you to go on existing provided you were quiet and made no trouble, and always treated him with the proper respect.

There was one evening, with which Rosalind illustrated the foregoing point, when she had without thinking picked up Conny's brandy glass and taken the first sip from it, when they were all sitting round chatting after dinner, and Aunt Christa had been altogether scandalized and scolded her in front of everybody for infringing (as near as one could make out) on her husband's dignity. And Conny? He had only smiled, while Aunt Christa went on and on, and finally he had asked Rosalind rather coldly if she desired some brandy of her own, which she did not and never had—and by that time she wished that brandy had never been invented and it was all she could do to keep from bursting into tears before them all.

Phoebe recalled the description of this scene with a shudder, and hoped that nothing like it would happen while she was there. She also determined contrarily that she would smoke cigarettes herself, though she didn't really care much for them, and drink wine and eat cheese—not considered a delicate thing for German young ladies to do—just to show Aunt Christa a thing or two about American women, who were entitled to do what they liked.

In Germany, Phoebe recalled drowsily, women weren't supposed to play games, or to hunt, or even to ride much, which would be more of a hardship for Rosalind than for herself. The German *Herren* considered that the Almighty had made pretty women to please their men, and their men did not like to see windblown hair and hot faces and muddy boots and short skirts on creatures designed solely to ornament life. . . . Rosalind's visiting cards had to be in German, Polish, French, and English. . . . Conny had put in a pink and gold bathroom for his bride . . . her sitting-room had been done over in apple-blossom pink and old blue, the walls covered with hand-painted silk . . . a special rosewood piano with a gold trim had been made in Berlin for her private apartments at the *Schloss* . . . one almost *has* to love a man who gives one not only one's bread and butter but diamond necklaces down to *here* and gold pianos, Rosalind had written during one of her more hopeful times . . . the castle was full of potted palms, huge ones like a conservatory, which were watered and tended like babies, and kept from draughts . . . and it had enclosed stoves of iron or porcelain which made less dirt and gave more heat and less comfort than open fireplaces, but Rosalind had had some of the fireplaces opened up and new, magnificent ones built into the rooms she used, and burned great logs in them . . . even in Berlin houses and flats with hot and cold water laid on were rare luxuries, and Rosalind insisted on staying at the Hotel Bristol in Unter den Linden when they went there because the impressive Louis XIV-style Palast Polkwitz in the Wilhelmstrasse had no bathrooms . . . but they always travelled in their own railway coach, often in a special train, with their own beds and linen and servants and food. . . . Conny had once been heard to say that he never went to see Shakespeare in London because the English knew nothing about him . . . surely that was sheer pose . . . at least it wasn't the time of year when one would encounter the Kaiser at Heidersdorf, and that was a relief, Phoebe thought, sliding into sleep . . . it would be fun to be there for a German Christmas, though, and see Rosalind as chatelaine handing out innumerable gifts to the lower classes, who curtseyed and said *Grüss Gott* . . . or *was* that what they said in Silesia . . . there had once been an awful row with Aunt Christa because Rosalind had taken the wrong, that is to say an inferior, lady to sit with her on the sofa because they wanted to talk about music . . . and just as she lost herself Phoebe was wondering if Aunt Christa would consider Rosalind's American friend sufficiently important to sit on the sofa beside Her Serene Highness the Princess Rosalind zu Polkwitz-Heidersdorf, who would not allow her husband's family to call her Rosa, German fashion. . . .

3

THE castle at Heidersdorf stood on a jagged crag overlooking what Rosalind had described as a perfectly sickening gorge, and the elaborate gardens had to be terraced three quarters of the way round. The road up to it was a looping gravelled avenue handsomely planted and pruned and swept for miles.

Rosalind held to Phoebe's hand in the motor all the way from Breslau where the train stopped, and they chattered like schoolgirls—for two people who had written to each other faithfully for years they still had a great deal to say, punctuated by exclamations of delight from Phoebe about the mountainous spring landscape through which they drove, and which Rosalind said was enough like parts of Scotland to make you ache. Warm weather had come early that year, and lilies of the valley were blooming in the woods like violets in Virginia, and the lilacs and laburnum were out. But as the motor swept up the long curving avenue towards the castle Rosalind suddenly burst out with something which lay heavy on her mind.

"Phoebe, I *am* so disappointed, but we've got family people coming next week, and if you don't *promise* to outstay them we shall have no fun at all! Darling, you don't simply have to be at Cannes at any definite date, do you?"

"No," said Phoebe consideringly. "No rush about Cannes, I reckon. What do you mean, family people?"

"Relations. In-laws." Rosalind made a face, and glanced at the chauffeur's back and lowered her voice. "When they come it's like walking on eggs—you get very careful and self-conscious, and you never know when something is going to set them off. The last time they all elected to use my sitting-room because it had just been done over and happened to take Aunt Nini's fancy, and so I couldn't play my piano because Conny said it disturbed their conversation. If they do that again next week I shall just have the piano moved into the library. Nobody ever goes there!"

"Shan't I be in the way during a family visit?" Phoebe asked doubtfully, and Rosalind seized her with tense little hands.

"But, Phoebe, you'd save my life by being here! If you can weather it yourself, that is! One has to just shut the door of one's mind and try not to think, or remember, or *reason*, while they talk! The conversation is all about other relations who aren't present to defend themselves, and about who is going to marry whom and how much more suitable two other people would have been for the engaged pair, and about who has just bought a new motor car and how much better all the other kinds would have been than the one he got, and about what *everything* costs, and how superior their own possessions are to somebody else's, and how *infinitely* superior *anything* German is to similar objects in England—and Phoebe, don't try to argue with them about poor old England, you must just choke it back and hold your tongue if it kills you, because it isn't any good to state facts to them, it only makes them worse. And *don't* mind if they go on about the war, will you, sometimes I think they only do it the way a nursery maid tells goblin stories, to scare themselves and everybody else into fits for the fun of it."

"What war?" Phoebe asked, bewildered.

"With England, of course."

"But there isn't any war—"

"I know, I know, but you'd almost think there *was*, to hear them! Just don't take any notice, that's all, and don't let them see that you're surprised or upset by anything they say. I've got so I can go mentally *blank* like a imbecile and let it wash over me—till all of a sudden I feel as though I've *got* to get outside and scream, and some day I will, and they'll send for a doctor and take me away in a straitjacket. Can you play *Skat* and pinochle and cribbage and those things?"

"No," said Phoebe without regret. "But I can play poker."

"Well, don't say that, for heaven's sake!" Rosalind cautioned her, and winced as the car swung perilously around a turn in the drive. "I *wish* he wouldn't take this road as though he was driving a flying-machine! Conny's always egging him on, and I know someday we're going right over the edge! And Phoebe, I do think I ought to warn you about Uncle Eugen, he will try to paw you, and he arrives on Thursday."

"Uncle Eugen," said Phoebe, fixing the name grimly in her memory. "He would, would he!"

"I may not have to put him next you at table," Rosalind went on anxiously. "Evelyn said he kept trying to get his leg over hers all during dinner last time she was here, but I can't always manage about the table, because in Germany people have to be seated according to precedence or they take offence and complain to Conny. He's in such a good temper today, by the way, and we shall have several more days all to ourselves anyway, before the deluge. I *entreated* him to put them off even a week so that your visit wouldn't be spoilt, and he came over all pompous and Prussian and said he could not ask the Count and Countess von Kittlitztreben to suit their convenience to that of an American miss they had never even heard of. Conny can be very trying in those moods. But on the other hand, he's had Laszlo come and do my portrait—at *great* expense—and it's hung in the grand salon over the mantelpiece and I really look very nice. And he's finally going to let me have my milk dêpot, no matter what Aunt Christa says."

"What milk dêpot?" Phoebe asked, for it had not been mentioned in the letters.

"Oh, just a place where the poorer women can get properly sterilized milk for their children," Rosalind explained. "You see, I do try to take an interest in our people here the way we do in the big houses at home, but it's very different from England, where all the tenants are friends with the family and like to be noticed and inquired into. Here they seem to think you're only interfering, and Conny's relations call it lowering yourself. But the way the poorer classes *live*, Phoebe, such conditions wouldn't be tolerated by *anybody* in England, and the way they have their babies—" Rosalind broke off sharply and her expressive little face grew rigid. Her hand was tense in Phoebe's. "Even the way I have *my* babies," she added under her breath. "I won't do it again, that way. I've told them so. If ever I have another baby it is going to be born in England, where the doctors are human beings."

Before Phoebe could say anything to that, and she didn't know what to say, the motor swung into the great forecourt of the castle and drew up at the foot of the stone steps. Lackeys in red livery smothered in silver lace, with powdered hair and white stockinged calves, ran out to open the doors and deal with Phoebe's luggage. She followed Rosalind up the steps and a man in a cocked hat with a staff in his hand came to attention as they passed him at the door and entered the great hall.

Phoebe received a confused and overpowering impression of a vast gilded ceiling studded with enormous crystal chandeliers, ranks of formal gilt furniture, palms, naked statuary, and mirrors, before Prince Conrad, wearing a lounge suit of grey English tweed, emerged from a door on the left and made her welcome in royal style, with a kiss on her gloved fingers and solicitous inquiries as to the fatigues of her long journey. He then set a possessive hand under Rosalind's chin and kissed her on the mouth and asked if she had had a lonely drive on the way in, and was she satisfied now that her dear friend had come at last—and Phoebe saw that Rosalind's face, upturned to his affectionate, searching gaze by the large, well-kept hand under her chin, was lit by responsive laughter and that her eyes lingered in his with a look of wifely coquetry and acquiescence in his proprietary air. But she *cares* for him, Phoebe thought, bewildered anew. And he's still in love with her. And they're *flirting* with each other before my eyes, as though I wasn't here.

A musical comedy maid in native costume, short bright blue skirts showing a lot of well-filled white stocking, a white apron, and a sheer white cap worn over dark hair in smooth plaits, showed Phoebe to her room and began to unpack her bags. When Phoebe had washed and changed into a soft tea-gown, the maid, whose name was Braga, opened the door on a footman who was waiting to guide the guest to Rosalind's sitting-room, where tea was just coming in.

They were, as Prince Conrad pointed out, temporarily very much *en famille,* but even so there were six around the tea-table, including Lieutenant Cuno von Tiefenfurt and Count Gerzlow, both smiling, attentive young men who were aides to His Highness, and Countess Malvida von Reisicht, the lady-in-waiting to Rosalind, rather a beauty in a buxom way. Aunt Christa was on a visit in Bavaria, which would end next week.

Little Prince Victor came in at the end of the afternoon, accompanied by his English nurse. He was a watchful, self-contained child of five, with his father's melancholy dark eyes and no resemblance to Rosalind in the rest of his baby features. He shook hands gravely all round, gave his mother a kiss by request, and was led away without a backward glance, having performed his daily duty and apparently taken no pleasure in it.

"But surely, Conny, you must have had more *bounce,* when you were that age," Rosalind commented when the door had closed upon her offspring. "They say he's perfectly well, but he's so quiet, and he always makes me feel very young and frivolous."

"Well, and aren't you?" her husband inquired, smiling.

"But isn't it a little *soon* for Victor to start disapproving of me?" she objected.

"It's the Polish blood in him, from my mother," said Prince Conrad complacently. "Very sobering—with a long history of tragedy and fortitude. He will make a fine soldier."

"I suppose so," said Rosalind darkly, and sighed. "If I had had a girl, do you think perhaps she might have been more like me?"

"God forbid!" said His Highness playfully, and pinched her cheek, and the company dispersed to dress for dinner.

Before that very formal meal was finished, Phoebe had become aware of an undercurrent between the Lieutenant and Malvida von Reisicht, noting with not altogether inexperienced eyes the signs of an understanding, if not a full-fledged affair. They made a very handsome couple, both young and *hoch-und-wohlgeboren,* and in a flagrant sort of way attracted to each other. Count Gerzlow, on Phoebe's right, was a sleek, effeminate youth who nevertheless undertook to make eyes at her in an unamusing fashion. Conny himself was all flattering attention to her least remark, and Phoebe felt herself being drawn out, just a bit, by Rosalind's quite natural eagerness to hear her tell of her own life in New York.

They wanted to know how many books she had written, and expressed incredulous surprise at the impressive total, and wondered where she had found the time, for they seemed unable to comprehend that writing books could be a profession and not just something with which to fill in one's leisure. They were astonished that she could give no statistics on the number of copies of each book which had been sold, and smiled indulgently when she explained that she did get royalty statements, yes, but she only looked at the final amount at the bottom and once it was banked forgot it, so long as the balance was on the safe side.

Malvida von Reisicht told a long and rather pointless story about a picturesque Bavarian cousin of hers who had always behaved just like a book, to the scandal of the rest of the family, and suggested that Phoebe might like to write a romance about him. Then Count Gerzlow recalled an incident in his own family history which he thought would look well in print, and Phoebe finally managed to convey to them that she never drew on real life incidents or things in the newspapers for her plots. Whereupon they all stared at her more incredulously than ever and demanded where, then, her books had all come from.

"Out of my head!" she said, with the faint irritation such obtuseness always evoked in her, and Prince Conrad said it was such a pretty head, too, to be so burdened with brains, and they adjourned with laughter to coffee and liqueurs in the drawing-room.

The men came too, for in Germany there was no decent interval, Phoebe discovered, when the ladies were left alone to compose themselves while their dinner partners drew together round the table and told stories over the port and the cigars. In Germany the cigars—and some of the stories—came into the drawing-room and the conversation remained general. She recalled how Rosalind more than once had complained of never being alone—not even in bed, Rosalind had added, during one of her desperate times—and Phoebe began to see how inconvenient so much household etiquette might become. She wondered how Rosalind had contrived to meet the train unattended by Malvida, and deduced from the conversation in the hall on her arrival that there had been some kind of argument about that, in which Rosalind had got her way. She was looking forward to a chance to settle down with Rosalind in private, no chauffeur, no lady-in-waiting, no Prince Conrad, and really chat about old times, and the people they used to know in England—which would of course be impossible with several other people sitting round getting bored because they had no part in such reminiscences, and besides they might draw wrong conclusions on matters which were none of their business anyway.

Before long she asked Rosalind to play. She had often sent over parcels of music from New York, including the scores of Fitz's musical comedies and all the best Victor Herbert songs, and other American compositions, and knew that Rosalind had enjoyed them. Rosalind went at once to the piano and played some Cadman and some MacDowell, while the Lieutenant and Malvida whispered on a sofa by the mantel-piece, and Count Gerzlow gazed sentimentally at the American guest, who ignored him rather pointedly. Just as she was making up her mind to say that the new composers were all very well, but what about Chopin, Phoebe noticed that Prince Conrad had a more than agreeable baritone voice, which was emerging from a mellow hum into the words of the last few bars of *The Land of the Sky Blue Water*, of all things.

"Conny always likes that one," Rosalind commented with a final lingering chord and an affectionate smile in his direction. "Come and sing your speciality, Conny." And she played the first notes of something lively which Phoebe did not at once identify.

In reply he indicated his half-smoked cigar with the ash still intact, and sat where he was, smiling, very much at his ease. But Rosalind grinned back at him, the best of friends, her fingers murmuring on the keys.

"Oh, please do," she said coaxingly. "Just to amuse Phoebe, because it's her first night here and we want her to feel at home, and it's the best of all the things you sing, you know it is."

Still smiling, Prince Conrad rose slowly to his magnificent height and strolled to the piano, near which Phoebe was sitting, so that he looked down at both of them as he leaned on the corner of it—and to Phoebe's amazement obliged with a spirited rendition of the Governor's song in *The Red Mill*—that strutting, genial, autobiographical tune about a man to whom every day was ladies' day, who was at their disposal all the while, whose pleasure it was double if they came to him in trouble, for he always found a way to make them smile . . . and who really should have married, but he never *could* see any fun in wasting all his time on one . . . "so *every* day is ladies' day with *me*. . . ."

Phoebe applauded instinctively, and the others all joined in, and he bowed his acknowledgments, chucked Rosalind lightly under the chin, and returned to his chair with the air of one who had condescended to amuse the children and must not be further imposed upon.

But he's a perfectly delightful man, Phoebe found herself thinking with enthusiasm. He's completely human, and he even has a sense of humor. That is, he was deliberately clowning the song, but without ever losing his presence, and he knew it suited him, too, with all its implications. I believe he's *fun,* Phoebe marvelled inwardly. Rosalind must have *tamed* him, and nobody ever thought she could. I never expected to *like* him . . . but I do. . . .

4

THE next day was hot and sultry. Directly after lunch, when Countess Malvida was looking thoroughly wilted and admitted to a headache, and Conrad had retired to his study with Gerzlow and the Lieutenant, Rosalind suddenly ordered round a carriage to take Phoebe and herself for a drive in the woods, where the wild flowers were in bloom. Malvida was firmly bidden to go and lie down with eau de cologne on her handkerchief, and the other two, both dressed in white with wide hats and parasols, set out together in barely concealed elation.

Rosalind said she still thought a carriage was nicer than a motor car if you just wanted to see things and not to arrive anywhere, and Phoebe, whose life in New York had become almost entirely motorized, agreed with her that an open landau was the last word in comfort and style. "Makes you feel like a queen," Phoebe said as they rolled away from the *Schloss* along one of the swept, curving avenues which led into the deep pine forest. "As though you ought to bow right and left to the populace." And then she realized by a fleeting expression on Rosalind's face that if you were a Serene Highness you did bow right and left to the populace, and there was a pause.

"I thoroughly enjoyed myself last evening," she said then, to break it. "I think your Conny is altogether charming, and not a bit what I expected. He unbent most gracefully, and his voice is excellent."

"He likes you," said Rosalind. "That makes all the difference. He was afraid you might be some kind of bluestocking, and was prepared to loathe you."

"Well, I thought he was a brute, and was fixing to hate him," Phoebe confessed. "Really, Rosalind, you've hardly done him justice all these years, and you never told me he could sing."

"He has to be in the mood," said Rosalind rather briefly. "We're too soon for the wild strawberries, I'm afraid—but you'll still be here when they're ripe, and we have them almost every day. This heat will do wonders, if only we don't get a cold rain to follow."

"But the Gerzlow boy I could do without," Phoebe continued, ignoring the weather, and realized by another fleeting expression on Rosalind's face that one must remember the two liveried men on the box, who might overhear, and the conversation at once became excessively botanical.

By the time they reached the cool depths of the forest where the fragrant boughs nearly met overhead and there was the scent of warm pine needles, Phoebe felt she couldn't stand it any longer and said in a lowered voice, "Can't we get out and walk a little way—so we can talk?"

"There's a place farther on with a bench," Rosalind promised, and when they came to where a tidy path led away to the left, too narrow for the carriage, she spoke to the coachman and they did step down and walk away from the landau, preceded by the footman, who carried cushions which he arranged on a rustic bench which commanded an artificial vista cut through the trees. Rosalind dismissed him and they sat down, Phoebe with a sigh of relief.

"Now, about that Gerzlow lad," she resumed firmly. "I'll stand for just so much from that kind, and he's begun to edge up on me already. The time is coming when I shall box his ears, with your permission, of course."

"Oh, Sigwart doesn't mean any harm," Rosalind assured her with a rather tired smile. "He isn't quite sure yet *what* he is, and he's trying everything on. He's better than the last one we had—*he* fell in love with Conny, and it got so uncomfortable we had to get rid of him, because Conny doesn't care for that sort of thing."

Phoebe blinked.

"Don't any of them ever fall in love with *you?*" she asked.

"One of them did." Rosalind sighed. "What a time *that* was!"

"What happened?"

"Oh, finally Conny had one of his rages and accused *me,* and Felix was too frightened to stand up and say it was all his fault."

"Accused you of what?" Phoebe demanded, frowning.

"Of—encouraging Felix, of course. But in the end Conny was very nice about it. He let Felix go back to Berlin unscathed, and then we got Sigwart. It's hard to say which way he's going to jump. Cuno yon Tiefenfurt, you may have noticed, has got off with Malvida."

"Are they going to be married?"

"Heavens, no, his people would never allow it. Poor Malvida isn't very well provided for."

"They seem to be very fond of each other."

Rosalind shrugged.

"They haven't much else to do," she said. "In Germany people seem to fall in love out of sheer boredom. But it doesn't really count, I always think, unless it happens *in spite* of everything—like you and Oliver."

"Oh, that," said Phoebe ruefully. "What a long time ago it was."

"Have you forgotten him?"

"No."

"Aren't you ever going to fall in love again?"

"I don't know. I've tried. I've *liked* lots of people, but—not quite enough. I suppose I'm a fool not to marry one of them anyway and have some sort of life," she finished with a doubtful glance at Rosalind, who had married someone she hardly liked at all, and it had turned out all right—hadn't it?

But Rosalind made no answer to the opening she had left, and sat poking the ferrule of her parasol into the gravel at her feet.

"Did you know Oliver was at Aldershot now?" she asked at last.

"No. Does that mean he's come back to England for keeps?"

"For quite a while, anyway, I should think. He's got his family there, and Evelyn saw them in London not long ago. She said he looked awfully fit, and Maia was just the same."

"And the child?" Phoebe asked.

"Like Maia, Evelyn said. Exactly. Isn't it a pity? And my Victor is all from Conny's side. I did want a girl, but I don't suppose I shall have another, it was very bad last time. There's something wrong with me, so I can't do it properly. They seem to think it's my fault, because I'm afraid. I don't know how one can *help* being afraid, especially—" She broke off, and Phoebe sat beside her, silent and embarrassed, wishing she had sufficient knowledge and experience to follow Rosalind into these dark mysteries and offer consolation or comparisons. "I'd like to see Oliver again—you can't be dismal long with him around," Rosalind went on after a moment. "I used to be rather like Oliver once, wasn't I?—back in my lighthearted days, I mean."

"My darling—aren't you lighthearted any more?"

"Not always." Rosalind shook her head, and her jaw was set. "I'm losing my grip, I think. Sometimes I get very sorry for myself, and that's a mistake. In fact, it's a crime. After all, I'm very well off here, compared to lots of people I know, and I have everything I could possibly want. Is Charles still at the War Office?"

"He was, the last I heard." Phoebe's eyes were compassionate.

"He must enjoy that. It would suit him. He's like you, he never married, did he?"

"No."

"Do you—think it is still because of me?"

"I do."

"It must be wonderful—to care as much as that about anybody. I never have. I've always envied you the way you feel about Oliver, no matter how hard it's been. If Charles loves me like that, I envy him too. I'll never know what it means now—to be in love that way. Everybody has the right to it—once."

"It's not much fun," Phoebe assured her wryly.

"No, perhaps not. But neither is it any fun to feel so empty—so *passed by*. Why don't you and Charles marry each other—then you'd both have something to go on with."

"Well, for one thing, it might not appeal to Charles," Phoebe tried to say lightly.

"I don't see why not. He must be deadly lonely at the War Office," Rosalind argued seriously. "And you must be lonely too sometimes, aren't you?"

"Deadly."

"Are you sure you won't go on to England now that you've come as far as this?"

"Quite sure."

"Imagine being free as air, the way you are, and choosing deliberately not to go to England," Rosalind said with a sigh.

"Would you like so much to go?"

"I'd give my immortal soul to go."

The words were low and not quite steady. The hands that held the ivory and gold handle of Rosalind's parasol were not quite steady either. Phoebe laid her own quick warm fingers over Rosalind's.

"Honey child—are you still so homesick?"

Under the broad, shady brim of her white hat Rosalind's eyes filled up and spilled over, and the tears rolled down her cheeks unheeded and dripped on the fine lace of her bodice.

"I used to think I'd get over it," she said slowly, with difficulty, trying to control her breathing. "I used to think I'd outgrow it somehow. They told me when I had a baby everything would change and I'd forget I'd ever had any home but this one. I've had two babies—and each time I thought I was going to die—and each time when I *didn't* die I thought maybe it was because I was meant to see England again—someday—not just Oliver or Mamma or Evelyn or Charles—not just the people I used to love and count on there when I was young—it's the *place*, and the way it's run, and the way it thinks, and the things it believes— I'd feel the same if there was nobody left in England who remembered me or cared what became of me. England is a state of mind, not just a country, and in Germany to be English is to be thought mad!"

Her face was shining wet with tears now, but because the bench could be seen from the distant carriage where it waited in the road she kept her head up and dared not use her handkerchief. Phoebe glanced over her shoulder at the two patient figures in cocked hats and polished boots, and rose, pulling Rosalind up with her.

"Let's go on round that bend," she said. "Let's go and sit on the grass and take our hats off and pick wildflowers and behave irresponsibly, as though this was Gloucestershire. Let's pretend they'll all be sitting round the fire at Farthingale when we go back to tea, the way it used to be—Bracken and Cousin Eden and Dinah—they all sent their love, by the way—Virginia, and Oliver, and Archie, let's pretend them all— even Charles, if you like. Speaking of babies, Dinah has started one at last, and is very pleased, though they're worried about her for some reason. It's due in September, so she can't come to England for the Coronation, and Bracken is going to just pop over for a couple of weeks in June. Of course Virginia is insufferable, she's got three now, without batting an eye, apparently. Archie's taking silk, did you know? That means they're prospering financially, I suppose. Does it also mean he'll be *Sir* Archie Campion, K.C.? Oh, *look* at the violets, I never saw anything like it, let's just go and *roll* in them—!"

With her arm around Rosalind's waist, they passed the bend in the path and the carriage was out of sight behind them. Phoebe whipped out her own handkerchief and offered it.

"C-can they see?" Rosalind quavered.

"No. They can't see or hear. Blow."

Rosalind mopped herself gratefully in silence, and Phoebe led her to a bank covered with moss and violets and they sat down. Phoebe took off her hat and threw it on the ground beside her, and after a minute Rosalind did the same.

"Conny hates me to cry," she said shakily. "And he can always tell. It's been months since I've given way like this—years, I think. Maybe it's seeing you again—not that I'm not *glad*—"

"It does take one back, to be together again," Phoebe agreed. She took a little gold powder-box out of her handbag and used the puff carefully on Rosalind's face, which was trustfully upturned to her. "There we are, darling. Now how about a bit of my lipstick?"

"Well, just a touch. So long as Aunt Christa isn't here. When we go to Paris Conny *likes* me to wear make-up."

"And in spite of everything, you do get along pretty well with him, don't you?"

Rosalind glanced at her oddly, around the mirror of the powder-box which she had taken into her own hand.

"I have to," she said, and became absorbed in applying the lipstick.

"But I thought—"

"When I first came to Germany," said Rosalind, and she was able now to speak unemotionally, as though they were discussing someone else, "I was a solid mass of rebellion. I hated everybody and everything. Conny's father died and I couldn't wear my pretty clothes, and I wasn't even allowed to play the piano because the servants would think it wasn't respectful. My lady-in-waiting then was a typical middle-aged *Hofdame* who reported everything I said or did straight back to Aunt Christa, who instantly tattled to Conny. But I've got Aunt Christa to thank, all the same, for my life being possible at all today—and not quite the way you might think! It dawned on me very soon that Conny was all I had in the world, and that he was really in love with me and wanted me to be happy with him. And it was perfectly plain that Aunt Christa was doing everything she could to make him stop being in love with me and be sorry he had married me. Even in those days I was bright enough to see that if ever Conny stopped loving me I might just as well jump out of the nearest window. So I began to fight Aunt Christa for Conny, and that made it fun, and so far I've won!"

"You've kept him in love with you, anyone can see that!" said Phoebe.

"Well, I did have the advantage of Aunt Christa," Rosalind remarked with her wide, disarming smile, a little more knowing now than it used to be. "I was his bride. When Aunt Christa had quite finished pointing out my shortcomings in the drawing-room after dinner, we went upstairs to bed—and then it was my turn."

"To point out Aunt Christa's shortcomings?"

"Nothing so easy as that," said Rosalind sweetly. "I learned how to please him. And it had nothing to do with Aunt Christa!"

"I see," said Phoebe. And belatedly she did.

"Besides—I suddenly stopped being afraid of him, and after that I was all right. I knew where I was. So you might say I've made a career of pleasing Conny, and I've got quite good at it. Because if you've got to live with a man as his wife, it is certainly much easier, to say nothing of gayer, to live with a pleased man than with a disgruntled one. The only trouble is that sometimes it's difficult to predict Conny, because he's only half German, and therefore not simple. The last time I cried, I remember now, was when Evelyn and Mamma went away after their last visit here, and we drove them to Breslau to put them on the train. Coming back with Conny in the motor, I got to thinking of what

Evelyn was going home to—and by comparison my life here at Heiders-dorf suddenly became unbearable and I began to snivel. Conny was marvelous that day, and let me cry all the way home without getting the least bit angry."

"Very kind of him!"

"Well, it was, really, because he hates to see me with pink eyes, and he says it's not very flattering to him that I can still be homesick. He can be very forbearing. And then the next thing you know he comes down on you like a ton of bricks for something much less, like playing the piano when Aunt Christa wants to talk. And that reminds me, I must get it moved into the library before she comes back, there will be less fuss that way. Do you think when we stand up we'll be all green where we've sat down?"

"Do we care?" asked Phoebe negligently, and stretched herself full length on the moss, reaching for the largest and fattest violet in sight.

"Well, we wouldn't have cared once, would we?" said Rosalind, throwing herself down flat too. "Isn't this wonderful, we always used to sit on the grass down by the tennis courts at the Hall, didn't we, and thought nothing of it. Do you know, I haven't had a tennis racquet in my hand since before Victor was born? I couldn't hit a ball now to save my life."

"I never could," said Phoebe, who was not a sportswoman. "But it was pleasant to sit and watch other people trying so hard. I wonder if Charles still plays polo."

"Of course he does, or he wouldn't be Charles."

The next half hour passed in aimless, comfortable chatter while they picked violets, bent over double till their hair-pins began to slide out. Then Rosalind remembered that it was just a little further along that the lilies-of-the-valley began, so they walked on and added lilies to their bouquets, which by now had begun to wilt in the stifling, unseasonable heat.

When they came back to where their hats lay on the mossy bank, their hair had come so loose they couldn't get them on properly again, and strolled along to the carriage carrying them in their hands, and were driven home that way. They arrived just at tea time, rather hot and tousled, but happy in a relaxed, schoolgirl way that neither of them had known in a long time.

Instead of turning into her own bedroom, Phoebe went on down the corridor to Rosalind's to get a book they were discussing. There they found Prince Conrad, who as their absence lengthened had begun to get a bit anxious. Phoebe was aware of Rosalind's English maid, Gibson, retreating discreetly through a further door as His Highness stood staring at them in genuine surprise and concern.

"Have you had an accident?" he demanded then, his eyes going from their uncovered hair to their flushed, shiny faces which needed powder, and their grass-stained, crumpled white dresses.

"No—just a childish afternoon picking flowers in the woods. Look" Rosalind held out to him the bunch of drooping blossoms, but he took no notice of them.

"And you drove back like this in an open carriage?" he exclaimed, and his raking glance missed no detail of their general dishevelment. "You have had the effrontery to return to my house looking like *gipsies,* for anyone to see?"

"But no one did see," Rosalind assured him lightly, casting down her hat on the sofa. "Except the coachman and the groom and a couple of footmen and the man at the door, and you know as well as I do they're all made of wood! Anyway, we've had a perfectly delightful afternoon being young again, and it's done me a world of good, and you like me to be happy, don't you? Smell!" And she raised the fragrant bunch of violets and lilies to his face with a smile of what seemed to Phoebe like calculated impudence.

But it worked. He caught her wrist in his big hand. His eyes were bright and searching on her face, and he seemed about to burst into forgiving laughter.

"Nine years married," he said softly, and his r's had got very German. "And still you can make my heart beat! It is bewitchment." His other arm clipped her round the waist, snatching her to him. "Am I master here—or slave? Answer me that!"

"How can you ask, when you know you'd have my head chopped off tomorrow if I annoyed you?" But she was smiling confidently, she was willing and pliant in his hold.

"You have annoyed me now," said Prince Conrad. "But whatever it is you have been up to, it is very becoming—"

Rosalind's face lifted ever so little—and then she was bent backward like a reed under his kiss. . . .

Phoebe found herself out in the corridor with hot cheeks, closing the door noiselessly behind her. She regained her own room in haste, rather shaken by what she had seen, and began to wash and change her dress for tea. In all the easy, affectionate, family life at home she had never witnessed so frank a demonstration of ownership as the one which had ended the uncomfortable scene in Rosalind's room. And she *dared* him, Phoebe thought fastidiously, splashing cold water on her face. She deliberately *enticed* him, because if she didn't he was going to be cross. She behaved like a—a mistress in a French play, and it *worked*. This whole place is second-rate Sardou, and if I'm not careful I'll be hypnotized into starting a flirtation with that little tick Gerzlow. . . .

When she had cooled off and Braga had helped her into a tea-gown, Phoebe went down to the green drawing-room where tea would presumably appear at the usual hour. She went a little self-consciously, for she felt like a chidden child who has got its playmate into trouble, and she felt also as though she had been peeping at keyholes. She wondered when they realized that she was no longer in the room. . . .

Gerzlow and the Lieutenant and Countess Malvida were assembled in the green drawing-room, and the silver kettle was boiling above its spirit-lamp when Phoebe went in. They waited another twenty minutes, making conscientious conversation on general topics, before their host and hostess appeared, both of them very self-possessed, very unconcerned, behaving as though they were not late at all. Rosalind was wearing the most fragile of chiffon robes, so fresh that it had obviously not even been sat down in. Their attendants, of course, made no allusion to the fact that the usual tea time was an hour gone. It was only Phoebe who was embarrassed.

5

DINNER was enlivened by a discussion between Prince Conrad and Rosalind regarding a musician named Schimmel who had been rescued from poverty by their good offices some time ago and put in the way of making an excellent living as a concert pianist. He was to fulfill an engagement in Breslau before long, and Rosalind wanted to ask him to stay at the *Schloss* as a guest, and play for them there.

"You forget," said Prince Conrad, "that we shall have other guests at that time."

Rosalind said she didn't see what that had to do with Herr Schimmel.

"Then you also forget that the man is part Jew," said Conrad patiently.

Rosalind pointed out that many good musicians were Jews. Mendelssohn, she reminded him, was a Jew.

"Nor would I ask my relations to dine with Mendelssohn," said Prince Conrad coldly, without in the least intending to be funny.

"But surely it doesn't matter what a man is if he can play so magnificently," Rosalind suggested.

"No matter what he does, however magnificently, it matters that he is a Jew," Prince Conrad replied, closing it.

Herr Schimmel was not mentioned again.

Phoebe's impression that she was living in an unproduced manuscript of one of the lesser French dramatists was augmented that evening by the uncalled-for behavior of Cuno von Tiefenfurt, who took root at her elbow in the drawing-room after dinner and began openly to pay her compliments and hang on every word she uttered, springing to light her cigarettes, and generally being a nuisance, while Count Gerzlow glowered ineffectually and Countess Malvida looked hurt and bewildered.

Phoebe's surmise was that the Lieutenant and Malvida had had a quarrel and he was only trying ineptly to irritate his *amie*. Then she became uneasily aware that Prince Conrad had noticed what was going on and chose to be amused. There was no opportunity in so small a group for any two persons to say more than half a dozen words to each other which were not overheard, so Phoebe's impulse to demand of her host that he keep his young men in better order was thwarted. And when in an effort to show the Lieutenant his place she devoted herself to entertaining Conrad exclusively, she was disconcerted to find that he responded with alacrity. So that the evening ended with all three men grouped attentively around Phoebe, while Malvida sat alone on the sofa and Rosalind dreamed melodiously at the piano and appeared to take no notice of any of them.

The difficulty of getting a private word with anybody weighed on Phoebe as she undressed for bed that night in her vast, gold-ceilinged room with the red velvet draperies, the French screens and the Persian carpet. Heidersdorf was not like the big English houses she had stayed in, where everyone wandered around all day as they chose, pairing off here and there and saying what they liked to each other. Talking to Rosalind was always complicated by Malvida's dutiful presence. Talking to Prince Conrad without an audience was apparently unheard-of. If it had been Archie's house, or even the Earl's, she could easily have found an opportunity to corner her host and say, Look here, you've got to call off those two young chumps or I shall be rude to them. An attempt to say the same sort of thing to His Highness looked very complicated, if not impossible.

Besides—Phoebe paused, hair-brush in hand, to gaze accusingly at herself in the mirror—judging by the evening's developments, Prince Conrad was not much better. There was no denying that tonight, under the noses of those two sulky boys and poor Malvida, she and Conrad had struck a spark. The first unexpected, exciting flash between two people who are going to be in some degree attracted to each other was not a new phenomenon to Phoebe any more, nor to him, she was sure. Tonight she had felt his personal magnetism and experience as the young Phoebe in London years ago was too ignorant to do. And his eyes looking into hers had been something more than friendly.

There must be worse fates, after all, she thought while she brushed briskly, than being maried to him. For one thing, one would hardly be bored. But the *nerve* of him, thought Phoebe, brushing. To look at his wife's best friend like that, as if— But of course no Continental is ever supposed to be monogamous, I don't suppose I'm the first. Women must be after him in droves. I wonder how much of that sort of thing Rosalind has had to put up with. Not from me, anyway, and that's flat. We'll see how he reacts to an American woman who knows how to dig in her heels. Beginning tomorrow I ignore him.

Tomorrow was the day Conrad had given his gracious permission for his wife's piano to be moved into the library. Having issued the necessary orders to the proper underlings, he withdrew into his study, signifying that he had no further interest in women's whims, and when the servants had done the job and retired from the room Rosalind and Phoebe and Malvida stood surveying the mammoth misplaced piece of furniture rather blankly. Rosalind touched the keys and said, "I do believe it will be a good room to play in." Malvida said, "Like a concert hall, rather. Dare we draw up a few chairs?"

"Let's make a conversation corner down at this end," Phoebe suggested, for all the furniture sat stiffly around the walls and facing outwards from against the big round center-table, in the German way. "If we brought that sofa and some armchairs into a group near this window it would be a little more homelike."

"Shall I ring for the servants?" asked Malvida.

"The servants would only be in the way," said Rosalind, rising from the piano. "There are three of us. Let's do it without the servants."

"But His Highness—" Malvida began.

"Don't let's *tell* His Highness," said Rosalind, laying hold of an armchair and pushing it across the carpet towards the window. "Perhaps if he doesn't see it till it's all done he will agree that it's an improvement. This room has always been a desert, it's time something was done about it."

For half an hour they pulled and pushed and puffed and enjoyed themselves. When they had finished, a small console table stood in the long west window, with books and flowers on it, and the sofa and several armchairs made a cosy group around it, near enough the piano for conversation with anyone who sat on its bench. Phoebe and Malvida threw themselves down into the chairs with sighs of satisfaction, and Rosalind played Strauss waltzes to them, while the almost forgotten clock ticked on towards lunch time.

Presently the door opened and Prince Conrad came in, pausing to gaze haughtily through his monocle at the rearranged library. The piano fell into guilty silence.

"We—changed things round a bit," Rosalind said.

"You did all this yourselves—without having in the servants to do it for you?" he demanded.

"Yes. It was easier than trying to tell them what we wanted, when we hardly knew ourselves till we experimented."

"Then put it back."

"Oh, Conny, please don't—"

"Put it back the way it was before your—experiment began."

"Don't you like it this way?" Rosalind asked pleasantly.

"It is not a question of what I like. The room can hardly be recognized."

"That's what I hoped," said Rosalind softly.

"The library must look like the library," said Prince Conrad, and he raised his voice. "No one else has seen fit to change it, these many years since I was a child. I will not have my rooms cluttered up like a cottage parlor. Put everything back the way it was. There is not much time before lunch."

Say Please, Phoebe heard herself thinking irreverently, but rather to her surprise this time Rosalind made no effort to coax him out of his bad temper. She said only, "The sofa was very heavy. Will you give us a hand with that?"

"Certainly not," said Conrad flatly. "You have torn the room to pieces without my help. You can therefore restore it to its former aspect, also without calling the servants' attention to such irresponsible meddling with the home of my ancestors. It is only twenty minutes till lunch time."

And he walked out and closed the door behind him with a snap.

For a moment Rosalind stood with her clenched fists resting on the keys and her head down. Then she straightened and met Phoebe's compassionate gaze and her slim shoulders rose in a small, humorous shrug.

"That's the German half of him," she said, and began resolutely to replace the furniture as it had been when they first entered the room.

Malvida looked near to tears, but Phoebe herself was trembling with rage. And only last night she had thought him charming and civilized and—well, civilized.

In silence the three of them pushed and tugged the heavy sofa and chairs into the original formal pattern. Phoebe's cheeks were scarlet, Rosalind was paper-white, Malvida was trying not to sniff. Then they went up stairs to wash their hands before lunch.

Just as Phoebe was about to leave her bedroom again, still molten with anger, there was a timid knock at her door and Rosalind came in and stood waiting while the maid Braga departed.

"I'm sorry you should see him at his worst so soon," she said then, without preface. "You were getting along so nicely, too, I thought last night. Please forgive him."

"*Is* that his worst?" Phoebe asked grimly, and Rosalind glanced at her, and away.

"I don't know but what it is," she said. "But I suppose by now you can guess the rest."

"Which is to say that by the time he's Uncle Eugen's age he'll be wanting to paw people too," Phoebe guessed brutally.

"I don't mean that at all," Rosalind protested honestly. "Conny has very good taste. I'm—always in the best of company. And when it's over he always tells me there is no one like me, after all."

"Rosalind, *really*—!"

"I know, I shouldn't mention it," Rosalind sighed. "But I'd feel such a fool not to, now that it's beginning again, and this time with you."

"Well, you certainly don't suppose it's *going* anywhere, with me!" Phoebe cried, not knowing quite where to look, for last night she had fallen asleep thinking of him, and at breakfast their eyes had struck sparks and his had lingered.

"I should be rather sorry if it did," Rosalind said gently. "Not that it need make any difference between you and me. I've often been quite good friends with people Conny has—had a fancy for. But he breaks so many hearts, always coming back to me. Please don't think I'm bragging, but—he *will* come back to me, you know."

"And you don't want to see my heart broken like the rest?" Phoebe put an arm around the small, straight figure and felt it tense with nerves and embarrassment. "Honey child—time has rolled on. Your friend Phoebe has turned thirty, do you realize that? And in all these years, her heart has been broken only once."

"Oliver," murmured Rosalind against her hair as they stood clasped, their cheeks together.

"Oliver. And anyway, I wouldn't have your Conrad as a gift, if you don't mind my saying so!"

She kissed Rosalind's grave face tenderly, and they went down the stairs with their arms around each other's waists. At luncheon His Highness seemed innocent, or oblivious, of having behaved like a brute, and likewise unaware that Phoebe would not even look at him.

6

WHEN Aunt Christa returned, and the absence of Rosalind's piano from her sitting-room was noticed and explained, Aunt Christa said that anyway it was Rosalind's place to be in the room when there was conversation in it, and not in the library mooning over music.

With the arrival of Conrad's relations, the Heidersdorf ménage went off the British schedule imposed upon it by its English chatelaine, and dinner was in the middle of the day. One did not wear formal dress for the evening meal, for it was remarked that only Englishwomen wore evening gowns as a matter of course every day of their lives, as though it was not in quite good taste. Much more food, and very German food, was served—the peas were cooked in vinegar and grease, and such strange delicacies as eels stewed in beer, carp in wine sauce, goose stuffed with apples, venison basted with sour cream and served with cranberry jam and vinegared beans made their appearance. Afternoon tea became coffee with a spirit kettle and a silver teapot as a sort of afterthought, so that tea as usual was defiantly partaken of by Rosalind and Phoebe, and sometimes, indulgently, as though to lend them countenance, by Prince Conrad.

Phoebe found that her lack of easy conversation German was no drawback, as everybody spoke fluent if somewhat Miltonian English with a strong German accent. Precedence removed her from her host's side at the lengthened dinner table, and dealt her Uncle Eugen as Rosalind had feared, and his behavior seemed likely to develop along the lines Evelyn had complained of. He was a gigantic, pudgy man who ogled Phoebe unmercifully from the beginning and addressed her facetiously as Missy, being under the impression that in America that was a form of pet-name. When he unfolded his napkin at table his wandering hand beneath the cloth sought for Phoebe's garter, and he sniggered joyfully when she gave him a look of outraged incredulity—and in jerking her knees away from Uncle Eugen she bumped them into Cuno von Tiefenfurt's on the other side, and instantly received an answering, sympathetic pressure. In the drawing-room Uncle Eugen still pursued her, professing not to believe that all that so beautiful hair was real, *hein?*

The company had now increased to fourteen, with Uncle Eugen's wife, Aunt Nini, their married son and his wife, their unmarried son aged seventeen, and two nondescript female cousins beginning with *von,* who were travelling with them. When Phoebe attempted to avoid Uncle Eugen she finally found herself in the sheltering proximity of Prince Conrad with unmixed relief. She asked him rather faintly if he would mind opening a window, as she was not accustomed to so much cigar smoke. He gave her a knowing smile like a wink, and turned at once to the heavy brocade curtains behind him, which had been drawn against the cool mountain air.

"Is Uncle Eugen too much for you?" he asked in a colloquial aside as she stood at his elbow waiting for a chance to breathe. "You have made a lasting impression, I see."

"Can't you save me?" she asked, and at the intimate amusement in his glance wished she hadn't and remembered that she was disgusted with him too.

"I thought an American miss was always capable of saving herself," he murmured.

"Now, don't *you* start!" she bade him crossly, and inhaled.

"I may say it, then—your so delightful little name—Phoebe?"

"Yes, of course. And I shall call you Conrad. It would be very silly if we go on being formal, I think."

"Thank you." And he made her a small, ironic bow, with implications.

"I never saw such a country for compliments," she complained. "It's enough to make one quite vain, except I think you do it automatically."

"But we have not always so much cause," he remarked with a gallant smile.

"You're just as bad as the rest of them, aren't you," said Phoebe cruelly. "Not much more subtle, really, than young Cuno. I'm getting most awfully tired of him."

"Then he shall be removed," Conrad assured her at once. "I thought he amused you."

"You thought nothing of the kind, you enjoyed seeing me try to cope with both of them. I warn you, I'll cope with Uncle Eugen in a way you won't like if you don't tone him down some."

Conrad threw back his head and laughed, so that Aunt Christa looked round inquisitively and said something behind her fan to Aunt Nini.

"Behave yourself, you'll have them all down on me," Phoebe said in a savage undertone.

"Oh, they are that already," he told her cheerfully. "In the first place, you are beautiful, foreign, unmarried, famous—you dress expensively, you travel alone, with money in your own right. Well, obviously, you cannot be all that and virtuous too!" He laughed again at her expression of angry, speechless surprise. "But you must not blame the boys too much," he went on. "It is naturally beyond their comprehension that a woman like yourself should be, by choice, without a lover." His look, direct and piercing under lazy lids, gave the word a capital letter. "They are anxious to convey to you that such a sad state of affairs need not continue—indefinitely."

Phoebe looked at him straightly and then said between her teeth, "For two cents I'd scratch your eyes out."

"My dear Phoebe, I hope you have not misunderstood me," he murmured, and she wavered, wondering if she had, and he added unexpectedly, "I have read that new book of yours you brought to Rosalind. And I should like to ask how you know so much about what goes on inside a man's head and heart. It is presumptuous for any woman to be so clever about a man. You have never been married?"

"No. And because you are dying to ask, I have never lived with one either."

His gaze rested on her thoughtfully, encompassing without the need of shifting its focus her shining, brushed brown hair, her sweet, serious eyes, that full lower lip, that young throat, and the slim bare arms in the low cut gown.

"What a waste," he said regretfully.

"Conrad, can you not close the window now?" Aunt Christa's querulous voice came across the room. "It is foolish extravagance to open windows when a fire is burning. The English, of course, prefer to live in a draught, and that is why they have so many weak chests, like King Edward, who died of it. Is it true, do you think, that the new King will be more lenient towards Germany than his father? Nini says that in Berlin there is now some hope that all this nonsense in London about our building a fleet to attack England will cease. Everyone in Germany knows that we must have a fleet to defend ourselves, or even to be a valuable ally to England, yes, in the event of a war."

"A war with whom?" Phoebe asked interestedly, glad of an opportunity to slip into a chair next to Aunt Christa, where she should be comparatively safe from Uncle Eugen's attentions. "Why should there be war in Europe?"

"Why, indeed?" said Aunt Christa with a shrug. "But one hears nothing else these days, and everyone knows that Germany is encircled by hostile nations who fear her as never before."

"Encirclement is becoming a fashionable word in Berlin," Prince Conrad said quietly. "As a matter of fact, Germany has been encircled ever since the Treaty of Verdun a thousand years ago. There is of course always the danger of coalitions, which was Bismarck's nightmare, but I am sure everyone agrees that a European war now would be an unspeakable calamity."

"*Now*, Conrad, without doubt," said Uncle Eugen's married son with unmistakable emphasis. "We are not at present in a position to come out of a fight with—let us say England—as victors. But in two or three years, when our fleet is built, then we can talk seriously to England."

"Say four or five years," said Uncle Eugen judicially. "When our arrangements in Heligoland are completed. Say about 1915."

"I am convinced that England will never attack Germany alone," said Prince Conrad conclusively. "And I do not think she will find allies in such an enterprise. In which case there will be no war."

"And anyway, the British Empire is breaking up," Uncle Eugen's married son assured them comfortingly. "Canada wants to join on to America, as everyone knows—Australia is going to declare her independence, I can promise you—India is seething to be free of British rule—things are brewing up against England all over the world. We have only to wait a bit. Soon we shall have nothing to fear from that quarter. They have no notion of administering colonies, and their economic system at home is childish—just one long bungle."

"Like their cooking," nodded Aunt Nini. "They have for a sweet a thing called gooseberry fool—ugh!—it is a good name!" She cackled delightedly at her joke. "Nothing they eat is not a fool!"

"When were you in England last?" asked Phoebe politely.

"Never!" said Aunt Nini with a sweeping-away gesture. "I would not go to England, there is nothing to see there."

"If England has so many shortcomings one wonders how it ever came to be a nation at all," Phoebe remarked recklessly, aware that Rosalind had warned her and was even now trying to catch her eye, and not caring.

"England has arrived where she is by seizing unlawfully everything she could get her hands on," said Uncle Eugen petulantly. "Now it is going to be our turn."

"To do the same?" Phoebe asked at once.

"To become great and powerful and rich," said Uncle Eugen, though he would have denied in the next breath that England was any of those things. "No young miss from America, however pretty, can have any idea of such matters. All you know of England is the hunting balls and the shops in Bond Street, *hein?*" He rumbled with his unctuous chuckle, bending towards her to shake a playful finger. "And the flirtations, *hein?* How about young Cuno, here,—have you seen in the English Army anything finer than our German lieutenants, Missy, answer me that one! No doubt you and Cuno have already much in common, *hein?* Ah, but if I were only Cuno's age, then you would have to watch out!"

"Eugen," said Aunt Nini, but without real reproof, seeming rather pleased than not that her husband was causing the American miss some embarrassment. "And will you be in Germany long, Fräulein?" she added to Phoebe somewhat pointedly.

"Not long now," said Phoebe with sweet obtuseness. "I have an aunt at Cannes, and I expect to go on there."

"It will be the wrong time of year for Cannes," Aunt Nini objected patronizingly. "It will be hot."

"I'm a southerner," Phoebe told her. "I like heat."

"Summer is the time to visit our German spas," Aunt Nini said. "And you should see our winters. You do not have such winters in America! Snow—you never saw such snow! And you should but witness a German Christmas—such toys—such music—such cooking—"

"I should like very much to have a Christmas here," Phoebe agreed, seizing a safer topic. "Perhaps sometime I can come again at Christmas time and see Rosalind handing out gifts to the school children—how many people was it you shook hands with once, Rosalind, and all of them belonging to the estate? You wrote the most fascinating letter, I remember, all about the reception down in the riding-school, and the children singing carols and the tree—and then how you had your own private English Christmas in your own rooms afterwards, with crackers and plum pudding from London, and your maid and the Scottish gardener's family in to share it."

There was suddenly an awful silence. Rosalind sat motionless, looking down at her clasped hands in her lap, while every eye in the room came to rest on her. Phoebe realized too late that she must have given something away, and glanced appealingly at Conrad. The look he gave her was remote, inscrutable, almost expressionless. She wondered if even Conrad had known about the English Christmas in Rosalind's rooms, with only a few homesick servants to share it.

"When was this, Rosalind?" Aunt Christa asked when the silence had lasted long enough.

"Oh, years ago," Rosalind said hastily, and it was impossible to explain to Aunt Christa that it was the year when Conny was spending all his time with the Grand Duchess Franziska and took no interest in how his wife spent hers, waiting for Victor to be born. "Conny said I might if I liked. He wasn't there."

"Why was I not told?" Aunt Christa demanded.

"I don't remember. Perhaps I thought you wouldn't be interested. It was so long ago the gardener's children who came to pull crackers that night are quite grown up now and have probably forgotten all about it."

"But it seems to me a very curious thing to do," persisted Aunt Christa offendedly. "To entertain the servants privately, behind my back, in your husband's home."

"I wasn't plotting to overthrow the Kingdom of Prussia, Aunt Christa," Rosalind said, goaded out of her better judgment. "It was just that I had hoped to go home that Christmas and it proved to be—inconvenient. So I—"

"*Home,* your home is *here,* how many times must I tell you, Rosalind, her husband's home is the only one a married woman has to call her own?" thundered Aunt Christa. "Always you speak of England as though you had left it last week, and for a visit only. You have a German husband, lucky for you, and a German son, and consequently a German *home*. England you have finished with, and England is finished, you will see! Give thanks that you live here in Germany where the future of the world will be born—for your children to inherit."

Again there was the silence, and they all seemed to be waiting for something, their eyes boring into the slim figure of Conrad's wife, who sat very still looking down at her hands in her lap. Again Phoebe stole a glance at Conrad, but his gaze was fixed on the ash of his cigar, poised in a steady, well-kept hand. A little muscle twitched rhythmically in his cheek, indicating suppressed anger—with whom? When the silence had become quite unbearable—

"Yes, Aunt Christa," said Rosalind, very low, without moving.

" 'Yes, Aunt Christa!' " mimicked that implacable woman, red and angry and restless in her chair. "Lip service! And behind my back— drinking champagne with gardeners and ladies' maids! What will our own servants think? What an example to set to Conrad's children!"

"Victor wasn't born!" cried Rosalind, and bit her lip.

"Or doubtless his English nursemaid would also have been invited to drink Conrad's champagne!" Aunt Christa took it up. "Our honest German nurse-girls are not good enough for the children of *die Engländerin!* We must have one over from London, in a fancy cap, who will raise us up milksops to play cricket—"

"*Quatsch!*" said Prince Conrad suddenly, and it was the first and last time Phoebe ever heard him use a German word in conversation.

Every head in the room turned to him as with that stupendous rudeness he rose and strolled easily, but with purpose, to his wife's chair and paused behind it, one hand resting lightly on its back, as he faced his astonished relations.

"I myself had an English nurse, as you know very well, as did Cuno, and the Emperor himself, for that matter," he continued with a parade ground rasp in his usually quiet voice. "Are *we* milksops? Do *we* play cricket? It is good for languages. And it is good for manners." He ran a cold, critical eye over Uncle Eugen's unmarried son, who was certainly not notable for grace of manner. "When Victor is told to do a thing, he obeys already like a soldier—thanks to that Englishwoman in a fancy cap, whose name is actually Smith. The English know how to bring up children. They do not know how to train an army, but their nurseries know discipline. With us, it is the other way around. Victor will have the advantage of both, and will do us all credit by the time he is commissioned—eh, Aunt Christa?"

"Yes, Conrad," said Aunt Christa meekly, and Aunt Nini nodded grave agreement with the head of the family who had just slapped them all down hard, as it was his place to do, and they adored him for it. And Uncle Eugen's unmarried son squirmed in his chair and grinned self-consciously under his father's considering eye.

Above Rosalind's head Prince Conrad glanced at Phoebe and if she read his look correctly it had a sardonic triumph, as though to say, You thought I wasn't going to stop them, didn't you.

7

EARLY June in the forest at Heidersdorf was indescribably lovely, but there was no childish gathering of wild strawberries by Phoebe and Rosalind. They viewed the beauty of the tidy pine woods and mountain lake sedately from a carriage driven along the endless avenues which wound through thirty square miles of private park—and the strawberries, small and pink and sweet, came to the dinner table in meringues, smothered in rich whipped cream.

Each time Phoebe mentioned Cannes and Aunt Sally, Rosalind implored her to stay just a few days longer, and the visit of what they privately called Uncle Eugen's travelling circus went on and on. Because of Cuno's now flagrant attentions to Phoebe, Malvida had taken to looking heartbroken and reproachful. Because of Uncle Eugen's uninhibited reactions to so much free, unmarried attractiveness and so much spirit too, Aunt Nini had inquired more than once about Phoebe's aunt in Cannes, whom she plainly by now regarded as apocryphal—and Conrad was more than once shaken by heartless internal mirth when Phoebe was forced to retreat almost, as it were, into his arms for protection from his ebullient relative. Even Uncle Eugen's married son had begun to show signs of taking notice, and his wife in revenge ignored Phoebe as far as possible, and looked at her with sidelong, spiteful, measuring glances, as though trying to see what Phoebe had that she lacked herself, she being years younger as anyone could tell.

Between Phoebe and Prince Conrad there existed a strange, unexpressed camaraderie, based on their instinctive understanding of each other, in which there was no room for illusions. He knew, beyond a doubt, that he would get nowhere with her now. She knew, with a watchful certainty, that he was always willing to try. Unfortunately to be kept at arm's length by so clever an opponent in the game as Phoebe was a new experience for His Highness, and he enjoyed it as he enjoyed all trials of skill—and even to look at from a respectful distance Phoebe was charming and added spice to his days.

During the first week in June Prince Conrad was summoned to Berlin by the Emperor, and the family awaited his return in a state of unsuppressible excitement. Aunt Christa prophesied that it would be the Order of the Black Eagle, with diamonds. Uncle Eugen, for unexplained reasons of his own, thought it was something to do with the autumn maneuvers, at which aeroplanes fitted with guns were going to be tried. Malvida, from some unguarded remark of Cuno's as he prepared to accompany His Highness, was convinced that at last it was war. And Rosalind confessed privately to Phoebe that she hoped it might be the offer of a diplomatic post—perhaps as Ambassador to Vienna—though of course Conny was still young for an Embassy. . . .

He returned a few days later, just at tea time, and followed by his uniformed aides came straight into the green drawing-room where the family was assembled. Very mysterious, very much at his leisure, he kissed his womenfolk all round, made Phoebe a rather special bow and a much more perfunctory one to Malvida, accepted a cup of tea from his wife's hand, and sat down with it, surrounded by an expectant silence.

"*Ach,* Conrad, how you tease!" cried Aunt Christa. "What did the All-Highest say to you? Have you nothing to show us?"

"To show you? What an idea!" said Conrad, playing up to her and sipping his tea, which he drank very hot instead of allowing it to cool first like the cautious British.

"Perhaps the interview was secret and confidential," Uncle Eugen suggested, full of meaning. "Our new weapons of war are not subjects to be bandied about the drawing-room by gossiping women, *hein,* Conrad?"

"I am not on the Imperial Staff," Conrad reminded him goodnaturedly, lifting his cup again. "Not yet, anyway."

Rosalind had been sitting with her hands locked in her lap, watching her husband's face. Now she leaned forward and said, very low, "Are you being sent somewhere on a mission?"

In exaggerated, humorous surprise, he returned his cup to its saucer with a clink and stared at her.

"They will burn you for a witch some day," he said. "How did you guess?"

"Where?" said Rosalind tensely, sitting motionless.

"Your clairvoyance doesn't tell you that as well?"

She shook her head mutely, her hands pressed together in her lap.

"Guess," he said, setting down his cup and taking a cigarette from the crested gold cigarette case he carried.

"Vienna?" said Rosalind, barely audible, and he smiled and blew out the match, and the rest of them sat watching this small intimate drama as though at a play.

"Rome," said Rosalind, with a sort of unwilling conviction, and then something in his face lit an incredulous hope in hers. "Oh, Conny, not—not—" She seemed unable to go on.

"I go to London for the Coronation," he told her, smiling.

"Conny!" Rosalind was out of her chair and bending over him, her small, trembling hands clutching his massive shoulders. "Conny, is it true? You're not joking—you're not—fooling me—?"

"It would be a pointless sort of joke, wouldn't it, to say I was going to London for the Coronation and then set out for Constantinople?"

"*London!*" cried Rosalind, and it was a hallelujah. She swung round to Phoebe, her arms outflung, her slim body in its clinging tea-gown seeming to vibrate and shimmer with joy. "Phoebe, do you hear? *London—at last*—oh, won't you change your mind about it now and come too?"

"But Conrad has said nothing about taking you to London with him," said Aunt Christa sulkily, for it was not the Black Eagle after all.

Rosalind turned back to her husband as though wilting in mid-flight. Her face went white in an instant, leaving her eyes wide and dark, her hands dropped to her sides.

"Conny—?" she whispered, and waited like a disciplined child who dares not be importunate for fear of failure.

"Victor is just getting over his cold," said Aunt Christa, her voice like a heavy hand imposing silence. "I do not understand how you can be so heartless, Rosalind, as to go dancing off to a foreign crowning and leave a sick child behind you. Everyone knows how delicate Victor is."

Rosalind gave no glance in her direction, but stood rooted, with her eyes fixed on Conrad, looking frightened and childish, and almost without hope. Her words came faintly, but with a rush.

"But, Conny, he's not ill any more, the doctor says he is recovered, and he goes out again—and—there's nothing I can do here even when he is ill, Smith won't let me go near him—he doesn't *want* me, I sometimes think, he's used to Smith, he'd rather have her, I'm sure—"

Conrad had risen and come towards her while she spoke, and he set his hand under her chin in the usual possessive way.

"Is this place then such a prison to you?" he asked gravely, with his habitual arrogant faculty of ignoring the existence of spectators.

"Oh, no, Conny, *no,* this place is—is my home," said Rosalind, remembered her duty with pathetic haste. "But it has been such a long time since I saw England—I—I—" Her lips trembled, and Phoebe could see the working of her slender throat as she tried to swallow. "—I would like a holiday there," she managed to say almost voicelessly, "—with you."

"I was not a week away in Berlin," said Conrad, looking down at her while the smoke from the cigarette in his other hand curled up around their heads, "and I was more bored than I can be in a month at home. For my own sake, I must take you with me, wherever I go." He pinched her chin as a caress, and there before them all she caught the big hand in both hers and pressed her lips to it in a gesture of abject gratitude and affection that opened Uncle Eugen's eyes and caused his son's wife to look down her nose, while Aunt Christa said *Tsck-Tsck,* and Phoebe went hot and cold with embarrassment that a woman could be so brought to her knees by a man who professed to love her.

When Phoebe still declined to consider going to London she thought she saw a gleam in Prince Conrad's eye which said that she did not dare because of him. And she wondered now and then, with a passing chagrin, if her obstinate insistence on Cannes might not look to him like the better part of valor, and assured herself that it was nothing of the kind, and that she had no use for him whatever and would not touch him with a barge-pole.

Nothing short of a command from the All-Highest would have made it decent for Conrad and his wife to leave Heidersdorf during a family visit like Uncle Eugen's, but it was necessary for them to start for London at once. By a small miracle of diplomacy, it had been arranged that the Crown Prince and Princess of Germany should represent the Kaiser at the Coronation, though Wilhelm had visited England earlier in the year for the unveiling of the memorial to his grandmother in front of Buckingham Palace, and King George had succeeded very well as his host. The German Embassy was of course packed out with the Crown Prince's entourage, and Rosalind and Conrad were to stay at one of the big ducal houses in Park Lane until they had time to formulate their own program.

Unlike the special envoys to the ceremony, Prince Conrad seemed to have no time limit on his stay in England, and assured Rosalind easily that she would have plenty of opportunity to see her friends and make visits at Farthingale and the Hall if she liked. I wonder what it means, Phoebe found herself thinking. I wonder why he's been sent. I wonder . . . what Bracken would say. . . .

She was to travel with them in their special train as far as Paris, and there she would turn southward towards Cannes while they took the Calais route to England. But it was with an oddly fatalistic feeling, almost without shock, that on the day before their departure from Heidersdorf she received a cable from New York: *Dinah seriously ill. Have cancelled sailing. Please go to London in my place send me Coronation story, that's a good girl. Name your price, I'll double it. Love.* BRACKEN.

Still with an absence of surprise that she could not account for, Phoebe showed the cable to Rosalind and accepted her enthusiastic invitation to accompany them all the way to London. Then she cabled Bracken: *Am on my way. Give love to Dinah. Address me care Virginia.* PHOEBE. Even while she wrote it, she entertained again the teasing query— Why was Conrad sent to London now? What would Bracken give to know? What would Bracken do to find out? How could she find out . . . for Bracken? . . .

She wrote out telegrams to Aunt Sally at Cannes, postponing her visit there, and to Virginia at Farthingale asking to be put up. And when that was done, she sat soberly at the writing-desk in her bedroom at Heidersdorf contemplating the unforeseen workings of Providence. Finally she went to stand in front of a mirror, searching her own image with anxious eyes. If Oliver was stationed at Aldershot it was no good saying she might not see him. She would. And how would she look to him, after these nine years? It was no good saying it didn't matter now. It did.

PART SIX

CHARLES

London.   *Summer, 1911.*

➤➤➤

1

THERE was no time for Phoebe and Rosalind to shop for new clothes in Paris on the way to London. Prince Conrad's special train was routed straight through to Calais and they were to go on from there by the turbine, which was said by Conrad in his zealous care for their comfort to be steadier than the Flushing or Ostend boats.

But Phoebe had bought a gay wardrobe in New York for her visit to Germany and the Riviera, and it was so long since Rosalind had been to London that everything she had was as good as new there. Judging by the mountains of luggage which accumulated in her apartments as her maids packed, she was adequately equipped anyway for a Coronation Season. There was even a *jupe-culotte,* which she had got from Paris at Easter time to enliven her convalescence—a delicious tea-gown variation of the debated harem skirt, in soft blue satin veiled with a beaded ninon tunic, so high-waisted and low-cut that the bodice was hardly more than a jewelled *ceinture* around the breast, and the skirt was subtly bifurcated with intricate drapery into trousers below the tunic. She was not allowed to wear it at Heidersdorf except when she and Conny were absolutely alone—but he was much diverted by it and inspired to call her his little blue-eyed houri from paradise, and to recollect sentimentally that he had always admired her in trousers. Rosalind intended to wear her *jupe-culotte* in English country houses, where she hoped it would cause a mild sensation and testify to the broadmindedness of her dignified Serene Highness husband.

They arrived in England during Ascot Week, and Archie himself

197

came down to Dover to collect Phoebe, while Prince Conrad and Rosalind were ceremoniously met by their ducal host's representative and
escorted to a reserved compartment in the London train. Phoebe was
gratified that Archie had got a reserved compartment of his own, so
that on the way up to Town she could ask questions and hear all the
family news.

He and Virginia had taken a furnished house in South Audley Street
for the Season, and the children were there too. He had booked a table
for Cup Night at the Savoy, and Phoebe was sure to see everyone there
that she used to know. Edward and Winifred had opened the St. James's
Square house and were giving a ball a few nights after the Coronation.
Their son Hubert was at a preparatory school for Eton now, as was his
cousin Lionel Flood, and each of them would soon be joined there by
a younger brother. Clare was determined that her next child, which had
ruined her Season by promising to appear in August, would be a girl,
and Clare usually got her way about things, Archie said, so the stork
had better watch out. Winifred had been heard to remark that it was
a mercy she herself was not expecting now, as it might have prevented
her from taking her rightful place as Countess of Enstone in the Abbey
at the Coronation, and putting on her coronet along with the other
peeresses as the Queen was crowned.

When they reached South Audley Street, where Virginia was awaiting
them, Phoebe was taken almost at once to the nursery, and was duly
impressed and enchanted by what she found there. Virginia had done
everything in the best possible style, producing her own counterpart in
dark, slim Daphne, now nine years old, while Irene who was seven had
red-gold curls like her Aunt Dinah, and Nigel, at two, was beginning
to look just like Archie and would doubtless, said Phoebe, be called to
the Bar in due course.

From Virginia, when Archie had tactfully withdrawn and left them
to gossip the night away, Phoebe learned that Dinah in New York
had lost her baby but was out of danger now. It wasn't just that she
was so small, she seemed to have injured herself some time ago, perhaps
with so much riding, and there had been anxiety from the beginning.
The doctors were saying now that side-saddles were very bad for one,
and a great many women were learning to ride astride, which Virginia
thought must be very uncomfortable, and besides, how would one look
from behind?

It was the most extraordinary thing, Virginia continued, but Clare was actually getting on with Mortimer Flood, and she didn't deserve to, either, for everyone knew she had only married him for his money. But he was kind, and well-meaning, and devoted to the children, and made money hand over fist, and Clare had her own motor car and a personal fortune in jewels and dressed at Lanvin and Worth, which was a good thing because she was putting on weight and losing her looks—

"Which you certainly have not done," Phoebe put in at this point, for Virginia was still slender though she had bloomed and ripened into more pronounced beauty than she had had as a girl.

"Nor have you," said Virginia promptly. "I like your hair done that way, wrapped round your head. Do you think mine would go up like that? Can you do it yourself?"

"Yes, I'll show you tomorrow. I've been thinking how we've changed, though—it's partly the styles. When I was here before our skirts trailed on the ground—it was a prettier line than now, don't you think—belts are so high we can't have any waistlines at all, and we're supposed to look smaller at the feet than at the hips. Rosalind has a blue *jupe-culotte* from Paris—so marvelously made you can't be sure the skirt *is* divided, but it is! She says it makes Conny laugh."

"Do you remember the cakewalk?" said Virginia dreamily.

"Don't I! That was the start of all the trouble for Rosalind!"

"Is there trouble? I knew there would be! What's he like, really?"

"He's only half German," said Phoebe, trying to be fair. "But sometimes that's more than enough! And his family—!" She gave a short, graphic account of life at the *Schloss*, at which Virginia crowed with heartless laughter until she finally broke off to say, "How does she *stand* it? But she must see how funny it is!"

"She does, most of the time, I think," Phoebe said. "But it isn't funny, you know, to have to live with it."

"Why on earth doesn't she come home oftener and get a breather?" Virginia asked in her innocence, and Phoebe said darkly, "That's where the German half of him comes out."

"You mean he won't *let* her?" Virginia cried incredulously. "But he promised!"

"She says he admits now he would have promised anything to get her."

"Why, the low-down, lyin', yellow hound-dawg!" cried Virginia furiously, and Phoebe nodded.

"He is, and then some. But—he can be very fascinating."

Virginia sniffed, and looked at her suspiciously.

"You haven't been flirting with Rosalind's husband!" she accused.

"No, indeed, I've spent my time trying to prevent him from flirting with me!"

"Is he *that* kind too?"

"Very much that kind. And jealous along with it. If I had to choose, I think I'd rather be Clare."

"We all said at the time, if only Rosalind would marry an Englishman!" Virginia sighed, and this brought them to Charles Laverham, who was still at the War Office.

Thus, roundabout, they reached Oliver at Aldershot—and then it was Virginia's turn again.

"Some day, somebody is going to lay hold of Maia and bang her head against the wall till her eyes and teeth fall out," said Virginia. "It might even be me. But never Oliver, poor lamb!"

Phoebe felt her stomach contract suddenly around a cold lump of lead, and said uncertainly, "As bad as that?"

"What we really ought to do," Virginia went on, "is to maroon His Serene Highness and Maia Campion on a desert island somewhere and let them get on with it together. Talk about jealous! Phoebe, I give you my word, I have seen her go and deliberately sit down between Oliver and some woman he was talking to on a sofa and ask what they found so absorbing to discuss! She calls him to heel in a room full of people, as though he was a bird-dog. Sometimes he doesn't come at once, and then she goes home without him and doesn't send the motor back. I've heard her make remarks in the worst possible taste before other people about his dinner partner or someone he was legitimately dancing with. I've seen her look at him like an assassin when he had merely made his manners to his hostess. I've heard her jeer at what she calls his conquests, and name names. I'm warning you, Phoebe, if you give any indication that you knew him years ago or were fond of him you'll have an embarrassing scene on your hands!"

"But, g-good heavens, does he have to put up with it?" Phoebe asked after a stunned silence.

"I think he's tried everything he knows," Virginia said. "He doesn't talk to me about it, of course, and I shouldn't dare to bring it up. But the last time they stayed with us Archie did try to get at him privately about the way Maia behaved, and Oliver admitted he was at his wits' end and said that it was really a sort of madness with her, and swore he had never given her any sort of cause. He says it first began to get really bad out in India after the baby died, and Maia imagined that she couldn't hold him, as she calls it, if she hadn't got a child. But now they've got Hermione, who is a *brat* if I ever saw one, and things are no better, and it's become impossible to ignore. I wouldn't have mentioned it except I know you and Oliver were great friends once," said Virginia tactfully, "and you must be warned for your own sake, to save unpleasantness."

"Oh, horrors," Phoebe said miserably. "Maybe we won't meet at all, I shan't be in London long."

"But they are coming up for Winifred's ball on the twenty-sixth."

"Oh. Well, I needn't dance with him, I suppose."

"It might be better if you didn't," Virginia agreed. "He does dance with people, of course, he gives in to her just as little as possible, but you're laying yourself open to spiteful remarks from her if you do, and he might let fly back at her if she ever got her knife into you—"

"Oh, how *awful*," Phoebe moaned. "Apart from Maia, how is he?"

"Much the same. She can't get him down, nothing can. You would never know to look at him that he wasn't ideally married and not a care in the world. Except around the eyes. They're a little tired."

There was a pause, while Phoebe sat trying not to wring her hands over Oliver or otherwise insult his bright spirit by pitying him, and Virginia tried not to watch Phoebe's telltale face, and finally said, "He worships the child—and she's going to look just like Maia, and screams with rage if she doesn't get what she wants. No Nannie on earth can cope with it, because Maia is always interfering and bribing Hermione with sweets instead of relying on any sort of discipline. I know, I know, everything I say makes it worse, but it's just a mess, Phoebe, and you had to know!" And then Virginia added, not altogether irrelevantly, "How's Miles?"

"All right, I reckon," said Phoebe, her mind not on Miles. "He's got a job at the College in Williamsburg now, and is living at Cousin Sue's house."

"That's nice for both of them, isn't it. Tell me about Gwen's babies."

"I haven't seen them, I'm afraid. Cousin Sue says Rhoda has Gwen's brown eyes, and the baby is fair, like Fitz. Belle's twins are eighteen, doesn't that make you think? And Marietta's Audrey is fourteen!"

"Good Lord!" said Virginia, appalled. "She was born the year I came out! Do you ever hear from Johnny Malone?"

"Sometimes. He's still at Madrid. He says there's going to be a war."

"Where?"

"In Europe. The Balkans first, according to Johnny."

"Oh, Bracken's been bleating about the Balkans ever since I can re-member!" cried Virginia impatiently. "Suppose the Balkans do have a war, it won't touch England!"

"The big countries might jump in," said Phoebe without much con-viction. "They call it Spheres of Influence, and the Balance of Power. Russia can't let Austria come too close on the west, and France would back up Russia, and Germany would help Austria—and so on."

"Who has England got to help?" Virginia asked skeptically.

"France, I should think. Certainly not Germany. What does Charles say about it now?"

"Charles has gone potty about aeroplanes. He wants the British Army to have whole fleets of them, mounted with guns, as though they were ships. To *fight* with, mind you! When it's all they can do to stay up!"

"It's a beastly idea, isn't it," said Phoebe with a shiver. "Well, at least I'll dare to talk to Charles about old times, he hasn't got a wife to shoo me off! Will he be at Winifred's ball?"

"Sure to be. But you'll see him tomorrow night at the Savoy. Lady Shadwell is bringing a party."

"Is she still *alive?*"

"Very much alive. She has promised Daphne to present her at Court along about 1918, and Daphne is practicing already."

2

Cup Night at the Savoy was perhaps the smartest, gayest evening of the London Season, and this was a Coronation Year. Everybody was wearing their best, drinking champagne with supper, greeting friends, talking horses.

Charles was there in Lady Shadwell's party, looking scrubbed and brushed and Army in his evening black and white—a little heavier in build and a little less tanned than Phoebe remembered him—but very fit. He came across to Archie's table and took both Phoebe's hands and said, "Welcome to London," and "You look beautiful," with such sin-cerity that she found herself clinging to him after the handshaking was over and begging him for a chance to *talk.* "Come and have lunch," said Charles at once, as though he had not a calendar full of appointments at the War Office.

"Yes, please," said Phoebe with undisguised eagerness.

"How about Monday?" said Charles.

"Yes, please," said Phoebe.

"One o'clock at the Ritz," said Charles.

"Thank you," said Phoebe. "Have you seen Rosalind?"

"Not yet. Am I safe to go and say Hello, do you think?"

"Do it anyhow," said Phoebe.

"Right you are. Monday. God bless." Charles moved on down the room, towering, serene.

There was a stir at the Duke's table as the men all rose when Charles paused there, and the host greeted him affectionately as "my boy" and Prince Conrad offered his hand in a friendly clasp. "Hello, Charles," said Rosalind, and Charles said, "Hello, nice to see you back in London. Going to be here long?"

"Until after the Twelfth, anyway," the Duke answered for her, and this was news to Rosalind. "They'll be coming up to my place in Scotland then, I hope."

"Indeed, yes," Prince Conrad assured them, smiling. "I look forward to some Scottish shooting again, and have brought my guns."

"Oh, good," said Charles. "Time enough to see something of you, then. How does it look to you hereabouts?" His eyes came back to Rosalind. "Pretty much the same?"

"It looks like heaven to me!" she said, laughing up at him. "I had no idea how homesick I was!"

"Mustn't forget all about us, you know," said Charles easily, and those were the last words he addressed to her that evening.

"Such a nice man," the Duchess remarked when he had returned to Lady Shadwell's table. "High time he married, though. Is that Selma Gluckston on his right? Would she do, do you think?"

"Usen't the name to be Glückstein?" asked a brittle little woman seated next to the Duke, who replied with dignified reproof, "Perhaps it was, my dear Lily, but her father makes much the best motor car England has yet succeeded in turning out."

"Well, she *is* quite pretty," conceded the rebuked one amiably. "This is the third time in a month I've seen her with Charles, which is pretty drastic for him, isn't it, he usually plays the field, rather."

"But surely she is a Jewess?" remarked Prince Conrad in surprise.

"Surely his people would raise objections to so unsuitable a connection?"

There was a longish pause. Then the Duke said obtusely, "Oh, you mean because of the motor cars. We are becoming very broadminded in England about families in trade, you know, nowadays. Have to be. That's where all the money is, what?"

"I should like to see Charles settled," said the Duchess smoothly and with nothing but kindliness in her tone, before His Highness could explain that he had not been referring to motor cars. "He would make some woman a good husband. I suppose it might as well be Selma, and no doubt she's willing enough!"

"Steady on!" said the Duke genially. "You might leave Charles something to say about it!"

"I'm afraid I shall have to, my dear," his wife replied in all good humor, and the subject was adroitly changed.

But by then Rosalind's hands were cold and unsteady, for one of them had lain briefly in Charles's big warm grip, and she was thinking, Thank God they've all forgotten, if they ever knew—and so has Charles —so has Charles—and she *is* a very pretty girl. . . .

At the Ritz on Monday Charles and Phoebe began with harmless gossip about who had got married or engaged or fallen out of love since last she was in London, and whose sisters and daughters were coming out this year, and whether Phoebe would see the Coronation Procession best from Archie's seats on the island in Parliament Square or from the War Office seats near Admiralty Arch, and what were the prospects for Goodwood—and then Charles said, turning a glass of Chablis in his big fingers, "I suppose you know that Oliver is pretty well done for."

Again Phoebe's insides went into a cold lump.

"How do you mean?" she asked faintly.

"Now don't try to put on a show, my girl, I know all about it. Years ago, when you and Rosalind both left England in the same week, Oliver and I had to sweat it out together."

"You knew about my letter—afterwards?"

"Yes, even that. You *were* a blazing idiot, weren't you!"

"Well, if it's any comfort to you, I've paid for it ever since."

"*You've* paid for it!" said Charles with rude scorn. "What about Oliver, married to a she-basilisk who has damaged his chances of promotion by her vicious tongue, and made him a social liability in half the houses in London!"

"Oh, Charles, it can't be as bad as that! Virginia said Maia was terribly jealous, but I can't—can't believe—"

"You'll find out," Charles promised with an awful sort of satisfaction.

"Would it be better if I arranged not to see him at all?"

"I suppose he could bear that too," said Charles bitterly. "It's about all that's left for him to come up against. And by now he ought to be used to the idea that you're a coward."

"*Charles!*" It was an incredulous yelp of pain.

"Forgive me for being frank," said Charles with irony.

"I suppose you mean it will make it easier for him if he sees me again now," she suggested coldly, and Charles grinned.

"Not in the sense that you aren't still a very desirable young woman," he admitted. "But to know you are in London and not to see you at all—" He shook his head. "I can only judge by myself, of course."

"Were those few minutes at the Savoy with Rosalind really any good to you?"

"You write books about people, don't you?" said Charles. "It's your business to know things like that, I thought."

She swallowed that meekly, and said, "Virginia thought I'd better try not to dance with him at Winifred's ball."

"Nonsense," said Charles.

"She said Maia might make one of her scenes."

"Let her," said Charles. "He'd have got the dance."

Phoebe lifted candid, troubled eyes.

"Worth it, you think?"

"Stop fishing," said Charles. "You're more beautiful and more disturbing than you were ten years ago. He's got the right to make what he can of that. God knows his pleasures are few enough these days. But you're not to pity him, you know. He isn't sorry for himself."

"He was so *gay*," Phoebe said softly, looking back. "That's what I remember best about him. He always made you feel gay too. It was just something inside him that *lifted*."

"He's still got it." Charles refilled her glass, and his own, and Phoebe raised hers, looking at him directly over the top of it.

"Do you want to hear about Heidersdorf now?"

"May I?" he asked in his gentle voice, and his eyes were unabashed and honest.

So Phoebe told him, with brutal simplicity, and he listened almost without comment, and without too obviously neglecting his food, for

Charles never did anything that was obvious, especially since he belonged to the War Office. None of it was really surprising to him, for he had spent most of his holidays during the past nine years travelling in Germany, and had made a point of learning to understand the nuances of the language, which he now spoke fluently, and his observation of the German character had prepared him for most of what he heard from Phoebe. He had always been careful to travel as an inconspicuous Englishman with an interest in picturesque ruins and spectacular views and quaint villages. He had avoided the diplomatic circles in Berlin and the big princely houses and the international set. Instead, he took rooms in odd, inexpensive places, and conversed respectfully with local authorities and bigwigs who condescended to him, and he asked polite questions and never argued with the answers, for fear of drying up the subject before he had learned all he could.

At first it was just a sort of hobby with him, a labor of love, a rather pitiful effort to acquaint himself with Rosalind's new surroundings and see for himself what she was up against. Then one day in London he had talked too much to a man at the club—an unusual thing for Charles, but it was raining and he was lonely—and soon he was sent for by his superiors, who asked him if he would care to go in for it seriously, now that he had started. Charles pricked up his ears. And that was how Captain, now Major, Laverham, V.C., Royal Horse Guards (Blue), seconded to duty at the War Office, became attached as it were in his spare time to Intelligence.

So he listened attentively, but without surprise, to what Phoebe had to say about life at the *Schloss,* recognizing in her a keen observer and a good reporter, waiting patiently for her to tell him without prompting the things he wanted to know. And finally she asked him the question he was expecting.

"Charles, what's all this about a war?"

"I'm afraid it's got to come," he sighed, and Phoebe stared at him.

"But those are Conny's very words!" she gasped. "How can you all just sit round *saying* that? Can't you get busy and stop it?"

"Does he want it stopped?" said Charles.

"Yes, I think he does," Phoebe said consideringly. "I think he's sorry. But he's the only one I saw in Germany that I could say that of."

Charles nodded.

"And he isn't sorry enough to do anything about it," he remarked. "But aren't *you?*"

"We in England can't stop it," said Charles. "We can only batten down and prepare to ride it out."

"You hear a lot about submarines in Germany," Phoebe told him. "Could they really sink a battleship?"

"They never have," said Charles cheerfully. "But then, we must remember that they've never tried, mustn't we! It's our fleet that worries Berlin, of course, so they dream of something that can destroy it. Personally, I think the real trouble in any future war would come from the air."

"Malvida said once," Phoebe recalled suddenly, "that Cuno said that Zeppelins could cross the Channel to London carrying bombs."

"Easily," said Charles.

"And when I said that sounded as though the fighting would be in England, which was nonsense, she *closed up,* as though she might have given something away, which I thought was queer, because usually they brag."

"Very interesting," said Charles. "And did you hear anything about guns mounted on aeroplanes?"

"Yes, I did, once. In connection with the autumn maneuvers. Are they really going to try that?"

"Oddly enough, it works." At this point Charles paused to give minute attention to the menu the waiter handed him for the choosing of a sweet. When that was disposed of—

"And I heard something about balloon-destroying guns carried on motor cars," said Phoebe, raking her memory. "Are they new?"

"They are if they can keep up with an aeroplane going at forty-five miles an hour," said Charles.

"You mean shoot down an aeroplane from the ground like a *pheasant?*"

"While it does its best at the same time to drop a bomb on you," he nodded.

"Charles, what kind of world is it going to be? I'm getting frightened. No country could survive a three-dimensional war like that! It would be wiped out in no time. There's no defence!"

"That's what they said when gunpowder was invented to replace the bow and arrow. Thick castle walls and slits out of which to pour boiling oil suddenly became obsolete—and there was no defence against the terrible cannon ball. But nobody's been wiped out yet." He grinned reassuringly and offered her a silver plate of little iced cakes. "We are

witnessing the birth of a new era—the air age. Try one of these, anyway.
You're all right, so long as the Atlantic doesn't dry up!"

"But I don't want to be all right if England isn't!" said Phoebe, realizing it with dismay. "If anything happens to England I want to be here.
I'll come back and fight too."

"It's still a man's army, my dear, thanks all the same."

"I could nurse. My grandmother Louise was a nurse in Richmond all
through the worst of it in 'sixty-four."

"And did she carry life-and-death messages in her hoop and save the
city?" he asked lightly.

"That was Cousin Eden," said Phoebe without smiling. "And it was
morphine she carried in her hoop, for the wounded. And the city was
taken."

Charles looked up at her from his coffee in astonishment, for some of
the tragedy and fortitude of the Confederacy were in the simple words.
Phoebe had grown up on the defeated side of that long war, where the
bitter knowledge formed part of her heritage. We didn't win—we lost—
we were beaten. Old wounds had not healed in the South. Poverty and
sorrow and humiliation lay at the back of Phoebe's childhood, because
they had lost. Beautiful Great-aunt Felicity had died in Richmond of
the fever—Great-uncle Ransom had had to go on without her, and without his livelihood, and his savings—Cousin Barry, another legend to
Phoebe, had been killed at seventeen—Cousin Dabney, who was one of
the idols of her early youth, had lost a leg—Father himself had been
long disabled by a Yankee sabre-stroke in the shoulder—Farthingale
plantation had burned to the ground but Great-uncle Lafe always loved
to tell of its great days when he was a boy—but Richmond was taken—
all that gallant effort and sacrifice, all that agony willingly endured—but
they had lost. . . .

"I'm sorry," said Charles gently. "It seems so long ago and far away.
But not to you, I realize that. Careless of me."

"England always wins her wars," Phoebe rallied. "Except one."

"Except one," he agreed, and they laughed together over Yorktown,
Virginia, 1781.

Phoebe felt a rush of tenderness for Charles, who was such a lamb,
and who knew so much more about everything, she was sure, then he let
on. Since Bracken was not there, and Oliver was denied to her, she decided to confide in Charles.

"Does it seem to you at all mysterious, the way Conny was sent all-of-a-sudden to the Coronation?" she asked, and with satisfaction felt his full attention swing alertly into focus.

"Was it sudden?" he said only, and she told him how the apparently unexpected summons to Berlin had come in the midst of a sacred family visit, and how abruptly a departure for England had ensued, and how unrestricted as to time and whereabouts His Highness appeared to be, now that he had arrived, for he was prepared to stay all summer while Rosalind saw her old friends and enjoyed herself.

Charles seemed to be waiting for her to go on.

"Well, that's all," she finished rather lamely. "But it did occur to me the last night at the *Schloss* that it was exactly the kind of thing that always brings Bracken's ears up. Do you think—by any chance—he's in the Secret Service?"

"Bracken?" Charles asked stupidly.

"No. *Conny.* Charles, you weren't listening!"

"I was listening very hard indeed." Charles studied her a moment, as though making up his mind about something. "My ears are up too, hadn't you noticed?"

"Will you help me, then?"

"To do what?" said Charles exasperatingly, his eyes on her face.

"To find out what he's up to—for Bracken."

"If he is up to something, Bracken is the last man I want to tell," said Charles.

"Because he's the Press? But so am I."

"Then I won't help you a bit," said Charles.

"But *why?*" she demanded.

"Now, look here, my dear, I don't say there's anything in all this," said Charles, very matter-of-fact. "But if there is—and you can shake Germans out of your pockets when you go to bed at night nowadays— if the blighter was sent here to Nosy Parker round amongst his wife's connections and take advantage of their hospitality, it is very important that he shouldn't be frightened off. Not yet, anyway. So just pretend not to notice anything, whatever happens, and don't go about warning people, will you!"

"But—"

"Please don't mention this to another soul. Promise?"

"But, Charles—"

"There's a man at the Home Office—I'll tip him off if you like."

"What good will that do?"

"They'll watch him. In a quiet way. If they think best."

"But if he hears people saying the kind of thing you've been saying about—about aeroplanes, and things—"

"Oh, he'll hear a lot of that, I expect."

"Wouldn't it be better if he didn't?"

"We might even hear something back," Charles suggested. "If the conversation were steered the right way, I mean. If he were encouraged to bait his trap."

Phoebe's eyes sparkled.

"Oh, Charles—*espionage!*"

"Shut up, will you, and don't talk nonsense!" said Charles crossly. "They'll probably laugh at me at the Home Office, but I'll give them the chance. Don't go and spoil it all by wagging your tongue, now!"

Phoebe promised, and soon Charles paid the bill and they left the Ritz, and he put her in a taxi for South Audley Street. She looked back and saw him turn away unhurriedly down Piccadilly. He had never batted an eye, of course. But there had been just that one electric instant when she had felt his riveted attention before he said, "Was it sudden?" And after that, his *excessive* stupidity. . . .

As the cab crept through the traffic towards Berkeley Square, Phoebe gazed blindly out of the window, wrapped in speculation—just what did Charles *do* at the War Office? A further query, still dim, still hardly articulated, was being born at the back of her consciousness—by her novelist's imagination out of her feminine intuition, as the stud-book would say— Suppose Conny was a secret agent—suppose Charles was his opposite number. . . .

3

By EIGHT o'clock on the morning of Coronation Day Phoebe had taken her place with Archie and Virginia in the stands which rose in Parliament Square facing the Abbey. Edward and Winifred had gone to their seats in the transepts even earlier, robed in crimson velvet and ermine and carrying their coronets. Conrad and Rosalind would arrive in the First Procession, which consisted of Royal guests and their suites.

It was the leaden sort of June day which England sometimes inflicts on a hardened population, and a cold wind fluttered the flags on the roof tops and tossed the garlands between the white Venetian masts along the route. Scarlet-coated soldiers were already lining the streets, with a good-humored crowd packed behind them. There was a spatter of rain around nine o'clock, and then the sun looked out—but it had gone away again before the three-minute gun sounded in the distance. Virginia hugged the upstanding chinchilla collar of her coat closer and shivered, and Phoebe was glad of the long fox stole and muff which she had decided at the last minute to wear over a cloth suit instead of the thin embroidered linen she had intended.

As Big Ben struck the half hour they heard the first gun of the salute, which meant that Rosalind was leaving Buckingham Palace in a State coach with her husband, following the Crown Prince and Princess of Germany. Phoebe's mind went back to the other Coronation, before any of this had happened and the world was young. Charles was the one in the Procession that time—and Rosalind had been with the rest of them at the window in St. James's Street—they had argued about which Guardsman was Charles, but Rosalind knew without his being pointed out to her—today Charles was sitting beside Selma Gluckston in the stands the other side of Admiralty Arch, Oliver was with Maia in the same stands, and Rosalind was a foreign Royalty. Only Archie and Virginia and herself were the same, and Phoebe's eyes rested on her companions fondly, as the guns boomed. Virginia turned, and read her thoughts. "Last time we had her safe with us," she said.

The braided trumpeters came into view, followed by the Life Guards on their black chargers. Then came the Guards' band, with its flourishing drummers, and the glittering string of State coaches, each with white-breeched, scarlet-coated postillions and footmen, the horses pacing proudly—Phoebe's eyes filled with quick, childish tears—it was so solemn, and yet so gay, and so beautiful—and they were all so much older and wiser and sadder than they had been when King Edward was crowned. . . . The coach which was said to contain the Prince and Princess Conrad zu Polkwitz-Heidersdorf passed in a gilded blur.

The Second Procession brought the Royal Family in State landaus, and the Princes and Princesses of the Blood Royal—smiling, fairhaired children in gala robes and ermine. The crowd cheered and waved and wept with affection and sentiment.

Then after another dull, chilly wait, and with a detachment of the Blues *en cuirassier* to lead it, came the King's Procession—more State coaches followed by the gorgeous East Indian Orderly Officers, mounted, the aides-de-camp and the Commanders-in-Chief and the Field Marshals with their crimson batons, the equerries and the escorts of Colonial and Indian cavalry—and finally the Royal coach itself drawn by eight cream-colored Hanoverian horses with braided manes and purple trappings—Lord Kitchener rode just behind it and beside the Royal Standard and was loudly cheered—then more equerries and more cavalry. . . .

Phoebe stood spellbound and choking till the soldiers lining the curbs fell out and the stands twinkled and shifted with movement as people rose to stretch and search out sandwiches and chocolate to make the best of a two-hour wait. Archie produced a flask of brandy like a conjuror. They thanked him devoutly and Phoebe began to scribble notes on a pad on her knee for Bracken.

Later, in a mighty anti-climax she pieced together from Winifred and Rosalind the scene inside the Abbey—how a shaft of sunlight shone through the clerestory and touched the gold plate on the altar—how the peeresses' gallery had glowed and glittered with crimson velvet and jewels and ermine and tiaras—how the unseen choir-boys' voices soared —how the Regalia was brought to the High Altar in solemn procession and then carried to meet the King at the West Door—the spine-tingling fanfare of trumpets heralding the Royal entrance—the King's grave dignity and the Queen's grace and beauty, and the touching moment when the young Prince approached his father and knelt to recite the oath in a voice still treble. . . . *I, Edward, Prince of Wales, do become your liege man of life and limb and of earthly worship; and faith and truth I will bear unto you, to live and die* . . . and the thoughts of all who heard him went back affectionately to his grandfather, and ahead prayerfully, for this was the future Edward VIII . . . and the King, visibly moved, set a fatherly hand beneath his son's chin when he received the kiss of fealty on his cheek. . . .

Once the Coronation story was finished and filed by cable and Bracken's enthusiastic acceptance came back, Phoebe's thoughts began to dwell anxiously on the night of the ball in St. James's Square, where she and Oliver would meet again, as old friends, with half their world looking on. By lunch time of the day itself she had stage-fright in the last degree and could not eat. Oliver and Maia were staying with Clare in Belgrave Square, and so without being obvious there was no opportunity to level off the worst of it by catching a glimpse of him before the ball began.

Phoebe dressed that evening in a state of grim calm, fumbling at things with cold fingers, furious and frantic with her own insurgent nervous system over which her will power had no control. Like Virginia, she had never suffered from the shyness so many girls must somehow live through and conquer, and tonight was worse than any début, and she did not know what to make of herself as she stood shaking in front of a long mirror in her room waiting for the motor to be announced.

As she had remarked to Virginia, a woman's whole outline had changed since Oliver saw her last. They had worn pompadours then. Now her chestnut hair was parted and dipped on her broad brow, with the ends wrapped widely around her head and held in place apparently only by a large jewelled pin either side. Her gown was of champagne-colored charmeuse, veiled to the knees with a chiffon tunic embroidered in gold sequins and cut in long points at the sides weighted with heavy gold tassels. The skirt fell from so high a waistline, and the square-cut neckline was so low that the bodice was largely a golden girdle and the sleeves were mere chiffon incidents without even a sprinkling of sequins to give them substance. Her eyes were dark with excitement, her cheeks were hot, and her mouth, with its full lower lip, was brightened with carmine. He might get a surprise when he saw her—but he could hardly be disappointed.

She wondered if her heart would come up through the roof of her mouth at sight of him, and how she could ever surrender to him so clammy a hand. I *will not* behave like this, she told herself futilely, I'm as wobbly as though I was coming down with something—maybe it's influenza and not Oliver at all. Things would have been bad enough tonight if he had had a normally happy marriage with a chance to become philosophical over what had seemed so tragic to them both nearly ten years ago. But it was impossible in the circumstances to tell oneself firmly that that was all over and done with. Maia had not taken the one road to make him forget his lost love—to lull him with kindness and affection and tact into comfortable domestic habit. Maia's fantastic behavior had left ample room in his life for the cherishing of an old ideal. And Maia's watchful presence would make every word and glance between them a hazard.

It has been said that in order to appreciate a woman's beauty you must behold her descending a staircase, and that is how Oliver's eager gaze first found Phoebe at Winifred's ball. She came down slowly, seeming very much at her ease, and chatting to Virginia at her side, who was wearing Nile green with a short tunic edged with marabou, and a green bandeau in her dark hair. A waltz was being played in the ballroom beyond, and above the laughter and music you could hear the lisp of dancing feet.

Oliver stood at the bottom of the stairs looking up and waiting for them to discover him, which did not happen till they were almost on top of him. Virginia saw his face as Phoebe's glance met his, and she told Archie later that she nearly burst into tears on the spot, so defenceless it looked, so young and shining with perilous happiness. But there wasn't time to cry, said Virginia, because she was so busy looking for Maia to head her off, and finally discovered her dancing with Charles, and asked herself rhetorically what they would ever do without him, and how on earth he had contrived to hoick Maia out on to the dance floor at exactly the right moment.

Silently Oliver held out his white-gloved right hand to Phoebe, and silently she laid hers in it. She came down the last step and stood level with him, looking up, her hand still in his. Composure had descended suddenly upon her, and she was thinking very clearly, she was sure, and her heart wasn't beating too fast any more, and her knees weren't shaking, and there was nothing to be nervous about at all, for Oliver was not disappointed and he had not changed. . . . The only trouble was that she had completely, between one breath and the next, forgotten Maia.

"I have been trying all day to think what I would say to you now," Oliver said.

"That will do as well as anything," she smiled.

"Not very brilliant, was it! But you always did take my breath away. When did I waltz with you last? Don't tell me. It was only a week ago."

Still composed, with the perfect equilibrium of the butler who has just finished off the champagne in the pantry, Phoebe crossed the open space between them and the dance floor and went into his arms.

"It's a new tune, though," she said dreamily. "*The Merry Widow.* Did you see it?"

"Three times. Have you seen the one at Daly's now?"

"*The Count of Luxembourg.* No, not yet."

"Let's go," said Oliver. "I'll make up a party. You must see Lily Elsie in the staircase waltz."

Maia returned to Phoebe's consciousness like an avenging goddess in a blaze of thunder and lightning, and she missed a step. What *had* they done? Where *was* Maia?

"Sorry," said Oliver, taking the blame for the break in their rhythm.

"My fault," said Phoebe. "I—just woke up."

He gave her a slanting look full of comprehension and said, "You've changed your hair."

"Don't you like it?"

"Very much. But I have to readjust my ideas." He studied it intimately as they danced. "How do you make it stay up?"

"Will power," said Phoebe, and they laughed foolishly, like children on a lark. With Oliver you were always wittier than you had ever suspected. Oliver still had something inside him that lifted and lilted like the violins. . . .

"Love that hovers over lovers speaks in song,
And the fingers' clasp that lingers close and long,
And the music answers swaying to and fro,
Telling you it's true, it's true. . . ."

"Oh, how *good* it is to be with you again!" she said impulsively, and his arm tightened as they made a swinging, exultant turn at the edge of the floor, and she felt his breath on her cheek.

"May I see you?" he murmured under the music.

"How?" she said hopelessly. "Where?"

"I don't know. No harm in asking. Couldn't we have lunch or tea somewhere?"

"Alone? We'd be seen. Somebody would run and tell her."

"Probably. Would you mind?"

"I was thinking of you, mostly."

"Oh, I'm used to it, you know," he said without rancor.

"Is she here tonight?"

"Dancing with Charles just now." He nodded across the floor and turned so that Phoebe looked that way.

Charles was not hard to spot. The woman in his arms was slender and danced easily. Her dark hair was parted and piled into heavy coils high at the back of her head, with a silver filet across it. Her eyes were long and narrow and set at an upward angle. Her skin was sallow and thick, and her mouth was small and would have been the better for a touch of rouge. But the whole effect of her, at that distance, was one of great elegance amounting to beauty.

"She's charming," Phoebe said hastily.

"She can be," said Oliver without much expression, and added in a deliberately impersonal tone, "She likes Charles. Makes it awkward, because I know he's never been able to stick her."

"He seems to be getting along all right."

"Oh, yes, they learn manners in the Guards! As a matter of fact, he timed this rather well, didn't he," Oliver remarked, amused, and laughed when her eyes came back to him in surprise. "Good old Charles!" he said. "He wasn't born yesterday!"

There was an edge to the laugh and the tone which had not been there once. Phoebe plunged.

"Oliver, is it as bad as Virginia says?"

"Knowing Virginia, probably not. But it's not very good, all the same."

"I'm so sorry," she whispered.

"Well, I tried," he said ruefully, and the music stopped. "Come and be introduced."

Maia and Charles saw them, and stood waiting at the side of the room. Reptilian, thought Phoebe involuntarily, with her dreadful facility for the right word, as she met Maia's direct look—her eyes are like a lizard's.

But Maia's lips were smiling, as she acknowledged the introduction.

"Oh, you are the one who writes books. I've heard a great deal about you from Oliver's family." Her voice was thin and pinched like her mouth, with artificial vowels. "I always thought it was odd we didn't meet the last time you were in England."

"I wasn't here long," Phoebe said casually. "You were off in the country somewhere, I think."

"With my poor father," Maia nodded. "Just think, we were convinced he was dying then, and now he's being very hearty and enjoying life with his second wife!"

"That's good," said Phoebe, and suspected that Oliver's lips twitched, and fought for safe footing on very brittle ice. "I think people ought to marry again if they're lonely, don't you?"

"It's rather an odd thing to say, when you haven't married even once yourself," said Maia with a measuring glance which questioned Phoebe's spinsterhood. "The next dance is ours, Oliver. Could you find me a glass of water before it starts?" She laid her hand on his arm, but Oliver stood like a rock.

"Are you all booked up?" he asked Phoebe. "How about an extra later on?"

She promised him the last extra before supper, and he walked away with Maia, smiling back over his shoulder.

"See what I mean?" said Charles grimly. "Let's sit this one out and recover, or is someone going to take you away from me?"

"It's Archie," she said, glancing at her card.

"Oh, good. Let's find him *and* the punch!"

Which they did, amongst mutual congratulations that it had been no worse. "Wait," said Archie darkly, when he heard about the extra.

"But she *looks* all right," Phoebe insisted as the three of them sat together under a potted palm on what Archie had hailed as the mourners' bench. "Surely you're all dreaming. There's nothing wrong with her."

"Oh, we don't say she goes for him with the carving-knife," said Archie, being fair, and then he frowned. "All the same, the seed of madness is there," he muttered.

"Archie, don't be *gruesome!*" cried Phoebe in horror.

"Well, dash it all, he's my brother. It's a nasty thing to have going on in the family."

Virginia sailed up then with Lady Shadwell's nephew, who would be the Earl of Nutfield one day, and who doted on Americans, according to Virginia, so Phoebe had to find him a dance, and the mourners' bench broke up.

The evening fled away and Phoebe was surrounded and the more she saw of Maia in her silver filet and white crêpe de chine gown sewn with silver bugles, dancing and chatting with other men besides Oliver, the harder it became for Phoebe to believe that there were women in London who preferred not to risk a dance with Oliver, and who begged their hostesses not to put him next to them at dinner for fear of Maia's tongue —and the surer she became that somebody was dreaming.

When the supper time extra came round, Oliver appeared at her side looking as though he hadn't a care in the world, and led her away to where the noble staircase curved upward, red-carpeted and lined with potted flowering plants and palms, and dotted with chatting couples who were sitting out.

"These cosy little cushions on the stairs must mean that Winifred has got Rosa Lewis in charge of the party," he remarked settling Phoebe under a palm out of hearing of the next pair. "Which also means that supper will be superb." He sat down beside her with a sigh of happy accomplishment. "Now. When can I see you?"

"I suppose we could always go back to the Tate," she said, only half in earnest, and he laughed.

"I could lead you round it blindfold," he said.

"Oh, Oliver, have you really been there again?" Her eyelids stung with tears.

"Again and again! I told you I would. They have got some rather nice additions since the time we saw it together."

"I suppose I *could* meet you there—feeling awfully guilty and clandestine," she said uncertainly.

"And enjoying it, rather?"

"No." She shook her head. "Not the clandestine part. It doesn't go with you. I'd rather flaunt you!"

"I believe you would, too," he said, as though such a thing as a woman proud to show that she was in love was a new idea to him. "Well, I've only got tomorrow, this trip. Three o'clock?"

"Yes. If you're sure it's all right."

"Quite sure," he smiled, and she saw that he must have kept some sort of life of his own—the club—the War Office—the bachelor chambers of people like Charles—where Maia could not intrude.

They were still sitting on the little cushions on the stairs and Phoebe was promising to go to Egypt some day and think of him, for he was always in love with the desert, when they became aware that the music had stopped and Charles was mounting the stairs towards them.

"Supper," he announced. "Hurry up, old boy, Maia's just sitting down and you're being paged."

Oliver went lightly down the steps with no visible ill-humor at the summons, and Phoebe followed with Charles to Virginia's table. Along about the third dance after supper, when Phoebe was just setting out with Edward on a one-step, she was surprised to find Oliver at their elbows.

"Be a good chap, and let me have this one," he said, and Edward surrendered his partner with a look which washed his hands of the consequences. They danced it almost in silence, and she was very much aware of Oliver's guiding arm and the way his breath came and went, and the crisp perfection, even at the end of the evening, of his white shirt-front and tie, while Oliver decided that it was lilacs she smelled of.

The music ended when they were near the door to the staircase hall and they drifted out, away from the dance floor, her right hand still in his left. Maia had just reached the bottom of the stairs, wrapped in a silver brocade and ermine cloak which set off her dark hair but made her untouched-up skin muddy and dull.

Oliver went straight up to her.

"I didn't know you were ready to go," he said. "I'll get my coat."

"Please don't trouble," Maia said, her face a mask of composed fury. "The motor is waiting to take me home." She turned to pass him, and he laid his hand on the fur over her arm.

"I won't be a sec," he said, and ran up the stairs.

She did not glance his way. Her eyes rested on Phoebe, who stood helplessly where Oliver had left her, unable even to attempt to escape now that the thing had begun to happen just as they all said it would.

"Perhaps you will see fit eventually to return my impressionable husband to me, Miss Sprague," Maia said, and her thin voice carried in the silence the music had left, as people filtered out into the hall to change partners and find places to sit out the next dance. "You may tell him that the motor has gone. I see no necessity to keep the chauffeur hanging about all night while Oliver amuses himself."

"Oh, Lord, here we go again," murmured Archie at Phoebe's side, but Maia left it at that and swept past them towards the door.

"Damn," said Phoebe without heat. "Oh, damn and blast. I was going to be so careful."

4

THEY spent an hour or more at the Tate the following afternoon, most of the time sitting on a bench and talking absorbedly of what had happened to them in the years between. When he returned to England from foreign service Oliver had collected all of Phoebe's books and read them hungrily, distilling out of them what he could of her growing, changing personality, wondering anew in his soldier's way at her minute and embarrassing knowledge of what went on inside people, and at the easy, amusing way the people she wrote about conversed together, just as you could hear people anywhere in a room only a little better, he would tell himself in perpetual astonishment that she could do it. At the same time he received from Virginia a very decided impression of success.

Now Phoebe sketched in some of the gaps for him, not consciously holding back anything, and came to the Coronation offer from the women's magazine and how she had refused it, she thought with wisdom, and gone firmly to Germany instead, and how Providence in the shape of Bracken in New York had caught up with her at Heidersdorf. When she told about what it was like at the *Schloss* he listened attentively but without Charles's pinpoint concentration. And if Phoebe did most of the talking it was because there was so much behind Oliver that would not bear talking about, and most of it was expressed in the way his body leaned to her as they sat on the hard oak bench, the way his eyes clung to her face, the way he listened and made her go on.

Phoebe watched him lovingly as she talked, and thought how little he had changed, though his eyes showed weariness as Virginia had said, and his dark hair was streaked with grey at the edges. And she thought, He's nearly forty—half his life gone, and I have had so little of it. She thought, What is it about this one man that holds me fast to him forever? And his quick laughter answered her, responding to something she hardly knew she had said, and his brilliant eyes caressing her face as he listened, and the lean, alert look of him on the hard bench, and the curve of his upper lip beneath the clipped mustache. . . . He was Oliver. He was good to be with, he was fun to talk to, he knew what she meant, he thought she was funny and beautiful and desirable, he made her feel like a queen. He was the only one she loved, because he had something inside him none of the others had—something quick and tender and acute, something light and keen and perceptive, something kind and uncritical and cradling, that closed round her like arms, and lifted. Oh, *Oliver* . . .

Then it was time for them to go. Oliver looked at his watch and glanced round the deserted gallery, from which even the attendant in a peaked cap had for the moment receded. She had taken off her gloves while they sat there, and now she began to put them on again. Oliver caught her left hand and held it to his lips—she felt them move against her fingers, and the prick of his mustache.

"There aren't words to say what it's meant to me today," he said quietly, "or how glad I am that things are going well with you."

"They aren't, particularly," she confessed, looking at him through hot, sudden tears. "Not in any way that matters much."

"My dear, you must make some kind of life—I suppose I should tell you to forget me."

"I've tried," she told him with trembling lips.

"You must try again."

She shook her head, looking down at her gloves, and bright tears fell on them as she tugged them into place.

"But, Phoebe, you were made for life, not a nunnery!"

"I don't exactly live in a nunnery in New York—I have friends, I—

even get proposed to sometimes. If I always say No, that's my own look-out." On a final effort she conquered her tears and looked him in the face with a rather twisted smile. "We're all going down to Farthingale with Virginia after Goodwood. Shall I see you there?"

"Oh, yes. I shall be at the Hall sometime in August."

"Once more, then, before I go home."

"Once more, anyway. This isn't good-bye."

They rose. He was going to be late for tea in Belgrave Square.

5

SUSSEX WEEK was hot and they all wore their prettiest dresses, and then everyone retired to houses in the country with expressions of relief.

Rosalind and Prince Conrad went to visit her sister Evelyn in Surrey, and then to Dorset, from where Rosalind wrote to ask if they might come to Farthingale a little later than they had planned, as they were now invited to visit a famous house near Oxford which Conny was anxious to see and they had to get it in before the grouse shooting began.

Virginia puckered up her brows, because that would bring them there the same week that Charles and the Chetwynds were coming, and while it wouldn't have mattered if they lapped over a day or two, and there was plenty of room, and it would be rather like old times again—she did wonder just a bit how Prince Conrad would fit in for the whole week. Then she thought of Selma Gluckston, of whom she did not approve and who was never invited to Farthingale, and wondered just how deeply Charles was getting involved with Selma, and if it mightn't be a good idea to cure him once and for all, just in case. And taking care not to consult Archie until it was too late, Virginia wrote back to Rosalind urging them to come just when it was most convenient, and not mentioning who else would be there the same week.

Archie when he finally heard about it advised her that she would rue the day. "No doubt," said Virginia unrepentantly, "but it will cook Selma's goose! He can't possibly make do with her after he's had another good look at Rosalind." Archie said that was Interference, and should be punishable by hanging.

The first few days of that dubious week went exceedingly well, and everyone was charmed with Prince Conrad's affability and good manners, and certain political and international subjects were prudently avoided in general conversation. To everyone's relief, Conrad seemed almost to seek out Charles Laverham's company rather than to resent his presence there, and Charles's attitude towards Rosalind was of course the last word in casual friendship casually renewed. If Conrad had ever been jealous of Charles there was no sign of it now, and Virginia, who would never have admitted to Archie that she had had her own misgivings, began to breathe easier.

Oliver and Maia were not at the Hall that week, but Clare and Mortimer had come down to await the birth of Clare's third child in her old home, and Mortimer accompanied Edward and Winifred when they drove over to Farthingale for dinner one night. It was dear old silly-ass Mortimer who put his foot in it up to the elbow, Archie told Virginia later that evening when he was trying to explain to her how on earth he had allowed the subject of a possible future war to get started in his own gun-room after dinner. Archie indignantly denied her brutal accusation that he had dozed off and let the thing get out of hand. He had merely turned his back for a minute, he said, to pour himself a whiskey and soda, and when he turned round again there was Mortimer saying something about putting your money into oil shares because the next war would be fought with petrol.

"You mean aeroplanes and that sort of thing?" suggested Tommy Chetwynd skeptically. "Charles here is always saying that we shall be bombed from the air in the next war, and I don't mind telling you it gives me the creeps, rather. We shall all have to live underground, or something. Beastly uncomfortable, what?"

"I was talking to a feller in the club last week," said Mortimer, oblivious of the fact that Archie was trying to catch his eye, "who said that we should have German dirigibles over London in no time if we got mixed up in another war." Then he realized, belatedly, the presence of Prince Conrad, and refusing to be disconcerted put him a straight question. "Does that sound to you like nonsense or not?" he demanded frankly.

"No. But first—why German, and why over London?" Conrad asked quietly. "Everyone now has dirigibles, have they not? Our Zeppelins are not the only machines of the kind. Why not say French dirigibles over Berlin?"

"Further to go," said Mortimer bluntly. "Neutral territory between, and all that. Besides, if France goes to war with Germany, England is bound to come in."

Prince Conrad raised his eyebrows.

"Bound?" he queried softly.

"Because Germany will have to violate Belgian neutrality to get at France, now that the French have got those forts along the northeastern frontier," said Mortimer, and Archie looked at Charles and they both looked away, because now they were in for it.

"I most sincerely hope you may be wrong about that," said Conrad gravely. "I should hate to think, for one thing, that the German General Staff would do anything so—uninventive as to invade Belgium."

"Well, there's one other way into France, through Switzerland," Mortimer conceded drily.

"I think plain commonsense would tell the German General Staff that the consequences of invading a neutral country would be too dire to contemplate," Charles remarked, and Prince Conrad gave him a quick glance and a nod, as though he agreed with that. "It wouldn't do them much good to get a clear road ahead from Belgium to Paris if they had the British Army on their tails all the way."

"Commonsense might also tell the British Cabinet that England would make money by remaining neutral," said Conrad thoughtfully, gazing at the amber liquid in his glass.

There was an embarrassed sort of silence, as though someone had said something very off color.

"But there *is* the Belgian treaty, isn't there," said Tommy Chetwynd uncomfortably at last. "That brings us in automatically if Belgium is molested."

"In that case, I am afraid Graf Zeppelin would have something to say to London before long," said Conrad, it seemed with regret.

"But, my dear fellow, our Army won't be in London, it would be on the Continent," Mortimer pointed out, and as Prince Conrad did not reply at once, looking down at his glass, waiting for his remark to sink in, Mortimer added angrily, "To drop bombs on London would be simply to murder a lot of defenceless women and children!"

"The British Army wouldn't like that, would it," suggested Conrad. "It would want to be at home, defending its families. And if an army goes home, the war ends."

"But no civilized nation makes war on noncombatants!" Mortimer insisted, shifting in his chair. "That's sheer, unbridled hate!"

"War is not a civilized pastime," Conrad reminded them patiently. "With man's conquest of the air, it will become still less so. But a short war, brought to a quick end because one side finds it intolerable, could be more merciful in the long run than the old-fashioned sieges which went on for months while people starved by inches."

"You mean it's kinder to blow people up than to starve them to death," said Tommy, wincing.

"And quicker," nodded Conrad. "But why on earth does everyone in England think Germany wants war? That is absurd."

"There's never been a war without at least one side wanting it," Charles told him coolly.

"True. But now that I have spent several weeks here after a long absence, it seems to me that the anti-German spirit in England amounts to foolishness." Conrad looked round at them, polite and correct and unargumentative, as though seeking enlightenment. "People whom I must take seriously, like yourselves, predict war with Germany. I confess I do not understand why."

"Because a big German fleet on top of the Kaiser's bad manners is too much to bear!" exploded Mortimer, and Archie slid down in his chair and buried his face in his glass. "The fellers who say Germany is building the fleet to protect her dear little merchant marine make me laugh! As long as Germany increases her Navy at the present rate of speed England has got to do the same, and sooner or later the lid blows off!"

"Then, of course, we come to the submarine," Conrad reflected. "An unknown quantity still. And I think with all of us"—he flashed a keen glance round their closed, guarded faces—"rather a dark secret. Nothing but actual warfare can determine its precise value as a weapon, I suppose. It is logical that you here in England should be preoccupied with the submarine. England without a Navy, or with a defeated one, could no longer exist. Whereas Germany without a Navy would still be Germany."

"I wonder if an aeroplane could spot a submarine under the surface," Charles threw in unexpectedly. "The Americans are using aeroplanes with great success on the Mexican border now—for scouting and mapping. And last May at Henley, as everyone knows, we were able to drop plaster-of-Paris bombs on a dreadnaught-shaped target marked out on the ground—and hit it from an altitude of a thousand feet going at forty-five miles an hour."

"But there's the question of flying range." Tommy was getting interested. "An aeroplane would never dare go far out to sea. Dirigibles could, they can stay up for hours—days, maybe. I'm for dirigibles myself, every time. Oliver says our new army biplanes are killing their pilots right and left down at Aldershot."

"This is the most bloodcurdling conversation I've heard in a long time," Archie observed from the depths of his chair. "You remind me of a half dozen housemaids all trying to top each other with gruesome stories of their great-aunts' operations."

"I think it is very illuminating," said Mortimer, with his usual imperviousness to hints or tact, "getting a foreign viewpoint like this. Now, with regard to invasion, how about Britain?" he resumed to Prince Conrad. "The First Sea Lord says it can't be done. What do you think?"

"But of course it can be done," Conrad assured him quietly, nursing his glass. "By a determined enemy, who did not count the cost, and with a superior air force, any country on earth can be invaded. Transportation centers could be pulverized, the civilian morale destroyed by loss of life behind the fighting line, panic and confusion created in the capital city—no government could hold out long, there would be a mass demand for peace. The country which is ruthlessly prepared to strike first and hardest is bound to win."

"But at what cost!" cried Mortimer. "The first country to wage war from the air on civilians back of the lines would become a pariah—an outcast among nations!"

Prince Conrad gave a small, unconcerned shrug.

"The country which wins the next war can make its own right and wrong," he said.

Just as Archie was thinking, I really must do something about this, the door of the gun-room opened and Virginia looked in, demanding what on earth was keeping them so long, and announcing that everybody wanted to dance and the rugs were up.

Charles, who had said so little, heard her with thankfulness and rose with alacrity. Charles had been suddenly visited with what he was inclined to consider a revelation. The blighter hasn't come here to snoop, thought Charles— he's been sent here to scare us. The next war must be made to look too horrible for words. That way we shall try and avoid it, while Germany, in their own homely phrase, stuffs its mattress. How childish they are. How Boeotian. Fatheads. Bogey-bogey-bogey, like one's nursery days. If only one could laugh. If only they didn't mean it. . . .

6

PHOEBE found Rosalind's childlike good spirits at being in England again rather heartrending, and had glanced more than once at Prince Conrad in the effort to comprehend him—for if he enjoyed his wife's radiant happiness as his expression of indulgent amusement indicated, why had he withheld the privilege so consistently and against his prenuptial promises?

That evening at Farthingale Phoebe determined to take it up with him. The gramophone was playing a waltz in the drawing-room, and she was strolling with Conrad in the moonlight on the stone-flagged terrace outside the long windows, cooling off after a romping polka. The casual ways of an English country house made many more opportunities for tête-à-tête conversation than had existed in the formal atmosphere at Heidersdorf, and every now and then he had been tempted to make what Phoebe derisively called in her thoughts "advances" to the baffling American who seemed to know every parry and counterthrust in the game at which he considered himself an expert. She took no particular pains to avoid him—she would not dignify his pursuit of her by being angered or frightened by it. She simply presented to him an impenetrably amused and efficient cold shoulder, and every now and then laughed in his face, which is always disconcerting to the most cast-iron masculine ego. When they danced together he was inclined to hold her much too close and so she had suggested the terrace. And now, before the moonlight could go to his head, she attacked him.

"You ought to let Rosalind come home more often," she began accusingly, glancing in through the window to where Rosalind was dancing in innocent mirth with Archie, seeming to float with sheer, uncomplicated happiness.

"It is difficult for me to get away from Heidersdorf now. I am a man of many affairs, you see," he replied without any signs of umbrage, and so she tried again.

"Then let her come alone, it would do her good," she persisted.

"A good German wife does not leave her husband and children to go junketing and flirting in London," he said, still without animus.

"She isn't a German wife, she's as English as the day she was born. And it's not children. It's only one."

"Ah, yes," said Conrad, and sighed his regret.

Phoebe scowled at him.

"You are a brute, aren't you!" she said almost admiringly.

"Why do you say that?" His eyes were on her, piercing, caressing, challenging. "I am devoted to Rosalind, as you very well know—as you are yourself. However, to me that does not constitute an insurmountable barrier to our being devoted—you and I—to each other." His bright, intimate gaze probed her defensive silence, meeting no response. "Without her my life would be very flat," he added as though stating a fact so obvious as to be negligible. "Without her I bore myself. It has always been like that."

"How about your boring her?" Phoebe asked bluntly, and he laughed with perfect good humor.

"Oh, I think not," he replied easily, and she saw that she had voiced what was to him a mere whimsicality.

They are impervious, she thought, pacing beside him in the pure white light with the sentimental music beyond. Germans are completely oblivious of any idea they don't wish to entertain. Nothing can get through their skulls that they don't want there. Even the best of them—and surely Conrad is among the best of them, she thought—have heads made of solid bone. It must be very comfortable—never to wonder, never to wish, never to doubt—always to *know*. But suppose, just once, they were wrong. I should think, if they were ever *proved* wrong, so conclusively that they could find no explanation, no way out, and had to face the fact that they were actually *wrong*—I should think their reason would totter. . . .

They had reached the far end of the terrace, where a vine cloaked the corner of the house beyond the windows, and turned to retrace their steps. Suddenly Conrad's arms were around her and his lips had caught hers by surprise. At first shocked into immobility and then swept by congealing anger, she merely stood, passive, stiff, enduring, until he let her go, and then said with what she felt was childish inadequacy, "Don't ever do that again. And I mean it."

"You are very exciting," he murmured. "You should learn to enjoy yourself a little."

As his arms slackened she wrenched herself out of his hold and stood back away from him, wondering how on earth she could convince him that she was not to be treated like this. He had her at a hopeless disadvantage, and he knew it. She could not make a scene. She could not return, angry and upset, to the drawing-room and give him away before his wife. She had to accept his presence amiably, and it would be difficult to extricate herself from her visit and leave the house for the rest of his stay there, without being obvious and calling attention to the situation he had made, which was the last thing she intended to do. Meanwhile, everything she could think of to say sounded like quotes from the sort of novel she would have scorned to write, and she suspected that in common with the rest of his countrymen Conrad had complacent doubts about her spinsterhood.

"We'll go in now," she said shortly, "since you can't be trusted to behave for five minutes. I wasn't brought up with your kind of man, and I keep forgetting that you're not a gentleman."

He chose to be amused, as always, at her insults.

"With a beautiful woman, there is only one kind of man," he remarked, falling into step beside her.

"In your experience, no doubt," she admitted. "But you might have the decency not to risk humiliating Rosalind before her friends. The music has stopped and they'll be coming out. For her sake, we're going to be found here making polite conversation."

"And how does our friend Major Laverham employ himself these days?" Conrad began obediently in the most casual tones. "He is no longer with his old regiment, I understand?"

"He's at the War Office."

"Oh? A Staff Officer, perhaps?"

"I really don't know," she said curtly.

"And does he still play polo in that so dashing way?" There was just an edge of irony in his voice.

"Probably. I haven't heard."

"He must ride around fourteen stone," Conrad remarked. "It must be difficult to find ponies up to his weight. I hear he has spent much of his time in Germany lately."

"Has he?" said Phoebe in genuine surprise, for when they had talked of Germany together Charles had never mentioned to her that he had any first-hand knowledge of the country at all. "Have you seen him there?"

"No. I thought it was odd I hadn't."

"Did he say he had been there?" she asked, puzzled.

"No. But we know in Germany that he was there. I thought it was odd he says nothing of it. Why do you not compare notes with him sometime, on your travels in my country?"

"Well, I've seen very little of it myself," said Phoebe, and thought, Good Lord, he's stalking Charles! What *are* they up to?

"If the subject were once opened," Prince Conrad murmured close to her ear, "I could then invite him to Heidersdorf, on his next visit. Do that for me, will you?"

"Why should you ask him to Heidersdorf?" Phoebe asked bluntly, looking him in the eyes, and Conrad's shoulders rose in the Continental way.

"His views are always interesting. One feels he is in touch with things here. A responsible man, shall we say?"

And one wants to pump him, thought Phoebe. I'd like to see it done. He's after Charles, even to the extent of throwing Rosalind at him. What *is* going on?

They all went off to bed early that night, as tomorrow was the first day of cubbing, and everyone who meant to go out had to be up at an unearthly hour. Rosalind had not ridden to hounds for years, and had persuaded Conrad to go too, and Archie was mounting them on his best. Phoebe was to ride Clare's bay mare from the Hall, and everyone said what a pity it was that Oliver and Maia had not arrived in time. Charles was to have one of the Earl's weight-carriers, and the Chetwynds always rode anything that was given them and stayed on no matter what happened.

The morning was cool and misty with sparkling cobwebs on the grass. The hounds were young and excited. The foxes were young too, and plentiful. The Field was small, and there were only a few motors and foot people at that God-forsaken hour. Prince Conrad made no secret of his preference for shooting grouse to killing foxes, but in order that Rosalind might enjoy herself he was now magnanimously allowing days to escape him which might have been passed at Scottish houses out with the guns. He rode correctly but without enthusiasm well back among the Field, while Rosalind had become in her pathetic joy almost a thruster, and was sometimes quite out of sight ahead of him on a long run. Penelope Chetwynd usually kept up with her, and Charles was always there on a big compact roan, and once when Rosalind took a ditch with a reckless flying leap he cried *"Over!"* in a mixture of praise and relief which startled him into hoping no one had heard, as he followed. She glanced across her shoulder with a grin which rolled time back, and they might have been boy and girl again, and Germany only a place on the map.

Their quarry having successfully gone to earth that time, they were ambling on towards Moreton on the way to the next covert when they came to a road with a stone wall either side and a sharp turn beyond some grey farm buildings huddled in the pale morning sun. Charles was just thinking that it was still early for motor cars when one shot round the bend to find the road ahead full of horses, and the fool who drove it let out loud squawks with its horn.

Charles's horse promptly stood on end and tried to fall over backwards on him, and when he had righted things there Penelope was saying with a rather hysterical giggle, "Rosalind's half way home." He saw the small flying figure in the next field, riding cleverly but pulling on a horse which was clearly out of control. He sat still at the edge of the road, watching. His teeth were set, but in the old days if he had gone after her and tried to help she would not have spoken to him for a week.

Most of the Field were still behind them. Archie came up at a trot, took in the situation, and went so far as to jump the further wall and pause there. Just then Rosalind's horse put its foot in a rabbit hole and went down, pitching her over its head. Simultaneously Charles shot out ahead of Archie, going full tilt, and reached her first.

She lay just as she had landed, half on her side, oddly crumpled, with her hat jammed on her head. She did not move as he knelt beside her, but when he turned her very carefully on to her back and straightened out her legs, running an expert hand along the bones, he saw that her eyes were open. She looked up at him silently.

"Where does it hurt?" he demanded. "Lie still, and tell me where it hurts."

"It—doesn't," she said with an effort, and her face contracted not with pain but with terror. "Charles, something's broken, I—haven't got any legs."

"Yes, you have, I've just counted 'em. You've knocked your head, I expect. I'm going to try to get your hat off now. Say if I hurt you."

The hat came off. Her head rested in his hand, the heavy dark hair loosened. The rest of the Field was arriving now, Archie first, then Penelope and Phoebe, Prince Conrad among the last. He ran from his horse to kneel beside Rosalind and laid urgent arms around her lax body.

"My treasure, speak to me!" he entreated at once, and everyone who heard him winced and thought *Germans!*, and Charles said sharply, "Don't move her, please, until we find out where she is hurt!"

Conrad brushed him aside and raised Rosalind in his embrace to a half sitting position, gathering her up against his shoulder. Charles made an instinctive gesture to prevent him, crying, "No, *don't!*" and Conrad said coldly, "Kindly keep your impudent hands off my wife!" Charles sat back on his heels and they were all forced to watch in helpless silence while Conrad put his right arm under Rosalind's knees and lifted her from the ground.

"I shall carry her down to the road," he said harshly. "Please find some sort of motor car to take her to Farthingale."

"It's over ten miles," said Archie. "Take her as far as the farm there, if you like, and we'll put her to bed and send for a doctor."

"I prefer to take her back to her own bed at your house at once." Conrad started down the slope of the field with his light burden, and as they went Charles saw that she hung limp and unconscious across her husband's arms.

Phoebe moved to Charles's side, where he still knelt on the ground, and laid her hand on his shoulder.

"Archie will see about a car," she said. "It's never any use to argue with Conrad when he's made up his mind."

Charles rose slowly and stood with his head down, brushing off his knees. His horse moved in a step and nuzzled at his elbow, sensing disaster. Charles laid hold of the reins blindly, but made no move to mount.

"They'll telephone ahead for a doctor to be at Farthingale," said Phoebe beside him.

"He's killed her," said Charles through his teeth.

"Oh, Charles—she only fainted, surely."

"It seemed to be her back. The only safe way to move her was flat on a stretcher. It was murder to pick her up like that. But I couldn't stop him. *Could* I have stopped him?"

"No."

"No. I tried." He stood staring at his stirrup leather, his big fingers fumbling at the buckle. "Try to go along in the car with her, will you? Try to be there when the doctor—" He raised his head and met Phoebe's eyes. "Try not to leave her. Make a blooming nuisance of yourself—but stick to her."

"I'll try, Charles." Phoebe turned to go, and hesitated. "You all right?"
"Yes. I'm all right."

With a glance which turned Charles over to his sister Penelope, Phoebe led her horse down the slope after Prince Conrad.

The doctor was waiting at Farthingale, and Phoebe, unaccustomed to illness and accidents, steadied herself with fervent inward prayers for strength, and helped Rosalind's maid undress her on the big bed. Her hands and knees were shaking, and she felt sick with shock and apprehension as Rosalind failed to regain consciousness. She remained resolutely in the room while the doctor made his examination, and he soon confessed himself to be in need of another opinion.

By that time the rest of the household had arrived back in other motor cars, and Archie led the doctor away to put in trunk calls to London for two other physicians he knew there, one of whom agreed to catch the noon train and bring nurses, the other to follow that evening.

Meanwhile Rosalind lay small and white and broken in the bed with her eyes closed, seeming scarcely to breathe. Leaving Virginia to watch, Phoebe slipped away to change her clothes and prepare for her vigil, nurses or no nurses. Charles had vanished at once into his bedroom, and Tommy was with him there. Conrad was in the gun-room drinking a whiskey and soda. Once he had laid his wife on the bed and seen Gibson, her maid, in charge, he showed no further desire to intrude. In fact, he appeared rather anxious to avoid Rosalind's room, and himself chose the refuge of the gun-room, saying that he would await the doctor's verdict there when he had bathed and changed. Phoebe saw the door close behind him with relief, but must have looked surprised, because Gibson said, bending over her mistress, "He is no trouble when she is ill. We have things all our own way then, praise be."

7

THE first doctor from London was unable to bring Rosalind back to consciousness, and the room was rapidly turned into a hospital by the two starched nurses working with silent efficiency while Phoebe sat on the window seat to be out of the way, with an open book in her lap, of which she did not take in one word. The second doctor arrived after dinner, which was brought to Phoebe on a tray, and they worked over Rosalind until midnight, while Phoebe dozed uneasily in an armchair in the corner, and woke with a start to find the first London doctor standing over her. She stared at him uncomprehendingly, and he repeated his question.

"Who is Charles?" he asked.

"Charles Laverham."

"Is he here in the house?"

"Yes, he—"

"Send for him," said the doctor, and turned away.

"I c-can't," said Phoebe, and scrambled to her feet to catch the doctor's arm. "What is it? Did she ask for him?"

"She is half-way conscious now. Twice she has said the name Charles, and that's all. If Charles will come and try to make her respond to him, we may get some results."

"B-but he isn't her husband," Phoebe threw out both hands against the doctor's sharp, cynical glance. "Oh, no—you mustn't think—she and Charles grew up together, and he got to her first when she was thrown."

"Then surely her husband would have no objection—"

"But he *would*," said Phoebe desperately. "Her husband is Prince Conrad zu Polkwitz-Heidersdorf. He—makes scenes," she added, and blushed miserably for Rosalind.

"Then keep him out of here," said the doctor, and walked back to the bed.

Ten minutes later he was standing over her again.

"Let's find out if Prince Whatshisname has gone to. bed," he said. "See if you can get hold of Archie Campion and ask him to smuggle this fellow Charles in here. It's a chance to hold on to her, and we need to take it."

Archie reconnoitred and found that Conrad's light was out in the small room over the back garden to which his belongings had been transferred earlier in the evening. Then Archie tiptoed to the other end of the corridor, routed out Charles, who was reading in bed, and hustled him in dressing-gown and slippers to Rosalind's door, where they found a nurse on guard. She remained there when Charles had gone in, to ward off nuisances, Archie thought, trailing back to his own room and an anxious-faced Virginia.

The doctors appraised Charles with a glance as he approached the bed.

"Try and rouse her," one of them said, and vacated his own chair at the bedside.

Charles sat down in it, utterly composed, and took one of the small quiet hands in both his.

"Rosalind," he said in his slurred, soft tones, and she moved her head on the pillow and murmured something.

"Again," whispered the doctor, watching.

"Rosalind, it's Charles. *Come* on, old girl, they want you to wake up."

Slowly her dark lashes lifted and she saw him sitting there.

"Hello," she whispered.

"That's better," said Charles easily. "Archie's gone and got a lot of high-priced doctors down from London to look at you, and the least you can do is cooperate."

"Am I—dying?"

"How can we tell, if you just lie there with your eyes shut? Of course you're not dying. You took a nice clean spill right over his head. I'd have done the same in your place. Nothing to make a fuss about. Doctors have to earn their fees somehow, and they want you to try to waggle your toes or something."

For the first time her gaze left his face and wandered vaguely around the unfamiliar faces beside the bed. Then she frowned slightly.

"Where's—Conny—?"

"Asleep, of course," Charles told her matter-of-factly. "Do you want him?"

"*No*—oh, no," she murmured, and her heavy lids came down. "Charles."

"Yes, I'm here," he said.

"Don't—go away—"

"What, without seeing you again tomorrow? Not likely."

The doctor's fingers were on her pulse. He nodded, and Charles slid out of the chair and the doctor took his place. Just inside the door Charles was confronted by Phoebe, who said, "Oh, Charles, you're marvellous!" and burst into tears.

"Now, now, hold up," he said, and put an arm around her. "You can't afford to cave in, she's going to need you. Will you promise me something?" He drew her further from the bed. "I can't hang about here in the circumstances, I'll have to bung off to Buckinghamshire tomorrow as planned. Promise you won't let her out of your sight while she's like this—and write me every day, will you?"

"Yes, Charles. I will."

"You won't sail for home, or go to Cannes, or anything like that till she's all right again?"

"I promise."

"Good. Now I can just manage not to go out of my mind."

Charles went back to bed and his volume of Conan Doyle, and Phoebe returned to her chair in a corner of Rosalind's room.

In the morning the doctors quite naturally made their report in private to Rosalind's husband, and the little group of rather silent men in the gun-room had had no official news when he finally entered upon them shortly before lunch and accepted a whiskey and soda from Archie's sympathetic hand.

"Well," said Archie, "do they think it's going to be serious?"

"It's very unsatisfactory," said Conrad, sinking into a chair with his glass. "I suppose these fellows know their business?"

"Oh, bound to," said Archie. "Very well thought of in Town, I assure you. Anything broken?"

"The spine is not actually broken, though it has been injured," said Conrad. "There is slight concussion too, and some internal damage. I questioned them very closely about that, and they are convinced that even if she is able to walk again there can be no more children."

The words struck the air of the quiet room with the general effect of high explosive. Archie came to first with the realization that he had not moved for he didn't know how long, and that Charles was standing at a window looking out, with his back to the room.

"If we are to believe these doctors," Conrad was continuing, "she is in no immediate danger of death, but cannot be moved for some time—perhaps weeks. I deplore the inconvenience to your household, my dear Campion, but your wife has been kind enough to say from the beginning that she wished to keep Rosalind here until she is quite recovered—"

"Oh, absolutely," said Archie hastily. "By all means. Best place for her—delighted to have her—do anything in the world for her, you know—"

"Thank you," said Prince Conrad in his most stately manner. "I am told by your physicians that there is no objection whatever to my keeping our engagements in Scotland and making my wife's excuses—they say there is nothing to be done here, except see that she has complete rest and quiet and does not attempt to move about, and the nurses will be kept on, at my expense, of course. Since I can do no more than that to hasten her recovery, I will depart as already arranged, on the Friday morning train."

"Uh—quite," said Archie, barely covering his astonishment at such coolness. "Very sensible of you, no doubt. It's a woman's job—nursing." And, Why am I saying this, he wondered—fatuous ass—it's catching.

"I will supply you with my Scottish itinerary," said Conrad, sipping his whiskey, "so that I can be reached at any time if there should be some sudden—necessity."

So Rosalind was left in peace, to everyone's satisfaction, and soon began to show a gradual improvement in color and spirits, though she was kept flat in bed and showed no inclination to try to move anything but her arms and could not even be propped up for meals. She was not surprised at Conrad's departure for Scotland, and seemed to feel no resentment at what looked to the rest of them like the most heartless conduct on his part.

"Conny never has any use for peope who are ill," she informed them cheerfully. "Each time the babies came—well, I hardly ever saw him at all, of course, once I began to lose my looks. And that time I nearly died of bronchitis, he simply went off to Berlin and left Gibson to cope. It wasn't fear of infection or anything like that—if you're ill you simply don't exist for him. It's really very convenient," she said placidly. "Gibson and I like it that way." But her smile, Phoebe thought, was piteous.

8

WHEN Charles at Lady Shadwell's in Buckinghamshire got Phoebe's letter saying that Conrad had actually gone, he at once went down to Cleeve Place, his uncle's house which was not more than twenty miles from Farthingale, so that he could motor over from there every day and back. He would sit a while in the drawing-room downstairs, receiving the small daily news of Rosalind's progress, seeming to derive some sort of comfort just from being under the same roof. He never asked to see her, and when it was finally suggested he thought it might be better not, though once or twice he was persuaded to just look in at the door and say Hello. Now that she was mending, the pain had begun, and she was often made drowsy with pills to give her respite.

Then one day he was commanded back after Rosalind's door had closed on his brief appearance there, and the nurse placed a chair for him close to the bed, saying that Rosalind ought not to talk much, and left them.

"Anything you want?" he asked after they had looked at each other a moment in silence. "Fruit—flowers—books—anything I can get down from London to cheer you up a bit?"

Her head moved a little on the pillow in negation.

"You've only got to name it," he reminded her. "One rather shopworn soldier entirely at your disposal."

The corners of her mouth lifted slightly.

"Please hold my hand," she said.

"With pleasure," said Charles, and took possession of the one nearest him where it lay on the coverlet. Her small fingers nestled gratefully into his warm ones. Her smile broadened.

"Tell about—what you've been doing," she murmured.

"Oh, much the usual sort of thing," said Charles, and began an account of his Buckinghamshire visit.

When the nurse returned half an hour later Rosalind lay a little on her side, curved towards him, asleep, her hand in his. The nurse was startled.

"Did you move her?" she demanded quickly, and Charles shook his head.

"She did it herself as she dozed off," he said.

"But—we've had to turn her," said the nurse. "This is an excellent sign, we must have you back again, sir."

Meanwhile London had livened up for the Little Season, and during the French autumn maneuvers a brilliantly beribboned case containing messages had been successfully dropped from an aeroplane on its headquarters objective, and all the English illustrated weeklies were printing articles entitled *War by Petrol* and so on. Archie brought back a story which was going round Town to the effect that Germans now visiting in England had begun to choose the country house they intended to live in before long while a conquered England labored to pay an enormous indemnity. And of course no one could help thinking of Prince Conrad and his tour of inspection, at present being conducted in Scotland.

In October, while the Scottish shooting parties were still in progress, the perennial Balkans boiled over in a war between Italy and Turkey, as Italy reached out for North African territory roundabout Benghazi and Derna. Charles, who had been spending some days in Town, drove over during the week end from Cleeve Place, looking rather grave, and said that things were humming at the Shop so he would have only the one day there—which rather dashed their spirits, for they were saving a surprise for him. Rosalind had been sitting up in a chair, carried to and from it by Archie or the youngest footman, and she was planning to receive him that way for the first time today, and the doctors thought now that she would be able eventually to walk as well as ever. But on the way up to Rosalind's room Phoebe gave him the rest of the news, which was not so good. A telegram from Conrad had just announced his arrival at Farthingale the following day, and while Rosalind had not said much it was plain to see that she was depressed and quiet.

"That's a nice thing to hand me just as I go in," Charles said, his hand on the outer knob.

"Well, you had to know, didn't you," Phoebe said sadly, and very soon left them alone together.

Rosalind was sitting in an armchair by the fire, a rug over her knees. She wore a warm velvet tea-gown with a froth of lace at the throat, and her dark hair was dressed as usual again, parted in the middle and drawn out in two wide wings at the sides into heavy coils high on the back of her head. For a while after Phoebe had gone it was hard for them to find anything to go on talking about, and then Rosalind suddenly gave up and said, "Charles, I'm terrified."

"What now?" asked Charles, with his lovely faculty of never turning a hair.

"Conny comes tomorrow—and he'll want me to get up and walk."

"Luckily they seem to think that's possible."

"But I can't."

"Have you tried?"

She shook her head.

"I just can't. I'm too frightened."

"That it will hurt, you mean?"

"No. Not that. He'll make a ceremony of it—I know him so well. The doctor will be here, and Phoebe, and the nurses—and they'll all be watching, and Conny will expect miracles, and I shall be shaking and sick with nerves and just go down in a heap on the floor before them all, and Conny will make a scene and say I didn't *try*—"

Charles's lips were set, but he said only, "Can't you tell him you want to be alone with him the first time you do it?"

"But I don't think I *do!*" said Rosalind, and her eyes were haunted. "So much depends on—on my being normal again. You see—if I can't walk—I might just as well be dead. In fact, much better. I mean, I shall just be left somewhere in disgrace in a chair at Heidersdorf and never see anybody but Gibson and Aunt Christa, and pretty soon I'll start to scream and scream—I've been so near it before—and they'll come and take me away in a straitjacket."

"Well, if you're going to be left somewhere, why can't it be here?" he asked reasonably.

"He won't allow that much longer. I belong to him. He'll take me back to Heidersdorf—I shall have to have German doctors—" She hid her face in her hands.

Charles sat a moment in silence, looking down at his own hands clasped tight in front of him. Finally he said without moving, "If you can walk, though—if you're going to get well—it won't be so bad, I suppose. You can bear it then."

And she answered, her face hidden, "I always have borne it."

"What would happen," Charles began, speaking slowly and carefully, "if you just told him tomorrow that you wanted to stay here in England—"

"He wouldn't listen—"

"—with me," Charles finished, and there was a long pause while neither of them moved.

"I—think I can bear almost anything now," she said simply, and laid her hands in her lap, looking at the fire. "But I won't let you, Charles. It would mean your whole life thrown away, for me. You couldn't go on at the War Office if you took another man's wife. You'd have to resign."

"I've got enough for us to live on without that," he said doggedly. "They can have the War Office, I've been there long enough."

"He would never give me a divorce," she said. "We couldn't be received anywhere. We should be outcasts."

"Last time I was down at Cleeve Place I had a good look at the dower house," said Charles. "Remember it? My Great-aunt Flora used to live there when we were children and we always went down to tea several times a week and had enormous cream buns. Remember what a pig you were about those cream buns? It's just as she left it when she died four or five years ago—with all the furniture in dust-sheets and the creeper growing out across the window panes. I got the key and went all through it, thinking how very comfortable one could be there. And I made up my mind then to offer it to you, along with myself, if you gave any sign of dreading to go back to Germany. Uncle Tim would let us have it like a shot, he's got no use for it whatever. We needn't see anyone there, if you don't wish to—not for months at a time. But our friends wouldn't let it make any difference, you know, in the circumstances. You see—Phoebe has told us quite a lot—and we're none of us blind, we can guess the rest. You haven't got to go on with it, my dear—if I can be of any use to you."

"Please don't say any more, Charles, I—mustn't listen."

"You feel you've got to stick to him, and take what comes?" He rose with a long sigh, and pushed back his chair. "I hadn't much hope of anything else," he said. "But anyway, you're going to walk."

She looked up at him, shrinking visibly.

"No—please, Charles, not now, I—"

"How do you know you can't if you haven't even tried? Come on." He held out his hands from ten paces away. "Nobody's looking now but me. I'll catch you before you can fall. Come on—try."

With her eyes fixed on his face, she pushed the rug from her knees and stood up slowly, raising herself by the arms of the chair. For a moment she wavered and reached towards his outstretched hands, but he stayed where he was, the length of the hearthrug between them. She made an uncertain step, then two more, and finally half ran, half fell into his arms, flung up against him and crying bitterly. Silently after a moment he lifted her off her feet and sat down with her in his lap in a big chair, holding her like a child, his lips buried in her hair, while she sobbed away nine years of loneliness and humiliation and fortitude.

When Phoebe returned to the room at tea time Rosalind was lying on the bed under the eiderdown and Charles sat near by telling stories. They explained that Rosalind had got a little tired sitting up and he had helped her to walk—*walk*, mind you—back to the bed. After tea, in Phoebe's rueful presence, he said Good-bye to Rosalind, for he was starting back at once to London to keep an eye on the Balkan War.

9

THE visit which Oliver and Maia were scheduled to make at the Hall had come during the worst of Rosalind's illness, while Phoebe had very little time to herself and grudged any absence from the room which would be long enough for riding or a dinner party. Oliver of course rode over more than once to inquire, and sometimes Maia was not with him.

There were brief encounters at the tea table and at the threshold of Rosalind's room, where they spoke of the invalid's progress, of Clare's baby (which proved to be a girl as ordered) and of certain repercussions from Conrad's Scottish tour—a witty widow with a fortune in jewels and a rather dashing reputation had discovered him with ill-concealed rapture and they were being photographed together for the society magazines poising sandwiches at shooting luncheons or grinning over the day's bag.

When Oliver came to Farthingale the last day before his return to Aldershot Maia came too, and remained downstairs in the drawing-room while Oliver went up to say a few words to Rosalind, who was still allowed only one visitor at a time. She clung to his hand and said, "Shan't I see you again?" and he had to tell her that Maneuvers were starting soon and he would be very busy.

His words echoed in Phoebe's mind as they reached the staircase on their way back to tea. Was it the last time for her too? She voiced the question before they came to the bottom step.

"Yes," said Oliver without qualification, and then added, "Isn't it *beastly!*"

She paused, her hand on the newel post, feeling suddenly a little sick, but wondering at the same time what more she could have expected.

"Oliver—" she began faintly.

"I know." His hand touched hers on the newel post and they both glanced at the drawing-room door, from which they could not be seen, but he took his hand away at once and put it into his pocket. "It's not been much good, has it. When do you go back to America?"

"I promised Charles to stay as long as she needs me."

"Good. I shall have a few days in London in December, but that will be too late, I suppose."

"I don't know. It depends on Conrad. He's bound to take her away as soon as she can be moved. Virginia will let you know when that is."

He glanced again towards the drawing-room door, bent quickly and kissed her hand where it lay on the newel post. When he straightened, they looked at each other gravely, with despair, and moved on in silence to the waiting tea-table and Maia's derisive, searching eyes.

That evening, when her supper tray had been taken away and the nurse was downstairs having her own meal, Rosalind lay looking up at Phoebe who sat in an armchair beside the bed.

"Well," she murmured, "now there are two of us." And she smiled at

Phoebe's inquiring glance. "I know how you feel about Oliver now. I said I'd rather, and it's happened. I want Charles." Tears of weakness and pain gathered behind her long lashes and rolled down her cheeks into the pillow. "Even when the babies were born, I wanted desperately to live and get well. But this time I don't seem to care. It must be the dope they gave me. I've lost my grip. If I've got to go on living without ever seeing Charles it's not worth bothering to do."

Phoebe took her hand.

"You've had a hard pull, honey. It won't look so bad when you're stronger. And you are getting stronger every day, you know."

"At first I thought I just wouldn't," Rosalind said. "But your body does what it likes, doesn't it. Mine is mending in spite of me. Remember that game we used to play about getting old together and reminiscing in our bath-chairs?"

"I do," Phoebe nodded. "Perhaps we still shall, who knows?"

"Then you'll come back to Heidersdorf sometimes? *Please* say you will!"

"Of course I will. Perhaps next summer. Even if there's a war, America won't be in it and I could still come to Germany."

"If there's a war I shan't be wanted there myself, and I should come home at once." said Rosalind confidently. "But there won't be one. There are too many intelligent people like Charles in responsible posts. The Emperor can't have a war all by himself, and besides, he'd be the first to back down if it came to fighting—bullies always are."

"Yes—I hope you're right," said Phoebe thoughtfully.

The next day after that Rosalind had begun to sit up in bed, and before long she was able to be moved to the chair where Charles had found her. Then Conrad came back, and she was beginning to walk a little, to his unconcealed relief. Early in December, looking fragile and rather frightened and very beautiful, she departed with him for Germany. He had bought her a long sable coat with a toque to match for the journey, and their private train would be waiting on the quay at Flushing.

Quite suddenly Phoebe was homesick. Virginia urged her to spend Christmas at Farthingale and see the fun with the children, and it seemed a reasonable, happy thing to do in the circumstances. And perhaps by then she could see Oliver again. . . .

She considered the prospect, lying awake in her room the night after Rosalind had gone and left her feeling bereft and useless and empty after weeks of exacting service to the creature she loved best but one in the world. She was no more good to Rosalind now, and she had never been any good to Oliver. It didn't seem, when she stopped to look at it, as though she was much good to anybody. This was unlike her, for she was not given to self-pity. But she wondered, lying unrelaxed and wretched in the dark at Farthingale, if Cousin Sue ever had times when she longed to do something to account for herself, to have something to show for the years she had already lived. Phoebe wanted to ask. Cousin Sue would know what to say.

I'm going home, said Phoebe to herself. I'm going back to Williamsburg and look at Father again, I've got some right to Father, anyway, he's mine. I'm going home and howl on his shoulder the way I used to when I was little. He'll know what ails me, he always has, but I was too spunky to admit it in the beginning. I was young then, I thought I could lick this thing alone. Now I know I can't. He must have been through something like this with Cousin Sue, but he married Mother and we've all been happy together. He didn't waste his whole life pining after something he couldn't have. Maybe I haven't exactly pined so far, but I'm not cured, I'm getting worse. And you *can* make a life, Oliver always said you could. Oliver's got a life, even with Maia, he's got a child, he gets a bit of hunting, he goes on laughing. Even Rosalind—she has Victor to show, and Conny is still mad about her in his own way. I wonder if she'll find it harder now, or if loving Charles will comfort her. It will be much worse, I should think. But how do I know, I've never tried it myself. Charles says it's my business to know these things, and I suppose it is. But Charles thinks like me, he goes on alone. Perhaps we're wrong, Charles and I. . . .

Perhaps I should have married Johnny, she thought, last time he asked me. He won't ask me again, Bracken has seen to that. Maybe I should have married Miles when I first got back from England, as I meant to do. But how do you know, till you've tried? Maybe even now it isn't too late for me to make something of myself—be of some *use* to somebody—maybe if Miles asked me again—oh, *Oliver* . . .

She sailed within the week, spent three days in New York shopping for Christmas presents for the family, and sped on to Williamsburg, convinced that there she might find sanctuary from something inside her which questioned and accused.

PART SEVEN

JEFF

Williamsburg.   *Summer, 1913.*

>>>

1

IT WAS an old-fashioned Christmas of the kind Phoebe had almost forgotten. Dinah was up again and able to travel, so she and Bracken came down from New York with Eden. Bracken's elder sister Marietta, who had married the Princeton professor, brought her husband and a daughter Audrey, very shy, with braces on her teeth, and a bookish boy turning twelve who wore spectacles. Miles was there, of course, having an assistant professorship at William and Mary now, so that he lived in Sue's house and occupied the same room his father had had as a boy. His parents arrived from Charlottesville, and his sister Belle, recently widowed, from Richmond, with her twins Calvert and Camilla, who were now eighteen, a handsome pair exactly alike and devoted to each other. Phoebe's own brother Fitz and his wife Gwen had two children, neither of whom Phoebe had yet seen—Rhoda was three and Stephen nearly two.

So it was a children's Christmas at Williamsburg too, with a tree and games and laughter and a great deal of food. But Phoebe couldn't help counting up. She and Miles were the only ones who hadn't got families, except for Cousin Sue—and of course Bracken, but that was just bad luck, and anyway he had Dinah, and couldn't bear to let her out of his sight for long, he had come so near to losing her. And Phoebe thought, If Miles and I had gone on with it ten years ago—if I hadn't been such a muddleheaded fool—if I'd stuck to my guns, and married Miles. . . . And Miles, a little adrift in his bachelorhood, much climbed upon by the young Spragues who after the fashion of children were strangely attracted by the person who made the least effort to secure their good will—Miles met her eyes across the room, Gwen's Rhoda dozing in his lap, and the look seemed to say, This one could have been ours.

Phoebe rose impulsively and went to him.

"Shall I put her away?" she offered. "The young ones are being rounded up for bed now."

"I'll carry her up, she's too heavy for you." He stood up with the drowsy child in his arms. "I expect they'll all be sick tomorrow."

"What matter, we're only young once!" said Phoebe, and Gwen came by with Stephen, saying, "Bring her up, Miles, they're dropping in their tracks!"

Phoebe watched them go up the stairs and realized with a new desolation that she had never put a child to bed in her life and would not know how. Even Cousin Sue was better off than that. Restless and troubled and very thoughtful, she turned back into the room. Fitz was playing the piano softly, for Belle's twins to sing duets. Camilla wanted to sing professionally, but they were all hoping she would outgrow it.

"Well, my dear—" Her father's arm came round her waist. "It's good to have you home again."

Phoebe hugged herself to him gratefully, and made no reply.

"Still running away from things?" Sedgwick murmured, and after a moment's indignation she gave a little laugh and said, "I suppose that's what it is. How did you know?"

"Because you're very beautiful—oh, yes, you are!—and very successful and very wealthy—according to our standards here—and very unhappy."

"Does it show as much as that?" she asked ruefully.

"More than I like to see."

"You lawyers are all too smart," she whispered, leaning against him. "This one isn't quite smart enough to help, is he?"

Before she could find a reply Miles loomed up on her other side, having deposited Rhoda on the bed upstairs, and said, "Like old times, isn't it, Cousin Sedgwick—having Phoebe here again. You're going to stay home a while," he added, looking down at her from his great height, "aren't you, now that you've come?"

"Yes—I think I am," said Phoebe soberly, and her eyes went round the bright room full of voices and music, and the faces she had known all her life.

Camilla ran over from the piano, attached herself to Sedgwick's elbow, and begged him prettily to come and sing with them. Like all female creatures of any age whatever, she always wanted to flirt with him, and loved to have him near her. Three-year-old Rhoda was the same, even if he was her grandfather.

Phoebe and Miles were left standing together and the music rose again, cruelly, on that most nostalgic of all tunes, even in its first youth, the *Merry Widow* waltz. Camilla's clear soprano soared, half a dozen other good voices followed. *When did I waltz with you last?* said Oliver. *Don't tell me. It was only a week ago. . . .* She turned sharply, so that her back was to the piano, and laid her hand on Miles's arm.

"The way I feel now I'll never leave Williamsburg again," she said. "Let's sit down somewhere, and you tell me all the dullest things you can think of about the College and what you do there and how you spend your days."

"It is pretty dull, I expect," he agreed with his habitual humility. "But I like it. And it might even be a nice change for you, after the gay life you've had."

"If I thought it was really dull enough," said Phoebe through her teeth, using all her will power to keep from covering her ears with her hands to shut out *The Merry Widow,* "I'd ask you to take me back."

"If I thought you meant a word of that," said Miles, "I'd catch you right up on it."

They stared at each other, both of them startled and a little apprehensive. Calvert and Camilla were dancing together now, singing as they swung by . . .

> "And the music answers swaying to and fro,
> Telling you it's true, it's true,
> I love you so! . . ."

Phoebe's beautiful lower lip came out.

"You mean—get married after all—the way we should have done in the first place?"

"We're only ten years late," said Miles.

"All right," said Phoebe, through her teeth. "What's ten years between friends?"

"Phoebe—you won't ever be sorry?"

"Not any more," said Phoebe cryptically, and Miles took her hand. "Shall we tell them?"

"Yes, tell them now!" cried Phoebe, and her eyes were very bright. "Let's scream it from the housetops! I've come home! I'm going to marry my first beau and settle down! *Stop the music and tell them now!*" Her hands went up over her ears.

Later that evening those who were staying in Sue's house walked home through the quiet, frosty streets from Sedgwick's house where the party was. Dinah and Bracken, hand in hand, still humming *The Merry Widow*—Dabney and Charlotte, his hand holding her elbow, his limp quite noticeable because he was tired, and even Charlotte's chatter silenced by her doubts about the thing which had caught up with Miles all over again—Belle with Camilla, shushing her too audible astonishment that Uncle Miles and Cousin Phoebe were in love with each other —and Miles, with Sue on one arm and Eden on the other. Sedgwick's house was big enough to hold all the rest of them.

Toasts had been drunk, and Miles was slightly exhilarated. It was the old story with Miles, as his mother well knew, but such a thing never occurred to him. There was something in his sober make-up, some shining skein of submerged adventurousness, which responded to the rich and strange. Virginia had caught and tangled it, in the pride of her first London Season. The Phoebe of the old days, simple and worshipping and shy, had never roused in him anything but kindly affection and a well-considered desire to establish himself with a home like other people in the most comfortable way possible and with as little inconvenience to himself as might be. But the Phoebe he saw tonight, with her hair wrapped around her head in an intricate sheath, with a perfect complexion discreetly enhanced, wearing a low gown which shimmered as she breathed—a Phoebe haloed by success, mysterious with travel and conquest and some tragedy, cast like a spent bird back into the scenes of her childhood—Miles's thoughts grew lyrical and his metaphors became reckless. For Miles was prone to worship, not to conquer, and his nebulous ideal woman was a cross between goddess and queen, and he would never have dreamt of presuming on his own mere maleness. Miles's ideal must always stoop to him with divine condescension, invite him into possession, and graciously, even grudgingly, permit him his privileges. It seemed to him that Phoebe, in consenting to live out the rest of her life in Williamsburg as his wife, had so condescended, and he was prepared, even eager, to spend the rest of his own life kneeling, in a suitably grateful attitude. It was not within the scope of Miles's comprehension that Phoebe, with whatever laurels on her childlike brow, only wanted a master.

But Sue, unable to keep step with his suddenly debonair stride, still dazed and fretful from the impact of the unexpected announcement which had broken into the *Merry Widow* music, was silently reiterating all the way home with an inward wringing of hands, Oh, darlings, *no,* that's not the way, it's all *wrong,* we'll all be *sorry.* . . .

2

BUT somewhat to her own surprise Phoebe was not sorry as the months slipped by and she settled back into the leisurely Williamsburg life as into an armchair. They went to Norfolk for a three-day honeymoon, and returned to Sue's house, where Miles had made of Ransom's library a private study which he and Phoebe now used as a sitting-room. She had no particular wish for a house of her own, when Sue had so much space going to waste and plenty of trained help, so that Miles's bride need have no housekeeping problems and could devote herself to starting a new book.

She found it a cosy sort of novelty, working at a little desk set up in Miles's study, with the typewriter on a nearby bridge-table, and Sue for company every day. The book was to be a real departure from what Phoebe Sprague's devoted public expected from her, though it was written with the same light touch, and no melodrama. But it was a pitiless picture of the Prussian type, both in its own home and loose in England among a tolerant society which would not or could not realize the Prussian mentality. It was not Conrad or Cuno or Gerzlow she was writing—but it was the essence of all three; their arrogance, and stupidity, and self-esteem; their picturesque uniforms and their deplorable manners and their brutal charm laid on with a sledge-hammer; and the uncritical, mindless, obedient complacence which they demanded and received from their womenfolk.

Miles as he read the manuscript chapter by chapter was disturbed and shocked and almost incredulous. Sue took it very seriously indeed, and noticed with satisfaction the increased maturity and sureness of the work. She was by no means convinced that Phoebe had not made a mistake when she married Miles, even though things were going far better than she had dared to hope. But when in the following November Phoebe began to feel very queer and learned without surprise and apparently without dismay that she had started a baby, even Sue began to wonder.

The prospect of the baby fitted in with Phoebe's new scheme of life, which was to be a good wife to Miles now that she had undertaken it, and to give him the home and family which she considered that her girlhood blunder had cheated him of. She had had little experience of illness and the inevitable woes and discomforts of her condition bore very heavily upon her, and the book began to suffer. Patiently, determined to do everything right and with a minimum of fuss, she laid the manuscript away—everybody said the first months were the hardest.

Christmas, 1912, found her quite miserable but uncomplaining, and nobody suspected that now she had begun to cast backward looks over her shoulder to the time, just a year ago, when she was still free, and had no obligation to Miles, and always felt well, and could write for six hours at a stretch if she wanted to. . . .

The enforced mental idleness, which drove her to novel-reading and embroidery and what she inwardly termed female conversation, and the new preoccupation with her own physical sensations, were rousing in her a slow, reluctant, but inevitable rebellion, and her high intentions began to recede into a mere dogged endurance of what she had let herself in for. She had practically asked Miles to marry her, and she wanted a child. Very well, then. Here she was. Everything according to plan. Just what she asked for. She was not going to change her mind *again*. No more running away from things. This time she was caught. This time she had burnt her boats. This time she was really done for.

Miles, who seemed unreasonably astonished, Phoebe thought, that any such thing had occurred, adjusted himself rather cautiously to the idea of being a father and at once gave his attention to the question of names. Phoebe, rather drearily aware that there would be lots of time, suggested that they wait and see which kind of name they would want. But Miles went into committee with himself and emerged convinced that if it was a boy it should be called Jefferson after the man who had built his beloved University at Charlottesville, and if it was a girl it must be named for its Great-great-great-grandmother Tabitha Day, who was still a lively legend in the family. Phoebe agreed listlessly, for it looked to her a long way to the christening. And she thought, At least it will never be called Oliver, and then she busied her mind resolutely for Oliver must have no part in Miles's child, and she would not allow herself to dream of him any more.

Snow fell the week before Christmas and Miles came home from the College with wet feet and began to sneeze. By Christmas Day, when all the family had gathered again, he had got one of his beastly colds which always settled on his chest and always caused endless anxiety and precautions. Anything like a bronchial attack shook him to pieces with coughing and left him exhausted and run down for weeks. But with a secret wish not to miss the festivities this year, which would include congratulations on his own approaching fatherhood, he insisted on going to Christmas dinner at Sedgwick's as usual. Afterwards, as they prepared for bed that night he confessed that he felt a little feverish. Phoebe was tired, and had troubles of her own, and felt she simply could not bear it if Miles was going to be ill now, and beyond a sympathetic murmur or two did nothing about it. Before morning he began apologetically to have a chill, and she woke Sue and they fixed hot water bottles, and as early as possible called the doctor.

Miles developed pneumonia, which they had all dreaded so often before, and early in January he died. Phoebe was stunned and incredulous, and actually too angry to cry. Sometimes she felt an impulse to wild, demonic laughter, and sometimes she wanted to stamp and scream with rage. Once more she had tried with all her soul to do the right thing according to the book of rules, and again she had been brutally betrayed. Nothing was fair, and nothing made any sense.

If Miles had died before the baby began, she could have gone back to New York with a rather wistful episode closed, and plunged into work and found herself again. But now she was trapped and forsaken. The relentless child would be born, the fruit not of a great love, but rather of her own good intentions, which as usual had gone wrong and wantonly boomeranged her.

She knew almost at once, in her uncompromising way, that now she did not want the child. There was no point in having it, with Miles gone. If she had loved Miles as she loved Oliver, it would have been something to cherish and adore. But poor Miles's child stood only for another well-meaning blunder on her part which she had to see through for its own sake. Miles's child stood for second best. Without its father, it had no place in the world.

She gave herself up grimly to the business of getting the thing over and living through it. She was thirty-two, and would not have an easy time. Since it had become impossible to go on with two kinds of creation at once and her book must wait, she read a great deal as a defence against thinking, nailing her mind to the printed page and forcing herself to comprehend it before she turned to the next. She helped to make the baby's clothes, sometimes with hands that shook with a kind of inner fury masked by smiling composure. She never gave way to tears or to the convulsions of frantic rebellion which tore through her like tornadoes without warning. And sometimes she tried to imagine what the little creature would be like, with such a heritage—Miles's diffidences and anxieties, her own seething self-control.

Her ordeal was cut short by the baby itself, which arrived at the end of May more than a month too soon. It was small and sickly and pathetic, but it had made up its mind to live, and so had Phoebe. And it was duly christened Jefferson at Bruton Parish Church, as Miles would have wished. Sometimes she wondered, even while she fed it, if it would always, all its life, seem to her a total stranger.

3

BY THE time she was well again, and able to go back to work on the unfinished book, the whole year with Miles had begun to have a curious, unreal quality, like a vivid dream—and she recognized in herself an echo of the summer in England when Oliver's vital presence had turned Miles into a shadow, and made her life in Williamsburg seem as though it had happened to somebody else. The out-of-focus mood persisted confusingly, just as it had followed her home to Williamsburg before and wrought upon her to send the letter to Oliver too late. Once more she was seeing double—the inviolate, insurgent thing that was herself, and the smiling automaton who moved through her days.

Including the baby, more than eighteen months of her life had gone by in a kind of fourth dimension over which she had had no control and of which she had only the haziest recollections now that she was back to normal again, comfortably bemused by a book, glued to a typewriter, turning out chapters which had apparently lain fallow in her mind only awaiting the day of release. This is either the best stuff I ever wrote or the very worst, she told herself, peeling off the pages, concerned that there seemed to be so little rewriting to do. Either I've lost the faculty of criticizing my own work, or I've got some sort of inspiration, she thought dubiously. Conny would hate being an inspiration. . . .

When Bracken arrived for Christmas that year she let him read the first half of the manuscript, and it made him blink. "Gosh," he said to Dinah in their room that night, for he had taken it to bed with him, "Phoebe is going to set the Thames on fire with this one. Everybody will run like hell from the serial rights, though."

Dinah, who was half asleep with her back to the light, turned over. "What's it about?" she asked, coming awake as she was always ready to do if Bracken wanted to talk.

"It's about Germans," said Bracken. "Germans at home, Germans in England, Germans anywhere. It's her own private declaration of war, and it's a daisy! She'll never dare to go back to Heidersdorf if she publishes this, I wonder if she realizes it!"

"Would they know?" asked Dinah.

"Of course they'd know, they never overlook anything!"

Bracken read on. Dinah squirmed round and lay with her cheek against his shoulder so she could read too. Pretty soon she said, "Golly!" and Bracken said, "I told you!" and turned the page. It was three o'clock before they put out the light.

Phoebe was delighted at Bracken's reaction to the manuscript and promised to get it down as fast as she could, and said she didn't care a hoot if everybody was going to be afraid of the serial rights. When he warned her that her name would be mud in Germany after the book came out she looked grave, for she had promised Rosalind she would come back, and already two summers had escaped her.

"I might go this year before it's published," she ruminated.

"You'd better, if you're going," said Bracken. "We'll get that war any minute now, and travelling might be difficult."

"Who is going to fight whom?" Phoebe asked with some sarcasm.

"Germany is going to fight England," he told her flatly. "It may not start that way, but that's how it will end. France—Russia—Austria—the Balkans—they're just also-rans. The main event is London against Berlin. To see who really rules the waves."

"England, of course," said Phoebe.

"Of course," he agreed promptly. "But she's going to have to demonstrate very soon. Somebody has to lick Germany and teach her manners. I only hope we'll have the sense over here to pitch in and help."

Phoebe stared at him.

"*America?*" she cried. "Fight *Germany?* I've been down here in the backwoods too long. What's going on in the world?"

"The Prussian so-and-so's have got their eye on the Panama Canal," said Bracken.

Phoebe didn't argue, though the words hit her plunk in the midriff, nor did she tell him he was crazy. Bracken never spoke without the book, and he and Dinah had been months abroad last summer. It was no good asking him how he knew. The chances were a hundred to one that he was right.

"I've just sent Johnny Malone to Berlin," said Bracken. "He speaks German now. I thought you'd like to know."

"Give him my love next time you write," said Phoebe.

"I wish I could," said Bracken, who had never approved of her marrying Miles.

4

It was the following June before the book was finished, and Phoebe took it up to New York herself, leaving little Jeff at home with Sue and his Mammy, who was Delilah's eldest daughter Rachel. She went to stay with Dinah and Bracken, who were soon to sail for their usual summer abroad. She wanted to buy some clothes and see some plays and get in touch with things again. And she had half promised to go on to Germany.

Bracken didn't come home to dinner the first evening she was there and Dinah explained.

"He's sitting up with the transatlantic cable," she said. "They've shot that Austrian Archduke who married Sophie Chotek, remember?"

"*Did* he marry her?" asked Phoebe, dimly recalling old scandals.

"Morganatically he did. She died with him, poor soul, at a place called Sarajevo. Bracken says this may be the kick-off."

"*War?*" cried Phoebe, thoroughly startled, and Dinah nodded.

"It's the time of year," she said vaguely.

"But—not because of Ferdinand and his Sophie Chotek!"

"He was Franz Josef's heir," said Dinah. "Bracken says anything can start it now. They're only waiting for an excuse. Things have been touchy there ever since Austria annexed some territory a few years ago."

"But I still don't see that England comes into it."

"War spreads, Bracken says. And they're all tied up in alliances and guarantees. England has got to stand by France, and France has got to stand by Russia, and they've both got to stand by Belgium—and so on."

"Wh-what about Oliver and Charles?" asked Phoebe, dazed.

"They'll be in it, of course. And so will Bracken—as a correspondent, the way he went to Cuba." Dinah's eyes were dark. "They get shot at just the same as soldiers."

"Oh, poor Rosalind—she always dreaded this so!"

"We never liked to say anything," Dinah began slowly, "but the chances of her getting out of Germany if they declare war on England are pretty slim. She'll be practically a prisoner."

"Can't we do something about it? Can't we get her out *first?*"

"How?" asked Dinah resignedly. "She *married* him!"

"I promised to go back," said Phoebe. "What if I sailed with you next week and asked her to meet me somewhere—Paris, or Switzerland, if she can't get to London."

"But, Phoebe, you've got the baby!"

"I don't think he'd miss me much, at his age. If I could get Rosalind to come to Paris for a few days' shopping, suppose, even if Conny came along we might be able to save her—"

"Darling, I don't think you quite comprehend," said Dinah gently, for living with Bracken made one a realist, "if war is declared Conrad will be mobilized—civilians can't travel about to shop—frontiers will be closed—France will be enemy territory for Rosalind."

"But there must be some way!" Phoebe insisted. "Let's get hold of Johnny in Berlin! Bracken could come at it some way through Johnny, and he could go to see her!"

But Bracken said firmly that Johnny had a couple of other things to see to just now, and two days later a cable forwarded to Phoebe from Williamsburg settled it: *Don't come. Don't try. Love always.* ROSA-LIND.

It looked for a while as though Serbia might be able to handle it, with a lot of tact and the grace of God. Dinah and Bracken sailed on the *Mauretania,* and Phoebe returned to Williamsburg feeling tied and help-less, and waited anxiously each day for the Richmond paper to arrive, hours ahead of the *Star* from New York.

It was from Sue's quiet house in Williamsburg that she watched the black cloud, at first no larger than a man's hand, gather above Europe as July ran out into August and the monstrous choosing up of sides began. Russia—Serbia—France—Belgium—England and the Oversea Dominions, the roll-call ran, against Germany and Austria-Hungary. It looked all right. It looked safe. But only Germany was ready.

In August Bracken's dispatches from Belgium began to appear in the *Star,* which Phoebe received daily. He had got out to the Continent in time to see the Germans enter Brussels on the twentieth—an army with banners and bands, breaking into the famous goose-step as it approached the Grands Boulevards—they had sent up a fresh army corps, replacing the battered troops who had done the fighting, to make the entry more impressive—the Belgian population stood on the pavement and watched it in stony silence, and though it was mid-afternoon on a showery summer day, the air was cold and black with hate, wrote Bracken, as the Germans took possession of the main squares and spread out through the captured city.

A week later Louvain was burned, deliberately set fire to, house by house, amid atrocities and terror. In Brussels it was hard to believe what the people of Louvain were suffering. Brussels had been merely over-run, as by locusts. Its occupation was orderly, though severe. Rheims fell on September fourth, was retaken by the French and then was pounded by German artillery for four solid days. . . . This was a new kind of war, wrote Bracken. German *Schrecklichkeit* was a new weapon. There were no rules to this war.

A letter from Dinah said she was working for the Red Cross in an office established in the ballroom of one of the big houses in Park Lane where young officers now getting killed in France had been waltzing a few weeks before. Charles had been promoted full colonel and given command of a cavalry regiment and was already in France. Oliver would be going out very soon as a brigade-major. Edward was rushing round London trying to get a job as somebody's ADC, and Archie would be chucked into the Judge Advocate General's department because he knew law, and was moaning that he would never see France.

In October there was a letter from Virginia:

> You'll never guess who has turned up in England (she wrote Phoebe) in a boatload of refugees from Antwerp! You see, my French being useful, I was asked to go down to Folkestone and help with the bewildered Belgian refugees who are streaming in there in such a state they don't even know their own names any more. Last Saturday I had just got back to my hotel after an exhaust-

ing day sorting out wailing children and broken-hearted women and a few wounded, when one of our assistants ran up to say would I please come back at once to the quay because somebody was asking for me. And it was *Cousin Sally!*

Of course the last anybody here heard of her she was safe in the South of France, but little, as Bracken is fond of saying, did we know! Had you people in Williamsburg any idea that Cousin Sally had had a daughter years ago in France, not by any one of her three lawful husbands, and that this Clémence—herself duly married— then had a daughter called Fabrice, who is now sixteen? (Clémence is dead, and so is her husband, and Fabrice has been brought up by Cousin Sally and calls her *belle-mère* because Cousin Sally still doesn't look like anybody's *grand'mère*.)

Fabrice was at school in Brussels, and when things began to look bad Cousin Sally went there to fetch her back to Cannes. But before they could leave Brussels mobilization set in, and made it impossible for civilians to travel, and the next thing they knew the Germans were right on top of them. I should have mentioned before—the whole thing is desperately complicated as you can see!—that with Cousin Sally beside Fabrice are her maid Elvire, a gaunt, middle-aged creature inclined to just sit and quietly drip with tears in the most pathetic way, and a very silent man, also French, forty-ish, in delicate health, who naturally had to be kept out of the Germans' clutches. So they all fled on to Antwerp, because that was the only train they could get into. And then Antwerp was bombed by the Zeppelins, and one bomb fell right at the end of the street where they were, and they *saw* the Zeppelin overhead, and saw the houses which were hit, and the dead bodies—and it was all just as we were told it would be, with vertical death and destruction as well as the old-fashioned horizontal kind, and Charles, God bless him, was right, and I only hope the right people listened to him in time.

Not long after that Namur went, and Antwerp began to be shelled by German artillery, and they had the most hair-raising escape down the Scheldt in a fishing-boat, which was one of the last to get away, with the city on fire behind them and hot flying ashes falling in their hair. They thought it was a boat going to Ostend, but it came straight on to England and landed them at Folkestone, pretty much done up, not having had anything to eat since the Lord knows when, and having lost every scrap of luggage except Cousin Sally's jewel-case, which Elvire managed to hold on to through everything. When our people at Folkestone began to ask Cousin Sally the usual rude questions about her resources and if she had any friends in England, she showed them the jewels—a king's ransom, I should think—and mentioned me as her nearest relative. And I was only ten minutes away from where she stood!

You can imagine the scene. I took them all back to my one bedroom at the hotel, which is packed out, and wangled a little cubbyhole on the top floor which the mysterious Sosthène could call his own, and left them to wash up and tidy themselves while I wheedled a decent meal for them in the dining-room, it being long after the usual hours for hot food. And now I have sent them all down to Farthingale to recover, while I get on with things here, rather wondering what the next boat will bring! Fabrice can wear the clothes I left at home, and no doubt will, and I've written Clare to help provide extras for the rest of them, until we can see where we are.

I can hear you shrieking, "But what's she *like!*" Well, she's exactly like what we have always imagined Cousin Sally would be. She must be getting on for seventy, but her figure and carriage are still young, and her hair is still red—very well done, too. And she does speak English with a French accent, just as Bracken told us she did, years ago. Of course her *maquillage* had run a bit, and her marcel had come loose, and she was tired and tragic and bewildered, but not at all confused, and never without dignity. If I had not happened to be there she would have taken them all to London and put them up at Claridge's and refurnished in Bond Street without delay. Tell Cousin Sedgwick he need have no anxiety, she's tough, and she's come through with her colors flying. What's more, I am convinced that the silent Sosthène is her property and not Fabrice's. The tenderness in his manner towards her is beyond words, and his concern for her comfort is like a lover's.

Bracken was at Brussels and Antwerp too, as you must already know, but in that mob they never saw each other—lucky for him! He left Antwerp in a motor car through Bruges to Ostend with a couple of British correspondents who simply had to keep one jump ahead of the Germans, and came on by boat to Dover. He had two days in London, most of the time asleep, though I believe he did something about a courier service as well, and has now gone back to Boulogne where our wounded are coming out.

The St. James's Square house is being turned into a hospital for wounded officers, and Dinah is doing whatever she can there, as I shall later on. Winifred is simply wonderful, and Clare has gone down to Gloucestershire to superintend turning the Hall into a convalescent home for soldiers. We do wish you were here, we could use you! I don't say anything about the sheer crowding horror of these days in England because you can read that anywhere and we keep too busy to think much about it. Archie is up in the Midlands somewhere doing I don't know what—*Captain* the Hon. Archie Campion, if you please!—and I haven't seen him for days and don't expect to for days more. London is pretty grim, with almost no light in the streets at night except for searchlights hunting for Zeppelins —everyone says we are bound to get them here before long, especially if we should lose the French Channel ports.

Do you still hear from Rosalind? She can't reach anybody in England now, so you are the last link. One daren't think what she may be up against these days, though Conrad's position will protect her to some degree. English people were roughly treated in Berlin when war was declared, and the Embassy windows were all smashed with rocks brought along by the mob for that purpose—you don't just pick up brickbats loose in the Wilhelmstrasse!—and a crowd stormed the Adlon Hotel looking for British newspaper correspondents, who had to get out the back way. Some Americans were mistaken for English and had a very lively time in the streets, and the Ambassador has been splendid. I keep wondering about Johnny Malone in Berlin—of course he is having the time of his life, though how he'll get his copy out nobody knows—there is no Western Union cable-landing in Germany, crazy as that seems, only one line which runs through the Azores.

Bracken saw the German Army pouring through Brussels for three days and three nights without stopping, like a mechanized caterpillar, with a dreadful mechanized *singing* in time to their feet—he saw the ruins of Louvain while they were still smoking— he saw the women's faces and the children—he talked to German officers and men—and he says it's nonsense to hope for a short war or an easy one. He says the Germans are a separate race, not quite human, with no margin for error. He says nothing will save us but being tougher and better trained and equipped and more determined than they are—and not getting rattled. He says they count on our getting rattled, and do everything they can to make us lose our heads and let each other down. He says there aren't any rules any more, the Germans always hit below the belt. He says sportsmanship isn't any good, with Germans, they only think you are a fool. He says Britain has got to throw the book out of the window and start slugging. And he says America has got to come in.

So heaven knows when we shall all be together again in the old way. But we've been sitting on the lid of this volcano so long it's almost a relief to find it has blown off at last, so that we can really get down to it. We shall win, of course, and teach Germany a lesson, but at what cost. I will do my best to keep track of things and let you hear often. Maia wanted to do her share, naturally, and they have taken her on at St. James's Square, but she's just as hard to get along with as she ever was—Winifred tells her off like a drill sergeant, but darling Dinah tries to be polite and I frankly avoid Maia, and it's all frightfully awkward and unnecessary and not at all the sort of thing one wants in a hospital where people ought all to pull together. At least Oliver will get a change! . . .

Phoebe sat holding the letter and staring at the desk in front of her where the galley proofs of the new book lay—the most timely thing possible to print, in its prophetic dissection of the German state of mind. Somewhere in the house little Jeff was crying, and she heard him without curiosity or impatience. Rachel was there to look after him, and always knew what to do. *We do wish you were here, we could use you.* . . . The most terrible story the world had ever seen was being enacted in France and England, and Phoebe Sprague was three thousand miles away.

Dinah and Bracken did not return for Christmas. By then the war had settled into a dismal stalemate in the trenches, a nightmare of mud and cold and snipers. Charles was reported missing in the fighting round Ypres early in November, where the cavalry had gone into the trenches with rifles and fought like infantry. Oliver had got a body wound at Wytschaete from which he was recovering in London. Rosalind's letters to Phoebe were few and brief, and sounded as though they had been dictated to her, or had been written under surveillance. Then they stopped coming.

The Lions' Den, which Bracken called Phoebe's private war with Germany, was published during the autumn in a whirlwind of publicity and made the expected sensation. She was trying hard by Christmas to begin a new book, and made nothing but false starts, because of a deep-rooted longing to write about London in wartime and she was not there to see it. She promised herself that when Bracken did come back she would go up to New York and make him tell her a lot of things he hadn't, for one reason or another, written for the *Star.*

Meanwhile little Jeff's first efforts to walk and talk, which so enthralled his grandparents, were more than likely to bring tears to Phoebe's eyes—Jeff didn't belong, and she was so sorry for him that it ached, and she strove constantly against a crooning, poor-baby love for him which was the most she could seem to feel. She was convinced that the family's poor-Miles habit had done irreparable harm, and her determination that there must never be a poor-Jeff atmosphere made her almost brusque with his baby griefs lest he should learn the self-pity which had cursed his father.

In April Dinah and Bracken were back in New York. Dinah had badly overdone it at the hospital and was ordered to take a long rest. Bracken too was suffering from nervous fatigue and from the restrictions, amounting to embargo, which Kitchener and General French had placed on war correspondents at the front. Everyone was now becoming thoroughly alarmed about Rosalind, who had not sent one word out of Germany for months.

Phoebe thought it over carefully and then packed up little Jeff and Rachel and took them along when she went to New York. She was not going to have it said in Williamsburg that she had deserted her child and gone off on a wild-goose chase. Dinah met them at the station with the motor, looking rather thin and white, and gazed with delight at Jeff in his mammy's arms.

"Oh, Phoebe, he's beautiful!" she said enviously. "I'm Dinah, Jeff—say Dinah—*please* do—*Dinah*," she insisted, pointing to herself.

"Diney," said Jeff, and hid his face in Rachel's neck as though aware that he had muffed the word, but Dinah was enchanted.

They could talk about Oliver in the car driving home, for Rachel and Jeff did not count. He was quite all right again, Dinah insisted, and was going to have a Staff job at the War Office now, so he would be safe and dry in London and they didn't have to worry. It was Charles they worried about—still missing, though the Red Cross at Geneva was trying to trace him—not reported prisoner—not known to be dead. It was the kind of thing that drove wives nearly mad. But Charles hadn't got a wife, and Rosalind wouldn't know. Phoebe confessed that she had begun to fight a lurking dread that Rosalind might not be alive. The *Schloss* was well back of the German Eastern Front—but Conrad would be away with his regiment, and who knew what might happen to Rosalind, left alone with Aunt Christa and the other terrible women of his family? Where was the maid Gibson and her promise to keep in touch? What became of the letters Phoebe still faithfully mailed to Rosalind? The old melodramatic sense of Rosalind's doom was heavy on her heart.

When Bracken came home to dinner he was taken straight up stairs to the room which Dinah had several years ago prepared as a nursery, and there was introduced to Jeff, who was just being put to bed.

"This is Bracken," Dinah told the baby, pointing. "Say Bracken, Jeff —*do* say it, darling—"

"Backers," said Jeff, and chortled at Dinah, who chortled back.

Bracken offered to shake hands gravely, and Jeff reciprocated, a little limp with surprise and drowsiness—he had never been invited to shake hands before. Phoebe stood looking down at them—Dinah kneeling by the crib, an arm along the pillow—Bracken leaning over the opposite rail—and all three of them and Rachel laughing like ninnies. Phoebe was conscious of the steady, triumphant growth of an Idea.

5

AFTER dinner that night, when they had settled cosily over coffee and liqueurs in the library, she sprang it on them.

"Bracken, I want to go to Germany and find out about Rosalind."

Dinah drew in her breath and looked at Bracken, who said quietly after a moment, "You have to have a passport these days."

"You can fix that for me, can't you?"

"I suppose so."

"B-but, Phoebe, what about the *baby?*" cried Dinah.

"Will you keep him?" Phoebe asked casually. "I needn't be gone much more than a month."

Dinah's eyes grew very large in her thin face, staring at Phoebe.

"Could I?" she whispered, as though afraid somebody might say No, it was all a mistake. Then suddenly her voice rang out like a peal of bells. "Oh, darling, *could I?*"

"He won't be any trouble so long as he's got Rachel," Phoebe nodded. "And I'll feel more in touch if he's here in New York with you." She turned confidently to Bracken. "How long should it take to get the passport?"

"Maybe ten days." He took the pipe from his mouth and knocked it out against an ashtray on the table beside him, like a good actor holding his pause. "There may be some difficulty about the German visa," he said.

"But I'm an American!" Phoebe bristled.

"You certainly are," Bracken agreed. "And you wrote a book called *The Lions' Den,* remember?"

"They won't know about that."

"Why won't they? Their Ambassador here can read."

"But it's not *important* enough!"

"How many thousand copies have been sold?"

"Quite a lot," she admitted with chagrin.

"Well, you must have a pretty fair idea how Conrad and his kind will react to that book."

"They'd be frothing."

"Well, there you are."

"Bracken, you don't suppose it would have anything to do with Rosalind not writing?"

"It might. She might be forbidden to have anything more to do with you."

"I've got to go anyway," said Phoebe obstinately. "It might just as well not be anything to do with the book. She might be ill, or—especially if Conrad is away she might be tyrannized over in a dozen ways. Maybe she isn't getting my letters, or can't get her answers out of the *Schloss*. Maybe they've sent Gibson away. You've got to help, Bracken, you know our Ambassador in Berlin, don't you?"

"I do. But he's not God." Bracken pondered, rubbing the bowl of his pipe with his thumb in a way he had. They both watched him, hanging on his next words. "I could get you as far as Switzerland," he ruminated. "You could go to Zurich."

"What good would that do?"

"I'll have Johnny meet you there. You can give him all the facts and all the questions—you daren't write 'em—and then wait there while he investigates."

"How?" asked Phoebe with some skepticism.

Bracken said after a pause, "He has been visiting prisoner-of-war camps with a secretary from our Embassy. He will arrange—through the Embassy—to visit the nearest camp to Heidersdorf. Being there, he will pay an innocent American call at the *Schloss* as an old friend of yours. We can leave the rest to him. Nobody can think of more inconvenient questions to ask than Johnny can if he smells a rat. Of course if he sees her without any trouble we'll know at once how things are. Anyway, it's the best I can think of at the moment."

Phoebe said she supposed it would have to do, but it wouldn't be like seeing Rosalind herself.

"The *Lusitania* sails about the first of the month," said Bracken. "I'll try and get you on her. There's some risk now, of course. The Germans have given out that they'll sink British ships anywhere near the war zone."

"That's what Charles used to call their bogey-bogey-bogey technique," said Phoebe lightly, and they began to talk of Charles, and of Tommy Chetwynd who had been killed at Neuve Chapelle in March, and of the Zeppelin raids on England's East Coast, and—with growing animation —of Cousin Sally, who was Phoebe's aunt, and who by some magic artifice looked very much today as she had looked when Bracken last saw her at Cannes in the year of the Jubilee.

"And to Sosthène," said Bracken solemnly, beginning to refill his pipe, "she is still the only woman in the world."

Dinah said Sosthène was a lamb.

"An expensive lamb," Bracken remarked. "They all went up to London and Cousin Sally sold a diamond bracelet on which they can apparently all live forever. She gave Sosthène a wad of money and he went to Archie's tailor. You never saw such a wardrobe!"

"Well, she also took Fabrice to *Lucile*," said Dinah, with a slanting look at him. "I didn't hear any complaints about that!"

"I protest," said Bracken, at work on his pipe. "Phoebe, I protest. There are several one-syllable Anglo-Saxon words for Fabrice, and the time is coming when I no longer refrain from using them. I admit Fabrice made eyes at me. Archie wasn't there, and she knows it's no use with Sosthène. I think in the circumstances I behaved very well, when what I really wanted to do was clout her one, hard."

"She's a flirt, eh," said Phoebe drily.

"That's euphemism," said Bracken, and struck a match, and Dinah giggled at him.

"He got a sort of *hunted* look," she said reminiscently. "Fabrice had got hold of that Southern phrase, kissing kin, and insisted Bracken was within the degree of cousinship to be kissed regularly on the slightest provocation, in order that Fabrice might demonstrate that she was a good little American!"

"How Johnny will love to hear about this," Phoebe said. "He always wanted to know more about Aunt Sally. Where are they now?"

"At Farthingale most of the time. Virginia being in London, that's an ideal arrangement."

"At least she's lucky they aren't penniless," Phoebe suggested.

"Well, yes, there are small mercies," Bracken conceded, puffing. "*Very small*," he qualified at once.

6

To DINAH the loan of little Jeff Day even for a month—and Bracken said it would be at least two before Phoebe came back—was rapture as uncomplicated as that of a child with a new doll. She had come safely past a dozen psychological pitfalls to a sane acceptance of the fact that she could never have a child for Bracken, and she never looked back now to a time soon after her marriage when she had started a list of names, both boys' and girls' to be on the safe side, and added to it when a new one struck her fancy—or to the time when at last it looked as though she might begin to catch up with the other wives in the family, and the bright nursery room on the upper floor had been made ready—or to the dreadful time when she lost the baby and almost died, and they told her she could not have another, and she felt only a blissful relief that nothing like that could ever happen to her again—or to the time, months later, when it began to dawn on her that she was letting Bracken down, by not giving him a son to carry on the newspaper as he had done for his father. That knowledge grew and worked in her until she went resolutely and ignorantly to the doctor and asked for an operation so that she could try again, and he had to explain that there wasn't an operation for a case like hers; whereupon the recent months of secret humiliation and self-abasement told on her and she broke down and cried, and the doctor in his wisdom told her what Bracken had said when the crisis came: "I can do without a child," Bracken said with white lips, "but without Dinah life's no good to me." Dinah looked up at the doctor, quivering, and gasped, "You *chose?*" and the doctor shook his head and said, "*He* chose."

Ever since then Dinah had held her head very high. Bracken chose. And he chose *her*. The doctor had given her back her self-respect, and thereafter she never faltered again, and ceased to feel secretly apologetic to Bracken, or slavishly anxious to please him, or abjectly afraid of not doing everything she could to make up to him for the one thing she couldn't. She became just Dinah again, gay and self-possessed and adorable. Bracken told himself that at last she had got over losing the baby, and he too became himself again, and stopped being a little too cheerful, to show her he didn't mind a bit, or watching every word he spoke for fear of reminding her, or dreading the sight of all the other babies in the family which might upset her.

The empty nursery stayed where it was, because they didn't need the room for anything else, and it was used periodically by Gwen's babies when she and Fitz brought them along to New York, and even by Virginia's the autumn she paid a visit there. Virginia remarked to Eden that Dinah was just like the women of their own family, who always loved their husbands better than their children, and made few bones about it, and Eden recalled with rueful laughter that her mother always used to say that Aunt Louise Sprague would have cut off Sedgwick's head to save Uncle Lafe's life any day.

Phoebe discovered with chagrin when the time came to leave Jeff and Rachel behind and sail for England that she minded it rather more than she had expected to. And then she wondered with her usual honesty if it wasn't more because of the tranquil way he had settled into his new quarters without seeming to care much whether she was there or not, than that she would miss him herself. Dinah had the inborn knack of playing with children and Phoebe hadn't, and it made no difference which of them was the mother, Dinah belonged in a nursery and Phoebe remained a visitor there.

On that last Saturday morning Phoebe and Dinah sat on the floor beside Jeff, who was busy with blocks, and talked for a bit over his head about food and fresh air and not too many new playthings all at once, and what Phoebe was to tell everybody in St. James's Square. Then Bracken called up the stairs that the car was waiting. Phoebe managed with some difficulty to plant a kiss on Jeff's cheek and stood up, straightening her hat.

"Don't come down with me," she said to Dinah. "He might suspect something and begin to howl. Good-bye, Jeff, you're in clover here, and don't you forget it."

"Say Good-bye to Phoebe," Dinah admonished him.

"Goo'-bye to Fee," said Jeff unemotionally.

"Wave your hand to her," Dinah prompted.

He waved his hand.

"Well—good-bye," said Phoebe rather flatly, and bent to kiss Dinah and ran down the stairs.

Then the one Jeff called Diney grabbed him and held him so tight it almost hurt. He endured it for a minute and then squirmed uneasily.

Instantly her hold relaxed, and she looked down at him with shiny beads on her cheeks.

"I mustn't break you, must I," she whispered.

He grinned at her. She grinned back. On a mutual impulse they fell again into each other's arms.

PART EIGHT

W*A*R

>>

1

$\mathbb{B}$RACKEN went on board with Phoebe and saw her luggage into the small inside stateroom on B Deck which she had all to herself, as she preferred it to sharing a larger one with a stranger. It was all he had been able to get for her at short notice.

While they stood together counting the bags his mind went back to the notice signed by the German Embassy at Washington which they had seen in the morning paper during breakfast—a formal statement that vessels flying the flag of Great Britain or her allies were liable to destruction in the waters adjacent to the British Isles and that travellers on the Atlantic voyage sailed at their own risk. Phoebe had asked at breakfast what that meant, and Bracken replied rather tersely that it meant submarines. Phoebe reminded him that the *Lusitania* was not a battleship. Bracken said she was a British ship, and asked Phoebe bluntly if she would rather wait a few days and go on an American liner, or a Dutch one. Phoebe told him not to be silly.

Now he looked at her gravely in the cramped little room, with the electric light bulb glaring down from the ceiling and the bustle of white-coated stewards and the passengers' cheery voices outside the open door.

"I wish I were going with you," he said. "Tell 'em I'll be back soon, anyway. Next month, probably. Not Dinah. She's had enough for a while. She and Jeff will have to hold the fort here."

"Then I may see you in London before I start back," Phoebe suggested, pleased.

"Very likely." He glanced around the cabin. "See that thing there?

That's your life-belt. Remember where it is, so you could find it in the dark. And if ever you think the ship has been hit, put on your life-belt and go straight up to the boat deck. Don't go without it. Wherever you are, come and get it first. See?"

"Bracken, you don't really think they—"

"No. Not really. But judging by myself, one's tendency would be all to rush up to the open air, one would have a fear of being trapped down here. That's why I'm telling you to remember the life-belt if anything happens. There would be plenty of time to come and fetch it. Then you're safe. You'll float." He grinned, and bent to kiss her. "Don't have bad dreams, though," he said. "This would be a hard boat to catch, even if they tried."

Holding to his sleeve she went up the crowded main staircase with him to the lounge, where they saw no one they knew, though the place seemed to be full of celebrities. Finally Bracken kissed her again, and went away down the gang-plank, trying not to think he was having some kind of hunch, trying not to keep telling himself that she looked so helpless and *young*.

Phoebe wandered about the ship, seeing familiar faces among the stewards, and renewing her memory of the luxurious layout of the public rooms. The last time she had sat in that very corner with a book the world was comparatively simple and at peace, and she was on her way to visit Rosalind at Heidersdorf as a welcome guest. The last time she had dozed in a deck-chair under a plaid rug they knew at least that Rosalind was all right. . . . Which reminded her that she must see to her deck-chair, and she had one placed well aft on the boat deck on the starboard side in the sun. A middle-aged lady who was obviously an experienced traveller was already tucked up in one near by, and was half way through a new copy of *The Lions' Den*.

Descending to the dining-saloon to make her table reservation, Phoebe accepted with smiling resignation a place at the Captain's table—she never took much satisfaction in playing the famous authoress—and the first night out went to bed very early, convinced that she had nothing better to do. Besides, a young man in a peaked cap and a knickerbocker suit had passed her three times on the deck before dinner, casting interested glances each time, and she did *not* feel in the mood for a shipboard flirtation.

It was a smooth voyage in warm spring sunshine, and the portholes on B and C Decks stood open to the rhythmic swish of white water under the keel, and the air in the lower passages was damp and salty and made Phoebe's hair curl. On the decks children ran about in summer clothes without hats, and people sunned themselves till they burned. There was some talk among the passengers of submarines, and the middle-aged lady in the deck-chair near Phoebe said she knew a man who had actually cancelled his sailing at the last minute because of that notice put in by the German Embassy, and then she pointed out another man who had had himself transferred from the *Carpathia* because he felt that a fast boat like this one would be safer.

She was one of those travellers who make a point of knowing all about everyone on board, and it had taken her no time at all to extract from Phoebe that she was the author of the book everyone was reading, and to volunteer the information that the interested young man in the peaked cap was of an old Philadelphia family and *very* wealthy, and was going to Geneva to do something splendid with the International Red Cross. Phoebe then relented and allowed him to be presented to her, as she felt that a friend at Geneva might be helpful later on.

Thereafter, though he tried visibly not to be a nuisance, young Mr. Kendrick was rather under foot, and Phoebe found him gay, a little cheeky, and—amusing. He was not exactly a handsome young man—his nose was too big, and his dark hair grew high—but he had a curling, humorous mouth and pointed, humorous eyebrows, and he made her laugh. More, he made her feel younger than she had felt for years.

On Thursday morning when Phoebe came on deck she noticed that they had swung out the lifeboats and uncovered them. The day passed uneventfully, with everybody saying that the trouble, if there was going to be any trouble, would come on Friday night as the ship ran for Liverpool across the Irish Sea. During the usual ship's concert, which took place on Thursday evening, the main lounge got rather stuffy because all the shades had been drawn, and the doors to the deck were closed to keep the light inside. When she and Mr. Kendrick went out for a breath of air after the program he said that smoking was forbidden on deck after dark.

Phoebe leaned her elbows on the rail beside his and he cheated so that their shoulders touched and the high white fur collar of her brocade wrap brushed his cheek, and he said, "Look, all you fishes and mermaids out there, look who's standing up here beside me—Miss Phoebe Sprague— the one that writes all the books." He cocked his head around to see her face inside the shielding collar. "*Miss* Phoebe Sprague," he repeated, and his eyes were bright and his teeth gleamed in his quirky smile. "How did that ever happen? Have you got a heart of stone, or something? It doesn't go with the books."

"Are you asking me, after five days' acquaintance, why I don't seem to be married?"

"I am. Provided that you aren't."

"None of your business," she said deliberately, after a moment.

"I begin to think it is." The friendly pressure of his shoulder against hers increased ever so little. "Because after five days' acquaintance I am falling in love with you."

"Now, Mr. Kendrick—" Phoebe straightened, with a smooth, aloof movement.

"I know, I know, How dare you Mr. Kendrick, and all that!" His voice was warm and easy, and he made no effort to follow her withdrawal, so that his very stillness against the rail held her where she was, less than a foot away from him. "Maybe it's *lèse majesté*. Maybe I should have put in my application through the Ambassador. Maybe I ought to show credentials. I come of rich but honest parents, I'm the only son, I learnt my law at Harvard, and I think America ought to be doing something about this damned war, and if she won't I will. So I bought an ambulance and bribed my way into the Red Cross with it. I'm twenty-six next birthday, and everybody says I ought to get married—"

"That's what everybody said about me," she broke in sharply. "And I did."

"You—did?"

"I'm a widow. I've got a son a year old."

"I—didn't know."

"You're not to blame for that. I only mentioned it because I want to say—because I like you so much I want to say, Don't ever let anybody talk you into it just because it's time. Wait till you just can't help yourself. And now, Mr. Kendrick, please take your old grandmother inside and send her off to bed before she can give any more personal advice."

She turned and walked briskly towards the door into the main hall, which was now masked by a dark curtain hung inside it. When he had seen her start down the passage towards her room Mr. Kendrick headed for the bar.

2

PHOEBE was awakened at an early hour Friday morning by the foghorn, and as she had been somewhat later than usual dropping off to sleep—largely because she had kept saying to herself, And I'm *seven years older* than he is, it's come to *that*—she buried her face in the pillow and moaned, instead of going down to breakfast. Presently the foghorn stopped, but by that time she was hopelessly awake so she rang for the stewardess and had breakfast on a tray. The stewardess said you could see Ireland now, on the port side, and the fog had lifted nicely.

Phoebe dressed at leisure and went up to her chair on the boat deck, and sure enough, there was Ireland, looking very green and solid. She rolled herself in the plaid rug and pretended at once to be asleep in case Mr. Kendrick came by. Pretty soon she did doze, so that the luncheon bugle took her by surprise. She was not hungry and stayed where she was, waiting grimly for the departure to lunch of a pair of small romping children whose pattering footsteps and artless voices had impinged every now and then on her pleasant coma. I'll let luncheon go, she thought comfortably. That egg will last me till tea time if I don't take any exercise. It will be nice and quiet here when everybody else has gone down to feed. I must teach Jeff not to run about and crow with innocent glee like the story-books when he is on shipboard. . . . She dozed again, on the almost deserted deck, and gradually became aware that lunch was finishing and people were drifting back again.

She was still only half awake when she distinctly felt a dull, heavy bump somewhere and raised her head sharply—the ship gave a long shudder, and instantly there was another shock, harder than the first, like an explosion somewhere below. A man's voice rose in a single warning shout, and the air was full of salt water and falling fragments of wood and even bits that rattled like metal. Some of it landed quite near her chair, and the rug which covered her was splashed with shining drops of sea water. Her mind was slower than her nerves, and she was trembling all over by the time she heard herself thinking, *We've been hit.*

She disentangled her legs from the rug with difficulty and stood up unsteadily. People were running towards the starboard side from all over the ship, and some of them were already hurling themselves at the lifeboats just forward of where she stood. The deck beneath her feet had tilted to that side, so that it was downhill to the rail.

Phoebe's mind was ticking now, but her legs were shaky and she felt a wild pounding in her ears which was her heartbeats. I mustn't be frightened—a big ship like this can't sink—my life-belt—Bracken said to get my life-belt—it's only as far as B Deck—there will always be time to get it—I'll be safe then—I'll float—

She walked firmly up the sloping deck and through the door into the main hall, where everyone else seemed to be hurrying out. She got down the stairs against the tide and turned towards her room, choosing the right one of four possible directions without hesitation. My passport, she was thinking clearly—my letter of credit, locked in the top of my trunk—my warm coat—the picture of Jeff on the bedside table—my gloves—

She reached the stateroom and pressed the light switch, noticing that her fingers fumbled and were cold, clenching her teeth with fury at these signs of her own weakness in a crisis. A ship like the *Lusitania* can't just go down like a stone, she told herself scornfully. Besides, we're just off Ireland. They'll see us from shore. They'll send out to pick us up in no time. It's only because I'm alone that I feel this way, if Bracken were here I'd be able to think nothing of it—it's frightening not to have someone to tell me what to do—times like these one wants a man around—a man that *belongs* to you—

She laid the life-belt on the bed and got her keys out of her purse and unlocked the trunk—put the passport and letter of credit into her handbag, and the little picture of Jeff taken on the lawn at Williamsburg —she wanted that to show Virginia—Virginia wasn't the only one who could have babies—she turned to the wardrobe to get her heavy coat— and the light went out.

Phoebe grabbed the side of the wardrobe as though the ship had lurched—had it?—of course not—and heard above the renewed thumping in her own ears the pound of running feet on the deck above. Then she snatched the life-belt from the bed and stepped out into the passage. Not only her own cabin light, but all the lights in that part of the ship had gone. There was a dim greyness and a damp smell of sea from the open portholes at the ends of the cross passages which ran to the outer tier of staterooms, and she thought, Somebody ought to have closed them. And realizing that now she had to walk in the angle formed by the floor and the side walls of the cabins, she thought, if we go on heeling over like this the water will pour in through the portholes—perhaps it's already coming in on the lower decks—that would sink us—

And the dread Bracken had foreseen of being caught down there took her by the throat, and she slipped and caught at the hand-rail, and said between her teeth, *Behave yourself!* When she reached the main square from which the central staircase rose, she found with relief that the lights still burned there, and there was no panic and no outcry among the people packed patiently, even courteously, on the steps which were now tilted sideways at such an angle that everybody had to hold on to everybody else. Half way up, a child had begun to cry and a woman's voice called "Harry!" and there was no answer.

Phoebe forced herself to stand quietly at the foot of the stairs, carrying her life-belt and handbag, waiting her turn for a footing on the bottom step, and trying fiercely to control the beating of her heart, which felt as though it had no anchor anywhere but was simply knocking about in her chest like a bird against bars, making her limp and giddy. She heard someone call out from above that the ship had found herself and the bulkheads were closed, and the danger was over. People around her smiled wanly and started shaking hands with each other, and a man said Well, that was near enough, and there was a little laughter. But they all stayed where they were, inching up the stairs. Then a quiet voice just behind her said, "There's a companionway further forward which is much clearer. Will you please come with me?"

It was Mr. Kendrick. Phoebe turned thankfully to follow him, and he spoke beyond her to the other people near the foot of the stairs.

"There's another way up which will be quicker," he said as though reasoning with small, frightened children. "Come along with us, and we'll show you."

A few detached themselves from the fringes and followed. Most of them simply stood where they were, clinging, desperately composed, seeming dazed.

"Take my hand," said Mr. Kendrick, and Phoebe reached out to him, ashamed of the clammy paw his competent grip closed on. "Never mind the rail, just straddle the angle—that's it—not far to go—the lights are out up here, but I know the way—"

She noticed that he carried three life-belts dangling from their straps in his free hand. He pulled her up the slanting companionway into the sunshine, and she turned instinctively towards the high side of the ship, towards land. The deck was full of confused, half-frantic people, running, calling, sobbing, or just aimlessly wandering, sometimes two by two. There seemed to be no ship's officers in sight, to bring order out of the chaos.

"This way," said Mr. Kendrick, and they half ran, half slid down across the sloping deck to starboard. "The port-side boats can't be lowered now, they've swung too far inboard. Let's get that life-belt on you, shall we? You get into it like a jacket. That's it. Now we tie the tapes. Like that. Very becoming. Do you want to try for a boat, or would you rather just take a chance?"

"Well, I—wh-what are *you* going to do?" As she spoke, the lifeboat on the davits nearest them suddenly let go by the stern, fouling its ropes, and spilled its screaming occupants into the water. Phoebe flinched and looked away, and felt his shoulder like a rock behind hers. "Let's stay here," she gasped. "Hadn't you better put on one of those belts yourself?"

A woman's voice cried out again for Harry, and now it held a note of fear. Kendrick turned quickly, and they saw her coming along the deck towards them, grabbing at things for anchorage along the way, dragging by the hand a small girl child who was whimpering with fright. She had no life-belts.

"Stay here," said Kendrick, hooking Phoebe to another companionway rail, and went to the woman who had lost Harry and offered her one of his belts. She shook her head, her eyes wandering beyond him.

"No, thank you, my husband has gone down for ours. He'll find us any minute."

"But just in case he can't find you in all this confusion—"

"No, thank you, really." She staggered away from him, dragging the child, dismissing him almost irritably with an impatient gesture, absorbed in her anxious search.

A very old gentleman, leading a very old lady by the hand, caught timidly at Kendrick's arm from behind.

"Have you got—extras?" he asked.

"I have, I've got two extras," said Kendrick promptly, and helped the two old people into the life-belts, assuring them that the ship would have been seen from the shore, and reminding them that the distant sails of fishing-smacks had been in sight all morning, and the lighthouse on Kinsale Head was just opposite.

But it was plain to Phoebe as she stood holding to the companionway rail that the ship was sinking steadily by the head, until now she realized with horror that a lifeboat filled with people but still on its davits was *floating* beside the outer rail, and no one had cast loose its ropes. If the ship suddenly settled the lifeboat would be dragged down with it. There was one steward fumbling with its bow-ropes, and no one to help him—he seemed to be hacking at them with a pen-knife. A man went past her wearing a life-belt, and his trousers were wet to the knees from the water in the lower passages.

Looking forward towards the bridge, she saw that the sea was now flush with the scuppers of A Deck there, and people clinging to the outer rail were being slowly forced aft by the lapping water, which gained and gained, so that those in front either let go and floated away or felt their way backward by holding on to those behind them. Phoebe was still being suffocated by her own heartbeats, but she felt very calm in spite of that, thanks to Mr. Kendrick, who was in a way taking Bracken's place and filling her need of masculine strength and presence of mind.

"We're going down pretty fast," she murmured when she felt him return to her side.

"Yes, we are. There will be a good deal of suction, you know, as she sinks, so you must try very hard to come back to the surface."

"H-how long—?"

"Any minute now, I should think. Those open portholes have let her fill very fast below. Take a deep breath when you feel her going, and fight like mad to come up. Your belt will help you. And try to get away from the ship as far as possible because there'll be a lot of débris. Just don't get rattled, and you'll be all right. That thing will keep you afloat for hours."

"Won't you please put yours on?"

"*Harry!*" cried the same voice again, with hysteria in it, and the child was crying.

Kendrick interrupted the woman's aimless progress for the second time, holding out his life-belt.

"Put your arms in this," he rapped out. "Quick. Do as I say."

"Oh, *no*—!" Phoebe began, and smothered her protest as the woman obeyed him, passively allowing him to tie the tapes.

"Take the child in your arms," he said, and shook her to make her hear. "Take hold of the child and hang on to her!"

The woman nodded blankly, and bent over the child.

"But that belt was *yours!*" cried Phoebe.

"Oh, I can swim," he told her with a confident smile. "I've won prizes, swimming. I'll be all right. Keep your head, now, and don't forget which way is up! Here we go, I'll try to find you again in the water—"

Phoebe was watching, suspended in time, while the edge of the clear green water reached for her feet, felt it cold around her ankles, felt it grip her knees—in her ears was a long sobbing moan which was the voice of the dying ship as she went down. Phoebe thought, The funnels —they'll smash us in the water— And then the world turned icy cold and there was no way to breathe.

Strangling, kicking, choking, she realized that something held her by the arm like a snake, and she was caught in an endless coil of rope which wound itself around her right side, burning her wrist and hand with its drag. She fought it wildly, painfully, and it let go, and she found herself gulping down fresh air again with her face above the surface.

Then something else hit her a grinding blow on the right shoulder and she cried out with the pain, and heard the cry echoed a dozen times as people on all sides of her thrashed and flailed about trying to catch hold of anything that floated, trying to make room for their own ghastly, contorted faces in the thick floating mass of loose débris—planks, chairs, hatch covers, crates, oars, loose boards and wooden railings, which made a sort of giant scum on the quiet sea. Caught in it, people were praying aloud and calling out for lost companions and shouting for boats to pick them up, and inevitably there rose again the high wild wail for Harry.

Vaguely mindful of Kendrick's parting words, Phoebe tried to push herself away from where she thought the ship had been, but her right side was utterly useless and an agony to bear and she knew there were broken bones somewhere. So she drifted, the life-belt holding her face upwards to the calm sunny sky, and she felt the cold water already numbing her feet, and wondered how soon the fishing-boats would come and begin taking people out of the water, and how many lifeboats had got away from the ship safely, and if there would be room in any of them for people in the water—wondered what had become of Mr. Kendrick, and for a moment entertained the idea of calling to him, but it would sound awfully silly to set up a howl for "Mr. Kendrick" like a page-boy, and she didn't know his other name. Besides, she didn't want to sound like that poor daft soul who had mislaid Harry. . . .

The sun on the water was dazzling, and there was a long, slow swell, and for the first time in her life Phoebe began to feel seasick. But I didn't have any luncheon, she protested to her insurgent insides, and at once lost what must have been her breakfast. The human sounds were diminishing all round, as she drifted, and the numbness reached her knees, and she couldn't be sure if she still had her shoes. The life-belt pulled and pressed on her injured shoulder till she almost wished it wasn't there. And gradually her thoughts got more confused and like a dream when you know you are dreaming but can't wake yourself up.

I'm glad Bracken didn't come with me, she thought, beginning lucidly enough. Dinah would be out of her mind with worry, and he is the kind to give away his life-belt too—nobody could swim long in this water— but what a story he would have got if he'd lived through it—there's nobody to be out of their mind about me, Jeff's too little, and I don't belong to anyone—not the way Bracken does—perhaps it's just as well, in case I'm not picked up at all—am I going to die now, like this?—will Rosalind ever know what happened to me, and that I tried to come?— why don't I seem to be frightened? of dying, I mean—it's the cold— and the way my shoulder hurts—no fight left in me, I reckon—if it didn't hurt so, I could splash, and make a noise—they'll think I'm dead —I might just get left here, when the boats come, if I look dead—

But at the first effort to move, to see where she was and what was around her, she sank back sick with pain and lay quiet on the water again, her eyes closed against the sun, her long brown hair floating.

I lost my handbag, fighting off that rope, she thought. A man is so lucky to have pockets—what time was it?—about two, we'd set the clock up again—when will they hear about it, in England—tea time—Virginia will start ringing people up—I wonder where Archie is—Charles isn't there to help—one always thinks of Charles—if she rang up the War Office— And the thought she had held back so long, the name she had forbidden her mind to utter, would not be denied—it reached her lips in a soft despairing moan as she lost consciousness—*Oliver.* . . .

5

THE news reached London in the late afternoon, first as a nerve-crisping whisper at the Admiralty, then as a low-voiced horror at the War Office—and shortly by some mysterious underground route it was carried to the crowd which began to collect at the Cunard office in Cockspur Street, where mute, white-faced clerks had no further information to give.

It came to Oliver from the grim lips of a young subaltern who brought some papers into his office for signature—"I say, they've sunk the *Lusitania,* sir—bang off the coast of Ireland she was—how's that for cheek?"

Oliver shook his head, picked up his pen—and paused.

"What about her passengers?"

"Sunk without warning, sir. Frightful loss of life, I should think. Survivors, if there are any, will probably be landed at Queenstown."

Oliver wrote his name on the top paper with a steady hand, blotted it, and said, "Come back in ten minutes."

"Thank you, sir."

When the subaltern had gone, Oliver rang up the house in St. James's Square, where Virginia was working as a V.A.D. in the wards, and asked if she knew what boat Phoebe was sailing on. Virginia told him.

"Why?" she asked then, when he said nothing more. "What's the matter? Oliver, are you there?"

And he had to explain.

He hung up on a stunned silence at Virginia's end, and sat a moment staring at the pen still in his hand. Very slowly then he traced his name again, and reached for the blotter. Then with a jerk he threw down the pen and started for his commanding officer's room. As he crossed the threshold his telephone rang, and he left it ringing, and it was finally answered by somebody from the next room, who made a note on Oliver's pad that he was to call his sister-in-law, Mrs. Archie Campion, at once.

The General was a compassionate man, for all his red tabs and power in office, and he listened silently with his eyes on Oliver's drawn face.

"You see, sir, the girl being a sort of relation of mine, quite young, and travelling all alone, I'm asking you for leave to go to Ireland tonight. My brother Archie is in France. I'm the only possible one to go and bring her on to England—in case she's hurt, that is, or—"

"Last train to Fishguard leaves Paddington about eight," said the General. "Takes three hours longer by Holyhead. Fishguard is a closed port, though—this is an Admiralty job. Sit down, I'll see what I can do on the telephone."

Oliver collapsed thankfully into the nearest chair, while the General spoke tersely to people at the Admiralty. It took a little time and patience, but it was arranged. By seven o'clock Oliver was in possession of his leave and his passes, and had borrowed money for the journey from everybody in sight because the banks had closed.

He rang up Virginia then and reported that he was off to Queenstown at once. Shirking an encounter with Maia in St. James's Square, he sent out for food and ate it at his desk, while further scraps of information trickled down the telephone. Fishing-boats and trawlers were out in the Channel working against the oncoming darkness, pulling people out of the water. Hundreds were believed lost. Hundreds of bodies might be brought in—women—children—the ship had gone down within twenty minutes after she was hit, no one could think why. . . .

He arrived at Paddington without luggage a few minutes before the train to Fishguard left, and sat silent and withdrawn in a smoking-compartment with a couple of civilians and a man he suspected of being an American journalist.

About three in the morning, at the last station before Fishguard, the Intelligence Police came through the train examining identity cards and papers. They passed Oliver's credentials without comment, but the American journalist was politely questioned and removed from the train. They drew up on the quay at Fishguard in the first grey dawn, and Oliver stepped down stiffly to see the steamer waiting in a busy hiss of steam, and a young Navy man sent by the Admiralty picked him out of the thin stream of passengers and luggage with a friendly query about his bags.

"I haven't got any," said Oliver. "Not even a razor on me."

"I'll lend you one," said the Navy man cheerily. "You'd like a cup of tea, I expect, and then you can get a spot of sleep on the way across, sir."

The steamer blew perfunctorily, and Oliver went aboard, piloted by his Admiralty chaperon who was inclined to treat him as though he was a bit decrepit. He drank the hot tea which was brought to him. He didn't sleep. But that was none of the Admiralty's business.

Fishguard to Rosslaire is the shortest route across the Irish Sea, and the tiny village is connected by rail with Cork and Queenstown. The journey through the green Irish countryside took several hours. Oliver endured it stoically, smoking the Admiralty's cigarettes when his own gave out, and staring blindly at the windows.

He was only now beginning to realize the quixotic, headlong thing he had done, rushing off like this to see for himself what had happened to Phoebe Sprague. The explanation he had given his General was in its way quite true. There was no one else to come, and she would be alone and frightened, perhaps badly hurt, perhaps— But Maia wouldn't see it that way, Maia would know why he had come. Maia would be sure now of a lot of things she had never been able to prove. And with the blank focus of his eyes on the window frame rather than the spring landscape beyond it, he couldn't feel that it mattered much any more, what Maia could prove. All that mattered was that Phoebe Sprague should be still alive when he got to Queenstown.

It was late forenoon when he arrived there, and survivors had been coming in all night. Some of them were still roaming the streets, clad fantastically in odds and ends, searching for lost friends and relatives, repeating the same names and the same questions hopefully, or desperately, to passersby on the chance of a clue.

Oliver joined them in a walking nightmare, and made his way first to the little Cunard Office on the quayside. There he found a huddle of half-demented survivors gathered round a list which was now and then added to, where it hung pinned to a board. Oliver took his turn at the list, which was pitifully short, and there was no one there named Sprague, or Day. His uniform and red tabs drew the respectful attention of the driven young man in charge, who said the hotels were full of people who might easily not be listed yet, as some of them weren't—weren't in a condition to give their names, as you might say, and then there was the hospital, and—apologetically—of course there were the morgues. "I should begin with the Queen's Hotel if I were you, sir," he finished helpfully.

The conviction was growing on Oliver that if Phoebe were—able—she would have got her name on the list or filed some sort of message by now. A visit to the post-office telegraph station in the square yielded nothing. There had been no message signed Sprague or Day. He went on, and entered the lobby of the first hotel he came to. Weeping, hysterical women, tense, overwrought men, silent, motionless figures, some rudely bandaged, lying on the sofas and in the chairs and even on the floor— the place smelt of vomit, and urine, and blood. He paced grimly among the oblivious crowd, looking into tragic faces distorted by grief and horror. She was not there. A sympathetic manageress gave him the register to search. It was worthless. He thanked her and left the hotel, drawing a long breath as he reached the clean, salty air of the street.

He was accustomed to war, and to the sights and sounds and smells of war. But this was not war, this was murder. These people weren't soldiers, trained to endure, these were civilians, old people, women—he realized with a separate shock that he had not as yet seen a child survivor. He walked on down the sunlit street, through straggling, odd-looking, seemingly aimless groups of people, looking for the next hotel, and came to the Town Hall, which had been turned into a temporary morgue with officers of the Irish Constabulary at the door. A woman was being led away from it, weeping into her hands. He paused a moment, and then with a jerk of his chin approached the door.

"I am looking for Miss Phoebe Sprague," he said, sounding to himself exactly like a hundred other voices he had heard that morning, and the man said stolidly, "We haven't got their names, sir. These haven't been identified. You may as well go in, though."

"No, don't go in—I've just come out, and she's not there," said a sensible voice, and Oliver turned to see a young man in a mussy knickerbocker suit standing at his elbow. "My name is Kendrick," the young man went on, holding out his hand. "Heard what you said, and I'm looking for her myself."

Oliver brought himself together with an effort and shook the young man's hand.

"You knew her," he said gropingly. "You were on the ship, of course—"

"We were standing together as the ship went down, and I couldn't find her—afterwards. I'd like to help you if I can."

"Thank you. My name is Campion. I'm a sort of relative. That is, our families are all mixed up together by marriage. I came over from London as soon as I heard."

"I've done the hospital," Kendrick said matter-of-factly. "And the Queen's Hotel. And this is my second morgue. Where have you been looking?"

"Just the hotel, and the telegraph office, and the office on the quay. They've got a list there, but she isn't on it."

"I know. Well, what next? There are several more hotels, small ones, and another morgue. Let's do the hotels first." Kendrick took his arm in a friendly way and started off across the square to where the door to what was hardly more than a pub stood open. "They were carrying some stretchers in there a little while ago. I figure she must be pretty well knocked out or she'd have been heard from by now. She had a lifebelt on—I saw to that. Mind the step, sir—"

The furniture of the tiny bar parlor was all pushed to one side to make room for several stretchers which had been laid on the floor. A local doctor, working in his shirtsleeves with a bloody basin on the floor near by, was kneeling beside one of them. Oliver and Kendrick stepped round and over him into the room, and there on the next stretcher lay

Phoebe, covered by a coarse blanket, her long hair, which always curled when it was damp, spilling off on to the uncarpeted floor. Her eyes were closed and she looked asleep except for the rigid line of her mouth and chin, set against pain.

With a little sound of pity and concern Oliver dropped on one knee and laid a cautious hand on the blanket over her heart.

"Phoebe," he said. "Phoebe, darling—you're all right now, we've got you."

Slowly her lids lifted and her eyes, smudged with purple shadows, gazed up at him. Her lips parted and quivered, but no words came. Kendrick stood looking down at them, aware of drama.

"Are you hurt?" Oliver was saying gently, and his hand drew back the blanket to reveal her right arm roughly splinted and a swathing of linen bandage round her shoulder. "Who did this?" he asked, and touched the splint.

"On the—trawler."

"Did they give you anything for the pain?"

"No." Tears welled up and ran down into the edge of her hair, following the track of endless other tears all night long whenever consciousness returned.

Kendrick laid his hand on the doctor's shoulder.

"Anything for pain?" he asked.

"It has run out," said the doctor, with a brief gesture of despair. "All gone, hours ago."

"The chemist?"

"All sold."

"The hospital?"

"Perhaps. But I've no one to send."

"Stay here with her," said Kendrick to Oliver. "I'll see what I can find."

When he returned from the hospital, bringing some precious little white pills, he found Oliver still crouched beside the stretcher on the floor with Phoebe's hand in his. They raised her head to a glass of water and she cried out with pain, and it was all they could do to help her swallow two of the pills. The doctor then set her arm with rough efficiency, and splinted it again, bandaged up her shoulder and said the ligaments were torn, with some damage to the collar bone though it was not broken. It would be painful and useless for some time, and she had been many hours in the water, and he advised the hospital at once.

"No," said Phoebe firmly. "I want to go on to London."

"I want you to," said Oliver. "But he may know best."

"Help me to sit up," said Phoebe. "Those pills are working. Hold my head straight—it's like a gigantic stiff neck—"

They raised her again with agonized care, and she sat groggy and shaking, with her good shoulder braced against Oliver, and tried to smile.

"If I have some food now I think I can get on my legs," she said. "I'm all right from the waist down. Just kind of numb. They took away my jacket to dry it and I never got it back. Can you buy me something to travel in? I'm still a bit damp."

It was now past the time for serving hot lunch, and Kendrick went away to interview the woman who ran the little hostelry. A bank-note changed hands, and Phoebe was helped out into the kitchen and placed in a big chair beside the hearth. Every move was painful to her, but Oliver fed her eggs and bacon and she drank hot tea with Irish whiskey in it, while Kendrick went out and bought her a tweed coat and a soft hat to match, and some hairpins.

Then the men retired from the kitchen, and the landlady twisted up Phoebe's hair into a bun and skewered it with pins and brought her a basin of hot water and towels and helped her to make what toilet she could in spite of the bandages. She had been wearing a good tweed suit and its skirt and linen blouse had stood the wetting well and were now mussily dry. Luckily she had not lost her shoes.

Revived by the food and drink and fortified by another of the little white pills, and most of all comforted by Oliver's presence in Queenstown, Phoebe felt sure that she was good for the journey to London. As Kendrick was an able-bodied male alien, the port of Fishguard was closed to him and he had to go by way of Dublin and Holyhead, but Oliver's General had arranged for Phoebe's entry by the route he had come, and Kendrick promised to turn up in St. James's Square on Monday.

"I don't have to worry about you any more," he said to Phoebe as he saw them off in a reserved compartment on the Rosslaire train, and he kept her left hand in his, looking down at her with his quirky smile. "It's up to the British Army now to get you to London, and you'll be in good hands." When Phoebe found nothing to reply to that which would de-compromise Oliver at once, Kendrick turned to him and said, "Well, good luck the both of you. And don't let the grass grow under your feet."

"Oh, Mr. Kendrick, please—!" Phoebe began anxiously. "Oliver isn't— we aren't—"

"Oh, all right, if you say so. But I've got eyes, haven't I?" he grinned, and left them with a cheery wave.

"I'd better write him a letter—he'll be at Claridge's," Phoebe said hastily. "I'd better tell him straight out that he's made a mistake—that you have a wife. Or else he'll make some kind of break in front of every-body when he comes to call."

"Don't worry about it now," said Oliver, and unfolded a rug. "Just put your feet up and lean back on this cushion and rest. I'm not at all sure I ought to let you attempt this journey yet."

"Think I was going to let you out of my sight?" Phoebe sighed, allow-ing herself to be tucked up nearly full length on the seat of the carriage. She smiled up at him over the edge of the rug. "How did you manage this, anyway, things being as they are?"

"I just walked out," he said laconically, folding the rug under her feet with a little pat.

"And will there be hell to pay when we get to London?"

"All sorts of it. Go to sleep."

"What did you tell the War Office?"

"That you were a sort of relative—young and helpless—travelling alone. The War Office has a very kind heart." He bent over her as the train began to move out of the station, one hand braced on the seat be-hind her head. "I should have given myself away just as badly if I had tried to stick it out in London till we knew what had become of you."

"You *have* given us away now, haven't you!"

"Yes, I suppose I have. Go to sleep." He kissed her lightly on the lips as she lay looking up at him, and then sat down on the seat opposite and opened a copy of the *Bystander*.

And almost before she knew it, lulled by the motion of the train and more hot food and little white pills, and most of all by the comforting, beloved presence near by, Phoebe fell asleep.

4

VIRGINIA was waiting at Paddington with a motor car, and by that time Phoebe was running a temperature of 102° and had to be put to bed with bronchitis and a torturing cough. During the wretched weeks which followed she never ceased to be thankful that she had managed to reach London before she collapsed, and even Maia was reduced to seething silence by the gravity of Phoebe's condition.

Thus Phoebe was spared the sort of scene which might have occurred if she had entered the house in St. James's Square with Oliver in any other circumstances, and only Oliver knew what he had to bear of innuendo and recrimination in private. He stuck pleasantly and firmly to his statement that it was only decent that some one of the family should have gone to Queenstown, and that he was the only one in a position to arrange it, and that without him she might have died there, alone, of the effects of the exposure from which they were still fighting to save her with the best care London could provide. And except for Maia's knowing silences and oblique, hostile glances, he considered that he had got off quite lightly.

The family had kept a few rooms at the back of the house upstairs for their own use, when they turned all the large reception rooms into wards. With Archie away, Virginia was living there, besides Winifred and Edward, and Phoebe was given a small maid's room at the top of the house to be ill in, and got what care could be spared from the wounded men downstairs. Before she had begun to rally enough to receive visitors Kendrick had gone on to Geneva, leaving her an address there at which he hoped she would communicate with him when she was able to come to Switzerland herself in the effort to reach Rosalind.

He was still incredulous, when he left London, that the American Government showed no signs of avenging its citizens who had died in a disaster which violated all known laws of warfare, and he made angry inquiries of Oliver about how to join the British Army if his own country would not fight. It was some satisfaction to him to learn on paying his respects to the American Ambassador in London, who was an old friend of his father's, that Mr. Page agreed with him openly that President Wilson's "too proud to fight" statement was a most profound and humiliating mistake. That unfortunate phrase at once made its way into stinging cartoons and music-hall jokes, and also caused astonishment and regret in the most responsible circles in France and Britain. On the advice of Mr. Page Kendrick reluctantly abandoned any idea of shooting it out with the Germans at once, and proceeded to Geneva to take up his Red Cross work—temporarily, he added, scowling.

As soon as she was able to risk a journey Phoebe was bundled down to Farthingale to recuperate, and left there in charge of Aunt Sally and what Virginia called her troupe. Tired as she was when she arrived there, Phoebe insisted on having tea with the others in the drawing-room before going up to bed, and as Virginia had accompanied her, it made quite a party.

Red-haired, full-bosomed, small-waisted, neat-hipped, Aunt Sally was a living miracle of vitality and good looks. She was made up like a Parisienne, clothed by the Bond Street branch of her favorite French dressmaker, and had for years thought exclusively in French, so that her English had become rather formal and was often a literal translation, which added to her accent lent charm and humor to her least remark.

Sosthène was silent only because he chose to be, and not because his English was less adequate than Aunt Sally's. He was a pale, bony man, with receding straight dark hair and eyes which Phoebe admitted could really be called smouldering—eyes which always looked a little sleepy under half-drawn lids, though they moved attentively from face to face round the circle. His lips were well-cut and smiled easily, deepening a line in his cheek which was a very masculine version of dimple. His teeth were white, his hands were beautifully kept, and although his clothes were strictly Savile Row he was a strangely exotic presence in the quiet room, handing the teacups for Virginia, taking round the cake-stand, making sure that everyone—particularly his Sallee—had what she wanted, and ignoring, not pointedly, not rudely, but just being oblivious to the little jibes and pecks he constantly received from Fabrice.

Phoebe stole incredulous glances at Fabrice, who at sixteen was quite the most exquisite creature one had ever seen, in a self-conscious and stagy way. Fabrice was like a badly overacted French ingénue in an American stock company, Phoebe thought. Her figure was delicious, and her tea-gown allowed it to show. Her face, apparently still innocent of make-up, was delectable, with enormous, heavily lashed brown eyes and a pouting pink mouth. Her young voice chirped like a bird, with theatrical French intonations on her English sentences. I see what Bracken meant, Phoebe thought. Dear God, what a *brat!*

After tea Phoebe was shooed off upstairs to bed and sentenced to having her dinner on a tray here. Aunt Sally's maid Elvire, who understood massage, came in to make her comfortable—with the result that Phoebe dropped off to sleep before dinner arrived, and again directly after she had finished it. And that was the first night since the ship had gone down under her that she did not wake, sweating, because she had dreamed that the clear green water was reaching for her feet again on a tilted deck.

. . . Phoebe thought the dream was childish and cowardly, and had not told anybody about it, but she had not had a continuous night's sleep in weeks until Elvire's knowing fingers had stroked and smoothed her nerves into relaxed slumber.

Elvire was there to help her dress the next morning, for although the broken bone was mending, the torn shoulder ligaments gave constant trouble and were still painful, and her right arm was nearly useless. At breakfast, Fabrice cut up Phoebe's bacon for her with a pretty air of ministering to the aged and infirm, and Aunt Sally discussed the news in the morning *Times* with Virginia.

When the first German onslaught last year had been checked and turned back short of Paris, everyone looked forward through the long, trying winter to the spring drive, when the weather would permit maneuvering, and when at last the German lines could be pierced, dislodged, and thrown out of France. But it hadn't happened that way. When the fighting flared again around Ypres in the spring the British were outgunned and outmanned and held on desperately against an enemy which everywhere was in possession of higher ground. The German lines wavered here and there but were never rolled back. And now in June the fighting was dying down again, both sides exhausted, and there had been almost no change of ground. Italy's belated entry into the war had made no noticeable difference to the Allies yet, and Russia was falling back instead of invading Germany from the east. French manpower was leaking away, and the old British Army was almost all dead, and the new one was not ready. It had begun to look as though the war would actually last through another winter.

The *Times* that morning said that the Germans had used poison gas again, near Menin, and the good God only knew, said Aunt Sally, what the Boche would conceive next. There had been another raid on the East Coast of England—Zeppelins—casualties and damage to homes— well, Aunt Sally knew already how that felt.

"We were all asleep that night in Antwerp," she said in answer to Phoebe's question. "In a hotel in the Place Royale. The Queen was asleep in the Palace on the other side of the Square. The first I knew was a terrific explosion—my windows shattered on the floor. It shattered the Queen's windows too. I knew what it must be, for it had not the sound of a bombardment by guns. That I have known well in my days. And soon we had that too, in Antwerp, when a few days later the Germans began firing into the streets and things began to catch fire. Twice

I have known a city to burn over my head," she said. "Richmond—none of you was born when Richmond burned." Her swift glance round their listening faces included Sosthène. "Bracken's father brought his Yankee soldiers to save our horses when the stable went up in flames. He went in first, to show them the way—shall I ever forget Eden's face while we waited. . . . We all thought Eden was wicked, to marry a soldier from the army which had beaten us. I myself married a man who had worn a grey uniform like my father and my brother. My pride would not have allowed me to do otherwise. I did not love him. The man I could have loved was killed. But he gave me the dignity of his name and what security there was left in the South after the war—and he got what he wanted." She sat a moment withdrawn, her jewelled fingers quiet on the handle of her coffee cup, looking back. "Eden made the better bargain then," she said matter-of-factly. "My time came later, though. Later I could allow myself not to envy Eden."

They waited spellbound, hoping for more. Sosthène's sleepy eyes rested on her fondly, the line in his cheek had deepened in a half smile. He must have heard it all a dozen times, Phoebe thought, but he listens—it's her voice he hears—he loves even her voice. . . .

"I thought that in Richmond I had seen the end of the world," Aunt Sally was saying. "My friends were dead, our money was lost, our property was damaged or gone—but see how one can be wrong! I had yet to live at all. The world does not end while one is still alive. You must have noticed that yourself, my love, when the ship went down." Her blue eyes, unfaded beneath their darkened lids, took Phoebe by surprise.

"Well, yes, I—but I think I only believed that at Queenstown," said Phoebe, and suddenly with Aunt Sally's eyes upon her she realized that Oliver had come to Queenstown, and she blushed like a girl.

Aunt Sally observed, was amused and interested, and let it pass.

"This war now," she went on. "Once more for me it is the end of security—habit—all the dear familiar, usual things. I may never see Cannes again, and all my treasures which are there."

"They will never get to Cannes," said Sosthène softly.

"But naturally," Aunt Sally agreed at once. "I, however, am now up-rooted—" She made a quick, Gallic gesture of pulling up. "—like an onion!" she cried, and the word slipped into its French form and became somehow even funnier, and they laughed with her like children. "So I am here, with those of my blood again. I see my brother's child." She gave

Phoebe a caressing glance. "I begin already to like what has happened to me. It is like before. The world goes on. One is still enchanted to live."

"I am glad we came to England," said Fabrice softly. "I shall marry an Englishman. I prefer them." And she looked under her lashes at Sosthène, who would not see.

"Ah, yes, we know quite well enough what you prefer," Aunt Sally replied rather crushingly, and to Phoebe's regret rose from the table. "And now, Virginie, let us do the flowers."

That evening while it was still daylight on the terrace, Phoebe left the others sitting in cane chairs waiting for the moon and went upstairs to the convalescent's early bedtime. In the hall, where the angle of the staircase cast a deeper shadow, she came upon two interlaced figures, one of them in the frothy pink of Fabrice's dinner frock and the other wearing khaki. Instead of springing apart guiltily at her approach, they were only sufficiently aware of her to draw deeper into the corner, moving as one, and as she mounted the stairs she heard a dreamy murmur and an intimate breath of laughter. She peeped again over the bannister. Fabrice was so given to the man's embrace that her light dress was only a pencil-slim streak in the twilight below the stairs.

Well, thought Phoebe in some astonishment and made a desperate effort to stay awake till Virginia came upstairs. When at last she heard low voices and the soft closing of doors, she got up and put a dressing-gown round her shoulders and pattered along to Virginia's room. Virginia was returning to London early in the morning and she had to find out tonight anything she was going to know.

"That was Archie's brother Gerald," said Virginia rather grimly, when Phoebe had asked what was going on here anyway. "He's been at the Hall on leave."

"B-but you said he was engaged to Lady Jenny Keane—"

"He's broken it off. Tonight he asked Fabrice to marry him."

"Oh," said Phoebe, and thought it over. "Well, sometimes it's better to find out in time. But Fabrice is so—very young, and so—so—"

"Yes, isn't she!" said Virginia, brushing out her hair with short, angry strokes. "Archie will be pretty sick about this. And Gerald is old enough to know better. Besides, he and Jenny were well suited to each other, till Fabrice went to work!"

"Does Aunt Sally—"

"No, she doesn't. They came out on the terrace after the moon was up, and said it was all fixed up and they were going to be married.

Cousin Sally said they were no such thing, as Fabrice is too young and Gerald is off to France within a week. Fabrice tried everything, coaxed and cried and stamped her foot in the *prettiest* way, but Cousin Sally can be firm! She sent Gerald packing, and ordered Fabrice off to bed. And do you know what she did when we all came upstairs? She locked Fabrice's door and took the key away with her!"

"Gosh!" said Phoebe, impressed. "Was that really necessary?"

"What do *you* think?" said Virginia.

2. *Zurich.*   *Summer, 1915.*

▸▸

1

On the day that Phoebe was finally able to start for Switzerland, the London newspapers carried the first report that the Germans had turned up at Hooge with another new weapon—liquid fire.

Bracken, who was on his way back to France with full correspondent's credentials and would accompany her as far as Paris, was angry and oppressed by the morning's news. He deeply resented the Wilsonian policy of writing notes to Germany, and felt that America was making a fool of herself in the eyes of the whole world, especially Germany. His open, cosmopolitan mind could not comprehend that anyone even on the safe side of the Atlantic could fail to see that now a civilization was involved, not just an altruistic principle.

They went by the one o'clock train from Victoria, the train which always brought to an end so many leaves, and they crossed the Channel on a little steamer full of civilian passengers, women and children, as well as uniforms. It sailed with its lifeboats swung out ready for lowering, and with look-outs posted to watch for submarine periscopes.

Phoebe looked more than once at the solid deck boards she trod on, and heard the steady pulse of the screw, and tried not to think about the leaden, stricken stillness of that other ship, going down beneath her. Bracken understood about that too. "This is like getting back on the horse right after it has thrown you," he said, and she gave him a grateful smile.

At the Gare de Lyons when Bracken put her into the express for Lausanne, where Johnny was to meet her, he said solemnly, "I know you won't take any notice of anything I say, but don't go into Germany yourself, do you hear? You haven't got a German visa, but don't try to get one in Switzerland, do you hear? Tell Johnny the known facts, and all your suspicions, and let him try to get to her. You wait for him at Zurich, do you hear?"

Phoebe said meekly that she heard, and stepped into the train.

Johnny was waiting on the platform at Lausanne, and took her to the new Cecil Hotel where she was to break the journey for a day's rest before they went on together to Zurich. And during that time they were to work out what could be done about Rosalind and line up the queries and possibilities resulting from her long, mysterious silence.

Johnny kissed Phoebe without asking permission, and said she didn't look like a survivor, and it was a little while before she could induce him to put his mind on the reason for her being in Lausanne. When he finally consented to listen to Rosalind's story he was at once caught up in its implications and regarded her as another Andromeda to be rescued from dragons. He jotted down the facts in his pocket notebook in cryptic pencilled memoranda as they talked—had she received the letters Phoebe kept on sending, and if so why hadn't she sent out replies, even after she was told to send them through the American Embassy since the other routes had apparently failed?—why hadn't she communicated with England as other people now contrived to do, through neutral channels in Sweden and Holland?—had Conrad left her at the mercy of his relatives at Heidersdorf and were they stopping her letters?—what had become of Gibson?—had Conrad seen Phoebe's book and was he so angry he had forbidden any further association between his wife and her American friend?—where *was* Conrad?—and if he was away at the front, as he ought to be, couldn't Rosalind slip away for a few days, as far as Zurich, for a brief meeting?

They decided to say that Phoebe had come to Switzerland for the Red

Cross, and not solely to see Rosalind, not to make too much of it, not to show undue anxiety, and being in Switzerland Phoebe would naturally hope that Rosalind could come and visit her—just for a few days—before her return to England; not having had a letter from Rosalind recently, she had asked Johnny to jog her up and remind her of her old friends. America was still neutral, much as Johnny deplored it. And Germany earnestly desired the good opinion of America still, and was polite to the American Press in Berlin. Johnny's visit would be an opportunity for Conrad to show an American that a woman married to a German was not a slave. It was a chance for him to show magnanimity, even if the book had annoyed him. . . .

Sometimes their arguments looked thin and futile, sometimes it seemed that only a tyrannical Prussian could find fault with them. When they were all neatly marshalled in the notebook and all the queries had been raised and all the possibilities thought of, Johnny gazed at it a while, memorizing it line by line, and then he tore the pages out of the notebook and held a match to them before he and Phoebe took the train to Zurich. Phoebe said Good-bye to him there, and settled in at the Hotel Baur au Lac to await his return with what patience she could find.

Johnny could not go charging up to the *Schloss* at Heidersdorf and demand an account of its chatelaine, though. He had to go all the way to Berlin and arrange with the American Ambassador to accompany one of the tours of inspection which were made periodically by the Embassy secretaries to prisoner-of-war camps scattered over Germany. He had accompanied more than one of these tours before now. And there was a camp, still unvisited, conveniently near the *Schloss,* so that from there he might reasonably motor over to pay a call on the dear friend of his boss, who had asked him to present his family's compliments to Her Serene Highness if ever he was in the neighborhood.

It was therefore on a warm morning in August that Johnny borrowed from the tactfully disinterested secretary the car with the American emblem and followed the steep, winding drive which climbed to the *Schloss* on its crag, drew up with a confident flourish on the gravel sweep, mounted the wide stone steps and presented his card to a surprised and doubtful footman in powder and knee breeches. He was admitted to the great hall, with its palms and mirrors and statues and crystal chandeliers, and left there on an unwelcoming bench while the footman carried his card away on a salver.

2

U<small>PSTAIRS</small>, in Rosalind's pink and silver sitting-room which had been recently redecorated as a birthday gift, Conrad was making a scene. But this time Rosalind knew exactly how the quarrel had got started, having screwed herself up through a sleepless night to re-open the subject which was sure to precipitate it—the prisoners' camp at Halkenwitz near by. What made any reference on her part to the camp especially precarious just now was that the Emperor had come to Eastern Headquarters near Breslau and would be a visitor at the *Schloss* for dinner and the night, and tomorrow morning Conrad as one of his ADC's was to leave again with him for a tour of the Eastern Front.

All she had done, in a final effort before Conrad's departure for an indefinite period of time, was to ask him once more for permission to visit the prisoners with little presents of newspapers, books, and tobacco —for *all* the prisoners, she kept repeating anxiously, as all nationalities were represented there, Russians, French, and British. It wasn't just that she wanted to pamper her own countrymen. *All* the prisoners needed little extras, and she would distribute them fairly, and it was part of the duty of the Red Cross, whose uniform she was entitled to wear, to alleviate suffering wherever it was.

"They do not suffer!" snapped Conrad. "They are well housed in a brick building which was once a factory. They are dry and fed and it is summer and they cannot be cold. What more can they ask?"

"But, Conny—"

"Kindly do not bring this matter up while the Emperor is here tonight. It would be extremely tactless. And I have told you before that I wish you to discontinue your Red Cross work. It only upsets you."

Rosalind was silent, while her mind went back unwillingly to the autumn day nearly a year ago at the station at Halkenwitz when the British prisoners arrived—she had never dared tell Conny why it had upset her so—not the real reason. She had been there on the platform with other women in Red Cross uniforms and brassards, because the train had been announced to contain German wounded on their way to a mountain spa which was converted into a hospital for officers. The Red Cross women went along the train handing up mugs of coffee and meat sandwiches to the wounded, and Rosalind was nearing the end of her car and just turning back when she was paralyzed by a voice calling distinctly in English for water.

She stared along the train to the car beyond the one she was serving—it was a cattle truck. She went towards it, unbelieving—it was full of British prisoners, many of them wounded, packed in so many to the space that the men could not lie down comfortably. The floor was covered with filth and there was a dreadful stench even in the cool mountain air outside.

With a gasp of horror she reached back to her trolley and snatched up a double handful of sandwiches and hurried towards the door of the cattle truck, which some German officials were also approaching. They did not recognize her, and one of them said roughly, "Not here, *gnädige Frau,* can't you see that these are prisoners?"

"But they're hungry just like the rest—they want water—some of them are wounded—"

"At the camp they will be fed," he answered, barring her way.

"But it's nearly a mile to the camp. How will they get there?"

"They will walk."

"Haven't you any motor lorries?"

"For *prisoners?*" He glanced at her sharply, with disapproval and curiosity, for her German was still not very good.

"But they're not *able!*" she cried, and stood holding the sandwiches and watching helplessly while the khaki-clad men, caked with dried mud, unshaven, hollow-eyed, many with bloodstained, dirty bandages, some incapable of standing unless supported by their comrades, some with improvised crutches and canes, were spilling out of the cattle-truck in obedience to commands bawled at them in German by a beastly-looking officer who carried a riding-crop and tapped his polished boot with it while he waited for the pathetic crew to emerge.

Word had spread through the town of the arrival of prisoners, and a crowd was gathering, mostly women and children, hostile, jeering, shouting insults and derision. The Red Cross women stood in the front rank empty-handed, making no effort to reach those who most needed their help. Someone in the mob threw a small rock and it struck one of the wounded Englishmen on the shoulder and he reeled, and a roar went up —a roar of amusement and satisfaction mixed. Other small missiles began to pelt in on the prisoners—handfuls of cinders, bits of brickbat, even eggs and potatoes from rifled market-baskets—thrown with good aim amid loud shouts of laughter and self-congratulation.

The camp officials meanwhile were knocking and herding the prisoners into a rough column for the march to the camp, and they began to move forward slowly, by necessity towards the crowd, which parted grudgingly before them, so that they were menaced from both sides. A few of the men looked back at their tormentors defiantly, none of them answered, none flinched, most of them seemed entirely unaware, helping each other along, exchanging a few inaudible words among themselves, ignoring their surroundings as completely as if they had been alone.

Clutching the sandwiches, Rosalind worked her way to the edge of the crowd and began thrusting the food at the men as they went by, until she was angrily swept aside by the officer, who knocked the last sandwich out of the hands of the prisoner with his riding-crop so that the bread and meat were ground beneath the marching feet. "But these are *my* men!" screamed Rosalind, so beside herself that she spoke in English. "You can't *do* this to my people—it's not *civilized*—"

A small boy ran out from the fringes and hooked his foot around a cane and pulled, so that the man who leaned on it fell heavily, and the crowd brayed with brutal laughter as at the antics of a clown. Before he could rise Rosalind was on her knees beside him, lifting his head to wipe away the dirt and blood where his face had struck the cinders, sobbing like a child with rage and terror, and crying out to him, "This is an outrage, I don't know what's got into them, I shall report it to my husb—*Charles!*" He lay there beside the track, helpless and bleeding—she threw her arms around him, holding his head against her breast, "Charles, *darling,* I'll get you out of this, I swear I will, don't you worry, my darling, I'll get you exchanged, I'll make them send you home—"

Hands gripped her shoulders from behind, dragging her up, other hands, those of his comrades, took Charles from her.

"*Prinzessin,* I must beg you not to interfere—"

"*Prinzessin,* if His Highness knew—!"

The weary, wavering column passed on. Charles, supported between two of his friends, one of them having recovered the cane, did not look back. She was never even sure if he had been aware of who she was. She stood, held on either side by her shocked associates of the German Red Cross, tears streaming down her face, until they led her away through an unfriendly mutter of *"die Engländerin,"* and put her into the motor and sent her home to Heidersdorf in disgrace.

Conrad was away at the time, but he had heard all about it, of course

—except that he still did not know she had seen Charles at Halkenwitz. She had written him a letter, all tear-blotted and frantic, when she reached home, all about the exchange and how they must let Charles's people know at once where he was—and then she tore it up. Almost too late, she had known better. After that she cherished some idea of getting into the camp herself, and finding out what conditions were like there, and seeing for herself how Charles was. But that was forbidden.

She was wondering now what would happen if she came right out with it after all, and said it was on account of Charles that she wanted to go to Halkenwitz camp. Well, what could Conny do? Charles couldn't be worse off than he was. Conny might even get him exchanged in order to hush her up. . . .

But Conrad broke their angry silence before she did.

"Anyway, you will doubtless lose interest in the Halkenwitz camp when I tell you that your friend Laverham is no longer there," he said, and for a moment she was speechless.

"H-how did you know—" she began.

"That he was there? Not from you, I admit! Three men escaped from the camp yesterday. He was one of them."

"Escaped—?"

"He will be caught, of course, and given solitary confinement in a common jail. They always are."

"You won't—have him shot?" she whispered.

"I'd like to. He is a very dangerous man."

"Charles?" She tried to laugh. "He's wounded—he's unarmed—"

"He is a British agent," said Conrad bluntly. "Did you know that?" His eyes raked her face.

"B-but he's just a soldier—"

"To the contrary. He spent a great deal of time here before the war began. Snooping for his damned War Office!"

"I—never thought—"

"So that is the kind of friends you have," he said, with a genuine Prussian sneer. *"Spies!* Kindly don't mention the escape of prisoners before the Emperor tonight. He would be very displeased. I want things to go as well as possible. Your mere presence here makes things difficult enough. Fortunately he has always had a weakness for you, even though you are an Englishwoman."

"Yes, I know," she murmured. "You used to have a weakness too. But the war has changed all that, hasn't it. I've become an enemy to you."

"It need not be that way," he said coldly. "I have told you a hundred times, if you will give up your obstinate English ways and learn to love Germany as your Fatherland—"

"I see very little about Germany to love these days," she said quietly. "Conny, why won't you let me go home?"

"Home?" he repeated, as though the word was unfamiliar to him.

"To England," she explained patiently. "You don't want me here. Nobody wants me here." Her voice broke, and then began to rise with months of accumulated hysteria. "I don't *belong* here, I've tried, God only *knows* how I've tried, but I can't do it, Conny, I can't *bear* it, *you've got to let me go!*"

"Control yourself, please," he commanded, with a glance at the door.

"I can't, I can't go on smirking and kowtowing and eating dirt because I'm English! I'm *proud* of being English, I'd rather be English than German any day in the week—"

He took her by the arm and shook her, saying, "Be quiet, someone will hear you!"

"I don't care, it won't be news to them, they all hate me for being English, they all spy on me and tattle and listen at keyholes! Maybe they think *I'm* a spy, like Charles! They know I hate it here, hate it from morning to night, hate dressing up and being ogled by your Prussian officer friends, hate having my hand kissed and seeming to flirt and play up to them, and I *loathe* pretending to be *flattered* because your sacred Emperor has a weakness for me—"

Conrad slapped her full in the face, a blow that made the room whirl round her. She stared up at him, transfixed and quivering, while one hand crept up to the place on her jawbone where the heavy signet ring he wore had cut the skin. He let go of her arm and turned away, and she sank into a corner of the sofa with her face in both hands.

At last he spoke, and his voice was silky.

"I suppose I must say I am sorry," he said. "But you really should not have brought the Emperor into our—private quarrel."

There was a discreet knock on the door and the footman came in with Johnny's card on a salver.

5

CONRAD dismissed the servant, saying, "Ask him to wait in the green drawing-room," and stood a moment with the card in his fingers. "And who," he inquired then, "is Mr. John Odell Malone?"

She did not answer, seemed not to have heard.

"Rosalind. Who is this Mr. Malone, Berlin correspondent of the *New York Star?*"

"I don't know," she answered automatically, her face in her hands.

"Isn't the *New York Star* that fellow Murray's paper?"

"Murray?" Her head came up slowly.

"The fellow who married Enstone's sister."

"Yes—Bracken Murray—is he *here?*"

"No, but a Mr. Malone is." He went to her, took her chin in his hand ungently and jerked her face up to meet his suspicious gaze. "Did you ask him to come?"

"How could I? I never even heard of him."

"Did you ask Murray to send someone?"

"Of course not, I—I don't know what you're suspecting me of now, but whatever it is I didn't do it! Maybe Phoebe asked him to come. I told you she'd wonder why she had no word from me. She probably wants to know if I'm dead!"

He dropped her chin and stood snapping the card in his fingers irritably.

"Then I suppose we shall have to see him," he decided.

"Now? I can't possibly."

"You must. Or God knows what sort of tale he'll carry back."

"What about this?" She touched the bruised cut on her jaw bone.

"Powder over it. Put on some make-up and that pink chiffon tea-gown and come down smiling, and he won't notice. Don't be longer than ten minutes, please." He walked out with the card, closing the door behind him.

When he had gone she sat a moment, wondering how she could bring herself to do as he demanded. Slowly her thoughts began to take form. Charles had escaped. And Charles was hardly more of a prisoner than herself. Charles had run for it, why shouldn't she? She had no passport— but neither had he. She supposed there were underground routes for prisoners. Charles would know about that, if he were a secret agent as Conny said he was, but she had no way of finding out. And Charles wasn't a German princess. She would have to walk across the border in her own identity, unless—unless she could find someone to help. Downstairs there was an American, perhaps sent by Bracken or Phoebe to see if she was all right. Somehow she must manage to convey to him under Conrad's very nose that she was not all right and wanted to get away.

Perhaps this Mr. Malone would help her, if he knew that. Bracken would have helped her, and this was Bracken's man.

Ten minutes later she entered the green drawing-room, smiling and wearing the magnificent chiffon tea-gown. But the bruise on her jawbone showed. She liked Mr. Malone as soon as she saw him—his grave courtesy, his level eyes, his unflirtatious admiration, his firm handclasp. He had come to tell her, he said, that Phoebe was at Geneva with the Red Cross people and wanted her to come to Switzerland for a visit, and as letters didn't seem to be very reliable any more she had asked him to mention it, if he was in that part of the world. And oddly enough, it had been quite convenient for him to do so. Unfortunately her husband seemed to feel, said Johnny, his eyes resting innocently on her face, that she would not find a journey to Geneva acceptable just at the present time. . . .

"I would love to go," she said, concealing her agony of desire, and lifted a glance of pretty entreaty to her husband. "Don't you think we might arrange it?" she asked.

"I am afraid it is impossible, my dear," Conrad said flatly. "With the Emperor in the East it is necessary that my house be always at his disposal."

"But it would be even more at his disposal if I were not here," she smiled.

"Ah, but the Emperor likes to see a pretty hostess," said Conrad with amiable conclusiveness. "So I'm afraid you can't be spared from your duties here as the angel in my home. Later on, perhaps—"

"But later on, Phoebe won't be at Geneva."

"You know I never deny you a whim unless I have no choice," said Conrad, and Rosalind shrugged as though resigning herself to the inevitable without too much regret.

"Let me have Phoebe's address in Geneva, so that I can write to her and explain," she said to Johnny, and turned away to an escritoire which held notepaper and pens.

Johnny thought fast, but he had stayed in Geneva himself and knew his way around there.

"The Hotel Beau-Rivage on the Quai des Pâquis," he said without blinking.

Rosalind wrote it slowly, bending above the escritoire with her back to them. Then she came towards him, saying, "Have I got it right, my memory is so bad," and showed him the paper she had written on. Beneath the address he read the hasty words: *Come back tomorrow at noon.*

"Yes, absolutely right," said Johnny, and their eyes met briefly, and hers turned away.

"Tell her I am so sorry and will send her a long letter," said Rosalind, folding the paper and tucking it inside the neck of her gown, and Johnny explained that he was going back to Berlin and wouldn't see Phoebe again for a while.

"She particularly asked me to convey her regards to your maid Gibson," he added.

"And I shall have to tell her that Gibson died last summer."

"Oh. She'll be sorry to hear that."

"I was very sorry to lose her." Rosalind's face was clouded and sad. "I'd known Gibson all my life, you see. She was one of the last links with my—with the time before I was married."

"But now you have good faithful German maids," said Conrad with firm cheerfulness. "Gibson was all very well when you were a young bride in a strange country, perhaps a little childish and lonely. But now this is your home, and it is right that our loyal people who were born here on the land should serve you."

"Yes, of course," she agreed listlessly. "How is Phoebe, Mr. Malone? Is she as beautiful as ever?"

"She looks very well now," said Johnny, and added with an eye to his effect, "She was on the *Lusitania.*"

The effect was forthcoming. Rosalind's hand went to her parted lips —even Conrad stiffened with surprise.

"Then lifeboats were successfully launched," he said, as though there had been some doubt.

"A few were, I believe, but Phoebe was not in one of them," Johnny replied briefly. "She was picked up out of the water some hours later, injured, and half dead, and has had a long illness."

"Here in Germany they gave the school children a holiday to celebrate the sinking of the *Lusitania,*" said Rosalind, and looked him in the eyes.

"I know," said Johnny, returning the look. "I was in Berlin, and I knew that Phoebe was on the ship. It isn't a thing I'd care to go through again."

"I didn't know," she said. "Oh, Conny, if it had meant Phoebe's death I should never have forgiven you!"

"Isn't that a little unreasonable, my dear?" He smiled indulgently. "After all, I am not a U-boat commander, but only one of the Emperor's aides-de-camp." He rose, and Johnny felt that the time had come for him to go. Prince Conrad made it even clearer. "It was kind of you to pay us a call, Mr. Malone," he said formally, and offered his hand. "If ever you are in this part of the country again we shall be delighted to see you."

Johnny had got used by now to shaking hands with people whose heads he wanted to punch and did it with good grace, and turned to Rosalind, getting another good look as he did so at that strange mark on her jawbone as though she had been struck. . . .

"Then perhaps I should say *auf Wiedersehen,*" he remarked, and briefly pressed the hand she held out to him, and went away.

4

THE Emperor and his entourage arrived at Heidersdorf late that afternoon, with a whirl of motors and a great clanking and jangling of accoutrement and an array of impressive uniforms. They were to dine and sleep there, and be off early in the morning to see the war against the Russians, which was going remarkably well.

Rosalind dressed for the banquet with great care, and this time it somehow happened that the bruise on her jaw hardly showed at all. Her fingers were cold and unsteady, and her eyes had strange little sparks in them. Charles had had a try, whether or not he succeeded. She herself could not do less. She had no papers, to cross the frontier into Switzerland, where Phoebe was. But the Emperor was here in the house, she would sit next to him at dinner, and with a *laissez-passer* signed by him you could go anywhere but to heaven. And the Emperor had a weakness for her, even if she was English. . . .

She was the only woman at the long, glittering table loaded with glass and silver and hothouse flowers, and lined with field-grey uniforms. Monocled eyes devoured her from every angle, but she devoted herself to the Emperor, who was in the best of spirits, his mustaches very upturned and militant. He had remembered her recent birthday, and he brought her a present, which he bestowed upon her publicly and with ceremony—an elaborately scrolled W in diamonds made as a brooch. Even as she accepted it with pretty surprise and confusion, and kissed his hand with the grateful humility of a loyal German subject, she was thinking how typical it was, how *Prussian* it was, that the initial should be his and not hers.

Every man in the room watched with his eyes on stalks as she replaced her own sapphire ornament, a present from Conrad, with the diamond W—every man present in his own imagination pinned the Emperor's gift on the front of her low-cut gown, as her own slim fingers, fumbling a little, fastened it there. But as the meal progressed and the wine circulated, their attention was discreetly withdrawn, and the Emperor began to pay her low-voiced compliments almost as though they were alone. He had never seen her more *intriguante,* more irresistible, he said, and what a truly fetching gown—his eyes wandered freely over her bare shoulders and down to where the diamond W rested between her small breasts. She was a woman to be greatly indulged, he remarked complacently, a woman well worth a little pampering now and then—

"Conny doesn't think so," she murmured, raising a limpid blue gaze to the slightly bulging regard of the All-Highest.

"Eh?—what's this?—are you two in an argument?" It was his bluff, favorite-uncle role now.

"Well, not—not exactly *that,* we're always good friends, of course. But I don't very often ask him for things—I have everything a woman could possibly want to make her happy." The long, innocent lashes swept down, and up again. "And of course I've already had my birthday present from him—he's had my rooms done over very extravagantly, and I'm extremely grateful. But there *is* something I want quite badly, and he says No. It's only because he doesn't understand—he doesn't think I'm clever enough to do anything on my own for Germany. But *I* think I could, if he'd let me try."

"And what is this great thing you want to do for Germany?" the Emperor inquired, amused.

"Oh, it's not great, it's only a tiny thing," she assured him modestly. "But I have an American friend, a well-known woman novelist who has great influence. She is now in Switzerland with the Red Cross, and she has asked me to come and visit her there, as it's been years since we've seen each other. Conny says I mustn't go because I am needed here, and I have my own Red Cross, and so on. But I think that's very shortsighted of him, don't you? Because if I write to her and say I can't come, she will think it is for a very different reason. She will think that someone in Germany is afraid of what I might say. She will think we have something to conceal, such as that our losses are too heavy, or—"

"But they are not!" he interrupted fiercely.

"Well, exactly, that's what I'm saying!" her soft voice agreed at once.

"But how much better if she heard that from me! How much better if a friend from Germany told her, quite simply, how well things are going here, and how confident we are. She would have to believe it, coming from me. She would write about it, and it would be printed in America that the wife of one of Your Majesty's officers was quite free to come to Switzerland to see a neutral friend, even though it's war time. They think over there that German husbands are tyrants, can you imagine that? I know very well that if I say I can't go, she'll be convinced that Conny is too selfish and domineering to allow it—or else that he's afraid I might give something away that I shouldn't. And actually it's only because Conny thinks I'm too stupid to do my little bit where I can and see that one American, at least, knows exactly how things are in Germany. And it isn't as though Conny would miss me, either, because if I had a passport I could go now, while he is away with you, and be home again before you return from the Front."

"Mm—well, I don't see why not," said the Emperor, eyeing with pleasure an elaborate dish which had just been set before him.

"Your favorite sweet, Sire," said the soft voice beside him. "I remembered from the last time that you liked it. That was what I thought of first when Conny told me you were coming today—the Emperor's *mousse,* I said to myself. He must have his *mousse* at dinner."

"Charming—delicious," said the All-Highest, with his mouth full. "And you want me to speak to Conrad, is that it, hm? Tell him you must have your little holiday and accomplish this important mission for Germany?"

"Oh, no, please don't do that, he would scold me for troubling you with such a trifle when you have so many bigger things on your mind!" she said, her blue eyes uplifted to him. "Conny *can* scold, you know, very hard!"

"Tsk, tsk," said the Emperor, and wiped *mousse* off his mustache, and went on spooning it in. "Well, no doubt sometimes you deserve it, eh?"

"Oh, doubtless, Sire, but not *this* time," she coaxed meekly. "This time I'm sure I could be of real use, if only I could just pop off tomorrow for a few days at Geneva. But I couldn't do that nowadays without a passport, could I? And I haven't got one. I suppose it would take quite a while to get one—unless you would help me."

"Mm?" He glanced at her sharply around his spoon.

"Is the *mousse* all right?" she asked with an anxious look. "Is it as good as it was the last time?"

"Delicious. Wish my own cook could make it. Must be some trick to it."

"It's quite complicated, I believe," Rosalind agreed, and added with an impish, intimate smile, "I could write it all out for you. Sire, I'll trade you the recipe for a *laissez-passer* to go to Geneva."

The All-Highest exploded with laughter, and retired behind his napkin. Rosalind waited, smiling, and he met her melting gaze above the edge of the napkin.

"That's a fair exchange, no doubt," he said. "But what about your Conrad, eh?"

"You give me the *laissez-passer* privately before you leave here," Rosalind suggested lightly. "And then tomorrow or the next day you just say to Conny, 'Oh, by the way, I sent your wife to Geneva. I think she might do us a bit of good there.' And by the time he gets back home he'll be so glad to see me again he'll forget to scold."

She could see that the idea appealed to the Emperor's God complex, and to his weakness for a joke, however feeble. To assist a pretty woman to play a harmless trick on her husband and then crow over him looked to Wilhelm like fun. And it always amused him to wield power with a stroke of his pen. Besides—the Americans were getting rather stuffy about this *Lusitania* affair, and a little bit of clever missionary work in the right quarters—

"Very well, I will give you your *laissez-passer*," he said magnificently. "And with it a few notations on things you might mention to your American friend. In fact, I will write out for you, not as coming from myself, mind, but as your own ideas, some points it would be well to make."

"Oh, please do," said Rosalind. "I'm sure you could suggest things I'd never think of. And you won't tell Conny till after you're well away from here?"

The Emperor gave her a roguish glance, which was rather as though he had pinched her cheek.

"I daresay it will slip my mind," he said.

5

MEANWHILE the Embassy secretary heard with a puckered brow Johnny's story of the paper on which Rosalind had written the address in Geneva. But he was a romantic young man, and he consented to return to Berlin alone and make no difficulties about Johnny's staying another day at the village inn. Johnny carried the credentials of a neutral correspondent and was nominally entitled to travel wherever he wished.

When it was then discovered that the Embassy car which had brought them to Halkenwitz wouldn't start, and Johnny suggested that he would get it seen to and bring it back to Berlin himself the following day while the secretary returned at once by train, his companion gave him a long speculative look and shrugged his shoulders. He knew that this was against the rules. But he felt that if Johnny Malone broke the rules it would be in a good cause. He made one last futile effort to cover the situation. "Remember, now, we're neutral," he said firmly. "You are *not* to have anything to do with escaping prisoners." Johnny assured him he wouldn't dream of such a thing. "And I shall catch hell if this is found out," said the secretary gloomily, and departed with his bag for the railway station, having given up all his spare cash at Johnny's request.

When he had gone, the car miraculously came to life again, and with Johnny behind the wheel rolled up in front of the *Schloss* at one minute to noon.

He was shown into the same drawing-room he had seen yesterday and there he found Rosalind, wearing a linen travelling cloak with a small hat and a motoring veil. She picked up a handbag from the table near by and came towards him with her hand held out as the servant announced him.

"It was very kind of you to suggest that I go for a drive with you to-day," she said casually. "I am all ready, you see, and it's such a glorious day that I had a picnic lunch put together so that we shan't have to watch the clock. My lady-in-waiting has gone to represent me at a meeting of our local hospital board, so she can't come with us. Walther, we shall want tea in the blue room about four-thirty," she added as she swept past the footman at the door, with Johnny just behind her.

He put her into the car beside the driver's seat and they waited while more footmen stowed away a large hamper at the back.

"Enough food for an army," she remarked for their benefit while this was being done. "I supposed you would have a driver."

"I always prefer to drive myself," he murmured as the car moved smoothly away from the steps.

"Thank God for that," she answered, as they were now out of earshot. "Could you possibly just drive straight through to Geneva without stopping?"

"As a matter of fact, Phoebe is at Zurich," he said, dazed.

"That's nearer, isn't it?" she remarked, accepting the mystery without comment.

"You mean you're just kidnapping me?" he asked with a little prickle of nerves at the back of his neck, and Rosalind laughed delightedly.

"Americans!" she cried. "They're like a breath of air! Mr. Malone, I want to get out of Germany. Will you help me?"

"Today?"

"Now. This minute. Please, you've got to, it's my only chance!"

"What about tea in the blue room at four-thirty?"

"By that time we shall have disappeared," she told him simply. "They'll wait till five before they think much about it. By six they will be alarmed and Malvida will start to have hysterics. By seven they will be sure there has been an accident, and the foresters will turn out to search. They will look for us all night, at all the bad turnings on the local roads. There are quite a lot of those. By morning they will notify the police, and try to telegraph Conny. With any luck for us they won't be able to get in touch with him till much later in the day. How far away can we be by then?"

"Let's see, must be a hundred and fifty miles to Dresden. We'd better leave the car there and take to the railway, since we're really in a hurry."

"Will it be much faster?"

"Night express from Dresden to Lindau—once we get across Lake Constance we're in the clear."

"*You'll do it?*"

"Couldn't ever face Phoebe if I didn't. Can't face Bracken if I do. I'll take Bracken every time."

"I'll bet Bracken would do exactly the same in your place."

"I'll bet he would."

She leaned back and drew a long breath.

"I can't believe it," she said.

"We haven't done it yet. How about your passport? I always have mine with me, luckily."

"I have a *laissez-passer* to Switzerland from the Emperor—written in his own hand."

"Is he in on this?"

"He thinks I want to go to Switzerland to convince Phoebe that Germany is winning the war. And he loves to meddle and play Providence. When I told him that Conny said I couldn't go and that he didn't understand what a lot of good I could do talking to an American writer, he instantly thought he could be cleverer than Conny and that it would be a good joke on him. And he even gave me a list of things to be sure and say to her!"

"I'd like to see that. Of course I'll have to talk you past the Swiss side somehow."

"Oh, we'll manage that," she said confidently. "I've been in and out through Lindau several times in happier days, and I'm sure to see someone I know and can tell a story to. There's only one thing." She hesitated. "I haven't got any money."

"I have," said Johnny.

"Enough for two?"

"I guess so. You'll probably have to sit up all night in the express."

"I shan't mind. You know—it's almost as though you *expected* something like this."

"I did expect something," Johnny confessed. "It's happened a little faster than I thought it could, but—we're on our way!"

"Won't Phoebe be surprised!"

"Not entirely," said Johnny, and reaching a straight road westward he let out the car.

"Conny will know why I've gone," she said, settling back into her corner. "That is—he'll know because I went with you and not in the usual way with half a dozen trunks and a couple of maids."

"And why did you?"

"Because I think he will try to stop me," she said simply. "Everything depends on when it occurs to the Emperor to tell him I have gone— or when he gets a telegram from Heidersdorf. If I had waited to pack and collect the entourage I'm not allowed to move without, he might had had time to do something. But he'll know now I'm not coming back. If he tells the Emperor that we may have trouble at Lindau."

"They won't be quick enough. And they can't be sure we'd go to Lindau."

"Hurry," she said quietly, and her hands were clasped tensely in her lap, her eyes were fixed on the road ahead.

"We don't want Dresden till after dark. Walk right up to the train just before it starts. Step out at Lindau tomorrow and catch the first boat across the Lake. Dinner at Zurich with Phoebe. Won't it taste good?"

She smiled faintly, and her face was small and white.

In order to avoid going to a restaurant in Dresden from which they might be traced, they ate the last of the sandwiches and other delicacies from the hamper before they drove into the city, and Rosalind let down her veil. At the station they left the car and walked together to the ticket window. There was a short queue and while they stood waiting Rosalind heard the man ahead of them ask for a ticket to Hanover. He spoke perfect German, but his voice stopped her heart. When he turned away from the window she stared up from behind her veil at Charles—wearing a rather shabby suit of German civilian clothes which were a trifle small for him, walking with a cane and a bad limp—Charles, in Dresden, buying a ticket to Hanover as though he owned the place.

Without lifting his eyes to her face, he stepped around the figure of a woman who seemed to be planted in his path and walked on, purposefully, towards the train gates, while she stood gazing after him. He had not seen her. If he had looked at her the veil was meant to hide her face. But it was Charles and he had got as far as Dresden and was heading northwards towards Holland—she had heard that some of them got away through Holland. . . .

Johnny's hand took her elbow and she accompanied him in stupefied silence towards the train for Lindau.

"You'll have to look as married as possible and nap on my shoulder," he was saying. "Sure to be other people in the compartment. I'll wire the Embassy from Rorschach on the Swiss side to collect the car. What's the matter, feeling faint?"

"I'm—all right."

"Hold up," said Johnny. "So far, so good."

All through that hot, endless night journey, as she dozed and waked and dozed again, she never quite lost sight of Charles, limping away from her towards the trains—after Hanover, what?—Bremen?—he'd never get out that way—Osnabrück—Amsterdam—she knew so little about the Dutch frontier—she wished she could see a map—at Zurich she could see a map—Johnny Malone would know how you got out through Holland, once she could ask him—darling Charles, so far, so good. . . .

She roused to find that Johnny had put an arm around her and held her gathered into the hollow of his shoulder, her face against his coat. Her small motor hat had slipped back and hung by its veil, her hair was loose—she suppressed the impulse to sit up quickly, and opened cautious eyelids. The seat opposite to them was empty now. She knew by the way Johnny held her, his body saving hers from the jerks and swayings of the train, that he was not asleep.

It was very hot, but the additional warmth of his guarding arm was infinitely welcome, his coat was harsh beneath her cheek, but her head fitted so exactly into the hard curve below his collar-bone—she thought, I've been married a dozen years and I never knew this about a man—I never knew you could be so comfortable—so *grateful*. And she thought, Why doesn't Phoebe marry him—I would, if I were Phoebe—maybe she will—you wouldn't ever have to worry about anything again—and unconsciously she nestled a little against the protecting shoulder, and his arm tightened round her reassuringly, and he thought, Worn out, and I don't wonder—brave as a lion, but all worn out—poor little mite, she's had a rough time—imagine roping in the Kaiser—that took nerve—imagine walking out of a palace like that with nothing but what you wore and no money—after all, I'm a total stranger to her—women are the deuce, I don't mind if I say it again. . . .

Through the window of the compartment Johnny saw the sun come up, red and angry and promising another hot day. He assisted a crumpled and apologetic Rosalind to recover herself and set off for the wash-room, and then he realized that his bag was still at the inn and he hadn't even got a razor on him, and must resign himself to arriving unshaven at Zurich for dinner. There was a restaurant car on the train, and when Rosalind returned looking remarkably fresh, he made her go and eat rolls and marmalade and drink hot coffee with him there.

At Munich, where the train stopped a long time, they knew they were still five hours from Lindau, and Rosalind sat tensely quiet while their compartment filled up again. But at last the wheels began to turn, and they looked at each other. The last lap.

6

PHOEBE, kicking her heels at Zurich, had no idea when to expect word from Johnny or in what form it would come. Probably he would have to travel all the way back to Zurich in order to speak freely and give her the real facts about Rosalind's silence. If Rosalind was all right—but she wasn't. She couldn't be. And if there was something fishy it might take him a while to find out. If she was dead—he wouldn't just send a telegram about that either. He'd come and tell how and when.

Meanwhile Phoebe reminded herself that it was an excellent opportu-

nity to learn all about Zurich, which might come in handy sometime,
remembering what a nuisance it was to have to write scenes laid in
Berlin when she had never been there, though no one had ever guessed
it—but she found the band concerts in the Stadhaus-Platz and the views
from the Quais and promenades and the Botanical Gardens and the
museums palled very soon when all her mind was concentrated else-
where, on the news which would come out of Germany.

And then one afternoon when she had returned to the hotel to freshen
up for dinner and was writing out some postcards for the children at
home, there was a knock on her sitting-room door, and as it was probably
the chambermaid with fresh towels she only said Come in, without looking up. And Rosalind herself opened the door.

Johnny was there behind her, of course, pretty well pleased with himself, and Phoebe warmly congratulated him on so Graustarkian an
exploit as the abduction of a Prussian Princess, however willing, in
broad daylight, and it was some time before they all stopped talking at
once and Rosalind's happy tears were dried, and they remembered they
were dying for dinner. Johnny went away for a bath and a shave, and
while Phoebe's clothes were all too big for Rosalind a tea-gown wouldn't
matter and they would have the meal served here in Phoebe's sitting-
room.

There was silence in the bathroom while Rosalind lay in a hot tub and
Phoebe pottered about the bedroom laying out fresh things for her to
wear, until finally Rosalind's voice came out through the open door
between—

"Phoebe, are you there?"

"Yes, honey, I'm here."

"Phoebe, I saw Charles." The words were cautiously low, a little
breathless.

"Saw—*Charles!*" Phoebe dropped everything and started for the bathroom door. *"Where?"*

"I saw him twice, as a matter of fact. He's a prisoner." Rosalind swished
up out of the water and wrapped herself in a towel. "You can come in if
you like, and hand me that dressing-gown."

"But this is *news*," said Phoebe, handing the dressing-gown. "He was
reported missing."

"He's still missing," said Rosalind grimly, and told about the scene at
the station at Halkenwitz, and about the other station at Dresden where
Charles went limping away from her, towards Holland—and how Con-

rad had said Charles was a secret agent, and how one could therefore hope that he knew of ways to get across the frontier—but her eyes were anxious and her teeth were set on her lower lip as she began to dress in Phoebe's things.

"He'll turn up safe," Phoebe reassured her. "They're nearly crazy in England because his uncle's sons have both been killed and Charles is the heir now."

"The heir to *Cleeve?*" cried Rosalind in dismay. "Charles a *marquis?* He'll hate that, won't he!"

"Don't see why, it's not one of the most impoverished titles," said Phoebe sensibly. "The tenants all love him, Virginia says, and he'll add tone to any coronation wearing four guards of ermine on his robe and a coronet with pearls and strawberry leaves."

"You always know the oddest things," said Rosalind, bending over her stockings.

"Well, I had to read up on coronations, don't forget!"

"Doesn't it seem a long time ago!" said Rosalind dreamily.

After she was safely tucked up in bed that night in a room next door to Phoebe's at the Hotel Baur au Lac, she went on thinking about Charles and the responsibilities of his inheritance. But it's nothing to do with me, really, she told herself firmly, for tired as she was, she couldn't go to sleep. Charles will be just the same, the title won't change him. Only now he'll have to marry, on account of the succession. I've forgotten who comes next after Charles, but it can't be anybody much. Charles will have to have children now, for Cleeve Place. But that's nothing to do with me, because even if Conrad divorced me I don't—don't ever want to marry again, not even Charles, and Victor is all the children I'll ever have. Anyway, I want to belong to myself now, and not to any man. . . .

And then, for the first time since Johnny had come to Heidersdorf, she thought, *But what shall I live on?* She had run away, burnt her bridges, hopelessly cut herself off, without a penny. Mamma wouldn't be pleased, she had only enough for herself. The idea of escape from Germany had excluded everything else. With a fine gesture of disdain she had left even her jewels behind. Everything had been so lavishly provided for so long she had actually forgotten it had to be paid for by somebody.

Well, I've got four languages, she thought. I can go as a governess. People like Virginia will let me teach their children French and Italian —I don't suppose anyone will want their children to learn German nowadays, and anyway my German still isn't as good as my Spanish, even, after all these years. Perhaps I can teach music too. I shall have to earn my living. That will be something new. . . .

But her mind kept on going back to Charles and his impending marquisate. Some woman will snap him up now, she thought. He's such a lamb. . . . She buried her face in the pillow. It's too late, I'm no good to him. But I can still see him sometimes. And that's all I ever really hoped for or wanted. I can see him sometimes. . . .

3. Farthingale.   *Christmas, 1915.*

>>>

1

ZEPPELINS had begun to get through to London now, working in from Kent and Suffolk, and on the night in September that Rosalind and Phoebe arrived a great deal of damage was done in the City, and casualties were heavy. They had reached St. James's Square before the raid began, and were having a cup of tea with Virginia in the upstairs sitting-room reserved for the family when the pom-poms started and the big Hyde Park guns began to speak. Virginia asked at once if they wanted to go down to the shelter in the basement, but Phoebe said No, she meant to get used to it, and anyway that was guns on the ground they heard and not bombs—so far.

"How clever of you to be able to tell the difference," said Maia, who had just come off duty in the ward below and was still in uniform.

Phoebe saw that she looked pinched and white and terrified, and discovered with humiliation that her own hands were shaking, and her heart had begun to knock about in her chest the way it had done on the *Lusitania.* She's frightened out of her wits, Phoebe thought contemptuously—so am I—but I won't show it—I'll die first—Virginia's all right—one must get used to it—

"Let's open the window and see if we can't see it," said Rosalind. "I think I hear a Zepp motor over us this minute."

"And if you do see it be sure to say that it looks exactly like a big silver cigar, won't you," Maia suggested tartly. "Everyone does. I'm for the shelter, myself, there's no point in showing off when there's no one to see." The door snapped behind her crisp skirts, and Virginia made a face.

"Funk," she said briefly. "She's wonderful with dressings, and has the lightest touch of any of us, so they can use her for burns and bleeding wounds—she can stand anything like that, things that would turn me inside out. The surgeons prefer her, and the men ask for her. I only hope there's never a raid when she's on duty!"

The door opened again and Winifred came in briskly, settling her cuffs for her turn in the ward.

"What a row outside," she remarked, and kissed Rosalind warmly. "Welcome to England, darling, we're doing this in your honor. You might have been safer where you were!"

"Don't you think we could *see* it?" Rosalind entreated.

"It's right over our heads by the sound of it," Winifred said unconcernedly, going towards the heavy curtains which masked the window. "Put out the lights, somebody."

The switch clicked under Virginia's hand, and the curtains rattled back on their brass rings. Winifred threw up the window and leaned out.

"There it is! Two of 'em, b'God!" she cried. "Why *can't* we shoot them down more often, you'd think they were big enough for our gunners to hit, wouldn't you!"

Phoebe forced herself to go to the window and lean out with the rest, her arm around Rosalind's waist. The sky over London was crisscrossed with searchlights, and the Zeppelins hung in the stabbing beams of light, one of them quite near, perhaps directly over Trafalgar Square. It *was* cigar-shaped, she thought wryly, and the lights turned it silver.

"It's not dropping anything now," said Winifred, watching intently. "We're making all the noise, here below. Why can't our *aeroplanes* get it, if the pom-poms can't? There must be some answer to them, England can't just sit down under this!"

"Why not bomb Berlin?" Rosalind remarked, gazing quietly up at the humming monsters.

"Yes, why not!" cried Winifred, and pulled them in and slammed down the window. "Would you mind if they did?" she asked over her shoulder as the lights came on again and she stood rearranging the curtains.

"Mind? Me?" Rosalind looked bewildered. "It's the ugliest city I ever saw, full of the ugliest people! And it's no good fighting this war with our gloves on, you know," she added matter-of-factly. *"They* won't!"

"Well, I'm glad to see somebody else as bloodthirsty as I am!" grinned Winifred. "Whenever I say something like that people raise their eyebrows as though I had forgotten my manners!"

"You don't want manners with Germans," said Rosalind. *"They* haven't any. If you're polite to a German he thinks you're afraid of him —which you usually are. But if you're ruder than he is, he thinks you're Somebody, and tries to be polite himself. And when a German is polite he licks your boots."

"Good Lord," said Winifred. "Well, you ought to know!" And she went away to the ward, her skirt crackling.

2

THE air raid made up Phoebe's mind for her. She was not going to leave England just yet. She wrote to Dinah asking her if she would keep Jeff over Christmas time, so that she could stay and be of real use at the St. James's Square hospital, and enrolled for V.A.D. training. Rosalind, who was judged too delicate for nursing, went to Lady Shadwell's house in Chelsea, which had been turned over to the care of convalescent blinded men. She read to them, played the piano to them, and made them sing with her, and they loved it.

And day after hopeful day slid by without news of Charles.

It was October when he turned up at last—telegraphed from Dover and then just walked into his old commanding officer's room at the War Office, leaning rather heavily on his cane and wearing the mussy suit of German civilian clothes which looked as though it had been slept in more than once. His General, warned by an almost-excited subaltern of Charles's arrival, looked up from his desk as Charles entered and said, "Well, you *have* been a time. Who's your tailor nowadays?" But he rose as he spoke, and their handclasp said the rest.

Charles's leg was found to be in very bad shape, with a damaged kneecap and joint which two operations failed to put right. Rosalind went to see him in hospital as soon as it was allowed, and except that he wasn't tanned found him looking much as usual. When she told him about working with the German Red Cross at the Halkenwitz railway station he said, "Then it *was* you, bending over me! I thought for days I must be clean off my rocker!" And when she told him about the ticket window at Dresden he said, "By Jove, yes, I did step on someone there at the wicket—was that *you* again?" And they laughed together, and their eyes held, and he said, "Not going back to Germany again—ever?" She shook her head. "God be praised," Charles sighed, very flat in his hospital bed. "Now I can put my mind on the war," he said.

But Charles was through with the war, for his right knee would be stiff as a board for the rest of his life, and his Uncle Cleeve died a few weeks before Christmas. Charles was given honorable discharge from the Army and advised to go down to Gloucestershire and be a big landowner and help win the war with his acres and his timber and his livestock and his farms.

Bracken was coming back from France to spend Christmas at Farthingale, and Archie got unexpected leave, so Winifred made Virginia take Christmas week for herself in the country. And with Phoebe and Rosalind, and Aunt Sally's troupe, they were quite a family reunion. It was understood that Charles would drive over from Cleeve Place for Christmas Day, and Clare was to bring the children from the Hall because Mortimer was somewhere in the North on his remount job—all the children except Hermione, who was being sent up to London with her governess to spend Christmas with Oliver and Maia there, and Hubert, Winifred's eldest, who was at Eton and would also go to London for Christmas.

It was the second Christmas of the war, but the shops were still full of presents and Phoebe's American dollars were lavishly drawn upon. They had convinced Rosalind that she needn't start her governessing quite yet, not so long as she was so useful at Lady Shadwell's, and Phoebe had insisted on putting a hundred pounds to her credit at the bank, for pin money, as Mrs. Norton-Leigh had behaved rather badly.

After a good deal of rambling talk about income tax and the cost of food nowadays, Mamma had finally consented to give her runaway daughter a minute allowance which wouldn't have kept a schoolgirl; and Rosalind's sister Evelyn, who was living in her little house in Surrey with her baby daughter while her husband was away in France, had his sister and his mother staying with her and made it quite plain that there was no room for Rosalind there. Rosalind had never drawn a check for herself before, and was enchanted with the privilege when Phoebe made it possible, and insisted that she could live for years on a hundred pounds. But before she knew it she had spent ten of it on presents for everybody, and forty more for clothes, which she really had to have besides the things Virginia found she could easily spare, such as a fur-lined coat. Rosalind could even wear Virginia's shoes, which was very fortunate as Virginia had such lots.

Meanwhile no word came from Conrad. He could have reached her through neutral diplomatic channels if he had tried. "I expect I'm blotted out," said Rosalind philosophically. "He won't ever acknowledge my existence again, even to divorce me."

That was just what Phoebe was afraid of, and she consulted Archie, who said that the English divorce laws being what they were, Rosalind could never get redress there.

"She worries that people will condemn her for leaving her child, even though Conrad has become impossible," Phoebe explained. "She thinks people may not realize that Victor has been sent away to school to fit him to become an officer—and to learn to hate his English mother, no doubt! She hasn't been allowed to see him at all since the war began."

"German boys never have much need of a mother, I fancy," said Archie. "It's not in the system."

"But if Rosalind can't get free of Conrad legally what about Charles after waiting all these years?"

"Would they marry now, d'you think, if she could?" Archie seemed doubtful.

"I don't see why not. Charles has been a monument of faithfulness, and poor Rosalind does deserve a bit of cherishing at last. To say nothing of what Charles deserves!"

To which Archie said, "Oh, rather," and the subject died.

Phoebe came face to face with her own responsibilities as a mother when Bracken arrived from France on Christmas Eve, muddy and gaunt, and with a growing reputation for graphic reporting, and found letters from Dinah awaiting him in accumulated mail. When he had read them and had a bath and a whiskey and got into fresh clothes and had a good think meanwhile, he got Phoebe alone and asked her flatly what she intended to do about Jeff. Phoebe at once looked guilty and apologetic and began to explain that she was going home in the spring, and sometimes thought she ought to go sooner, but there was so much to do here, and she was just beginning to feel she was of some use—

Bracken interrupted.

"Suppose Jeff didn't exist. Suppose you'd never had him. What would you do, stay on here indefinitely?"

"Well, yes—perhaps I would. As long as I was needed, anyway. I might even have got out to France to nurse. But—"

"Then suppose you give Jeff to Dinah and me. Go to France. Do what you like. He'll be safe."

"G-give him—?"

"I mean let me adopt him legally and make him my heir, provide his schooling, bring him up as my own, train him to inherit the paper some day and run it as I took over from my father. He'd be fixed for life, with a good job to grow into, and you wouldn't have to—worry."

"But, Bracken, I can afford to send him to college and give him a start in whatever he wants to do."

"Sure, I'm not saying you can't. And if ever he wants a job that way, I'll give it to him. But—Dinah is inclined to abase herself because we haven't got a son, and Jeff would fill up that gap and I should think everyone would be better off. Don't let that word adopt scare you. It's a mere legal formality, to protect his rights in the estate. It wouldn't make any difference between you and him—and he would always have a home with us, and Dinah to look after him when you aren't there, and a father besides, if he'll consider me as one."

"I suppose he'd soon forget me entirely," Phoebe said thoughtfully.

"My dear—forgive me, but he has already forgotten you."

Phoebe looked at him quickly as though to deny it, and then away, her lips rather set.

"You must think I'm—pretty heartless," she murmured.

"No," he assured her evenly. "You weren't in love with Miles. That was the heartless part."

"I tried to be. I *meant* to be."

"And you've tried to be a mother to Jeff, but trying isn't enough, Phoebe. Dinah isn't trying. Dinah has no choice. And she has become so wrapped up in the child that her one dread in life is the day you come to take him away. Let her be really happy and able to look ahead for him and lay plans. Let her pretend he belongs to her. Anyway, it's all in the family, isn't it! And whatever you do now, you'll never want him the way Dinah does. You'll never have any idea what it will mean to her to give him up. And to me, incidentally."

Phoebe gazed at him with troubled, honest eyes.

"I must be what they call an unnatural mother even to consider it," she said.

"Then you do consider it," he put in alertly.

"I don't know, I—Bracken, since I came back to England it seems more and more as though I was never married to Miles at all! It's all receded so far I feel as though Jeff is the result of some kind of hasty— *indiscretion,* instead of a respectable marriage! And letting you adopt him seems to make that worse, somehow. The servant girl's mistake!"

Bracken grinned.

"You read too many novels," he said. "Let us have Jeff, and I'll get you to France with the Belgian Red Cross—right up into the base hospitals where you can hear the guns. The British won't allow their nurses near the front, but the Belgians are not so fussy. As a nurse you can go places and see things that are barred to me as a correspondent. And if you keep a journal you will come out with a perfectly whopping story. All I ask is first publication rights, you can have the book to do as you like with."

"How generous of you," she remarked with affectionate irony, and pondered a moment, her eyes on the bleak winter hills beyond the window.

She knew that Bracken was offering her what was to him the most attractive proposition he could imagine. Bracken would perjure and steal and cheerfully risk his only neck for a good story. It would never occur to him that she didn't herself desperately want to be where she could hear the guns, which she was sure would set her heart to knocking about in her chest again, or that the prospect of nursing men straight from the ambulances with undressed wounds only filled her with dismay. She could do it, of course, if she had to. People got used to it. They even got used to having the wounds. And it was a thing worth doing, where she could be really useful. With Jeff provided for, she was quite free again to be useful where she could.

Free again. It is my curse to be free, she thought rebelliously, forgetting that she had never really liked being tied to Miles and Jeff. She had done all she could for Rosalind, who was fast regaining her old lightheartedness. There was nothing she could do for Oliver, who had never lost his. In London there was always the possibility, disturbing, distracting, secretly desired, of seeing him again now and then. Once they had simply run into each other quite by accident in Pall Mall and on a carefree impulse had had lunch together at Prince's, and so far as they knew had not been seen by anyone who mattered. But they couldn't go on doing that sort of thing, deeply satisfying and innocent as even that much of each other's society was. Not unless they were prepared to find themselves in an open scandal of Maia's making, and that would ruin Oliver at the War Office and be bad for Hermione. . . .

She sighed.

"All right," she told Bracken. "I might as well." . .

"Good," said Bracken, and his eyes were kind and comprehending. "There's one thing about the guns," he added consolingly. "They do take your mind off things."

5

CHARLES was the last man to feel that he deserved anything from anyone, but he arrived at Farthingale on Christmas morning with his arms full of presents and determination in his soul. Everyone was most awfully glad to see him, and made the most terrific fuss of him, and he was put next to Rosalind at luncheon. Looking down at her face laughing up at him during the meal, he said approvingly, "You're getting fatter," and instead of taking offence she replied that it was because she was so happy. "I feel—oh, years younger! I feel so—so *light!*" she cried, and made an embracing gesture of floating. He noticed that she seemed surprised, as though any woman who left her husband should be covered with remorse and shame for years.

Farthingale wasn't a big house, and it was pretty full, but somehow between tea and dinner by a curious coincidence everybody was taken with a need to write letters or have a bath or a nap or a walk before dressing, until Charles and Rosalind were left quite alone in the library. She was knitting in a corner of the sofa by the fire, and said that as soon as she had turned the heel she must think about dressing. Charles strolled over and closed the door and she noticed as he came back towards her across the room that though his smooth guardsman's carriage was forever spoilt by the limp, his back was as straight and his hips as narrow as when he had returned from South Africa fifteen years before.

"That leg of yours," she remarked casually. "Is it all right now?"

"As right as it will ever be. I shan't be able to hunt, you know."

"We shan't have any horses for years."

"Looks that way, doesn't it."

"Will it go on *forever*, do you think?"

"No. But for another two years anyway."

"The *boys*," she said, knitting. "Boys like Gerald Campion and younger—oh, much younger, one keeps forgetting he's all grown up. Virginia says he's in love with Fabrice."

"Oh? Let's hope he outgrows that."

Rosalind laughed her knowing, childlike chuckle.

"You're all so hard on her," she said. "But you must admit she's pretty!"

"Is she?" Charles was standing on the hearthrug looking down at her. "I suppose I'm permanently blind to every woman but one."

"That's very sweet, Charles, but you must find some nice girl and have a family now, on account of the title."

Charles made a sound, half laugh, half gasp, surprised, amused, a little horrified, and replied, "Oh, bother the title, Buffy can see to that, he comes next after me."

"Buffy?"

"You remember my cousin Buffy, Uncle Aubrey's son. He used to come to Cleeve for the holidays when we were kids."

"Oh, that red-haired little beast I chased round the herb garden with a cricket bat and he slipped and cut his chin on the gravel and howled so loud they all thought I'd murdered him?"

"That's Buffy! He wears the scar to this day, but I don't think he howls when he's hurt, he's a major in a Hussar regiment now, and won all sorts of glory on the Northwest Frontier. He's married the nice girl already, old Lord Bollard's daughter, and they have two good-looking boys, who must come from their mother's side. So the title is provided for, you couldn't ask for better."

"But isn't Buffy rather an ass, all the same?" she objected.

"Well, yes, he is, rather. But not more than I am, d'you think?"

Rosalind looked up at him on the hearthrug quite seriously.

"I wonder if you have any idea how good it is to hear somebody say something like that again," she sighed.

Charles, who wasn't conscious of having said anything, moved to the other end of the sofa and sat down.

"Do you remember the last time you were here I tried to talk you out of going back to Germany at all, and you raised a lot of silly arguments about my reputation at the War Office and so on?"

"Yes, Charles."

"Well, all that won't wash now, you see, because I've left the War Office and the Army for good. I've closed up Cleeve for the duration and am living in the dower house with a housekeeper and a couple of maids. Do you remember the dower house?" he insisted gently.

"Very well."

"Do you remember how in the small drawing-room two sofas face each other across the fire, and the tea-table was always at the end of the right-hand one, where Aunt Flora sat—and it was China tea in shallow flowered cups with gilt handles, and there was a tiered cake-stand called a curate, with cucumber sandwiches and Dundee cake and some kind of brittle molasses things with nuts in them—"

"And cream buns."

"Yes, and the sunset came in the west window and made a sort of pink glow against the marble mantel and on your white dress—"

"Fancy your remembering that!"

"It looks just the same now," he said. "Aunt Flora is gone. But you could be there, pouring out the tea—if you'd come."

"But, Charles, I—oh, it's no good, my dear, he'll never divorce me!"

"Well, suppose he doesn't."

"You mean—come anyway, as—as your—"

"As the only woman I've ever wanted."

Rosalind sat motionless, staring down at the knitting lying in her lap. The room was so quiet they could hear the wind outside, and the small sounds of the wood fire. He waited patiently, his eyes on her averted face. And when the silence was no longer bearable as they were, she laid down the knitting between them with a quick, decisive gesture and rose, not looking at him, and he stood up too, remaining where he was while she walked away from him, her head down.

"No, we couldn't do it," she said at last, very low. "A thing like that is impossible for a man in your position, with your responsibilities. You must find someone else—someone who would be—respectable—"

"Rosalind, I want no other woman at my side but you." His soft, slurred tones were a little more emphatic than usual. "Perhaps by the time I am gathered to my fathers still a bachelor you will believe that. But it would be much nicer for me in the meantime if you could take it in now."

"But—think how it would *look*, Charles! Our close friends like Archie and Virginia would understand, perhaps, might even encourage

us. But what about the others? What about your own people there
at Cleeve, they'd have a right to resent me, I couldn't face them—"

"There isn't a family on the place that doesn't remember you and
inquire after you, and ask me when you are coming back."

"The simple ones, perhaps—but remember the vicar's wife. I should
be cut by the vicar's wife!"

"I doubt that, in the circumstances. I'll ask her, if you like."

"And there's Mamma—and Evelyn too. I can't *think* what Mamma
would say!"

"You listened to Mamma last time, have you forgotten? You have
fulfilled the bargain she made with His Highness," said Charles, with
his teeth on edge. "He's had fourteen years of your life, and what has
he made of it? If he came to you now on his knees, making the kind
of promises a man in love will make, would you go back to him?"

"No, *no*—!" She put it from her with such vehemence, with both her
hands, that his eyes narrowed on her, and he took a step forward.

"As bad as that, was it," he said.

"He won't come for me—it isn't that—if the war ended tomorrow he'd
never want me back—it isn't that—"

"Well, then? Even people without imagination must have some idea
what it means to an Englishwoman to be married to a German these
days. If it's only that you're afraid of what people will say—"

"About *you!*" she entreated. "*I* don't matter. If you weren't Cleeve
now, if we could live quietly somewhere—"

"I never wanted to be Cleeve, God knows," he said quietly. "But somebody has to be, and I was always round the place, you see, they all know
me, and can count on me, while Buffy's still something of a stranger
to them because of the regiment's being in India so long. At a time like
this they need something to hold on to—"

"Yes, and if you bring home another man's wife—"

"I shall bring home Miss Rosalind. They've never called you anything else."

"No." She shook her head. "Later on, perhaps, if you—if Buffy can
take over at Cleeve and you still want to—to go away somewhere with
me, where it wouldn't matter—"

"What, as though I were ashamed?" He was smiling.

She gave him a long, incredulous look from across the room, and
then came to him slowly, and when she reached him she offered both
her hands, which he took in both his, looking down at her.

"You're very good to me," she said humbly.

"Am I? How?"

"You haven't made a scene, or—been offended, or tried to—to sweep me off my feet—"

He gave again that half-embarrassed gasp of laughter, as though she had said something too fantastic to be taken seriously.

"What good would that do?" he asked.

"None. But how did you know that?"

"Horse sense, I suppose," said Charles, and Rosalind threw up her chin and laughed as once she had never expected to laugh again. "Someday you're going to love me—I hope—if I behave myself, that is," Charles explained. "But it doesn't take much intelligence not to shove myself at you until then."

"How I feel about you isn't the question, Charles—not any more." She stood with her hands in his, feeling all his patient strength and devotion flow into her, up her arms and through her body till it sang. "There was a time when I would have said it was no use at all—that the power to love anybody had gone out of me, if I had ever had it. I'd got sort of numb inside. But now—well, I'm all pins and needles again. Seeing you did that. And as for loving you—" She leaned against him, pressing her face into the rough smoky tweed of his coat. "—more than anything else in the world, when everything seemed so hopeless, I only wanted to see you again—"

" 'Fraid there's not much to look at, now you come to it," said Charles contentedly, and laid his arms around her.

4. London.   *Autumn, 1916.*

>>

1

PHOEBE left for the Continent early in the new year with Bracken, who delayed his return in order to take her with him after the necessary interviews at the headquarters of the Belgian Red Cross at the Savoy in

London, and at the American Embassy, and the inoculations, and the
red tape.

Via Boulgne—which was full of British khaki and French blue, with
a white hospital ship at the quay, and where Bracken left her—via
Calais, and Dunkirk, she arrived in less than thirty-six hours at a hospital which had once been a big summer hotel in a straggling Belgian
seaside town so near the front lines that in the darkness the red flames
of the guns could be seen across the reverberating sands, and a search-
light playing over the water revealed the British gunboats on guard off
shore.

Though the hospital belonged to the Belgian Red Cross, most of the
nurses were English, said the starched night nurse who introduced herself as Sister Ida, while Phoebe followed her along corridors filled with
wounded on stretchers awaiting their turn at the operating rooms. Many
of them were caked with mud and filth, and the floor and stairs were
mired from the feet of the bearers. The wounded were brought in at
night, when the ambulances could travel more safely, and often arrived
at the hospital not more than twenty minutes after they had been hit—
others had lain for days unattended in No Man's Land. Only the worst
cases were allowed to remain here. The rest were given dressings and
nourishment and sent on to the hospitals at Boulogne or in England.

The bedroom assigned to Phoebe was a tiny cubicle on the top floor
with a heavily curtained window facing the sea. Sister Ida said that
Phoebe was just in time for supper with the night nurses, and nodded
wisely when she replied that all she wanted was to go to bed.

"You shouldn't have had to travel all that way alone the first time,"
she said, and came back in ten minutes with a cup of tea in one hand
and a hot water bottle in the other.

When Phoebe protested against such babying, Sister Ida advised her
drily to make the most of it, as she was expected to go on duty the next
morning. Phoebe began to explain rather nervously that she was only a
probationer, and Sister Ida laughed.

"Bless you, most of us are only half trained," she said, "but there are
no probationers here. We're all called Sister, and we all do anything that
comes along. You start tomorrow with twenty beds in the same surgical
ward I'm in—and you're expected to help with the dressings anywhere
else in the ward. I'll be coming off as you go on, but I'll wait and show
you round a bit if you like. You'll soon get the hang of it here, hospitals
are all pretty much alike, don't you think?"

The door closed on her friendly smile, and Phoebe was left alone with the sound of the guns, which so far she was too exhausted to find very alarming.

She slept restlessly, and woke in the dawn hearing aeroplanes over-head—French ones, she decided, going to the window, and stood a minute wrapped in her coat and shivering in the unheated room, gazing at the view which was to become so drearily familiar. Her room looked out to sea over the wide, level beach where there was no surf, and scattered fishing-boats had been abandoned just above high tide when theii owners went to war. There were a few twisted, wind-blown trees, and a quantity of long dry grass, and a huddle of rather ordinary little villas with sandy gardens. A few able-bodied Belgian soldiers were already about—orderlies, men on rest or in reserve, perhaps convalescents, all looking shabby and cold and undersized. The guns around Nieuport still muttered, and the window-casing jarred rhythmically as it had done all night.

Remembering Sister Ida's promise to show her round, Phoebe dressed quickly in her uniform after a hasty, chilly wash, and found her way downstairs. A passing surgeon, red-eyed and sleepless, glanced at her sharply, a broad peasant woman on her knees scrubbing the muck off the stairs gave her a shy Good-morning in Flemish.

Sister Ida met her in the lower corridor and Phoebe saw in the morning light that she was pretty in a faded way with a sweet, confidential smile. She was introduced to Matron and conducted through the rooms on the ground floor, including the ones where the operating was done. The big hotel parlor was converted into a recreation room, with a gramophone to amuse the convalescents, and a place where the nurses off duty could write letters—its windows faced on the flat, windy beach, with the flat white line of the incoming tide on the sand. Even here there was the familiar hospital smell of drugs and disinfectant.

In the wards she saw for the first time victims of the war who were not soldiers—women caught in the bombardment of a nearby market town and maimed for life, children who had lost limbs. A priest passed soundlessly, bestowing smiles and confidence as he approached a cot with a screen set around it. A nun sat motionless beside a sleeping child. . . .

Sister Ida's low voice ran on, describing the cases which would be in Phoebe's care—the boy with the bandage across his eyes was very young and frightened, and often cried out in his sleep—you had to be patient,

it comforted him to hold on to your hand, and a cup of hot milk sometimes helped him to doze off again—there was just a chance of saving a
little sight in one eye—most of them were very cheerful, even in pain—
as they got better they always wanted to talk, but no doubt Phoebe
had already noticed that!—changing the draw-sheet for the Scotsman
with the gangrenous leg was always a terrible business, it took three of
you, and even then he screamed with pain—the littlest baby had died
in the night, but as it had lost both arms that was probably a good thing
—if somebody would send out some rubber air-cushions it would be a
great mercy—and a bit of chocolate would help too, the food was so
dull, and eggs were hard to get—they had only eleven thermometers
for a hundred and twenty beds, and there was always a shameless grab
for the odd one—some new Belgian girls had just arrived from the London training school, but couldn't be trusted with temperatures and res-
pirations, and it took two hours for one Sister to do the whole ward. . . .

This was to be Phoebe's life, all through the spring and into the summer—while the long battle of Verdun began and ebbed without advantage to the German attackers, who in the end cried sour grapes and published fabulous figures of French casualties and prisoners, to prove that
it was immaterial whether or not Verdun was taken—the Germans
themselves having recklessly spent forces which would never be replaced, and without breaking the French front or luring the Allies into
a premature offensive.

The winter gales gave way to a hot sun which glared pitilessly on
the tin roofs of the pavilion wards and the hot breeze blew sand into
everything, and swarming black flies had to be brushed out of the wounds
open to be dressed, and then they crawled on the food. Matron wrote to
the Belgian Committee in London for something to be done about the
sanitary conditions, but nothing happened, and the garbage was left
standing uncovered for hours in the heat. There was no ice, there were
no cold drinks and no electric fans, and the men lay gasping for breath.
There were never enough pajamas to give them a refreshing change
often enough. The head nurse got ill, simply overdone, and several of
the Sisters dropped in their tracks, so that the ones who were left took
thirty beds apiece and forgot what it was to sit down.

Phoebe bore it all without complaining, in a kind of fierce resignation.
She was no good for anything but this any more, these were the people
who needed her, she might as well be here as anywhere else, and the idea
of quitting never occurred to her because there was no one to fill her

place. Her feet gave out, like everybody else's, and she went on duty each day with them tightly bandaged. And then one morning towards the end of that dreadful summer, she woke with a flaming sore throat and sharp pains everywhere and the room went round while she tried to dress.

She had no sooner got downstairs than she was sent back up again, and then was carted off on a stretcher like a *blessé* to the Isolation Villa with a temperature of 103°, and had scarlet fever. For days she knew nothing except that the bedclothes were on fire and that she was always thirsty, and that she was going to die there alone, and she wished she had drowned, because of the way the sun beat down on the sand, and the flies woke her every morning crawling on her face, going from one infectious case to another. . . .

Then gradually, against all the odds, the fever broke and her racked body began to mend, and she was able to be sent away to a villa near Boulogne to recuperate. Bracken came to her there, thin and worn himself, but smiling and capable and *kin,* and once more they made the journey across the Channel together, and up to London—which was under the threat of gas bombs now—and thence to Farthingale and a glorious feeling of home and family once more.

2

VIRGINIA came down for Phoebe's first week-end and brought all the latest news. Aeroplanes as well as Zeppelins were raiding England now, and Dover in particular was having a bad time. The summer fighting on the Somme had filled everything up with new casualties and the hospitals were all overworked. Archie was doing a job in Paris and had not been seen for weeks. Clare was running the convalescent home at the Hall and had just had another son. Winifred was perfectly splendid and did the work of two people at the St. James's Square house, where they had made another ward by clearing out the library. Maia was sure that the Germans would use gas over London and had got them all gas-masks, which everyone doubted would be worth anything.

Things had got so touchy and difficult between Maia and Winifred, Virginia said, that it had been arranged for Maia to work at Lady Shadwell's house in Chelsea for a while—she was good at reading to the blinded men, and they seemed to like her well enough, they were grateful to anybody, poor lambs, though it was hard on Lady Shadwell's staff having her there, for Maia was edgy and unreasonable all the time now, and admitted that the raids were getting on her nerves. Clare had heroically invited her for a spell of duty at the Hall for a change, but Maia refused to leave London so long as Oliver was at the War Office, which was no doubt very wifely and commendable, said Virginia, but at the same time very trying for everybody, including, she should think, Oliver.

Rosalind was back at the Chelsea house herself, having said firmly that Charles or no Charles she could not sit down comfortably in the country and fold her hands in the middle of a war. She could play to the men by the hour, and they loved it because she always gave them what they asked for, from Bach to *Tipperary,* and encouraged them to sing, and everyone knew that a good ringing song, with everybody joining in, was wonderful for keeping the spirits up. She sent Phoebe her love by Virginia, and hoped to get down to Farthingale herself for a few days later on, but a new batch of men had just come in, some of them in bad shape, and she was needed.

As for the war, which Proebe had somewhat lost track of, the German situation on the Somme was now so desperate that they had begun to loose whole flocks of Zeppelins on London, though very few of them got through. Royal Flying Corps boys who had mastered the difficult business of taking off and landing in darkness went up to meet them, and Zeppelins were being brought down in flames all over the place, with their German crews roasted, Virginia reported callously, beyond recognition. In Belgium the invaders had resorted to slave raids on the conquered population for labor at home, and were conscripting men in Poland for the army. The British Coalition Government was in what Bracken tactfully termed disesteem, and people said Mr. Asquith would resign soon, and that man Lloyd George was always making trouble. And on the other side of the Atlantic, President Wilson was running for a second term.

Mention of Mr. Wilson always aroused Aunt Sally to caustic comment. His behavior since the *Lusitania* went down was in her eyes both indefensible and humiliating, for Aunt Sally considered herself still an American even though she gave it the French pronunciation in the feminine. His unfortunate remark that America was not concerned with the causes of the war had earned for him her violent enmity, and there was a similar reaction in more official quarters, the difference being that Aunt Sally said what she thought, and perpetually apologized to

Sosthène for the affront to his countrymen which was implicit in the President's intimation that one side was no better than the other—his total inability to comprehend the issues at stake.

Sosthène, it was now known, had been barred in his youth from doing his military service by a constitutional delicacy which made it impossible for him to ride or climb or dance or attempt anything which taxed his endurance, and therefore he was useless in an army where men much older than he were doggedly holding out in the trenches—and since an operation a year ago he had been compelled to the life of a semi-invalid.

No one had any idea how long the association between him and Aunt Sally had been going on, but it was very evidently based on mutual devotion, in his case expressed by a touching tenderness of manner and countless small, watchful services, and on hers by a fierce protectiveness and an anxious attention to his diet and peace of mind and the danger of draughts. She plainly regarded President Wilson as a blot on Sosthène's personal landscape, and never failed to knife him at every opportunity for not throwing America's fresh strength and conclusive weight into the struggle which had ravished France and was claiming all the best men in England.

"This Meester Weelson," Aunt Sally would say, scorn exaggerating the French twist to his name. "He is a village schoolmaster, who reads copy-book nothings from a blackboard—out of date—out of contact—out of his brains! We shall never redeem ourselves as a democracy. George Washington must revolve without doubt in his grave! Lafayette—has this Weelson ever heard of Lafayette, do you think? Your Grandmother Tabitha Day, Phoebe, was a protégée of Lafayette, do you remember?"

"Well, yes, Aunt Sally, but she was a little girl at the time—"

"Have I said she was not? My great grandmother, it was, as a matter of fact, your great-great. How time slips away when one is happy as I have been. Gran adored Lafayette, that I remember well—he came second after the man she married, who was his friend. What Gran would say to this Weelson I dare not think! Jefferson she had no fear of speaking up to—and the Randolphs when they quizzed her. Gran was not afraid of anything, not even the Yankees when they came to Williamsburg. I am glad she did not live to meet a Boche." She brooded a moment, looking back, her fine, veined hand loaded with rings tapping the arm of her chair. "How is it that such an imbecile as this Weelson should be born in the State of Virginia, the cradle of all our liberties? A man without statesmanship—without even tact, or usual international good manners!—without bowels of compassion! What is he made of, and he a Virginian like the rest of us! He belongs better in Berlin, where they breed boors, and I should like to see him sent there!"

Sosthène reached out and stilled with his own gentle hand the restless fingers on the arm of her chair. A long look passed between them, naked with love and understanding. She smiled.

"I know. You do not like me to break my heart. But it is for the State of Virginia I have pity—one hangs one's head in shame—so long a tradition of great men, and now *this!* Ah, well, it is soon over—he will not be re-elected."

"But, darling, Hughes doesn't say anything about putting us into the war either," Virginia reminded her. "And it has to be either Wilson or Hughes, they say."

Aunt Sally clenched small white jewelled fists.

"Where are our *men?*" she cried. "What have we stood for, all these years, but what the Allies are fighting for now! Freedom from tyranny—freedom from *bullies*—it is the *Germans* again, just as it was when Gran was a little girl and we fought a German who happened to be King of England! It is always the Germans who cause the trouble, what is it about Germans that they must molest and oppress? Why are not Germans *people?*"

"They have never been civilized," said Sosthène, who so rarely spoke. "They were never conquered by Rome. They remained barbarians."

Phoebe stared at him. It was a viewpoint.

"Say that again," she commanded.

"It surprises you?" he asked with his courteous, underisive smile.

"Well, yes—I hadn't thought of it like that."

"One is perhaps inclined to forget that even here in Britain there were four hundred years of the Pax Romana," he said gently. "In Germany, no—only the Vandals and the Goths. Every so often they burst out. It is in the breed."

"May I use that?" Phoebe asked, the professional in her stirring. "May I quote you?"

He gave his small, amiable shrug, his quiet hand still covering Sally's. "It is not original," he said, amused.

Bracken had put his foot down on any more of what he called Phoebe's Belgian nonsense, as though he had not suggested it in the first place, and was arranging for her to go to a hospital near Paris, where the life would be a little less murderous and he hoped she would have time and strength to do some writing on the side. She was not fully recovered when the summons from there came late in the year, but she insisted on starting for France immediately for fear someone else would get her job, she said naïvely—bitter fighting was still going on in the Ancre valley and the French were starting an attack at Verdun.

She spent several days in London, and the last evening before her departure she went round to Chelsea to say Good-bye to Rosalind. As she stepped out of the taxi in front of the house she heard the drone of motors overhead and the guns in the north of the city had already begun. The driver cocked an eye upwards.

"Jerry's back," he said cheerfully. "You'd think they'd get tired of it, wouldn't you, all the good it does 'em." And then, as the Whitehall guns took up the tale, "Better skip inside, miss—what goes up must come down!" And he was off towards the Embankment with a reckless scrape of gears.

Phoebe ran up the steps and rang the bell, and the maid took her to a sitting-room two flights up where Rosalind was expecting her. The ground defence was getting noisier and the first dull crunch of a falling bomb shook the windows as they greeted each other.

"Just in time," said Rosalind in relief. "I was afraid you might have to take shelter somewhere on the way, and our evening would be gone. I suppose these little London shows look pretty feeble to you after being in Belgium."

"We were never actually bombed at the hospital," Phoebe said. "There were German planes over us a good deal of the time, but they never made any serious effort to flatten us. It was always much worse on the road coming and going than while you were there."

"The men say it seems worse here in London," Rosalind told her. "Just because it's not the front. Some of them who stood up to anything that came along in France are inclined to go to pieces here, because it's *London* and ought to be safe. And of course not being able to see makes everything more frightening." She paused a moment, listening to the din inside. "Would you mind going downstairs while this is on?"

"No, but I'm not really nervous—" Phoebe began in some surprise.

"Oh, it isn't that, it's the men," Rosalind explained. "You see—this is Maia's night on duty—she's supposed to be reading to them, but she can't be heard above this row, and anyway—"

"Anyway, what?" Phoebe demanded, following Rosalind out into the upper passage.

"Anyway, she's no good in a raid," said Rosalind flatly, and the words were drowned by the loudest crash of all, and Phoebe saw from above that the great crystal chandelier which hung over the staircase was swinging as though in an earthquake.

"Could that thing come down?" she asked casually, and a turn in the staircase brought them level with it, and then beneath it, as they descended, and Rosalind glanced up.

"Well, it never *has*," she remarked wryly, and laid a quick hand on Phoebe's arm as they reached the floor above the street level, where the big front drawing-room had been turned into the soldiers' recreation room.

Through the wide, arching doorway they could see the men sitting about in comfortable chairs with their canes beside them, in the patient immobility of the blind. Some of them still wore their bandages, others looked quite normal except for their attitude of waiting, their lack of free movement, for they were all still new to the business of finding their way about in the dark.

Just coming out of the door was Maia, wearing her nursing dress, with an open book still in her hand. She halted when she saw them, and backed up against the door-casing. She was white to the lips and there was an odd glitter in her eyes.

"They can't—can't hear me in this noise," she gasped, on the defensive. "It's no good my staying here, I can't shout above this!"

"Go down to the shelter," said Rosalind curtly. "We'll stay with them."

"But I couldn't make myself *heard*," Maia repeated breathlessly, and Phoebe saw that her teeth were inclined to chatter and that her fingers gripped the book till the tips were white. Another bomb shook the windows and the whole house seemed to shiver and settle, and Maia dropped the book and ducked against the wall, flattening herself to it. "It's the *noise!*" she cried, and began to babble. "Even with a thunderstorm, I can't stand the noise, you know I've always been afraid of thunderstorms, even when I was a child—you think I'm a coward, but I've always had bad nerves, and there's nothing I can do for the men while this is on, they won't even know whether I'm there or not—"

"Get down to the shelter," said Rosalind through her teeth. "Go on down where you belong, and sit with the kitchen maids and be *safe!*"

Maia fled, sobbing, her hands over her ears, towards the lower flight of stairs which led to the main hall and the entrance through a green baize door to the servants' quarters and the cellar refuge where the maids gathered during the raids.

Rosalind turned in the doorway, facing the tense immobility of the helpless, waiting men, and she crossed swiftly to the piano, calling out, "How about a song, boys, let's drown them out, we can make more noise than that if we try!"

The piano banged gaily into

"Raining, raining, raining,
Always blooming well raining—"

while Rosalind's trained voice rose steady and true, and the men's voices followed. And then the world rocked round them with a mighty concussion and the long windows above the street blew inwards and shattered behind their heavy velour curtains with a lingering tinkle of glass, and the air was full of plaster dust and the smell of explosive, and all the lights went out except a pair of candles on the mantelpiece.

Once more they all heard Rosalind's confident voice: "That was a close one, but we're all right here! Sit still, everybody, there's glass all over the place. Wait till we can get some more light and brush things off a bit. Don't anybody move!" And she added to Phoebe, who was beside her at the piano, "There are candles in the wall-brackets. Hurry and light them from the ones on the mantel." And as they each snatched up a candlestick she whispered, "I'll bet that one shook her up! She must have been still in the lower hall when it hit!"

Phoebe carried her candle to the door and stopped there, staring into the darkness where the staircase had been. The great chandelier had broken away from the ceiling four stories up and struck the steps, carrying them down with it as the staircase wall buckled inward in a mass of masonry which had fallen straight through the lower hall to the basement. Even the floor of the upper passage where she stood sloped precariously towards the chasm, and plaster fragments were still sifting down from the jagged hole above.

Slowly she turned back into the room, where Rosalind was moving briskly about with her candle, dusting off with her handkerchief the heads and shoulders of the men who had been near the window, in case of glass splinters, requiring them all to sit still and not cut themselves, making light of the smashed room which they could not see, and the lack of illumination. Soon the rescue squad would arrive and begin to dig in the wreckage below, where it seemed impossible that there could be anything living, and somehow the men must be led out to new quarters for the rest of the night and many days to come. Silent, com-posed, with her serene hospital mask as firmly in place as though the men she tended still had their eyes, Phoebe set down her candle on a small table and bent to run her fingers lightly over the collar and hair of the nearest man, feeling for glass. He snatched at her hand and held on tightly.

"Where did it land?" he asked, turning up his bandaged face to her anxiously. "It *was* close, wasn't it! Were we hit?"

"Oh, no, nothing as bad as that," she reassured him gently. "It must have landed somewhere further along the Embankment. All we got was the blast. The chandelier in the hall came down all over the stair-case, and we'll have to stay here till they clear it away, there's a lot of plaster down."

"Lucky we were all in here when it happened," he said. "I remember that chandelier, I used to see it often. Lucky there was no one under it."

5. *France.*   *Spring, 1917.*

▶▶

1

PHOEBE left London on the following day, and slept exhaustedly in the train all the way to Folkestone, after being up most of the night. She knew they had sent for Oliver, but before he arrived she had gone with a motor full of blinded men who were to be put up temporarily at Clare's house in Belgrave Square. By the time she had got them settled in there, Rosalind came round to say that everyone had left the house in Chelsea.

Two maids had been got out of the basement alive and taken to the hospital. Maia, who had not reached the shelter, must have been instantly killed. Phoebe wondered if anyone had told Oliver that Maia had left her post during the raid, was in the act of leaving it before Rosalind and herself had offered to stay with the men in her care. Knowing Rosalind and Virginia, she thought he was pretty sure to find out sometime, but hoped he needn't know.

The French hospital to which she was now assigned was a small chateau on the Versailles side of Paris, which was owned by a member of the old *noblesse* who some years ago had married an American woman. Widowed during the first fighting on the Marne, the American *comtesse* had turned the chateau into a convalescent home for soldiers, and Phoebe found its gilded salons full of cots in rows beneath shrouded oil portraits and tapestries and chandeliers, and its extensive gardens peopled, even in winter, with muffled figures in wheel-chairs and on crutches, taking the air.

The routine was comparatively easy after life at the Belgian front, and although she was lacking a typewriter she began to keep her notebooks again. Most of the women with whom she worked were Americans who had married in France, and when soon after her arrival news came that Mr. Wilson had been re-elected Phoebe heard a lively echo of Aunt Sally's angry bewilderment and humiliation that America, champion of liberty, should stand smugly by, wrapped in aphorism, while other men fought and died for the cause she had always been so ready to defend.

"We went galloping off half-cocked to Cuba to rescue a lot of unwashed niggers from Spain," said the Comtesse, who was Charleston-born, "but France and England, who are our own kind, can bleed to death and we don't lift a finger! What Germany has done makes Spain look like a guardian angel! Where's Roosevelt? Surely *he* hasn't gone soft like all the rest of them! If that man Hughes, whoever he is, had come straight out and said he'd lead us into war instead of writing Notes he'd be President now, or my name's not Mary Rutledge!"

When Bracken looked in at Christmas time Phoebe showed him her notebooks and he groaned. It was good, he said, it was great stuff, but they couldn't print it, it would have to wait a bit. Mr. Wilson in his latest speech, still wearing the mental white robes of the Great Peacemaker he considered himself to be, had called upon both sides to state their aims and explain what they were fighting for—thus, said Bracken, grinding his teeth, suggesting that the Allied aims had not all along been public property, thus implying all over again that he saw little to choose between Germany's ruthless aggression and the defence by France and Britain of martyred Belgium and their treaty obligations, which the German Chancellor had named scraps of paper. Mr. Wilson argued for an immediate "peace without victory" and no hard feelings, thus proving that there was no substitute for commonsense, said Bracken, who was shackled and gagged by the tight Allied censorship which prevented even correspondents from reporting the general reaction, or their own, to the latest Wilsonian *bêtise*, for fear of worsening his opinion until he might begin to side openly with Germany. Instead, the Allies issued a clear and patient list of their terms, and Germany returned vague blusterings about "negotiations."

They went to a great deal of trouble about Christmas at the chateau, and each wounded man had a little pile of presents, each wrapped separately—cigarettes or chocolate, a pipe, or a penknife, a packet of notepaper, a fountain pen, or a photograph frame, a linen handkerchief, a nail file, or a new toothbrush—the ingenuity of the Comtesse was boundless, and everything pleased them, for wounded men are strangely like children, uncritical and grateful for little things, and the wards were full of laughter and festivity.

Bracken had brought Phoebe some bonbons from Paris and some silk stockings, for which he received an extravagant hug, and Oliver sent her a gold-mounted fountain pen from Asprey's done up with a box of notepaper. The card said simply *With love from Oliver*. The gift spoke for itself, and Phoebe took the hint, feeling a little self-conscious as she sat down to write the second letter she had ever sent him in their lives, for it was impossible not to recall the first, and its disastrous consequences. With Phoebe Sprague, the authoress, looking over her shoulder, she tore up two false starts which sounded exactly like an authoress not writing a love letter—and on the third attempt succeeded in saying how delicious it was to have a present from him, and in telling something of her surroundings and duties without committing *belles lettres*.

Early in the year the Germans, taking heart from the prospect of another four years of Wilson, and in need of whatever consolation they could find, overplayed their hands as usual, by an announcement that unrestricted submarine warfare would now be resumed without regard to the pledges extracted from them by former Notes from Washington. They justified their action by saying that their peace offers had been rejected and that the Allied Blockade was illegal, for Germany was feeling the pinch of the British Navy.

And then to everyone's surprise, perhaps Germany's most of all, Mr.

Wilson gave the German Ambassador his passports. It was a diplomatic break only, and not a declaration of war, as was hastily pointed out. But it was a sign that some glimmer of enlightenment was at last beginning to penetrate the President's self-isolation from realities. Perhaps it resulted from an aroused public opinion, as the sinkings without warning piled up in the public conscience and the curtailment of American overseas trade skimped the American pocketbook, and people realized that they were being dictated to by a foreign Power which took upon itself to say where American ships could go and where they couldn't, and what about this freedom of the seas which the Barbary pirates had once attempted to interfere with? And perhaps in part it was the result of Ambassador Page's tireless efforts to open his old friend's reluctant mind to the facts as he saw them at his London post. But—

"We should have done as much when the *Lusitania* went down," said the Comtesse.

2

MEANWHILE, Phoebe's correspondence with Oliver remained entirely unpolitical and concerned itself more than once with the weather. He had replied at once to her Christmas letter, on his club notepaper. She tried to imagine him at a desk in the silent writing-room, his greying head bent above the lean brown hand which guided the pen in its small, tidy script which was so amazingly hard to read, its *m*'s and *n*'s and *u*'s and *i*'s and *e*'s all alike with an occasional tail or *t* for a clue. Sometimes it took half an hour to decipher his brief letters, and then, she would ask herself rather hollowly, what had she got? For Oliver was not one of those people who had the knack of getting himself down on paper. Born of a large, letter-writing family scattered all over the map, who described voluminously everything that happened to them or entered their delightful heads, always with the happy suspicion that it would be read aloud amid gales of laughter, and with an eye to that effect, and herself wielding a free and racy pen, Phoebe felt a schoolgirlish disappointment with Oliver's letters. All the sparkle and vitality of his presence escaped on its way to the page, all the warmth and wit of his love dwindled into inarticulateness. *I'm just a thick-headed soldier,* he had said in the only other letter she had ever had from him, all those years ago, *and I don't know how to write letters.* He hadn't learned, in the interim. He began with *My dearest Phoebe,* and ended with *Yours, Oliver.* In between, she would decide petulantly, was practically nothing.

So that, longing to let herself go and escape for a bit from the chateau and its load of pain and grief, she must suppress the impulse to Do-you-remember and I've-always-wanted-you-to-know, and write in the same matter-of-fact vein that he did. And as a consequence Oliver at the other end felt always a little dashed, without knowing why, for he had never been really sure of her except while he held her in his arms, and he was inclined to assume still less in his replies. Until finally Phoebe heard herself thinking, Maybe it's been too long—maybe by now there's somebody else. . . .

This went on till April, while more and more ships carrying Americans were sunk without warning, and at long last, rising suddenly to heights of righteous indignation, President Wilson made his eloquent declaration of war. Paris and London put out the Stars and Stripes on their balconies, and the Comtesse said with satisfaction that she never knew he had it in him, and the following day a letter came from Oliver, written in Paris where he had just arrived with his General for a conference at Headquarters.

> We shall be here only a few days, [he wrote] but with any luck at all I shall have tomorrow evening free and shall come out to see you after dinner, if I may. Will you try to arrange for a quiet spot where we can talk privately? Soon you can safely turn over your half of the war to your army and come back to England, so I hope to put an end to all this letter-writing nonsense.
>
> Yours,
> OLIVER

And that didn't sound, did it, as though there was anyone else?

All that day Phoebe was especially kind to the men in her charge, with a more than customary touch of gaiety which twice brought Gallic compliments on the brightness of her eyes. It was the old Oliver-feeling, the excitement, the giddiness, the *lift.* She recognized it with relief, for she had had time to outgrow it by now. The Comtesse, suspecting something more than a visit from an old friend, obligingly lent the privacy of her own sitting-room where Phoebe was waiting, wearing her Red Cross uniform with her hair nunnishly hidden by the white veil, when Oliver was brought to the door and left there.

He stood a moment, still holding his cap with the red Staff band, his gloves and stick, just looking at her. Then he dropped them on the nearest chair and came towards her.

"I never know what to say when I see you again," he confessed, and his arms went round her, hard and possessive. "Must I say anything?" He bent and kissed her, and after a moment's surprise she answered him as she had done before, going all of half way. "That's better," he murmured, and his lips moved on across her cheek and eyes.

"It's—disconcerting," she got out shakily. "I mean I wasn't—couldn't be sure—"

"*What?*" His arms tightened masterfully in the way she had never forgotten, till she gasped with the pressure on her ribs and flinched closer to him, laughing with what breath she had left. "What weren't you sure of?" he demanded, looking down at her, half amused, half angry, his face only inches from hers so that she could see the dancing amber flecks of light in his eyes and curve of his upper lip beneath the small mustache.

"Well, I mean—in your letters you d-didn't—"

"You know I can't write letters," he said reasonably. "That's why all this has got to stop now. Your country's in it, you don't have to fight your own war any longer, I know how you've felt about it, but now you can rest a bit. We'll find someone to take your place here and bring you home where you belong, where I can see something of you. I'm such an old crock now I'm stuck at the War Office, I'll not get back into the fighting at this rate. And you are going to marry me, aren't you, say, sometime this summer?"

It was not a question, or at least he knew the answer, but he waited for her assent, for a girl should always have the chance to say No. While the transparent thought ran through her mind that it wouldn't be a year this summer, and the equally luminous idea that she didn't really care if it wasn't, he smiled ruefully and said, "It's war time, my dear—and soldiers are always in a hurry." He laid his hard, cool cheek against hers, with his lips at her ear, and whispered, "Must I wait *forever?*"

"No!" she cried quickly, and felt her knees dissolve. "I didn't mean—oh, *Oliver!*"